Art and the Revolutionary Human Fruit Machine

Alex Pankhurst

Earl's Eye Publishing

ART AND THE
REVOLUTIONARY HUMAN FRUIT MACHINE
first published in the UK in 2012
by Earl's Eye Publishing,
PO Box 11086, Dedham, Colchester CO7 6WG
www.earlseyepublishing.co.uk

Copyright © Alex Pankhurst 2012

Alex Pankhurst is hereby identified as the author of the work
in accordance with section 77 of the Copyright Designs and Patents Act
1988
All rights reserved.

A CIP catalogue record for this book is available from
the British Library.
ISBN 978-0-9518133-2-4

Printed and bound by Impressions Print and Publish,
Somersham, Cambridgeshire, UK

By the same author:

Fiction
Scoffing the Primroses – ISBN 978-0-9518133-1-7
a novel for those who love gardening,
admire village living,
and relish the quirky side of life.
Available in paperback at £13.99, or as an ebook

Really lit up the day for me and stayed in my mind.
John Carey, Emeritus Professor of English Literature,
Oxford University
Great fun, extremely readable. One of the funniest
passages in any novel this year.   *Sunday Times*

A delightful tale. You'll either rush to discover the
finish,or linger, savouring each page.
                            www.thebookplace.co.uk
Very amusing.   It's wry, it's sardonic and deliciously
so. I couldn't put it down.   *Eastern Daily Press*

Readers' enthusiasm:-

'I immediately wanted to share the pleasure with friends.'

'More of the same, *please.'*

'So enchanted by your book I must urge you
  to write a sequel.'

'It's the best book I've read in a long time.'

'I've just ordered my seventh copy.'

Non-fiction
Who Does Your Garden Grow? UK edition, out of print
North American edition ISBN 978-1-893443-08-2
Stories and characters behind many favourite garden plants
Available in paperback and as an ebook

Acknowledgements
To everyone, friends and strangers, who helped with
fact-finding and test reading for this book, my warmest
appreciation, especially to the owners, skipper and crew
of the wonderful sailing barge Victor.

Author's Note
Rundleston exists only in my imagination.
But those living along the Stour and Orwell estuaries
may recognize some elements of the story setting,
with affection.

Chapter One

'I've cracked it. Our troubles are history', Ben informed his mother cheerily. 'Had this great idea for the maltings. It'll do up the building and bring in *stacks* of cash.'

From the sewing machine, Nora regarded her elder son with sceptical affection.

'But we've tried so many things, I really don't think...'

'No, no, this one can't fail', he assured her, dropping the shop's float in the safe behind the sitting room door. 'Got it all worked out. Or will have by Saturday. I'll tell you about it then.'

'Ben, there's something you should know...'

'Sorry, must rush', he folded the rug back and headed for the door. 'Flitch has asked me to crew on the Hetty Jane tonight.'

'Would you have time to clear the gutter – you did say you would', she called after him. 'Only it's dripping on customers.'

'Hope it got the right ones. Okay, I'll do it first thing tomorrow morning', her departing son assured her. With a sense of foreboding, Nora heard him hurriedly descending the stairs to the ground floor flat.

She would have to tell him. Tomorrow.

'Mornin' Ben', the driver of a scruffy Land Rover greeted him outside the shop early next day, 'you still on for this evening then? Installing that stove in the hulk Danny laughingly calls a tug.'

'Oh hi, Flitch.' Ben lent the ladder against the guttering and glanced teasingly across at the pony-tailed passenger. 'It had better work, Danny. You won't get us taking the damn thing out again.'

'Fancy a trip to Woodbridge?' enquired Flitch, noticing a car draw up behind his trailer. 'We're collecting a boat with a post through the hull. What would I do without people who can't steer!'

It was certainly tempting. A lads' day out, pub lunch, boatyard scenes for his sketchbook, but... 'Sorry', Ben concluded regretfully, 'I'm supposed to be clearing this gutter, and then minding the shop for an hour or so late morning. And this afternoon I've got to... well anyway, see you tonight.'

'That dude's got life worked out,' Danny commented as they moved off. 'Helps in the shop a bit and the rest of the time he can paint or sail, do what he damn well likes.'

A school crossing lady stopped the traffic and a couple of pupils trailed across. 'Yeah. No children costing him the earth' Flitch agreed feelingly, 'no mortgage, no wife to nag at him. He's a lucky sod.'

Ben Banding would have agreed, although this rosy picture ignored a private scar, and the worrying problem looming over him and his mother in the shape of the disused family maltings. It was down to him as the concerned man of the family to do something about it before it sank them both. But his new idea would turn the whole situation around, he was sure of it.

He looked young for forty-one. Wiry, with dark, curly hair and a determined chin, at rest his expression tended to a wistful incomprehension at the world, like a soft toy whose owner has grown up. He and his shaggy, cross-breed sheep dog Bodger were a familiar sight about the small East Anglian town of Rundleston, where the Bandings had lived and worked for generations. Along with other families they'd prospered from grain malting and the sailing barge trade, when the town had boasted three huge maltings, a brewery, warehouses, chandlers, sail loft and small shipwrights. The big curved wharf would have been crowded then with craft loading and unloading, the alehouses full of men hot and thirsty from shifts raking the grain and loading it, and boatmen telling tales of storms and sandbanks and bargemen's rivalries.

A gust of wind overturned the plastic bucket awaiting the gutter's detritus, and it rolled towards the road. As he went to retrieve it he pictured the estuary on the far side of the building whipped into little waves by the sudden breeze, with maybe a distant sail heeling over. He knew all the water's moods, and how the colours and atmosphere changed with the tides and seasons. Just now, the warmth of May was making the fields and woods on either side so lush and green it was like a shout of exultation. But there'd be no going out in the boat this afternoon, he decided, testing the steadiness of the ladder before climbing up. He'd do a last inspection of the maltings and make sure he'd got all the facts needed for the planning permission. Then he could tackle his mother with the business plan tomorrow.

His scruffy jeans and trainers were all that could be seen of him through the window as Nora Banding unlocked the shop door from the inside a few minutes later. He was a good lad, even if they had their differences, she thought, bending down painfully to pick up the mail. It would be even better to have him settled with a nice wife and growing family. The past twenty years had indicated painting was her son's passion, yet Nora still retained faint hope of marriage for him. And grandchildren for herself. Her solution to the maltings problem might prove just the help he needed in finding the right girl, she reflected with satisfaction. The family's greatest financial problem would be taken off their shoulders, he'd meet lots of eligible girls, and it would be excellent for Rundleston too. Good all round.

The brown envelopes were mostly invoices, and she put them on the counter to look at later. Better to concentrate on the meeting later today, she told herself, wondering again whether she'd done right to act behind Ben's back. He would be upset, but it was for his own good. And only a

3

couple of hours to go now before the signing. No going back after that.

She was tipping out a bag of change when the first customer approached and paused to converse with the legs. Nora smiled to herself. Mrs Simpson had an unmarried daughter with, according to Ben, an irritating laugh and the personality of a dust mite. But then he was rude about all the Rundleston potentials his mother had hopes for, and the girlfriends he chose himself ended up marrying other people, tired of waiting. Out of the corner of her eye she saw black stuff from the gutter splatter onto the pavement, and heard Ben's exclamation of apology, which she hoped Mrs Simpson would take as genuine. His mother wasn't fooled though, and was torn between sympathy and irritation. Alienating customers was hardly helpful when the shop needed all the trade it could get. Especially since the new supermarket was making such inroads into their stationery sales.

Mrs Simpson hastily entered the shop and headed for one of the card carousels, followed a few moments later by a second customer, and Nora sighed inwardly. Dedicated chatters, both of them.

'I was hoping to buy two of these birthday cards, but there's only one left – have you got any more?' Mrs Simpson held up a card depicting a busy scene with two coasters unloading timber next to an East Coast sailing barge, the wharf dominated by a six-storey maltings with distinctive hat-like kiln roofs. The artist had caught exactly the feeling of a bright and breezy day, sun-sparkled water reflected on the hulls, light and shadow playing on men's arms and faces, and the soft sheen of a gull's wing as it perched on a post in the foreground.

Nora fetched another pack from the store room, noting that they were nearly out of stock.

'It's such a wonderful picture of Rundleston', its admirer commented, 'I'd love to buy the original – but Ben doesn't sell his paintings does he?'

'Well, no, he's quite… obstinate about it.' Nora took the money and rang up the sale. 'In fact I had to bully him into getting that one made into a card.'

'I see him around the place with his sketchbook', Mrs Simpson continued, confident that the other customer wouldn't mind waiting, 'and I think thank goodness someone is capturing the old town – Rundleston's changing so fast'.

'That bit of the wharf is where they've built the yacht marina, haven't they', the woman behind put in helpfully, nodding at the card. 'And them maltings they're all flats now. Such a shame. My dad used to work there.'

'Have you seen the price of them!' Mrs Simpson included both of them in her incredulity. 'Seems it's mostly Londoners buying them. What do they want to come here for?'

'Yes', Nora agreed on all points, and suffered a squirm of doubt about her plan for their own empty maltings. What if she was doing the wrong thing? It would mean a big change for the town, as well as for the family.

Shutting up the shop at the end of the afternoon, she felt a sense of release. The deed was done, the agreement finally signed. But her relief was dwarfed by a greater apprehension. How was she going to tell Ben? The matter was urgent, otherwise he'd hear about it from someone else.

She closed the door at the rear of the shop and stood for a moment in the passage behind. Sometimes in dreams she found herself back in the house as it was when the children were young, before it was divided up. Turning the old place into three separate living areas had taken years and a good deal of money, even with Ben doing most of the work, but the end result was well worth all the hassle, she thought with

5

satisfaction. The large attic rooms had been converted into smaller bedrooms with en suite bathrooms, plus a sitting room, and although she'd resisted the idea of doing bed and breakfast, the money had proved a lifeline, especially now the shop was barely making a profit.

Ben had turned the ground floor behind the shop into rooms for himself. Although too low for a glimpse of the river, he had good-sized windows looking on to the walled garden, making it quite light. When you went in, which she never did unasked, the impression was of untidy comfort. It was his den, and he could make as much mess as he liked there. An adult son still living at home needs his own private domain, she'd realised.

Her flat on the middle floor was the best and largest as it included the area over the shop, and from her sitting room bay window there was that wonderful view out over the estuary. Always something to look at – birds and buoys and boats – the scene constantly changing with the weather and the state of the tide. You could waste all day just gazing. In past centuries Rundleston's other successful families had bought land and built big houses on the outskirts, but the Bandings had simply picked the best site in town and built on and up as they needed.

The reason for the town's growth was that the river's deep water course swept up against the land, allowing coasters to dock. But opposite their house the channel turned and wandered across the broad estuary, leaving the other half of town with mud flats at low tide and a little beach where the stream, the rundle that gave the place its name, gurgled into the river. Generations of children had paddled joyously in it, while their parents enjoyed a drink outside the town's waterside inn, the Spritsail Barge, known universally as The Spritty.

The Banding's house straddled the divide between the fashionable part where traders and captains had built handsome houses, and what had been the working area. The

6

position was ideal for the shop, which had originally supplied necessities for bargemen – everything from paint and turpentine, shackles, nails and tools, to gimbals and brass lanterns – and the building's history was reflected in the name it bore, Chandlers.

Looking at the new layout and picturing how it used to be she reflected that everything changed – people, places, businesses.   After all, as a young wife she'd been responsible for a big change herself, overcoming the resistance of her father-in-law to changing from chandlery to cards and stationery. And in past years the shop had more than paid its way. Now it was like swimming against a strengthening tide, and Nora was beginning to wonder how long they could keep going.

But the most pressing problem was how to tell Ben what she'd done about the maltings, she thought, climbing the stairs. And Tony in London as well – not that he would care in the slightest. Were ever two brothers more different? Opening the door to her light-filled sitting room, she looked up at the portrait of a handsome man, beautifully painted by Ben, from a photograph, of his father at the helm of a sailing barge.

'I wish you'd been here to advise me, Mike.'   The sentiment was hardly logical, since if her husband had been alive, what to do with the family's old maltings would have been more his problem. But Ben would find the decision more acceptable if Mike had made it. Nora sighed, hoping he'd realize it was for everyone's benefit, his own especially.

Ben was at that moment preparing to leave the building in which, unknown to him, he was now a trespasser. He'd spent a couple of hours, clarifying exactly how the conversion to a gym could be made, and composing the wording of a business plan. A real businessman would have called it a naïve outline, with no cost analysis or market research, but Ben was pleased with it, and would have liked to tell Nora about the idea that evening. The sooner her worries about the building were ended the better. But he'd promised to help hoist that cast iron stove into the old tug that was Danny's home. It would have to be the next day.

He locked the man-sized door cut into a huge entrance gate, and looked up at the imposing building. Between each of the five storeys ran rows of fancy brickwork, the corners and arched windows picked out in light colours, each keystone proudly bearing a sheaf of barley in relief. A rain-soaked planning permission announcement dated March 2007 was taped to the silvery wood of the door. Just history, now that it had been refused, Ben reflected, and part of him was glad. This piece of his family's past deserved better than being turned into flats. The request had only been made out of desperation, and the council's decision was right – there were too many flats already in Rundleston, what with two of the maltings plus the old brewery all now converted.

You'll have a new lease of life, he promised the place. His latest scheme would bring in rent and be a great success, he was sure of it. He'd talk to Nora about it tomorrow morning, Ben thought, with pleasurable anticipation. Before the shop opened.

He and Bodger found Nora putting a cloth on the table in the dining room at eight o'clock next morning, ready for the bed and breakfast guests. His mother's grey hair and middle parting combined with a kindly expression somehow put him in mind of a benevolent ewe, although he always felt guilty at that thought. And he was trying to ignore her increasing signs of age.

'I've come to tell you about this ace idea for the maltings', he announced, after greeting her.

'Er, Ben, there's something I need to tell you…'

'How much duct tape have we got in the house?' he interrupted.

'Duct tape? Well I think there's a roll in… What do you want it for?'

'Wrapping up the maltings. Bind it up with duct tape – it'll be an artwork', he teased, helpfully fetching the tray of cups, plates and saucers from the kitchen. 'Really put Rundleston on the map. And bring in oodles of cash.'

Plonking the tray down on the table he grinned at her. 'No, actually I've found someone who wants to turn it into a gym and health club. Great for the town, especially with all the new people in the flats. And this man's willing to foot the conversion costs and make good the roof, in return for a low rent.' He laid the places, adding, 'I reckon we could word the agreement so that we got a share of the profits as time went on. Or else put the rent up in line with its profitability.'

His mother looked at him fondly. Having married one idealist and brought up another, she'd concluded they were lovely people. Just needed managing that's all.

'It's too late Ben', she told him gently. 'I wanted to tell you last night but… Yesterday I signed an agreement giving the building to the town.'

If she'd announced it was going to be used as a tap dancing club for snails, he couldn't have been more taken aback.

'*You've given away the maltings!*' He stared at her in disbelief. 'How could you do that? How *could* you!

'It's not as if we haven't tried all sorts of things', she faced him challengingly across the table. 'Animal feed store, furniture depository, antiques centre – they haven't even covered the upkeep, have they?

But he wasn't listening. 'Why didn't you talk to me? I'd have told you about the health club plan. This one can't fail.'

'It's for the best, really it is', Nora insisted. 'We're just pouring money into keeping it sound – well trying to. This way we can afford to have Betty part time in the shop again. And that would help us both. Besides I haven't just given it away without strings.' She paused for effect. 'The condition was that they use it as a venue for an art festival.'

'What!'

Nora got out the salt and pepper, while he took this in. 'An art festival would give you lots of publicity', she assured him encouragingly. 'I won't interfere with the running of course, but as a home-grown artist, they'd be bound to ask you to exhibit.'

His chin jutted obstinately. 'I wouldn't put any of my work in for something like that.'

'Why ever not?' She couldn't conceal her impatience. 'Ben, what's the use of all those wonderful paintings up in your studio if nobody sees them!'

The familiar theme was usually unspoken. But it was so galling to produce a brilliantly talented son who refused to let the world in on the secret. As well as solving the maltings problem, a local art festival would surely break the logjam, and be the start of recognition for Ben. If he wouldn't help himself, she would do it for him, and now he was refusing to cooperate. It was infuriating.

'What *are* you going to do with them?' she demanded.

He walked over to the side window looking across the yard to his studio above the garage. 'They're ammunition', he said shortly

'Ammunition? Against what?'

'The lot of them. Especially that louse Oliver Rabson. One day I'm going to show him up as a cynical, money-making scammer.'

'Oh don't be so dramatic.' Nora never understood why the famous man's name seemed to set off an allergic reaction in her normally easy-going son. It was almost as if his animosity was personal.

'When is this going to happen, pray? And how?'

He'd turned back to the task in hand, and opened the cutlery drawer. 'I don't know when. Or how. But somehow I'll get back at that bastard.' He was promising himself now. 'And I need those paintings.'

Bodger had looked up questioningly at the raised tone, and a floorboard creaked overhead.

'Keep your voice down Ben', urged Nora, 'there's a nice woman and her disabled son staying upstairs. Look, come and have supper with me tonight, and we'll talk about things.' She gave him a placating smile. 'Please don't be mad at me about this maltings decision. Not only does it take all the worry away, but I'm sure an art festival will be wonderful for you as an artist, whatever you say. And great fun. You'll see.'

Chapter Two

Oliver Rabson was browsing through computer pages of the 2007 Queens Art Academy student degree show. The gauche and strident images on screen contrasted markedly with the plain tastefulness of the office in his Georgian London house. A full bookshelf faced two comfortable looking chairs on either side of a low onyx-topped table, while a row of filing cabinets and sophisticated printer-scanner occupied wall space behind his mahogany desk. This was tidy, and devoid of ornament except for an exquisite silver model of a bicycle, which his staff lived in fear of damaging. An antique bracket clock ticked placidly on the mantelpiece beneath an imposing mirror, and morning sunshine streamed through the big window at the far end from where he sat. On the table lay a remote control for the widescreen television behind electronic doors, and the cream walls of the elegantly proportioned, carpeted room were devoid of any art. Nor was there a single photograph giving any clues about the man and his context.

Asked to guess his background and occupation, a stranger might have taken in the prematurely silver hair, deep-set, intelligent eyes, strong mouth and heavy brow accompanied by an air of impatient authority, and opted for a banker, a general or perhaps a media tycoon, probably a scion of an influential family. When he was younger Oliver Rabson made a point of pricking such assumptions, but these days he didn't bother. His life story was well enough known and he was simply 'Rab', the newspapers had no need to elaborate. Everyone knew the name and that he, together with Charles Saatchi, dominated the world of modern art.

As the clock chimed nine, a perfunctory knock at the door preceded a plain middle-aged woman, her round, shiny face not enhanced by frizzy brown hair and a pair of unflattering spectacles. Most women would have spent much time and effort in trying to mitigate nature's unfairness, but possessing intelligence, organizing ability and a steady personality, Rab's PA had chosen to major in those qualities instead. Like a stumpy tug allied to a glamorous liner, she knew herself to be plain but indispensable, and was secure in her comfortable dowdiness.

'Ah, Pauline', Rab addressed her without glancing up, 'have a look at this one. What do you think?'

Over his shoulder she considered the lurid swirls of colour interspersed with giant yellow safety pins. 'It's rubbish.'

'Yes of course it's rubbish', her employer snapped, and immediately regretted it. He wasn't usually short with Pauline, they were a good team. 'But as we know the worse the stuff looks the easier it is to hype as cutting edge', he continued in a more moderate tone.. 'And I rather think this one might be brandable. Depends on the artist's personality. Could you do some fact-finding about...' he scrolled down the screen to find the student's name, "Peter Johnson" this morning, before I go to the exhibition. We'd have to change that name for a start.'

'I'm really pushed for time at the moment', she protested, 'I'm trying to get some information from Tootsie Smalt for the Sotheby catalogue, but she's being impossible and Sotheby's are getting jumpy. That show you're curating in New York is turning into a complete nightmare, and the shippers say they can't...'

'Well get that girl of yours to find out about this guy', he interrupted, 'shouldn't be beyond her for goodness sake.'

'She's left', Pauline informed him bluntly, putting a folder of opened post on the desk. 'That's why I'm up to my eyes.'

'Left? But she's only been in the job a month.'

'You shouted at her last week, if you recall. Reduced her to tears. She says she's not coming back.'

'That's pathetic. People have to take me as I am', Rab resumed his perusal of student offerings, 'after all you don't resign. At least not for the past fifteen years.'

'I'm saving it up', retorted Pauline darkly, heading for the door. 'Waiting for when it will create maximum nuisance.'

She half opened the door then turned, in time to see a suspicion of a smile on her employer's face. 'And talking of maximum nuisance, the fact that there isn't any back up is a real problem because I need to take a few days' holiday shortly. And there's no way we can recruit a new secretary in time.' An unspoken reproach about bullying yet another member of staff into leaving hung in the air.

'Nobody "needs" a holiday', he countered sarcastically. 'It's a modern idea whipped up by the tourist industry. Surely you can postpone it.'

'Not this time. My son Tommy has reached the age limit for his special school now', she told him stiffly, 'and I've been worried sick about what was going to happen to him. As you know he's only got me.'

The telephone rang on his desk and she hesitated, but he ignored it. 'Go on.'

'Well I've found this wonderful place, Rundleston Grange in East Anglia, where they live in a supervised community

13

and do whatever work they can to help support themselves. They've accepted him, and I want to go down and see him settled in.'

'Oh.' He had the grace to look discomfited. 'Look, come and sit down.' He motioned to the nearest armchair as he got up from the desk and walked over to the other one. 'I just might have the answer – I was going to talk to you about it later anyway.

You know that table at the Ivy you booked for lunch tomorrow – you did remember?'

'Of course'.

'Did you wonder who I might be meeting?'

'It's not my place to take an interest in your social life', she protested righteously, though on this occasion her curiosity had been aroused. The procession of beautiful, shiny girls that Rab squired around had long since ceased to interest her. She could have told them their ambition of marrying the famous multimillionaire was doomed to failure – they would last about six months before being superceded by the next hopeful. But he had instructed her to keep tomorrow afternoon clear of everything. Now that was unusual.

'You may know I was married years ago' he began hesitantly, 'and we had a daughter – Natasha'

'I've spoken to your ex-wife once or twice on the telephone...'

'Well I'm afraid I haven't had anything to do with the girl since we split up - when she was little more than a baby.' He sensed Pauline's disapproval and added in explanation, 'To start with I was too angry. And later Gaye made sure I wasn't part of her life. Kept saying Natasha didn't want to see me – and she might have been right. Gaye's had so many boyfriends perhaps the child thought of me as just another 'daddy'. The whole thing was awkward.' Rab picked an invisible piece of fluff off the armchair. 'I just paid the bills, made sure she had a good education, anything she needed. Not that Gaye is short of funds, seeing as she

14

took a good few million off me.' Resentment stirred as usual, and he fought against it. 'Anyway Gaye now says Natasha would like to meet me.' He looked up. 'Hence the lunch date and the clear afternoon. Father has rapprochement with long-lost daughter – what sort of time do these things take?'

'How old is she?' enquired Pauline, trying to picture the scene. Perceiving one of London's most eligible bachelors as nervous family man was taking some adjustment.

'Twenty-one – just graduated from Oxford with a degree in Politics, Philosophy and Economics.' Conscious of the stark contrast between their respective offspring, he went on quickly, 'Gaye says Natasha's going off round the world with her boyfriend next summer when he finishes at university, and she doesn't know what to do in the meantime. Suggested I could give her a year learning all about this business, and I don't see why not. I'll pay her of course. And she might as well start by helping you. That'd fill the gap and give us time to appoint someone else. How would that be?'

Pauline had never seen her famously acerbic boss so unsure of himself. It was a revelation. 'Sounds an excellent idea', she agreed, standing up. 'I shall look forward to meeting her – always assuming she says yes. Let's just hope she does.'

It had never occurred to Oliver Rabson that his daughter might turn down the wonderful chance he was offering. Brought up sharp by this possibility he called after his PA as she reached the door, 'Oh and Pauline – I promise not to shout at her.'

Natasha's bed was covered with discarded clothes – what the hell do you wear to meet your father?

'What about this?' she asked, striking a pose in the doorway of her mother's office, 'you don't think the skirt's too short?'

Gaye turned from an invoice she was preparing on the computer, and assessed her critically, imagining the first impression Natasha would make on an apprehensive Rab. Fully aware of the glamorous girls always photographed at his side, she knew it was important their daughter struck a different note.

Lord, it was like looking at herself twenty odd years ago. The same long-lashed grey eyes, the delicate nose that was the hearts desire of all rhinoplasty candidates, even that boyish, tousled blonde hair, emphasizing Natasha's sweetly feminine face. But where Gaye's teeth were perfect, her daughter had a small, endearing gap in her front teeth which, she reproached herself, she ought to have had fixed. Except that it served to enhance Natasha's baby thrush, child woman effect – an unbeatable look, as her mother had cause to know. The checked browny-pink skirt revealed just enough knee above dark, suede boots, and a maroon velvet jacket completed the demure yet strokable effect.

'No, that's perfect', she said, 'although the top could do with something at the neck. My tiger stone pendant would be just right.'

But Natasha lingered. 'I'm not sure I want to go through with this – playing the dutiful daughter', she protested doubtfully. 'Why does he want to see me now, when you've always said he didn't want anything to do with me? What kind of father does that make him? He abandoned us.'

'Perhaps he had his reasons', Gaye took a headed sheet off a pile and placed it in the printer. 'He's never stinted on money for you, you know'.

'Pff, money!' scoffed Natasha, with the disdain of one who'd never felt the lack of it. 'He's got gazillions. And I don't like modern art, it's stupid.'

An idea struck her and she smiled. 'I shall tell him I'm serious about becoming a representational painter.'

'The art may be stupid', her mother printed off the invoice, 'but it's certainly very profitable. Maybe you could spend some time working for him – you'd meet influential people and learn a lot. If he offers that it would be an astute career move.' Gaye turned to her. 'Look sweetie, I really think you should do this. You're an adult now and I want you to meet your father and be on good terms with him'.

Natasha gave her mother a sideways look. That endearment usually indicated insincerity. And this suspicious change of attitude towards him – what was that about? But admittedly she did have a year to fill, and not much idea what to do with it. It was also embarrassing admitting that she'd never even spoken to her famous father.

'And if you don't hurry, you'll be late.'

Resignedly Natasha went to fetch the pendant from Gaye's jewellery box, leaving her mother gazing into space. Rab was going to be putty in her hands, she mused pleasurably, picturing the year ahead. Now that would be useful.

The summer sunshine filtered through high cloud, leaving the day pleasantly warm, and Rab decided the walk from Berkeley Square to Covent Garden would do him good, as well as giving him time to prepare for the forthcoming encounter. The more he'd thought about it, the more uneasy he'd become. Why, for instance, hadn't Natasha made contact herself? It's what he'd have done in her shoes. What if Gaye was up to something?

He passed the familiar Dover Street galleries. The art world was something he understood, but women? A dead loss, in his experience. The good looking ones were only after money, the whole damn lot of them. Gaye had been the first to teach him that harsh lesson. Tricked him into marriage by getting pregnant – she knew what she was about. His money was the result of years of hard work, and Gaye had taken half of it simply by lying on her back and lying about contraception. His anger against her burned deep as a pit fire, and he'd vowed never to get trapped by a woman again.

Perhaps it was that anger which had poisoned the relationship, giving the marriage no chance, he reflected now. They'd bought a handsome house in The Boltons, but he took to staying away, leaving Gaye to cope with the baby on her own. Except she employed a nanny, enabling her to go out to parties and stay on the art scene. She even began organizing events commercially, just to spite him, he reckoned, since they were generally gallery openings and the like. If they attended the same one he would ignore her, and he'd never taken an interest in the baby, he remembered shamefacedly. To him the child was a symbol of how he'd been trapped by a scheming woman. Soon he'd ceased to come home at all, and two years after the wedding, they divorced. Gaye sold up and bought a house in Richmond overlooking the river. Oh yes, she'd done very nicely for herself.

Outside The Ritz a well groomed woman and her paunchy partner were disembarking from a taxi, and he smiled wryly. Glamour was attracted to money as birds to ripe cherries. Now that he was famous as well as wealthy you could see the greed in girls' eyes as they flirted with him at art previews and parties. Vying for the attention of a not particularly good-looking fifty-year old? They were little more than prostitutes, by his reckoning, and found themselves treated as such.

Scorning the underpass at Piccadilly Circus he waited for a gap in the traffic heading up Regent Street, and glanced at the statue of Eros. Love. When you were young you believed in love. Until you were disillusioned. Would this grown up child he was about to meet be idealistic, or would she have been hardened by Gaye's succession of lovers? And how do you tell your daughter that her existence was the cause of her parents' enmity?

You don't, was the sensible answer. Keep off that whole area, he decided. Ask her all about herself and her life. In return he would tell her how he'd made his money through hard graft and intelligence. He was proud of the fact, it was part of who he was, and important that she know.

A cyclist passed him, bravely weaving through the traffic on a lightweight, modern model, and Rab ran a knowledgeable eye over it. The machines had come a long way from when, as a schoolboy, he'd started mending people's bicycles after school and in the holidays. The surprise baby of parents who'd long given up hope of having children, they'd scraped by, denying themselves, in order to afford new school uniform, books and outings. The young Oliver Rabson responded by earning as much money as he could with his bicycle repairs. He'd inherited mechanical flair from his father, a railway maintenance engineer, and gave good service to customers. That, plus an understanding of human psychology passed on by his teacher mother, meant plenty of business. At sixteen, as soon as he could leave school, he'd opened a shop, selling new models made cheaply in Eastern Europe, and offering a discount for old bikes traded in. The scheme went so well that he opened another couple of shops, and was soon receiving more old bikes than he could sell, so he began shipping them out to Africa, where there was an eager market. Trouble was, the buyers couldn't always pay for them.

The smell of coffee wafted out from a café in Shaftesbury Avenue as he walked past. It had been a lucky day when that Kenyan contact had offered to trade a load of coffee beans for the bikes, and he'd accepted, not even knowing how he could sell them. A lot more profitably than the money he would have got for the bikes, it turned out. And so, by accident, he'd found himself with a second business – importing commodities such as cocoa, maize, coffee and tea, often in exchange for bicycles which had cost him nothing.

That had grown swiftly and given him the capital to extend his bicycle and, by now, motorcycle, shops, until by 1984 there was one in every sizeable town. To the City's surprise he had then sold the chain for £52m, and the commodity business not long after for a further £38m. Why? people asked, and he wasn't sure of the answer himself. Except that it had felt the right thing at the time.

What to do next? He was still only twenty-nine and with more money than he would ever need, even after Gaye deftly removed a big chunk of it a year or so later.

The buzz about Young British Artists was starting and, now divorced and restless for something to occupy him, Rab had looked at the stuff being produced and decided it was mostly tasteless grunge that he would have been ashamed to collect and display.

But as Charles Saatchi began buying up the work of what had become known as the Young British Artists Rab realized that the rules of commodity buying and selling could be applied to modern art. Indeed it was the perfect commodity. You controlled the supply, because although there was masses of the stuff, it only became valuable when you bought it. That made the artist 'hot', and his work was then worth whatever you said it was. The trick was quietly to sell on the object, which by that time your ownership had given additional caché. And if occasionally the hype didn't work and something failed to find an eager buyer, you could give it to a public gallery and receive tax relief on the stated worth, which was probably twenty times what you paid for it. You simply couldn't lose.

What made it more beautiful, besides a buzz from the sums involved, was making fools out of people who thought they were astute. A few of them knew the score and flipped the stuff fairly swiftly, but mostly the newly rich bought just to show that they could. Rab might fall into the new money category himself, but he prided himself on his confidence and good judgement. No-one would be able to persuade him that spending several million pounds on something requiring zero skill that could be knocked up in a morning would enhance his lifestyle and display how wealthy he was. He didn't need to prove anything to anyone.

Except perhaps his daughter. He felt more uneasy and disconcerted about this forthcoming meeting than he had for a good many years. It was unknown territory.

He reached the restaurant ten minutes early, to make sure Natasha didn't have the embarrassment of waiting alone. And seated at his favourite table watching diners arrive, he wondered how he would recognize her. Would she have his hazel eyes and the dark hair he'd had when young? Perhaps he should have asked for a photograph. But the moment she came in the door he knew, and felt a stab of dismay. God, it was going to be Gaye all over again.

But instead of Gaye's calculated charm, the grey eyes that met his were artless and full of fun, and Natasha's smile as she reached up to kiss him was joyfully mischievous.

'I've looked in the books and there's nothing about what to say when you meet your father for the first time', she sparkled at him.

His answering smile was relieved. 'We'll make up the rules as we go along, shall we.'

Chapter Three

Luckily Gaye took swift action when the press and paparazzi began gathering outside her Richmond house where Natasha had sought refuge. She asked if her daughter could slink along the tow path at the back and up through a neighbour's garden. Then arranged for a taxi to collect her from there. It was undignified and shaming, and Natasha was trembling as she shrank into the back seat, holding up a newspaper to hide her face as the cab drew away. She felt as if the delicious cake she'd been eating for the past year had turned out to have a large, black, slimy slug in the middle. A half bitten one at that.

She'd had such a wonderful whirl of a year as her father's protégée. There were art parties, private dinners and charity fund-raising affairs to go to almost every night. He'd taken her to the exhibition he was curating in New York and she'd been to Sotheby's and Christie's, learning how prospective buyers were wooed, and attended their prestigious evening auction sales. She'd enjoyed several glorious weeks on his yacht, being nice to various people he'd invited. Rab had given her the use of one of his flats and a generous dress allowance as well as a salary, and it was wonderful shopping for beautiful clothes and showing them off at all these occasions.

When Rab hosted parties at the gallery house next to his real home, she'd helped him by being especially charming to the guests he wanted to impress, to ensure they were eager to spend millions on some piece of art that Rab was regretfully 'letting-go'. She was also now a veteran of the preview gallery parties he was invited to, and could murmur about 'layers of engagement', 'the juxtaposition of inner and outer worlds', 'spiral momentum' and 'expanding the possibilities of interpretation', with the best of her fellow guests, as they gazed at some strange offering. If in doubt, you said, 'I'm enjoying the fact that it's all coming at me', or 'there's a nice dynamic with this'. And 'edgy' was a very useful word.

Surprisingly well known faces went to these gatherings too. At first she'd been overawed to be introduced to rock stars, politicians, chief executives of famous companies and people whose faces she'd only known from film and television. But rubbing shoulders with the famous had now become familiar, and the discovery of her own power to charm had really boosted her confidence. When a man was speaking, rapt attention, eyes fixed on his, and a hint of a smile was the default stance. If for some reason that didn't have the usual effect, then a slow, full-beam smile straight into his eyes caused meltdown, she found. It was as if she had some invisible, intoxicating power, and the lift was better than any drug. Of course it was just a ploy to help her father's business, even if they started to chat her up in earnest. After a few besotted men had tried to take things further she'd arranged for Charles to be invited along to these parties as well. He was happy to work the room talking easily, and could be hauled over and introduced as her boyfriend should the need arise.

The warmth of the relationship with her new found father was also a source of great pleasure. His account of why he hadn't kept in touch was the complete opposite of her mother's, and had caused a rift between her and Gaye. How could she deliberately have deprived Natasha of a father? As a child growing up with man after man introduced as a 'special friend', who either ignored her or, worse, insincerely made an elaborate fuss of her, she'd longed for steadiness in a man. Someone who was always there, strong and caring. Who loved her. And she'd observed Gaye's shallow and pleasure-orientated existence with distaste. Natasha had vowed never to be like that, and surprised her contemporaries at Oxford by working hard and steering clear of the drinking and parties.

Getting to know her father as an adult had been a rewarding process. She'd found Rab to be rather distant at first, but proved herself to be intelligent and hard-working in the office, as well as an asset on the social side, and gradually earned the approval she craved. Although he had never put it into so many words, she felt there was a strong bond of love between them. He'd chosen to have her on his arm at the Berkeley Square Ball, and she'd thrilled to the pride in his voice as he introduced her, 'My daughter, Natasha.'

Now Natasha closed her eyes. Oh God. What must Dad be thinking? The shock news of Charles's arrest had come last night, and she still didn't want to believe it. Accused of supplying drugs to numerous well-known names, the report on the news had said. If it was true, she knew for a fact that he'd met quite a few of them at art parties. And it was she who'd got him invited.

Gaye had already given her a grilling. 'Was she on drugs?' No, they'd been offered but she couldn't see the point, and Charles had never tried to persuade her. 'Had she known that Charles did drugs?' Well, yes. But she'd thought it was only for his own use. She had no idea he was dealing. 'Hadn't she thought it odd that a student never had money problems?' The answer she'd given was that he came from a good family, they had a large manor house and estate in Somerset, she'd just assumed they were well off.

This might have satisfied her mother but, as the taxi crawled through Chiswick, Natasha reflected that it was only a half truth. She knew very well that his parents were struggling with the upkeep of their house, and wasn't proud of the fact that it had given her some satisfaction. The family might have a pedigree stretching back to William the Conqueror's Sock Drawer Keeper, but her father could have bought them out without even noticing the absence of such small change. Charles's parents clearly regarded her as socially inferior, but at least the financial imbalance helped to redress things her way. An uncomfortable thought obtruded. Had Charles taken to drug dealing partly because she had money and he didn't? And if so, did that make this situation any better? Because the conclusion otherwise was that she, Natasha, was a hopeless judge of character. He'd proved to be treacherous, shamelessly using her and her contacts. She wanted to confront him and shout 'How *could* you?'

But there'd be plenty of time to analyze her relationship with Charles. The pressing thing now was to prepare for a session with an angry father. Gaye had been adamant that she had to go straight to Rab and talk things through. 'I've phoned him and he's expecting you. He'll know what to do to keep you out of the papers', she'd said. 'But don't let him bully you.'

Twelve months ago Rab would have scoffed at the idea that any female could affect him so much, but the past year had been happier than he could remember. It was as if before he'd been living with blinds drawn, and Natasha had brought light and warmth into his life. Her lively intelligence ensured that it was a pleasure teaching her how the business worked, and she got on well with everyone, particularly Pauline. When he hosted dinners and parties next door he watched her aiming her charm and beauty at prospective buyers in a subtle assault they stood no chance of withstanding. And at gallery showings and events he'd been proud to be accompanied by this lovely girl, his daughter. Teasing, beautiful and vivacious, she was simply a delight to have around.

And now this.

He'd made an urgent phone call to his PR guru, who'd assured Rab he'd do everything he could to take the heat off, adding reproachfully that prior warning of the scandal would have made all the difference. Pauline had been asked to come in early and buy all the newspapers on the way, but he knew, with unhappy certainty, that the story would feature in every one. How could they resist?

Now she spread the papers across the office carpet, and the headings shouted at him, each one like a hyena rushing in for a bite. "Rab's Girl in Drugs Shock", "Art and Drugs Link", "Drugs Scandal for Art Tsar". How could she have betrayed him? His lovely Natasha. He felt as if he'd been lacerated by a favourite kitten.

'Did you know any of this', he asked Pauline tautly, when they'd finished searching the papers. Had he been so besotted with his daughter that he hadn't seen what was clear to others?

'No. Of course not.' She knelt down and began cutting out the offending pieces. It would be important to keep a record. 'And what's more I'm certain she's not on drugs herself. My belief is that she probably didn't know what that boyfriend of hers was up to. She's surprisingly naïve in many ways.

Please God that was true. Rab paced the floor. 'That little shit! I always wondered what Natasha saw in him.'

'He was never invited to a party next door, you know', Pauline assured him. 'That should put you in the clear. Any drug contacts he made were at other occasions.'

'But these are high-profile people he's been supplying. When he comes up for trial the papers will be full of it won't they. And the Rabson name will be dragged into it all over again. It could hardly have come at a worse moment.'

Pauline looked up. 'When would be a good time?'

'What I mean is, just as we're launching the Rabson perfume and fashion brand, the name will be in the papers for all the wrong reasons.' Rab glanced down at the article that was being cut out and groaned. 'How can I keep her out of this? And what am I going to say to her when she arrives, for heaven's sake? Do I come the heavy father and tell her she can't continue to be seen with me? Oh God.' He slumped down in one of the armchairs. 'Pauline, you're a woman. I need your advice.'

It had not escaped his PA that one of the reasons they worked well together was that the relationship was akin to a marriage. Overtly the dominant partner, he relied on her intelligence and initiative, and she knew she had his respect.

'They won't be so inclined to rope her into it if she's been out of the public eye for some time,' she observed quietly.

'You're right. She could stay on the island, have an extended holiday. Journalists are not exactly thick on the ground in the Virgin Islands, and the staff would make sure they didn't land anyway.

'She'd be awfully lonely', Pauline countered. And the poor girl would feel she'd been banished. It's not as if *she's* done anything wrong, as far as we know.'

'Well what are you suggesting – a nunnery?'

26

'The countryside is as good as a convent as far as the national press is concerned. How about you opening a gallery out of town – and putting Natasha in charge of setting it up?'

'A gallery! What the hell would I want with another one – the whole of the house next door is one bloody gallery, stuffed full of art works as attractive as a rotting rat. The public think I live in the place with my collection.' He smiled wryly. 'It'd send me round the twist.'

'No, that wasn't what I had in mind.' She folded a newspaper and added it to the pile. 'I was thinking of a shop, selling prints and the odd original piece. It'd show you haven't given up on her and can trust her with a new project. You could tell Natasha it was something the business might pursue if the venture was successful – a gallery in every region perhaps. It won't make any money of course, so after a while you can say it was an interesting experiment and close it down.'

He stared at her. 'You might be onto something. Worth thinking about anyway.'

Getting to her feet Pauline remarked, 'You know, I think for Natasha this whole situation might turn out … ' she stopped and shook her head.

'What were you going to say?' he demanded.

'No. You won't like it. She's your family, and it's none of my business anyway. It doesn't matter.'

'I'll be the judge of that, shall I.'

She hesitated. 'Well, Natasha's changed in the past year. When she first came she was a sweet and charming girl, innocent and natural. Now she's discovered the effect she has on people, men especially. And it's… well, it's a change for the worse.'

'Are you saying it's my fault?' He was incredulous. 'That Gaye's managed to bring her up beautifully, and in one year I've somehow ruined it all.'

27

'No, it was bound to happen.' Pauline picked up the pile of newspapers and put them on the low table. 'You can't look the way she does and not have people react. But you actually put her in situations where using her charm was pleasing you, and I just think that's a pity. It was as if you were encouraging her to alter her personality.'

Was that a fair accusation? Rab looked back over the past months, and was struck by an unpleasant thought. Gaye knew only too well how to use her charm for her own ends. Was he turning his lovely Natasha into another Gaye, manipulating, superficial and vain?

'My God, you could be right,' he said unwillingly.

And she's not really had to work', Pauline continued, walking over to the window. 'Apart from a bit for me, here in the office. Give her a taste of the real world, with proper responsibilities and amongst ordinary people. It'll be good for her.'

'Mm. Oxford might be the right place for a gallery', he mused. 'And she knows the place. It wouldn't be fair to plonk her down all by herself in some strange town.'

'Actually I have another suggestion.' Pauline was looking down at a motorcyclist cruising slowly past the house. 'How about Rundleston?'

'Where?'

'It's a small town in East Anglia – where my son is. I've been going down there quite a bit for the past year, staying in a Bed and Breakfast. Sometimes I take him out, but it's a charming little place and in fact I'm thinking of renting a cottage of my own for weekends. So there'd be someone to keep any eye on her and offer support.' She turned towards him. 'It rather looks as if the first member of the paparazzi has appeared. He's just parking his motorbike.'

Rab looked at his watch. 'When's Natasha likely to get here? Fairly soon if the traffic's not too bad. Still, it'll be next door they'll be laying siege to. We can create a diversion and let her slip in here. This Rundleston place –

isn't that where Lyndon Scroby has bought a house? I seem to remember him telling me about it.'

'Yes, he's gutting some redbrick pile nearby. I met him in the High Street the other day.' She smiled. 'He couldn't get over seeing a face he knew – I think he's moved there for a bit of privacy.'

'It'll seem an odd choice for me to set up a gallery, won't it?'

'No, actually Rundleston's getting quite buzzy,' she assured him, standing to the side to remain unobserved from the street. 'There's a new marina, and that's popular with the sailing crowd. And some large industrial buildings have been converted into luxury flats which Londoners are buying, so there's potential for contemporary art sales. Plus', she added encouragingly, 'as it happens they're holding an art festival this autumn. It'll be a useful test for Natasha.'

'Hm. Well, it's a possibility', he said, as a another way forward occurred. 'Plenty of my American contacts would have her to stay. One of them has a ranch in Montana the size of a small country. Nobody would know she was there.'

Pauline knew better than to push her suggestion further, and in any case there were more urgent things to attend to.

Nevertheless, sending their beleaguered daughter to an insignificant pimple of a place was one of several ideas Rab subsequently discussed with Gaye on the telephone later that day, and it caused the most adverse reaction.

'*Rundleston!*' she exclaimed, as if he'd suggested Natasha spend a year on a sewage farm. 'Oh I don't think that's a good idea at all. Definitely not.'

This might not have been the most advisable of strategies.

If his ex-wife was dead against it, his idea of setting their daughter in charge of opening an out of town gallery immediately commended itself to Rab as the best possible course of action, although he was mildly surprised she'd even heard of the place.

Yes, he decided, after putting the phone down. Natasha should to be given a project to work at. Do her good perhaps, rubbing shoulders with ordinary people. After all he didn't mix with the glossy rich at her age. Pauline could take some time off and go down there to ensure everything went all right. He nodded to himself. This might after all be the making of his little girl.

The past year had not been a good one for the Banding family. The business's takings were continuing to decline. Most of the town shops were fighting what was, as they saw it, unfair competition from the new supermarket, which could often sell goods cheaper retail than the shopkeepers could buy wholesale. The greengrocer next door had finally given up, resulting in a knock on effect on their own business. The empty premises meant that fewer people walked past the window, to be pestered for a small toy by a grandchild, or suddenly reminded of a prickly relation for whom a birthday card was a tactical necessity. And when they needed sticky tape, notepads or envelopes, potential customers tended to throw them into the trolley while food shopping at the supermarket.

Nora was finding running the shop a struggle physically as well as financially, as the prolapsed disc in her back became an increasing problem. The doctors had finally said an operation was needed, and the constant pain was getting her down, but how could she take the time off? Betty, their part-time assistant, had been re-employed, but couldn't do more hours because she minded her grandchildren. Ben was solicitous, and helped in the shop more, but he was exasperatingly unreliable, promising to do an afternoon, only to spend it in his studio above the garage, absorbed in some painting and oblivious to time. Relations between them hadn't completely mended either over the gifting of the family maltings to the town, something she herself didn't want to think about, the way things had turned out.

In fact no-one could quite put their finger on how Rundleston's art festival changed its character. It just quietly happened, as if a goose egg had disappeared under the warm feathers of the organizing committee, and eventually a flamingo had chipped its way out.

All were agreed that this was a chance for Rundleston to gain favourable publicity, bring in tourists and make a mark in the nation's diary. Even before Nora Banding's gift of the maltings had been formally accepted, initial approaches were made to bodies such as the East of England Regional Assembly, the Tourist Authority, Arts Council and the Lottery Fund, who were likely to offer grants. Chairman of the town council, Harvey Drail, then set up a working party to take things further, and it was they, under the energetic leadership of his wife, Arabella, who had put together detailed proposals for the character and funding of the arts festival.

Arabella Drail would have come top of most people's list of the town's most indefatigable organisers, as the Rundleston Players and the Old People's Welfare Group could attest. So this was not nepotism, although in truth his home life would have suffered otherwise. It was up to her, she felt, to ensure Rundleston made the most of a great opportunity, to transform itself into a town most people knew about, instead of somewhere that had to be looked up on the map. And when she was made chairman of the committee running Rundleston's art festival everything fell into place. One of the celebrated Young British Artists, Lyndon Scroby, had just bought the Drail's old house outside Rundleston, and that meant a hotline to the pinnacle of the art world. He could smooth her way to all these famous names, his friends. If, given luck, they graced the festival with their works, maybe even their presence, that would enormously increase the amount of publicity the event received. It promised to be really good for the town, far better than the old fashioned art that Nora Banding had in mind, which the press would hardly mention.

Thus the pitch to the bodies being asked for grants was shifted, emphasizing that it would be a showcase for cutting edge, modern, exploratory art. There would be at least one work by Lyndon Scroby (Arabella was hopeful about persuading him anyhow). There would be portraiture in the modern idiom, sound installations, and performance art. The visitor would be invited to explore space and time, light and colour, redefining the boundaries. Besides challenging art work and video competitions for local schoolchildren, the visitor would be drawn in and become part of the art.

Arabella had no idea what half this stuff meant, but Lyndon helpfully guided her on what she should put. 'No-one's going to challenge it', he assured her, 'in case they look ignorant. And basically it means you can do what you like.'

Ben observed the way Rundleston's arts festival was shaping up with bitterness. That the whole art world was united in deriding what he did had been obvious for years, and one day, he'd told himself, somehow, he would make the world see this stuff for the garbage it was. But at least the excesses and absurdities took place far away from him. Now to have it invading his beloved home town and, worse, being housed in his own family's former building, was like opening the bedroom door and discovering someone had covered every surface with day-glo orange fur and purple nodding dogs.

The temptation to say, 'I told you so', to his mother was strong, but he resisted. Although she tried to hide the pain her back was giving, she looked tired and drawn these days, which made him feel guilty. The part of him that was a dutiful and caring son knew he should offer to take her place full time in the shop. But that obligation was fighting everything in life that he enjoyed – spending hours in his studio working up drawings into paintings which satisfied his soul, helping Flitch in the boatyard, taking Bodger for long walks, sailing the family boat, or sketching things that inspired him.

When Ben saw the shadows and colour of evening he had a compulsion to capture it. Children crabbing on the quay with sunlight dancing on their faces, the rippled reflection of the Hetty Jane, or light streaming through a window – they were like switches to him. The images energized him, he simply had to capture them. And somehow in his hands and brain was the ability to transfer them to paper and board, and then to compose them into a picture that didn't just echo the originals, it transformed them into something magical. He felt he was a conduit for a wonderful gift, giving meaning to his existence. It wasn't just a hobby, it defined him. What he produced was part of how he saw himself, an artist. True, he had in past years spent time converting Chandlers, and running or overseeing various businesses at the maltings, but that didn't detract from who he really was. If I take over the shop though, he told Bodger, then that's what I'll be. A shopkeeper in a small town. And I'm bloody not. It was an intractable problem, and he responded by trying to ignore it.

Nora had no knowledge of his inner struggles, but she was wondering if circumstances weren't combining to give her a window in which to have her back operation and still keep the shop and the B & B businesses going. Pauline Mansard, the nice woman who'd been staying odd weekends for the past year, had telephoned to ask if she could please take the rooms for several months. She herself wouldn't be there all the time, but a young girl who was under her wing, would be. The situation sounded intriguing and Nora was dying to find out more, but Pauline wouldn't elaborate on the phone. They were arriving tomorrow and she would doubtless find out then. The good thing was that the continuity would mean much less work. Indeed Pauline had said they would pretty much look after themselves. And now today Nora had received a letter that might just solve the shop problem for a

33

while. Things were looking up if she could just sort them out satisfactorily with Ben.

To save her back he had insisted on doing most of the work that evening getting the rooms ready, and as she dusted the furniture it seemed a good time to broach the subject.

'Do you remember Madge, the girl who helped in the shop in the school holidays ten or eleven years ago?'

'Skinny kid with freckles and ginger hair?' he ventured, opening the cupboard door on the landing in search of the vacuum cleaner, Bodger immediately pushing his nose in curiously.

'Well I'd have called it auburn myself, but yes. And she must be late twenties now, married with a nine year old child.'

Ben was unwinding the flex. 'What about her?'

'She's written saying she wants to come back to Rundleston. Seems her husband has gone off with someone else and the house is being sold. She wondered if she and the boy could come and perch in our rooms until she sorts out a job and somewhere permanent to live.'

'Well she can't, can she.' He put the plug in the socket. 'You've just let the rooms for the whole summer.'

'Ah, the thing is I've had an idea', Nora told him carefully. 'If I lend them my flat free of charge, then in return I can ask Madge to look after the shop while I'm out of action. It'll give her time to sort herself out, and would really help us. It's perfect.'

'Just one teeny problem. What happens to you?' He delayed switching on the machine, but, with a little stab of shameful dismay, knew the answer that was coming.

'Would you mind if I moved in with you, and slept in your spare room? We could store your stuff in the garage couldn't we? Oh no', she remembered, 'all the Rundleston Players' costumes are in there. I must remind Arabella Drail to find somewhere else for them.'

'I'll move my things into the studio', he told her generously, trying not to think how cramped that would make his small sanctuary above the garage. But listen, it's better if you stay where you are, and put whatever-her-name-is in my place – Flitch'll let me sleep in the foc'sle of the Hetty Jane for a while. In fact he might be quite pleased – some drunks tried to cast her off the other night. Bodger would give them second thoughts, wouldn't you boy.'

'Goodness, no need for that, it'll only be temporary', she hastened to assure him. 'Just a week or two.'

'Okay', Ben smiled at her, pleased to think that his mother would soon be back to full health. Life could then resume its pleasant rhythm.

Nora had been expecting Pauline's arrival mid afternoon, and asked Ben to be on standby to take over the shop. In the event it was just before five-thirty that her car stopped outside the entrance to the yard at the side of the house, and Pauline got out to open the big wooden gates. She seemed to be alone.

'I'll give her a cup of tea, she'll be tired', Nora said, having summoned Ben, adding, 'After you close, it would be nice to come up and say hello.' Her casual tone belied the great hope that now dominated her thoughts. A girl, from London, the thinking went, she and Ben would inevitably see a lot of each other. Things could happen... Maybe, cross fingers, this would turn out to be her future daughter-in-law. And the mother of longed-for grandchildren.

She greeted Pauline at the side door that led into the yard. 'I thought there'd be two of you', she said, disappointed at not setting eyes on the girl destined to charm Ben out of his bachelorhood.

'Natasha's coming in her own car, so she has transport when I'm not here. She'll be arriving shortly', Pauline told her, retrieving her handbag from the passenger seat, before shutting the car door. 'I wanted to put you in the picture first.'

Over tea and biscuits, looking out over the estuary, she filled in the background to her sudden request to take the rooms for the summer, Natasha having been tasked to set up a gallery, which would conveniently keep her out of London. But it wasn't long before she detected anxiety on Nora's part.

'Oh dear. I didn't know you worked for Oliver Rabson, and this girl's his daughter. It could be a bit of a problem.'

Pauline looked questioning.

'It's my son, Ben – you've met him I think. He paints.' She indicated the many striking pictures on the sitting room walls, which Pauline had noticed the moment she entered. Well the thing is, Oliver Rabson's his bête noire. He hates all this contemporary art stuff, you see, and he's particularly taken against Rabson for some reason.' But her desire to match make refused to lie down. 'Could we pretend she was someone else, or just not tell him her surname?'

'No, that wouldn't work, I'm afraid. The gallery's going to be called 'Rabson's'. Still, they won't have much to do with each other will they', Pauline made light of the situation. 'But I can just introduce her as 'Natasha' if you like.'

Ben had a pleasant evening planned. First a decent walk for Bodger to Woodshey Bay. Then crewing for Flitch, taking the Hetty Jane out on the tide before docking at the quay where passengers would embark next day for a birthday party trip. If he was lucky, Flitch's wife Tricia would be aboard and rustle up a meal in the galley. Otherwise he could have a companionable pint and a pie in the bar of the Spritty afterwards.

He left Bodger in his flat with an encouraging, 'Won't be long boy', and went upstairs to his mother's sitting room. He found her chatting to Pauline, and did his bit with small talk before starting to make his excuses.

'Oh you haven't met Natasha', Nora forestalled him. 'She's just gone upstairs.'

At that moment the door opened, and into the room came a beautiful girl. She was a sight to turn any man's heart over, and Ben's duly missed a beat as his mind turned cartwheels.

It was her! Couldn't be... He stood still, frozen in disbelief, as if watching the Mona Lisa step from her frame sporting a Manchester United shirt and a death's head tattoo.

'Hello, I'm Natasha Rabson', the girl greeted him with a smile, observing a man more than usually struck by her appearance. Pauline had said she would find the Rundleston natives unsophisticated.

God! *No!*

Ignoring her, Ben walked past. '*Bloody hell!*' he muttered, opened the door and disappeared down the stairs.

After apologizing for his behaviour, and settling their guests at the top of the house, Nora found him in his flat, packing things into a sailing bag.

'Ben, that was extremely rude...' she began.

'You can tell the ginger kid she and her brat can come as soon as they like', her son cut short the reproaches. 'I'm moving out.'

'Moving out? But why?' Nora was bewildered.

Ben looked up and managed a shaky grin. 'Don't worry, I'll be around', he reassured her. 'It's just best if I don't stay here.'

Chapter Four

Natasha was delighted when Madge moved in to the ground floor flat with son Jamie a fortnight later. After the first week Pauline had gone back to London, promising to come down at weekends, leaving Natasha unhappily alone. Her father had given her the project of opening a gallery, and there was plenty for her to do now that she and Pauline had decided on the empty greengrocers shop as the right premises. Designing the layout, getting quotes from shopfitters and electricians, liaising with her father's legal people about company names, leases etc. was keeping her busy during working hours. And she exchanged emails with Rab and Pauline every day. But how was she supposed to spend the long evenings?

Rab's publicist had done a good job of heading off the press, and she was already yesterday's scandal, but even so she was under orders not to go back to London, or divulge her whereabouts for the time being. So although plenty of friends kept in touch, she couldn't describe what she was doing, and feeling, only general chat. Charles had been bailed, and kept sending her emails asking where she was, declaring his love and pleading for them to meet and talk things over, but she didn't reply. Whatever explanation he came up with, he'd proved untrustworthy, and there could be no going back. She missed the glamour and excitement of her life in London though. Most nights there'd been some party or gallery showing to dress up for, and now there was nothing. And no-one to talk to, except Nora Banding, who'd suggested Natasha make full use of her flat's kitchen. She mostly bought something that could be quickly heated up there, or made herself an easy meal. And then she was usually invited to stay and keep Nora company.

She found herself fascinated by the thrilling paintings that hung on the flat's sitting room walls, some oils, others watercolours, all beautifully framed. Any one of them would have been a privilege to live with, a room full was almost too much. The portrait of Nora's husband hung above the mantelpiece, and opposite it was one of her in the garden, hair light brown then, but the same sweet expression. Next to it an oil of a ploughman, tractor outlined against a dark and threatening sky, a mass of seagulls turning and weaving in the air behind him as he hurried to beat the coming storm. You could almost hear their raucous clamour, the artist had caught them so beautifully, yet in no way was the style dully photographic. Another depicted an old man in an ancient jersey pulling on the oars of a rowing boat, the light glinting on the whorls of water made by the blades. The sense of movement frozen in time, and the character on the old boy's face made it a painting to treasure.

'That's Herbie Luffe. He was a great old bargeman', Nora commented, seeing her interest. 'Ben was very fond of him.'

There was an awkwardness when Ben's name was mentioned. Nora was embarrassed at the boorish way her son was behaving. If he dropped in to see her and found Natasha there he'd retreat hastily, as if he'd happened on a five foot tarantula, mumbling about coming another time. She thought of explaining that he hated the modern art espoused by the girl's father, but that hardly seemed an adequate explanation. Besides, it would have been impolite, seeing that Natasha was herself opening up a gallery to sell the stuff. It was a pity that this charming girl, daughter of a multi-millionaire to boot, should be too young for both her sons, but it was mortifying that all Ben could do was rudely give her the cold shoulder. When he came to do his hours in the shop she chided him about his bad manners, but he refused even to discuss it. This unhelpful attitude did however succeed in killing off his mother's lingering hopes of marriage for him. It was like expecting a primrose to bloom in August, she finally realised. Just not in his nature.

Natasha was hurt and puzzled by Ben's obvious antipathy. She was also nettled. She couldn't ask Pauline or Nora, 'Why doesn't Ben like me?', because it sounded conceited. After all, why should he? All the same, as the beautiful do, she'd become accustomed to the fact that people were favourably disposed towards her, and took it for granted that men would behave as if she was the Piper of Hamelin, especially when singled out for a special smile. But on her landlady's son it was having the opposite effect. He might be gay of course, but that didn't fit either. She'd met plenty of gay men at art parties, and got on perfectly well with them. They liked aesthetically pleasing things.

It occurred to her that perhaps this woman, Madge, could cast light on the situation. As someone who had grown up in Rundleston, and worked for the family, she must have known them well.

Natasha was out when Madge arrived on the Friday morning, but knocked on the door of the ground floor flat later that day. It was opened by a girl wearing jeans and loose top, hair as auburn as a sunburnt fox, drawn back from her face with a brown velvet ribbon. She had very blue eyes and her pale skin was covered with freckles jostling for space, like duckweed on a pond. Besides the striking looks, there was a willowy elegance about her, and an aura of calm strength that Natasha immediately warmed to.

'I'm planning on a Chinese takeaway this evening', she said, after introducing herself. 'Can I get one for you and your son as a flat warming present?'

'What a kind thought, thank you. It's just me actually, Jamie won't be here till Sunday – he's with his father this weekend. But yes please, that would be lovely,' Madge smiled at her warmly. 'I'll certainly be ready for it – might be just about straight by then.'

Ben's large living room echoed his mother's above, but with sash windows through which you could climb out onto a paved patio. But where Nora had a dining room and two good-sized bedrooms over the shop, his flat was restricted to bedroom, kitchen, bathroom and another, smaller, room which had been full of stuff, transferred in the last few days to his studio above the garage. Nora's spare bed had been moved down, to make a bedroom for Jamie, and both rooms now had a spread of cases and boxes in various stages of being unpacked.

Four plain wooden chairs clustered around a pine table in the window bay, where that evening Natasha put the hot foil containers of spicy-smelling food. While Madge located plates, forks and spoons in the kitchen, she looked around with interest, trying to gauge the personality of the owner from the furnishings and décor.

An imposing ship's clock mounted on mahogany ticked away on the back wall, and between it and a large, brass-bound barometer was a beautiful wooden half-round of a sailing boat, its smooth hull showing off the grain to perfection. Like Nora's room, eye-catching paintings adorned the walls. A study of Ben's father hung above the mantlepiece, but this time he was seated, drawing what looked like marine plans of some sort. There was an atmospheric depiction of a ramshackle boatyard, a rotting hulk and huge rusty anchor in the background, one man operating a small crane, while another guided the boat it was lifting. And there were paintings of sailing barges, creaming up the river under full sail, or at anchor, reflection gently oscillating on quiet water as the crew rowed ashore. A long bookcase stood against one wall, next to an old television, and a saggy, comfortable-looking sofa and armchair faced the fireplace. The carpet had probably once been green, and the curtains were autumnal colours, with touches of cream to match the walls. It was a mellow, masculine room, Natasha concluded, belonging to someone who liked comfort and tradition, cared not at all about fashion, and had a strong sense of colour.

41

The two women found each other easy to talk to, and Natasha had soon confided the background to her situation, concluding indignantly, 'I don't want anything more to do with Charles. He just used me to make profitable contacts.'

In return she learned that Madge, having separated from her husband, was undecided about joining her parents, who had emigrated to Canada, or settling in her home town of Rundleston, if she could find a job.

'What kind of job?' asked Natasha, but Madge wasn't clear about that herself.

'I was doing business studies at university', she explained, 'with a marketing bias. And then', she grimaced, 'I went and got pregnant in my second year. So Luke and I married, and there wasn't any need for me to work, he was storming his way up in advertising.' Madge smiled self-deprecatingly. 'So I don't know what I'm fit for, but I'd be content with part-time work for now. It's important that Jamie has as much stability as possible. And I'd like him to have the sort of experiences I had, instead of suburbia. Rundleston gave me a lovely childhood.'

This was just the right moment to ask about the Bandings, thought Natasha, as they cleared their plates off the table and carried them into the small kitchen.

'What happened to Nora's husband? He looks quite young in those paintings.'

'Oh that was terrible.' Madge was putting the plates in a washing up bowl, while Natasha began hulling some early strawberries. 'He was drowned in a sailing accident. I was only about seven at the time, but I remember it clearly. My grandfather was the Banding's last manager at the maltings, so we knew the family well. And the really sad thing was that Mike was trying to save his son, who'd gone out when he'd been told not to, and had capsized and got trapped underneath the dinghy.'

'Ben?'

'No, his younger brother Tony. And he survived, because he was in a pocket of air, but Mike's foot got caught in a rope and he drowned.'

'How awful'

'Ben was away at art school, I remember. And of course he came home at once. He and Tony never did get on, even before the accident. My mother used to say they were living proof that nature beats nurture every time. But the fact that Tony had caused their father's death just made things that much worse. So poor Nora not only lost her husband, she then had warring sons as well.'

Madge found two bowls in a cupboard, and Natasha shared the strawberries between them, as they talked, then carried them back to the table with sugar and a carton of cream. None of this information helped in understanding Ben's hostility, but Natasha decided it might help to discuss it.

'Taken a hate against you?' queried Madge, after having the situation explained. 'That doesn't sound like Ben. He's really nice natured. Lives for his art of course – and no wonder', she gestured at the walls. 'From what Nora says she could do with him taking more responsibility for the family shop, but there isn't a nasty bone in his body.'

'Perhaps I imagined it', Natasha conceded, feeling rather foolish.

'Well now that you mention it, Nora did say he'd been behaving oddly. How intriguing.'

With her appealing, childlike beauty, Natasha's face would have had nightdress advertisers in transports of delight, Madge reflected, looking at her. Not to mention prompting fond, if not fondling, thoughts in most men. How was it that Ben Banding was apparently not only resistant to such an attractive girl, but actively hostile.

'If there's something eating him I'll soon find out', Madge assured her, delicately slicing a large strawberry in half with her spoon. 'I'm being shown the ropes at the shop on Monday, after Jamie starts at his new school. Going to have two days with Nora to get the hang of things before she goes into hospital, and Ben's promised to do after school hours and help as much as he can.' She laughed. 'And he'd better not try being rude to me.'

Madge was taken aback at the state of the shop. From her schooldays doing Saturday and holiday work there, she remembered it as a busy place, with so many customers the Bandings had needed help. Now there was a run-down, sad feel about it, and trade was clearly slow. But apart from its lack of bustle, everything seemed just the same. As before, the big racks of birthday cards took up two of the walls, with free-standing carousels dotted around the shop. Wrapping paper hung on the same metal arms, the notebooks, typing paper,envelopes and 'fancies' hadn't moved. Nora always kept a shelf for displaying seasonal goods, and despite it being May, some calendars and diaries lingered there, marked 'Half Price'. Just as always, the till on the the curved wooden counter was tucked into one corner, so's to get a good view of the door as well as the back of the shop.

Obediently Madge listened to Nora's instructions, while thinking much could be done to improve the situation. Had they considered stocking printer cartridges, for instance, and special paper for people printing out photographs? She did ask, but Nora's answer was vaguely negative.

'Oh I don't think there's much demand – and they'd take up too much space.' She sensed Madge's disagreement, and added wearily, 'I stick to what I know. Perhaps that's part of the trouble.'

'Would you mind if I got some in as an experiment?'
Nora patted her arm encouragingly. 'You do what you like Madge dear. You know, in a funny way I'm looking forward to going into hospital. Not the operation of course – although I'm hoping it will get rid of this constant pain – but having a rest and a complete break. And I certainly don't want to be thinking about the shop. So you have my

blessing to do whatever you think best. It's really kind of you to help us out like this, and I know how capable you are. Ben'll sign cheques for the business.'

If Nora was stale and tired, Madge surveyed the shop with optimism. It was a challenge. She felt sure she could get the place profitable again. After all, what was the use of a business studies degree if you couldn't pull round a failing family shop in a small town? She took the shop accounts back to the flat that first evening, and after Jamie had gone to bed, drew up a rough business plan. 'Unique Selling Proposition', she wrote in a spiral bound notebook. 'Prints of Ben's paintings.' And why not offer a framing service? He already had the necessary equipment.

She had mentioned this possibility to Nora. 'Well', she'd responded doubtfully, 'you'll have to ask him. I don't think he'd be keen.'

It was odd seeing Ben again after more than a decade. Like the shop, he didn't seem to have changed, whereas Madge felt she'd become a completely different person. Back then she'd been a raw schoolgirl, respectful of a thirty-year old man. Now she was approaching thirty herself, a divorcee, or soon to be, with a child of her own. She'd moved on in her life, while he seemed to have stayed in the same spot.

When Jamie reached the terrible twos and staged spectacular tantrums, Madge had learned to be firm but kind, to distract and, when necessary, negotiate. For some reason these valuable skills were not on the curriculum of her business studies course, but she now proposed to put them into practice on a grown man.

Ben drove his mother to hospital on Wednesday morning, then came back to the shop to give Madge time off for lunch. She returned to find Bodger snoozing behind the counter, and his owner looking bored.

With Nora gone, she was really in charge now. Time to get cracking.

'I don't like framing', was Ben's immediate response to her suggestion. 'It's not difficult to make a decent job of it, and it's quite fun making my own, but I'd rather not do more than that.'

Faced with Madge's arrestingly blue eyes and reproachful look, he straightened a box of key rings on the counter that had no need of exact alignment with the till.

'I'm not suggesting you slave over it when it's a glorious, sunny afternoon and you'd rather be out sailing', she said. 'Shall we just put a notice in the window about framing and see what happens?'

'Well...hmm.'

'There's not likely to be a great rush', she added persuasively. 'And it would bring in money.'

He could hardly object, and smiled at her shame facedly. 'Yes. Sorry, I'm just being lazy aren't I. We can offer the service if you want.'

First battle won.

Encouraged, Madge decided to engage on a second, and more important, front. 'You know what would give this shop something unique', she said lightly, 'cards that were prints of your lovely paintings.' She smiled at him. 'I specially like those barge ones in your sitting room. They'd be really popular.'

'No', he gave his decision with finality. 'They're paintings, not greetings cards. I'll be back at three. Come on Bodger.' He held the door open for an approaching customer, then disappeared down the street, the dog at his side.

Ben turned down Loft Lane towards the river. The tide was just on the ebb, a breeze ruffled his hair, and sun glinted on the water invitingly. But there'd be no time for a sail this afternoon, if he needed to be back in the shop later. 'We'll go for a w... perambulation instead, boy', he informed Bodger, 'after a bite in the Spritty'.

46

The Spritsail Barge was one of those pubs everyone loves, but for different reasons. Quaint and picturesque, it was a gift for tourist brochures, featuring photogenic families laughing happily. For newcomers and those with boats in the nearby marina, it meant they could sit at tables outside admiring the view, and comment, with apparent knowledge, on passing yachts, and sailing dinghies being launched from the hard. To the locals it represented continuity, having always been a favourite haunt of bargees, dockside workers, boatbuilders and maltsters, who were welcome in their work clothes. The main bar's wooden floor was rendered unpalatable to woodworm by centuries of mud and salt water, and the walls which might once have been cream, were now toffee coloured courtesy of the smoke, both from customers and a log fire that in winter provided communal warmth. A small bay window jutted out over the water which, at high tide, lapped the pub, and the cushioned sill was a prized seat. Old photographs of Rundleston were displayed, along with a ship's wheel, framed charts, pennants of barges long gone, and brass port and starboard lanterns that in a smarter pub would have been polished. Also a blackboard with today's lunch offerings.

The place had been Ben's second home all his adult life, but now it was a vital refuge. The cosy, uneventful life that cocooned him was being torn away, piece by piece, leaving him disconcerted and vulnerable. The first shock was his mother's gift of the family maltings, now, insultingly, to be the venue for a festival of modern art – the very antithesis of all he valued, and the reason that the world despised his painting. Then That Girl appeared. In his own house! The face of his dreams, the person he adored, his lost – no, *stolen* – soul mate, was here. But the face belonged to another person, and another generation. Worse, she was Oliver Rabson's daughter. Just looking at her was upsetting, but on top of that was the reminder of how so many years had passed without him noticing. How could Gaye be the mother of That Girl, when in his mind she was as young and beautiful as that herself? Now his own mother was suddenly ageing visibly, and the skinny ginger kid had turned into a woman, with a nine-year old son for heaven's sake, and was wanting to change everything at the shop. The convivial familiarity of the Spritty was one of the few certainties left in his world.

Flitch's wife Tricia was doing her usual lunchtime stint behind the bar when he and Bodger came in, and automatically began drawing a pint of Jahney's. Ben might have been more than a decade older, but she felt motherly towards him, and didn't like to see him miserable, as he clearly had been these past couple of weeks. His normally relaxed and cheerful self had changed. Best not to ask why, she'd thought, and Flitch didn't care. Bodger might be soft as a kitten, except where hares and rabbits were concerned, but he had a deep, intimidating bark, and the Hetty Jane now had excellent night time security for the price of a few showers and the odd load of washing . Flitch'd be glad for the arrangement to last all summer. But Tricia reckoned some rift with his mother was behind Ben's request to stay on the barge, and now Nora had gone into hospital he would surely move back to Chandlers. Illness transcends rows.

'Well, who's got the troubles of the world on their shoulders?' she greeted him, pulling on the pump handle a second time to make sure of full measure. 'Don't worry, your mum'll be just fine.'

'Oh. Yes', he responded absently.

'When she comes out of hospital will you be moving back home?' she took his money in exchange for the beer.

Ben explained about someone currently occupying his flat in return for minding the shop, and the guest rooms on the top floor being fully let.

'But your mum's got a spare room – you could stay there couldn't you?

'No, I *couldn't*', he answered with an unguarded emphasis that immediately aroused Tricia's curiosity. This was a man who didn't do strong feelings. A friend of hers once had ambitions of becoming Mrs Ben Banding, but finally gave up, reporting that though he was a lovely man, sweet and kind and sensitive, he seemed emotionally frozen. It was as if he was somehow waiting for the perfect woman, who probably didn't exist and never would.

'Why's that then?'

'Oh. Um…' Ben pocketed his change, floundering for an explanation. 'It's this creature who's taken the room upstairs, and uses the kitchen. She's the pits. Spoilt little rich girl who thinks modern art's just wonderful. Going to open a gallery next to us.' He took a pull on his beer. 'Huh! You know what I think about that rubbish! I'd just rather keep out of her way.'

Too late, another explanation occurred to him. 'Oh, and Tony's coming down to see Mum as soon as she gets home, so he'll need the room.' He made a face at Tricia, knowing she would understand. 'Never rains but it pours.'

Chapter Five

Tony duly arrived at Chandlers on Saturday afternoon, only to open the big double gates and find to his annoyance that there was no room in the yard for his car. Parking on a yellow line, he marched into the shop demanding to know why. With no observable pleasure at his brother's arrival, Ben explained that the extra vehicles belonged to the B&B guests and the girl temporarily in the ground floor flat.

'Well, two of them will have to move', Tony declared impatiently. 'I can't leave the Z4 out in the street – too much of a temptation for the local chavs. Where are they?'

'Don't know about Madge. You'll probably find the other two in the old greengrocers next door', Ben informed him. 'They're opening up a modern art gallery', he added stonily. 'You should have a lot in common.'

Natasha had relayed to Pauline, down for the weekend, what she'd learned about Nora's missing son, who apparently worked in the City for Grashes bank, and both of them were mildly curious to meet him. They were discussing what security measures the gallery would need, when there was a loud knocking on the door, and there stood a man in chinos and expensive leather jacket. There was a clear family resemblance with the same curly brown hair, but instead of Ben's puzzled appeal, his brother had an assessing, up-for-it expression, and a mouth that hovered on a smirk . Enquiringly, Pauline opened the door.

'I'm Tony Banding', the man informed her, without bothering to hold out his hand. 'I need to park in the yard, so I'm afraid you'll have to mo... Oh!' A lovely girl had appeared at the woman's shoulder. That in itself would have warranted a change of manner, but incredibly, this was someone he recognized. That face had been in the papers recently, and surely she was familiar from gallery openings... Could it be... Christ almighty, it was! Oliver Rabson's daughter. Here, in Rundleston!

'I was just saying, I'm Tony Banding', the tone had altered, and he smiled into Natasha's eyes as he proffered his hand, followed up with a more perfunctory shake for the old biddy. I just thought I'd come and say hello. Contemporary art's a particular interest of mine. I'm in charge of Grashes' art collection.'

This wasn't entirely true, but they weren't likely to check, he reckoned.

Tony chatted for a few minutes, revealing what the Rabson girl would undoubtedly recognize as impressive knowledge, then went back to the shop. He looked up at the familiar frontage and shuddered. Thank God he'd got away. He couldn't imagine how his lacklustre brother was content to stay in the place where he was born. Small town mentality, that was his trouble. Good thing one Banding had drive, talent and ambition.

And luck. He could hardly take in this fantastic turn of events. Natasha Rabson had been glimpsed at art gatherings, but he'd never managed to wangle an introduction. Now here she was, unbelievably, staying in his family house! Beautiful, unattached, and heir to mega millions. Play your cards right, he told himself, and Tony old son you've *really* landed in the jam.

He went into the shop. 'Best if you shift the Ford', he told Ben, without waiting for him to finish serving a customer.

'Well you'll either have to mind the shop while I do it, or wait until five thirty', was the calm response, as Ben rang up the sale. 'Or you could shift it yourself, of course – the key's in the kitchen drawer.'

But Natasha Rabson might assume it was his car, if she saw him driving a very ordinary Ford. And serving behind the counter of a two-bit stationery store just didn't bear thinking about. Accordingly the shiny, black BMW Z4 remained parked in the street, unmolested, until six o'clock.

Next morning Tony was torn between wanting to fetch Nora from hospital, thus proving himself to be the most devoted of sons, or letting Ben do it while he had the chance of rubbing shoulders with Natasha.

'Well Mum won't be able to sit very comfortably, so she'll need to go on the back seat', Ben pointed out.

That ruled out taking Tony's two seater, and meant he'd have to drive the Ford Fiesta. Decision made. It was Ben who went to collect their mother.

Pauline had discussed with Natasha whether they should intrude on the homecoming at all. After all, they weren't family, only paying guests, although both of them got on very well with Nora. But Pauline reckoned they could make a real contribution by preparing an appetizing lunch for her to eat with her two sons, then tactfully disappearing.

Pauline poached some salmon, and Natasha made a salad to go with it, followed by fruit salad and cream. Tony's offer of help came at the price of listening to how indispensable he was to the bank in advising on what art to buy, arranging their corporate entertainments and talking to clients who'd been invited to come and view the art collection. He also managed to convey a laudable sense of financial responsibility towards Nora.

'I'll buy Mum a new, flat screen television', he announced, surveying her old square-faced one as if he'd never seen it before. 'And I wonder if it would help her to have one of those chairs that raises and lowers electrically. They're expensive of course, but that doesn't matter.'

The meal ready, Pauline and Natasha stayed only long enough to greet Nora and welcome her home, then escaped to eat their own lunch at the Spritsail Barge.

'You wouldn't believe siblings could be so different would you', remarked Pauline, after they'd ordered food, and brought their drinks to a table outside in the sunshine. It was a warm day and the place was busy with young families. Boats lolled sideways on mud exposed by the ebbing tide, which had lengthened the little stream as it ran down beside the hard. From the boatyard at the other side of the sailing club came the whirr of a motor and the clanging sound of metal striking metal.

'We'd probably have squabbled all the time, but I always thought it would be lovely to have a brother or a sister', Natasha said wistfully, watching as a young family raced toy boats in the stream's chuckling water, mother and son versus father and daughter. 'When I was a child I longed to be in a proper family.'

'It's surprising Gaye didn't marry again and have more children'.

'Not really'. Natasha was clear-eyed about her mother. 'If she'd married again she might have lost out on Dad's money – although perhaps that's an unkind thing to say. And of course the Rabson name opens a lot of doors for her as an events organiser.'

'Perhaps she just didn't meet the right man to settle down with.'

Natasha shook her head. 'To her chasing and being chased by men isn't just a sideshow, it's what life's all about. If there's one thing I'm determined on, it's not to be like that.'

Remembering the deliberate flirting with Rab's prospective buyers, Pauline was glad to hear it.

'I always felt as if I was excess baggage, getting in the way of the great game. And she said my father didn't want anything to do with me, so…'

She didn't need to finish. What kind of mother would put her own shallow interests first? wondered Pauline, looking at Natasha's face and picturing her as a child, forlornly seeking affection. If she'd been mine I'd have loved her, she thought with compassion.

Father and daughter's boat was bobbing its way into the lead, and they were cheering it on, the girl jumping up and down with excitement, grabbing at his hand.

Natasha watched with a half smile. 'At least I've found my Dad now. Best thing that's ever happened to me.' She sipped her cider. 'Friends are all very well, but they don't *belong* to you, like family do.'

'Rab's delighted too', Pauline assured her. 'He's been happier this past year than I've ever seen him.'

A young lad arrived carrying their plates of ordered food, and there was a pause in the conversation while they sorted things out.

'There was something I wanted to ask you', Natasha continued, when he'd gone back to the bar. 'It's Dad's birthday soon – what on earth am I going to get him? He's so difficult to give to. You know him better than anyone. Suggestions please.'

'Well, let's think…' The wonderful paintings on Nora's walls were still fresh in Pauline's mind. 'Why don't you get Ben Banding to do a portrait of you? He's obviously very talented, and your father would it love it.'

'That's a great idea!' Then her face clouded. 'Ben doesn't like me though, does he.'

Pauline couldn't imagine any man resisting the charm of her young companion, especially if she'd put her mind to softening him up.

'Oh I'm sure he won't say no', she declared confidently.

Natasha wondered how best to approach Ben with her request.

'The problem is I hardly ever see him', she told Madge, 'he seems to do his best to avoid me.' She didn't like to admit it, but the experience of someone actively disliking her was novel, and disconcerting. 'Sometimes I meet him going up to his studio in the morning, or visiting Nora, but he's only got to see me and he scuttles off. You'd think I'd got the plague or something.'

'Why not ask him when he's minding the shop after three?' Madge suggested. 'He can't very well escape then.'

'Well it might be a bit tricky with customers coming in and interrupting', Natasha was doubtful, but it did seem the best opportunity. So next afternoon she entered the family shop to find it empty except for Bodger, snoozing in his basket behind the counter, but sounds of activity came from the store room at the back.

'Hello Bodger', she walked over to stroke him. Lots of people did, but he responded by a lift of his shaggy head, tail wagging, an honour reserved only for those he liked.

Hearing a voice, Ben emerged to find That Girl waiting for him.

When young he'd been taken to a play in which the villain hid behind a smiling mask. It had given him bad dreams for months, and Natasha caused much the same disturbing effect. Here was someone who was an enemy, who loved all that he loathed, and was setting up a gallery right next door to sell the high priced tat that was modern art – a two fingered gesture at the very mainspring of his being, by the daughter of a man he hated. Yet she had a face so like the image he treasured.

He froze at the sight of her, and she was reminded of a hedgehog defensively curling into a ball.

'I've come to ask you something.' She smiled at him hesitantly, and Ben felt disorientated, as if in a timeshift. It might almost have been Gaye.

'I love the paintings in your mother's sitting room, and I wondered if... that is, do you... would you perhaps paint a portrait on a commercial basis?'

'No, I'm sorry I don't do commissions.' But his curiosity got the better of him. 'Who's the subject anyway?'

'Um, well it's me actually. To give to my father for his birthday', she added hurriedly.

He reacted as if she'd asked him to cut off one of his hands with a penknife. 'You want me to paint you – for your father!' He stared at her in disbelief. How could life be this cruel.

'Oh no. No, absolutely not. You don't know what you're asking.'

The door opened admitting a customer, and Ben seized on the arrival with relief. 'Can I help you?' he enquired unnecessarily. The man had been in earlier seeking a ballpoint refill, and, unsure of the right one, had gone home to fetch the biro itself. Ben went with him to the display, and began discussing fine versus medium tips with unnecessary dedication to customer satisfaction.

Next time he looked round she'd gone.

That evening Natasha knocked on the door of the downstairs flat to pour out her woes.

Madge was sympathetic. 'I don't know what's the matter with him', she complained, getting together the elements of a packed lunch for Jamie, who was going with the school to a Shakespeare play in London next day. 'I'm trying to pull the shop round, and he's okay with modernizing the stationery stock, and broadening out into things like photograph frames and some toys and puzzles. We're getting in a photocopier for customers and that should be popular. But I've hit a brick wall about doing anything commercial with his paintings.'

'Turn that down a bit, can't hear myself think!' she called to Jamie, whose homework in the sitting room was apparently aided by strident music. 'It's not as if Ben will lose the copyright or anything', she continued. 'I've got a quote from a specialist printer, and I'm looking into selling them wholesale too. They'd be a real money spinner, I'm sure of it. That card of Rundleston Nora bullied him into having done is our best seller. And prints – people would love to have them on their walls.'

'According to Nora, Ben's got hundreds more paintings up in his studio', Natasha informed her, leaning against the worktop.

'Has he!'

'She said he showed his work to a couple of London galleries years ago and was told to push off and not waste their time. Nobody wanted that sort of art any more. And...' she shrugged, 'he took it badly and has kept what he painted to himself ever since.'

Reaching for the cling film, Madge paused, 'I'd love to see what he's got up there.' She thought for a moment. 'But that thing about the galleries makes it all the odder that he should snub you – after all you wanted a portrait done because you *liked* his work.'

'I think maybe it's what we're doing, Natasha had been trying to work things out herself. 'I suppose it is rather rubbing his nose in it – a Rabson gallery right next door.'

'Mm. And you are the daughter of one of the kings of modern art.' Madge opened a drawer, hunting for a plastic teaspoon.

'Actually Dad says very rude things about contemporary stuff. To him it's just a commodity that wealthy people can be persuaded to spend millions on to prove how rich they are.' Natasha laughed. 'Willy wavers, he calls them.' A thought struck her. 'I'm sure there are still galleries that would be willing to show Ben's paintings though. Pauline will know – I'll ask her.'

'And perhaps we could take them some examples,' Madge suggested. 'That would prove you were on his side.'

'The trouble is we can't borrow any of Nora's pictures – he'd notice. What about a couple of the ones in this flat? No, that would be stealing, technically, wouldn't it.'

They looked at each other, both struck by the same thought.

'Do you suppose Nora might have…'

'…a key to the studio?' Madge finished the sentence for her. 'Surely she will. We'd have to let her in on what we're doing anyway and get her permission. Are you up for it?'

'Yes, as long as we do it together. And we'd need to be certain Ben wouldn't find out.' The thought of incurring his wrath as well as dislike was scary.

'Tell you what', suggested Madge, 'tomorrow Jamie won't be back till late, but I haven't told Ben about the trip. So he'll be minding the shop from three, and well out of the way.' She smiled. 'How's your burgling skills?'

Nora was touched by the amount of attention and all the good wishes she'd received in hospital and afterwards. Besides Ben, who came to see her every day, numerous friends visited and others sent cards, and she'd received so many flowers, including some from Natasha and Pauline, and an enormous bunch of lilies from Tony, that it was a wonder there were enough vases.

Now, feeling rather a fraud, she was surrounded by flowers, the lilies' scent almost overpowering, and every visitor seemed to bring more. She'd been afraid of being completely laid up, and was pleasantly surprised at how much she could do. It was painful to lie on her back, she couldn't bend down to pick things up, and baths were forbidden until the stitches came out. But she could stand and walk without pain, and heat up the meals stored in the freezer, enabling her to refuse all culinary help offered by Madge, Ben and Natasha . Kind though it was of them, she valued her independence, and it was encouraging to be as normal as possible. 'Be playing tennis in six weeks', the consultant had assured her cheerily, unaware that her main hobby was sewing,. Sitting at her machine was uncomfortable, which was a particular nuisance as she wanted to get on with making costumes for the Rundleston Players. The sewing machine was a faithful friend, and using imagination and skill to create whatever costumes they needed was satisfying. The Players were suitably grateful, and Nora felt it was a good use for the talent she somehow possessed. Ben, bless him, had now solved the sitting problem, by buying one of those special kneeler seats secondhand, advertised on the post office notice board. She was comfortably perched on this, back straight, when Madge and Natasha popped upstairs to see her that evening, and explained their mission.

'Yes, there is a spare studio key. You'll find it on the back of the kitchen door − on a hook'.

Madge went off to get it, and Nora gave them her full blessing.

'I think it's a wonderful idea', she told Natasha enthusiastically. 'I've always said Ben should have put his mind more to selling his work, but he wouldn't. He's very private about his painting though – don't let him find you up there, or you'll be in big trouble.'

The two women felt as if they were planning a heist. Giggly and conspiratorial, they decided to wait until three-thirty, for no particular reason except it intensified their sense of precautions needed against the danger of discovery.

Natasha had postponed a flooring salesman's appointment, leaving the afternoon free, and rather guiltily they ascended the outside wooden staircase that led to Ben's studio above the garage. Madge turned the key in the lock of the glass-panelled door, and cautiously they went in, their nostrils assailed by the smell of linseed and turpentine.

It was a surprisingly cramped space, the problem made worse by the pile of cardboard boxes and plastic storage chests cluttering the far end, although they hadn't been allowed to obscure the window. Light also came from a big skylight in the sloping ceiling, and a special artists' lamp craned over a large, wooden easel, on which a painting of market stalls was in progress. On the table beside it a sketch book lay open, from which Ben was obviously working, an array of more old sketch books on the shelf above. Beneath it in one corner was a blanket nest, clearly belonging to the dog, next to an old tea trolley, once white, on which stood an array of pots and tins, aerosol cans of fixative and jars of pencils and brushes, plus a paint-smeared music centre. A small chest of numerous shallow drawers also fitted underneath the table, and two more folding easels. There was a box of frames, backing boards and glass, and a foot-operated machine for framing. The other side of the narrow room was entirely taken up by black-painted plan chests with wide drawers.

'That's where the paintings are likely to be, don't you think?' Natasha pointed. 'How shall we play this?'

They decided to take one chest each at a time, and riffle through the contents of the drawers, taking care not to disturb the order, and just to take out any pictures that really seemed extra special. The trouble was there were so many.

'Look at this!' or 'Isn't this fantastic!', they kept exclaiming to each other, 'We must have this one.'

It was light that seemed to inspire Ben – filtering through trees, gleaming on water, highlighting people's faces. It was a beautiful presence, and his composition was perfect, creating a magical combination. The paintings were simply inspiring. And in all his depictions, even landscapes, there were either people or animals. Natasha's favourite was of a man sitting quietly in a summer field at sunset, while around him a group of sheep grazed placidly, the whole sky glorious shades of orange, outlining their shapes in mellow light. It was peace and beauty on oiled paper. The one that had Madge most entranced was of a mother holding the hand of a young child as they walked down a woodland path, shafts of sunlight slanting through trees dressed in their wonderful October livery of yellow, copper, green and gold. A mother herself, with her own autumn colouring, it really spoke to her.

'It's criminal that nobody sees these.' She was stunned at what they'd found. She had no education in art, but Ben's paintings gave her the same feelings as a Monet exhibition she'd visited – delight over his take on the world, admiration and awe at the skill he possessed in hand and eye to create paintings that made you want to look and look. Madge was now convinced that Ben was not just a good artist, he was a great one. What's more this wasn't the work of a sad loner. It had to be someone who observed people acutely and reproduced them in paint with affection.

'Surely we've got enough now.' Knowing that he already disliked her, Natasha was particularly apprehensive about being caught trespassing in Ben's private den. She gathered her choices together, and went to the door, peering out nervously.

'Just one more', Madge insisted. 'I haven't looked in the bottom drawer of this chest.'

It was stiff, and she had to force it open. Quickly she flicked through the layers of discarded paintings. They were lovely, but Natasha was right, they had more than enough to show a gallery. She was about to close it again when her attention was caught by something underneath, wrapped in tissue paper. Curious, she took it out, a board by the feel of it, slightly smaller than A3. Folding back the wrapping, she stopped, staring, and called to Natasha .

'Come and look at this! Ben must have done a portrait of you after all. It's brilliant – although…no, there's something not *quite* right about it.'

A young woman with wide, long-lashed grey eyes and tousled, honey-coloured hair was looking sideways at the viewer, the curve of her cheek accentuated by a teasing smile. Wearing a low-cut, soft pink dress, her long, slender neck was adorned by a silver chain on which hung a brown-stone pendant, the light catching it echoed by the sparkle in her dancing eyes. The artist had exactly captured the girl's freshness and beauty, creating a celebration of youth and attraction.

'Let me see.' Natasha took the painting and stared at it, mesmerized. Then her own grey eyes widened, as she took in the significance of the painted jewellery. It was a tiger stone pendant that she'd worn several times, but it had only ever been borrowed.

'No', she shook her head slowly, 'it isn't me.' She raised her gaze wonderingly to Madge. 'That's my mother.'

Chapter Six

Madge enjoyed her lunch hours away from the shop. No business or child to think about, no obligations, just the chance to be herself, back in the place of her own childhood. For the past eight years, as she and Luke grew apart and their marriage deteriorated, the commuter town surroundings seemed to be stifling her spirit. Rundleston was different, she'd told herself. It was a proper community, people knew who you were and cared what happened to you. We'd be happy in Rundleston, she'd told herself, Jamie would love it.

But now, walking the streets, she was trying not to admit that the rosy vision she'd harboured was a little out of date, like a tape recorder in a world of CDs. Jahney's old brewery had become a large complex of flats, none of the maltings were working buildings, the High Street shops had largely changed, and of course strangers were now living in her parents' old house. It still hurt that her father had accepted that job in Canada eleven years ago. Common sense said her parents could do what they wanted without bothering what their daughter thought, now she was grown up. Nevertheless it seemed like a betrayal, and she felt the loss of her childhood home deeply.

It had recently occurred to her though that she'd done exactly the same to Jamie, just at a younger, and more vulnerable, age. His face now had that closed down look which was hiding deep unhappiness. She should have tried harder to keep the marriage together, she reproached herself, even though Luke and she had such different outlooks that there was nothing left between them. After the first shock she hadn't blamed him for having an affair with someone at work, in fact it was almost a relief that he'd provided a way out. But if she hadn't been so keen to come back to Rundleston, perhaps they could have kept up appearances and held together for Jamie's sake.

Reality was obtruding in other ways too. Luke agreed it would be best for Jamie if she didn't work full time, at least to start with, and his payments to her were generous enough not to need to. The plan had been to have a part-time job which would use her business studies and marketing qualifications, and she'd pictured herself easily finding an interesting niche, during school hours at least, as soon as Nora was fit to go back to the shop. Trouble was, the only possibility so far had been till work at the supermarket. Not only was a degree surplus to their requirements, but Nora's complaints that the place was undercutting them unfairly meant she just couldn't consider it.

Sometimes she sat at the top of the little beach at the other end of the town, and watched mothers chatting to each other while their toddlers played. There was no-one she knew among them, but she'd been thrilled to discover that a good friend from school, Tricia, was still around, behind the bar of the Spritty at lunchtime.

It had been Tricia's ambition to become a top chef. She made a face when reminded of it.

'I did do a catering course at Ipswich, but late night working in one of the hotels there wasn't really my scene. Then I got a job here in the kitchen – and married Flitch.'

Madge vaguely remembered him. A large lad, son of the family that owned the boatyard, he'd been mad keen on sailing, and spent much of his time doing up their remaining barge.

'Took him years', Tricia reported, 'and a deal of money. Now the Hetty Jane's got to earn her keep. We organize voyages down the estuary for bird watchers, school trips and birthday parties. I do the catering, and Flitch skippers, with Danny or Ben Banding as crew.

'Ben's sleeping on the barge at the moment isn't he – that's why Jamie and I have got his flat.' Madge was still unclear as to why this had happened, and hadn't liked to ask Nora.

'Yes, in the foc'sle. Told me he didn't want to stay under the same roof as some spoilt bitch from London.'

Tricia broke off to serve a couple of customers, leaving Madge to reflect on this information.

'I think that may not be the whole story', she remarked when their conversation resumed, and told Tricia how she and the 'spoilt bitch', had discovered a portrait of Natasha's mother in Ben's studio.

'Really? His lost love, do you think? Ooh I do like a bit of romance. Flitch wouldn't know what that was if it bit him on the bum. Bless 'im', she added for form's sake.

'I don't know. Natasha's dying to ask Ben about it, but can hardly pin him down long enough to pass the time of day, let alone have an in depth conversation.'

Tricia thought for a moment. 'We've got a barge trip booked on Sunday, and the girl who usually helps me is going to a christening, so I'll be shorthanded. How about you and whatsername coming as galley hands instead? Ben's crewing, so, she'll have him trapped.' She smiled meaningly.

It was a great idea, which Madge was sure Natasha would love. 'But I can't, I've got Jamie', she explained regretfully. 'It's my weekend.'

'That's not a problem, he can come as well – we're not up to passenger limit.'

Madge was thrilled with the idea of a trip on the Hetty Jane. One of the reasons for coming to Rundleston was to show Jamie there was more to life than suburbia, but so far he appeared uninterested in any of its attractions. She was aware that he was not finding it easy to fit in at his new school, and going on a barge as a member of the crew, however loosely, would surely be something in his, and Rundleston's, favour.

'Oh wicked!' he exclaimed when she told him. 'But... I don't know anything about sailing.'

'I'm sure we won't be expected to do any actual rope pulling, and these barges aren't your little tippy jobs, they're really sturdy', she assured him. 'They used to carry huge loads up and down the coast, sailed by just two men and a boy.'

The library provided a book about Rundleston and the East Coast barge trade, and they walked to the boatyard on the far side of the pub to look at the imposing Hetty Jane moored against a pontoon, and soon he couldn't wait for Sunday to come round.

Natasha liked the idea too, picturing herself lounging on deck after their duties were discharged, rather like on her dad's yacht. She was bound to be able to chat to Ben. How to broach the subject of his connection with Gaye was something not easily solved though, without giving away the fact that she and Madge had trespassed in his studio.

'You could say your mother has mentioned she knew him, and take it from there', suggested Madge, and this seemed the best way round the problem.

The forecast for Sunday was for a breezy day, largely overcast, with the possibility of showers. Tricia mentioned that one of her two helpers, an old school friend, would be accompanied by a child, so Flitch would have a life jacket ready. But she hadn't divulged their identities. Men couldn't be trusted with secrets, and Ben was helping bring the barge round to the quay on the Saturday.

A short while before the party passengers were due, Ben was thus completely taken aback to see Madge, son Jamie and Natasha boarding, loaded with boxes, tea towels, napkins and containers of food, and disappearing below.

'What's she...they, doing here', he asked Flitch, who shrugged. 'Helping Trish. I've said the boy can sit on deck.'

Flitch liked taking birthday party trips. Everyone was in the mood to enjoy themselves, and even if it rained they could be relied upon to have a good time below decks in the

Hetty Jane's cavernous saloon, leaving him to enjoy skippering the craft he loved. As the passengers arrived they went below for a welcoming cup of tea or coffee, and when the head count was complete, Flitch sent Jamie to check with Tricia that all was well below decks before starting the engine.

Casting off and manoeuvring the eighty-two ton sailing barge away from the quay and swinging her out through a narrow gap into open water was a delicate operation, and he and Ben worked as a practised team, while most of the passengers watched, and Jamie sat excitedly on the aft hatch amid coils of rope like sleeping snakes.

'Who's he talking to', he asked Ben, as Flitch radioed the coastguard with their itinerary and passenger count. 'What's that?' he pointed to the GPS screen. 'How old is she, and what did she carry?' He was full of questions and, between crewing duties, Ben found himself enjoying answering the freckle-faced boy, with hair as red as his mother's. After about ten minutes Flitch decided the breeze was strong enough to cut the engine.

'Drop out the main to the sprit', he instructed Ben. 'That's fine', as the maroon canvas unfurled and filled above them. The faint vibration ceased, leaving just the soothing sound of the slap of waves against the hull as the barge, powered now by the wind, surged placidly through the water. White bubbles frothed away on either side, Rundleston grew gradually smaller behind them, and the woods and fields of the estuary edged slowly past.

Below decks, Natasha and Madge were discovering that catering for twenty people in the cramped galley was also a skill, of a different kind, and they were the obedient crew to Tricia's captaincy, washing up cups, unpacking the buffet and laying the long saloon table. Once the passengers had been summoned from on deck, the two girls helped serve the food, pour the wine and clear away empty plates. They made a striking pair of waitresses, and enjoyed playing their role to the full, joshing with the guests and the fifty-year-old whose half century was being celebrated.

Jamie, Flitch and Ben had sausages and mash brought up to them.

'Do you like living in Rundleston?' Ben asked the boy, whose face was glowing not just from the wind.

This clearly wasn't a welcome question. 'No', his expression changed to a scowl. 'It's boring. No-one wants to be friends, and there's nothing to do.'

It hadn't occurred to Ben that Rundleston could be seen in that light. He thought back to his own childhood. 'I used to go sailing, and crabbing on the quay – that was great fun. We collected driftwood in a little rowing boat – and had barbecues at Woodshey Bay up river. We'd dig for worms and go fishing. And race – there's the regatta in July.'

He was waxing nostalgic now. Nora would have reminded him of the numerous times he'd infuriated her by squabbling with Tony all afternoon, or moaning, 'There's nothing to do, I'm bored'.

'But I can't do any of those things. What's a regatta?' asked Jamie.

'That loose line needs cleating up,' called Flitch, nodding towards the mast.

As Ben went forward to sort it out, he realized how much he owed Mike, who'd enthusiastically showed his sons how to do half the things he'd just listed, and by the time he returned a decision had been made. Madge was helping out the family by manning the shop for Nora. Her boy was unhappy and in need of some help, so he would return the favour in kind. It would be a sacrifice of time, but she, and the boy, deserved it.

'Tell you what', he suggested kindly, 'I'll teach you to row. And sail.' He glanced teasingly in Flitch's direction. 'We'll have you skippering one of these some day.'

The sun was refusing to come out, and every now and then there was slight moisture in the wind, giving it a chill edge.

So after lunch, most of the women guests stayed below, comfortably engaged in family gossip, while the men clustered by the bow, enjoying the scenery and relaxation with their own kind, glad to cast off their party manners.

There was so little room in the galley that everything had to be washed and put away immediately, and Natasha appointed herself chief washer-upper, while the other two unpacked the birthday cake and laid the cups and plates for tea. When they were all straight Tricia suggested Madge and Natasha might like to go on deck to cool down.

Madge went to sit by Jamie, who animatedly began explaining about mainsails and spritsails, marker buoys and depth gauges, and Ben found himself face to face with Oliver Rabson's daughter, the girl he'd been trying for three weeks to avoid. Hair dishevelled, her face was red from the heat of the galley. At least she could work.

'You haven't brought your dog today?' She sat on the hatch cover in front of him as he stood, one hand grasping the rail.

'No. Not on paying trips, there might be people who don't like dogs. He's with my mother.'

'Why's he called Bodger?'

This wasn't too bad. She was just a girl after all, making polite conversation. She couldn't help who her father was. Or that she looked so like her mother.

'Because he's a bodged job', was his practised answer. 'I got him from a friend who breeds bearded collies. Unfortunately there was a rough collie down the road who must have come visiting...' His eyes creased in a smile. 'They take a dim view of true romance in the Kennel Club. So he gave him to me.'

True romance, she thought. What a lead! No, better not.

'This is a wonderful way to have a birthday party, really different', she remarked. 'Bit of a bummer that mine's the end of February though. Could be a touch chilly. But there's a big heater down there and Tricia says it's great for evening do's. Pity I didn't know about the Hetty Jane this year.'

'Wouldn't you have wanted something a bit more glitzy for your twenty-first?'

'Oh that was last year', she informed him. Deciding that now was the moment, she kept her tone casual. 'When I told my mother that I was coming to Rundleston, she said she knew someone here.' Natasha looked up at Ben innocently. 'She said it was you.'

Gaye had talked about him! Only recently!

She saw him grip the rail till his knuckles whitened, but after a pause the voice was even.

'What else did she say?'

Whoops, dangerous ground. Uncertain what on earth to answer, Natasha was rescued by the skipper's interruption.

'Can you take that mainsail in a bit.'

Ben went to haul in the sheet as asked, only to find when he returned that Natasha had disappeared below decks, suddenly overcome with zeal for helping Tricia, whether she needed anything doing or not.

Since his mother's operation, Tony had taken to coming down to Rundleston most weekends, much to Nora's surprise. An enormous widescreen television now squatted in her sitting room. Its aesthetics were debatable, but the picture was certainly better than on her old one. She'd had to dissuade him from buying an expensive, electric 'riser' chair, on the grounds that she was only temporarily an invalid, after all. And now he was talking about buying her a car with more comfortable seats, which would be easier to get in and out of. Nora was touched that her younger son should want to go to so much trouble and expense on her behalf, and it was good that his self-imposed exile seemed to be ending. Perhaps his inner devils were loosening their grip.

69

Driving back to London Tony reflected how odd it was that for all these years the thought of Rundleston had repelled him, and now he felt drawn to it. It was as if some powerful magnetism had been reversed. But the reason wasn't hard to look for. It was a stunning piece of skirt who could be the making of his life.

A session on the internet had revealed all the press coverage, so now he had a better picture and could fill in the missing pieces himself. Natasha Rabson's boyfriend had been touting nose candy to the art glitterati. The newspapers didn't say so, but clearly as a result she'd been rusticated by her father. To Rundleston, of all places – it was like finding a Ferrari in a hen house. A rich city girl, used to mixing with the smart set, must be feeling decidedly out of place in a half-horse East Anglian town, he reckoned. But that was all to the good. She'd be more susceptible to a bit of sophistication in the form of Tony Banding, someone who shared her interest in modern art and understood the glamorous world she came from.

The thought stroked his ego, which some might have said had no need of encouragement. And although he tried to concentrate on plans for getting the girl, his mind kept straying excitedly to the enticing possibilities of becoming part of the Rabson empire. The resulting art contacts and introductions to so many potential clients would ensure the bank put him in charge of its modern art collection – having given the current old fart the heave-ho. That in itself would mean being in on all the corporate entertaining, since the usual excuse for a client-enticing bash was the opportunity to view the collection. And he'd be sent to all the art fairs to help woo high-net-worth individuals into becoming wealth management clients. Elevation to the board would only be a matter of time. Oh yes, his luck was in.

Strange thing, luck. He reflected on it as the dual carriageway stretched tediously ahead. You had to fight it when it turned on you though. The sort of bad luck he'd suffered at the age of sixteen would have ruined most people's lives. But not Tony Banding. It had made him stronger and more determined.

Any competent therapist would have identified this way of looking at the tragedy as a defence mechanism, but Tony had no time for psychobabble. He'd simply vowed to make a success of his life, to make Nora glad that if one of them had to die, it was he who'd survived the accident. And Ben's hostility and reproach had mutated in Tony's mind into jealousy. Accordingly, the will to soar was now a compulsion. He would show Nora and Ben what drive, brains and ambition could achieve. He would be very much the favourite son.

It wasn't long before he'd seen the potential of taking an interest in the bank's art collection as a way of getting noticed at Grashe's. Revealing that he knew someone who wanted to sell a Lyndon Scroby painting had done the trick. The curator hadn't asked too many questions either, after learning that the seller wanted to keep it quiet, through financial embarrassment. Now, as part of the bank's collection, it was valued at seven million pounds.

Peanuts of course, compared to the stuff that Rabson bought, and was known to sell on. And he, Tony, would be his son-in-law, he thought with relish. All he had to do was hook the girl. Should be a piece of piss with no competition around. But how to go about it? He'd need to flash the cash so she realized he had plenty of his own, and wouldn't be on her guard. But the usual ploys to impress, like weekends in Monte Carlo or New York wouldn't wash while she was having to keep a low profile. She must be bored though, and he could use that. She was unattached at the moment too. Couldn't be better. He imagined giving Natasha his long, appreciative look followed by a slow smile, a practiced ploy that he prided himself never failed.

It was annoying that she hadn't been around today – gone on some barge trip Mum had said, when he casually enquired. Well he could do a damn sight better than that. Newmarket races with a champagne supper afterwards should go down well. A day out at Silverstone, and maybe some culture if he could bear it. Better check out the dates of Aldeburgh Festival.

He glanced at his image in the mirror with satisfaction. Forty next birthday, just a few grey hairs to lend gravitas, but perhaps it was time to settle down. He was older than her of course, but she'd naturally look up to him, he flattered himself, and he'd be able to mentor her about art. This rosy scenario pleased him, although it rather ignored her influential father who didn't just know everyone in the modern art world, he was a colossus.

The plan had everything going for it. He, Tony, would be the one with serious wedge, married into a famous family, and giving Nora grandchildren. She and everyone in Rundleston would see what a brilliant success he was, compared to Ben, who was such a loser, no-one was ever going to marry him. His elder brother had as much chance of becoming rich and famous as a lame donkey winning the Derby.

While Tony was driving back to London, his stunning piece of skirt was discussing the ramifications of the day's barge trip over coffee with Madge, after Jamie had gone to bed.

'It was really awkward. I just didn't know what to say when Ben asked about my mother', Natasha related. 'And you should have seen his reaction. I'll have to talk to her and find out what it's all about. She's back from the Bahamas today.' She put down her mug thoughtfully. 'And we need to take those paintings to show a gallery – Pauline's given me the names of a couple of possibilities. Perhaps I could do that at the same time.'

'I thought you were under orders from your father to stay out of London. Wouldn't it be better if Pauline took the paintings to a gallery? And you could talk to your mother on the telephone.'

'No, I've been emailing Dad about progress with the gallery, and he's happy for me to come up for a couple of days and look at what stock we could offer.' She added proudly, 'I'm dying for him to come and see what I've done'.

Madge guessed from the little girl 'look at me, Daddy' tone that she was desperate for his approval. 'Is he going to come?' she enquired. 'The organizers of the art festival will be green with envy if so. Apparently they're having an uphill task getting anyone to take their beanfest seriously.'

'Yes, but not until the gallery's really ready.' Having let him down over the Charles thing, Natasha was determined to get everything just right, now Rab had entrusted her with a task. 'He's said he'll come and open it.'

The following day, while Natasha was up in London, Madge went to see Nora in her lunch hour. She found her surrounded by silky, scarlet material, which she was making into a sumptuous cloak, adorned with gold braid and sequins.

'It's for the Rundleston Players new production', Nora explained. 'Arabella Drail's written a play based on The Emperor's New Clothes.' She indicated the cloak. 'Lots of lovely costumes for all the courtiers of course. I sometimes wonder', she added with a naughty twinkle, 'if some of them aren't in it just for the chance to gad about in glamorous togs.' She paused. 'No, that's probably unfair. The last thing she wrote was called Reginald Rabbit and the Woodlanders, and they all had to dress up as woodland animals. You've no idea what a nightmare those costumes were to make! They're still in our garage. Goodness knows what they're going to do with them.'

Madge was glad to see her looking so much better, and in good spirits.

'Yes, I'm definitely on the mend now', Nora assured her, 'soon be bounding around like a young goat.' She laughed. 'Well an old nanny anyway. In fact I've decided from tomorrow I'll do afternoons in the shop to take some of the pressure off you and Ben. It's been really kind of you to help us out, Madge dear.' She smiled at her affectionately. 'But you said you wanted to find proper work. Has anything suitable come up yet?

As Madge was explaining how disappointing her job search had been up to now, there was a perfunctory knock on the door and Arabella Drail swept into the room. Other people might walk through doors, but Arabella made entrances. A woman determinedly fighting time, she had unrealistically black hair with a long Mary Quant-type lock on one side, half hiding one eye. To emphasise the effect, that part had been dyed a silvery mauve. An actress in her youth, as people had no difficulty guessing, she saw life as a perpetual drama. The success, indeed the creation, of the Rundleston Players had been entirely due to her. Now the organization of the art festival was a heaven-sent opportunity to play a starring role amidst the luminaries of the art world.

'Ben let me come through the shop', she announced, closing the door behind her and advancing across the room.

Nora wasn't best pleased. Apart from the fact that she preferred her visitors one at a time, relations with Arabella had never rested on more than the fact that their respective families went back a long way in Rundleston as business rivals and occasional partners. That and mutual need between the two women – the Players required costumes, and Nora was a talented seamstress who enjoyed making them. Following the sale of the Drails' large house with outbuildings, Nora had kindly stored them too. Personal rapport didn't come into it.

When she'd gifted the family maltings to the town, Nora hadn't stipulated what kind of art festival should be held there. She bitterly regretted that now. It went without saying, she'd thought, that it should be art as understood by most people, creations they would admire, want to buy and put on their walls. But as the event elided into a modern art jamboree, she felt very let down, and held Arabella Drail largely responsible. On her side, Arabella appeared unaware of any rift in their relationship.

Nora introduced her two visitors.

'Madge was just saying how difficult it's proving to find anything part time in Rundleston which would make use of her business and marketing degree.'

'Marketing?' The word acted like 'walkies!' to a dog. 'You know about marketing!'

'Well, er...it was part of my degree, but...'

'I think,' Arabella pitched her voice deeper, and gave every word extra significance, 'this might be Rundleston's lucky day. What the Art Festival needs now is someone to promote it, to get it mentioned in the media and talked about in the art world. Our sponsors are adamant the organizing committee should step up the marketing side, and we have grants that will pay for someone part time.' She waved her hand at Madge. 'Just the job for you!'

'Oh... um...'

'Now don't say no!' Arabella's idea was now gathering momentum, like a wave approaching the shore. 'You'd need to liaise with the Tourist Authorities and the media. Get the festival mentioned abroad – we want lots of foreign visitors. Plus people down from London of course. And', she paused dramatically, 'we are going to have a *tremendous* opening party for all the movers and shakers in the art world. You'll meet Anyone who's Anyone.'

Madge's calm personality didn't often give way to fluster, but found herself floundering for a response. Knowing Nora's caustic thoughts about what was planned, it would be rank betrayal. Worse than the supermarket. On the other hand, as employment to fit in with current circumstances it could hardly be better.

'Come and see me and we'll talk about it', commanded Arabella, taking the confusion for reluctance, which was never wise after she'd decided on a course of action. "R.I.U. Arabella", the committee had taken to calling her behind her back. Resistance Is Useless.

Chapter Seven

Ben didn't forget his promise about teaching Jamie to row.

'The tide'll be just right this evening', he told Madge, as he relieved her in the shop at lunchtime next day. 'The water should be up to the beach about six o'clock, and according to the forecast it'll be flat calm. Perfect.'

Actually the prospect gave him no pleasure. He was feeling low and disconsolate, and disinclined to mix with anyone. All he really wanted to do was shut the studio door, lose himself in a painting and not have to think.

But by the time Nora came to take over for her first afternoon, the sun had burned through the morning mist and it was a glorious day, with just occasional timid clouds causing welcome zephyrs off the water. Too nice to be closeted in the studio, as he had been all morning, framing. But his soul was in need of soothing, so instead he took a sketchbook and sat on the little beach, with his back to the warm retaining wall. He tied Bodger to a rusty bolt and the dog lay, sensing disquiet, head comfortingly across his knee.

The water on the incoming tide was still far away, but several small children were enjoying themselves on the sand. Their proportions were so appealing, quite different from an adult's. One little girl, face shadowed by a sun hat except for light on the tip of her nose, was with her father, and together they were building an elaborate castle of upturned buckets of sand. They made an attractive subject, and his pencil was soon recreating their lines on the page.

But drawing wasn't helping his state of mind as he'd hoped. That conversation on the barge had stirred up thoughts that refused to settle, as if they were bucketfuls of mud thrown into a clear water pond. Gaye had told Natasha about him. But what had she said? And what did she look like now? She'd been several years older than he was, so late forties. He put down the pencil, trying to picture her, then shied away from the task. The image in his mind was too precious to be sullied by reality, imagined or otherwise. Did she think about him, of what might have been, if Oliver bloody Rabson hadn't seduced her? If it hadn't been for that thieving bastard, Gaye would surely have been here, in Rundleston, sitting on the beach with him, looking forward to their own grandchildren playing on the sand. The rose-coloured notion didn't bear thinking through. It would mean his ethereal, beautiful, fun-loving Gaye had spent the last two decades in Rundleston, living...where? In Chandlers with his mother? In a little terraced house? No, no. The practicalities didn't matter. They'd have found a way somehow to be happy. Soul mates do.

The small girl patted the sand down with her spade before passing it to her father who turned the bucket over, and there was a crow of delight as the resultant shape emerged. I could have had a daughter, thought Ben. That could have been me.

Bodger sat up alertly as a labrador scampered on to the beach, its owner standing on the wall above them, calling uselessly. Sandcastles having no significance in its exuberant, doggy mind, the interloper tore across the edifice, scattering sand in all directions and scaring the small girl, who burst into tears. The young man put his arms round her and his cheek against hers, then, while offering soothing words, he surreptitiously tickled her tummy. Like magic, the tears vanished, replaced by a delicious gurgle of laughter, and she looked up at her father with such transparent adoration that it stabbed Ben to the heart, leaving the image imprinted on his mind.

I can't stay here, he thought in confusion, packing up his things. 'We'll go to Woodshey Bay. You'd like that, wouldn't you Bodger.'

It was their favourite ramble at any time of year, but now in early June, the countryside was simply intoxicating, as if it had forgotten that winter had ever been, and would come again. Walkers went past the sailing club and through the boatyard, which Flitch felt jeopardized security, but there was nothing he could do about a public right of way, and in any case they were almost all locals. The path then marched across a couple of fields, this year planted with broad beans, the fragrance of the flowers coming in waves on the warm air. At the far side it entered the woods that were Bodger's idea of paradise. There was a large warren on the southern edge, and soon excited barking indicated that his favourite sport of chasing rabbits was underway. Majestic oaks, chestnuts and wild cherries towered venerably above, an occasional fallen trunk reminding of storms past. The pathway wandered, sometimes down by the reeds and sea lavender, with the raw smell of wet mud wafting from the river, then, where seeping water made that route too boggy, up the slope, winding through the trees, till the estuary was just a sparkle of water or a glimpse of white sail through gaps in the green canopy.

Woodshey Bay was a curved bite out of the woodland, where shore mud gave way to sand. Boyhood memories of building fires on the beach, frying sausages, and, on occasions, camping had given the bay a special place in Ben's heart. But today, as he sat on a tree root, now a pillar, water having washed away the surrounding bank, the usual magic of the place wasn't working. Not only had a recent high tide deposited an unappealing covering of plastic bottles, cartons, bags and wrappers, but something had happened or been said that was troubling him. Quite what the problem might be he hadn't been able to identify, but his feeling was that it had to do with that Natasha girl.

The woods were alive with the sound of baby birds squeaking, calling their parents for food. *Weep! Weep!* Ben specially recognized that one among the others, and looked about for the young bullfinch. There'd been a bullfinch nest in the garden the year his father died, he remembered. For days the fledglings had called from Nora's borders, their insistent command accentuating the awfulness of the family's loss. Hell, it was twenty-three years ago this week. His father would have been seventy this year. Ben shook his head. Impossible to imagine his youthful, active father so old.

Weep! Weep! Ben peered closer into the patch of brambles the sound came from. Life was hard, as the young bullfinch would soon discover learning to fend for itself, and it had his sympathy. He'd felt like a baby bird himself, nineteen and suddenly wrenched away from art school to cope with the enormity of what had happened at home. Nora was distraught with grief, so it had been Ben who'd had to deal with the police and the coroner, organize the funeral, sort out legal matters, talk to solicitors and accountants and be his mother's prop, while keeping under control his own devastation. And resentment. It had been all Tony's fault. *Weep! Weep!* Yes, the bullfinch had it right. And as if things couldn't get any worse, when he finally returned to London, it was to find that Gaye had gone off with some rich art patron. Was about to get married, for heaven's sake. How could she! Her betrayal had left what happiness he might have hoped for in ruins, and he'd given up on art school in distress, and run back to the comfort of Rundleston. They weren't teaching him anything anyway.

He picked up a stick, bent down and in the damp sand idly drew two eyes, smiley mouth, a long neck and curved cheek. Gaye's face. Or was it Natasha's? And then, as if a trigger had just been pressed, the nebulous trouble in his mind took shape. Natasha had said she was twenty-two in February. *And that all happened twenty-three years ago.* Could that louse Oliver Rabson have got Gaye pregnant? And *that's* why they were in a hurry to get married!

Bodger came loping back to check where his master had got to. Absently Ben gave his soft head a stroke, deep in revelatory thoughts. Would that make Gaye's treatment of him any better? He considered. Perhaps. It was horribly hurtful and disloyal of her to sleep with someone else, but if she had, and then found herself pregnant... He crossed out the face and, almost unaware of what he was doing, drew the simple rounded shapes of a baby. But then why hadn't she explained as much to him when he came back to London in July? It would have helped. Better than bluntly saying it was all finished and she didn't want to see him again.

May. April. March. 'The end of February might be a touch chilly.' His stick paused, mid drawing. Wait a minute. Was it possible that we... That she could have conceived before he'd left London? No. Bloody hell. That would make Natasha *his daughter!* He felt as if he were a cat in a tumble dryer, dazed and confused, head banged by every revolution of his thoughts. But Gaye would have told him. Surely. What kind of woman would hide fatherhood from the man she loved, and pass the child off on someone else? Not the sweet girl he adored. She simply wasn't like that. Not his Gaye.

Hold on. The tumble dryer was slowing and he took a hold of himself. He was leaping to conclusions, there was a much simpler explanation. Natasha was probably a premature baby. That'd be it.

Far from soothing his troubled spirit, the walk to Woodshey Bay had left him in turmoil. How was he going to find out? And what would he do if... He could hardly encompass the discovery of an unknown child. But it wasn't until he was halfway through the bean field on the way back that something else seeped into his mind, and he suddenly stopped, causing Bodger to bump into him. If Natasha is mine, and that bastard Oliver Rabson thinks she's his, he thought aloud, can I use this to get even with him for shitting on my life? Could this be my moment?

As soon as Jamie had eaten and done his homework, Madge took him along to the hard beside the Spritsail Barge, where Ben was waiting with a small fibreglass dinghy.

'I won't stay and watch', she told him, as Jamie struggled into a lifejacket. 'it'll only embarrass him.'

It was almost high tide, and the water had stealthily floated all the moored boats on its way to the shore, swinging them round to point downriver. The weather forecast had been right, there wasn't a breath of wind, and the water was invitingly still, shiny as glass. The tables outside the Spritsail Barge were crowded with animated drinkers enjoying the warm evening, and the race officers at the sailing club were left gazing at an array of dinghies out on the water floating with the current, sails flapping dejectedly.

Ben had never taught anyone to row before, but he found Jamie an eager pupil, and before long decided that the boy could safely practice on his own within the confines of the shore and the mooring posts. He'd taken the precaution of borrowing from Flitch a tender with an outboard, so he could speed to the rescue if anything went wrong. It was gently beached, the water lapping round its stern, and Madge returned to find him sitting in it, occasionally calling instructions or encouragement to her son who was handling his craft with increasing confidence. The dog was splashing about in the shallows.

'He's doing very well', Ben told her, as she took off her sandals, delicately stepped into the boat and settled herself in the stern facing him. She had long, elegant feet, he noticed, and hadn't spoilt them with nail varnish.

'This is really kind of you.'

'Not at all. It's been a pleasure.' And somewhat to his surprise, it had.

'I need to consult you about something.' Madge had been wondering how to tackle this, and reckoned there probably wouldn't be a better moment. She told him about the job offer from Arabella Drail, with whom she'd subsequently had more detailed discussions, and how Nora had now generously given her blessing.

'She says I can act as a fifth columnist', Madge concluded with a smile, 'and dish all the dirt. But I know how you feel about the way this festival thing is going, and rubbishy modern art in general, so I won't accept if you'd rather I didn't.'

'Well it's nothing to do with me.' Ben raised his voice and shouted to Jamie, 'Keep out of the way, there's a boat coming in!' He watched the boy take avoiding action, called, 'Well done', then continued, 'Doesn't matter what I think.'

'It does to me', she insisted. 'It's a question of loyalty to you and Nora. You've been so good to us – making your flat available and everything. I really appreciate it. But I've got to do something about earning some money and renting somewhere, possibly even buy a little house.'

He looked at her, the evening sun burnishing that striking hair drawn back from her face, and automatically considered what colours would reproduce it. 'Are you going to stay here then? Jamie was saying you might go to Canada. He doesn't want to, by the way.'

'No, nor do I really. My parents are set on it and pressing hard. But if we went he'd lose touch with his Dad, and I think that's not fair on Luke, my ex, and especially not on Jamie. Boys need fathers, don't they.'

His eye on the boy, he said, 'In answer to your question, this stupid art festival's going to take place whatever happens. It'll be a farce, but if you can make some money out of it, that's fine by me. You go ahead.'

Madge smiled at him gratefully. 'Thank you.' It was generous of him, she thought.

She would have to reveal their studio raid, and now with Ben pinned down and no possibility of interruption, it seemed the right time to come clean. Well no, best to keep Natasha out of the line of fire and accept all the blame herself.

'There's something else to ask you, but I have to start with a confession. I, um, borrowed some paintings from your studio.' She saw his expression and hurried on, 'No, listen, please. Nora said it was okay, and your paintings are so brilliant they deserve to be a commercial success.'

'Commercial success? You must be joking.' His tone was bitter. 'The art establishment's so involved with the dross being churned out that anything remotely realist gets laughed to scorn.'

'Well being secretive is hardly going to help, is it. Why shove all those fantastic paintings into drawers and just leave them? What's the point? What were you going to do with them?'

He was beginning to feel uncomfortable at being asked to explain things best left unsaid, and was anxious for the conversation to end.

'Shall we call that a day, Jamie? You must be getting tired', he called, but the boy showed no sign of having heard, and Ben found himself encountering Madge's challenging look, and something approaching amusement on her face.

'Nice try', she commented, recognizing his attempt to change the subject.

Indignation rose. Hell, she was the one who was in the wrong for trespassing in his private domain, and now she was getting at him. And she obviously had no idea of the futility of trying to change an art world that ridiculed artists like him.

83

'Listen', he said sharply. 'The Tate – a *national* gallery – paid over twenty-two thousand pounds for a tin of human excrement that some guy said was art. These days shit is art, and what I produce is treated as shit. Why? Because there's money in it. Anybody can churn out the stuff that people like Oliver Rabson pay millions for. It doesn't take any talent, so there's lots to sell.'

'I'm sure your right, but...'

'I *am* right! Proved it to Tony once, when he was spouting all this art gobbledygook. He challenged me to produce a Lyndon Scroby lookalike, and it took precisely two minutes. Soon shut him up.'

'I'd like to see that. Where is it?'

'Oh Tony went off with it.' He gave a snort of derision. 'Probably got it framed in his flat now. He likes that kind of thing.'

Jamie had become entangled in a mooring chain and Ben stood up, shouting instructions. Sitting down again, he apologised, 'I'm sorry to sound off at you, and it probably seems conceited. But when you've got a talent in your fingers and your head, it's just a fact. Heaven knows I'm useless at anything else.' His smile was rueful. 'Drawing and painting are.. well, they're my life. They give me peace. And it hurts to have it held in contempt by a bunch of cynical, money-grubbing confidence tricksters.'

As if a protective layer had been torn off, Madge was being given a privileged glimpse of the bruised and vulnerable man beneath. It made him seem younger than her, not thirteen years older, like a small boy in need of comfort. Her maternal instinct stirred, she asked gently, 'So what are they for, all those beautiful paintings?'

'I don't know.' He shrugged helplessly. 'I thought perhaps one day my time would come...'

'Are you doing a Vincent?'

'A what?'

'Vincent van Gogh never sold a single painting. It was his sister-in-law, wasn't it, who went into marketing overdrive after his death, and made him famous. I'll be your sister-in-law, as it were. Except you don't have to die', she smiled at him. 'Just give me permission.'

'I don't like hype', he responded mulishly. 'The modern art market is all hype and nothing else.'

'There's a difference between puffing rubbish, and making sure people know about something wonderful', Madge countered, realizing, disconcertingly, that this was a re-run of the arguments she frequently had with Luke over advertising. Only she used to be on the other side.

'But paintings like mine would sell for very little', he objected. 'The art establishment would see to that. They've got too much to lose if fashion turned.'

'The general public aren't taken in by all this contemporary blurb though', she countered. 'They still want something attractive to hang on their walls. They may not be able to pay much, but there are more of them. So I was thinking of prints. You don't lose the copyright', she assured him, 'and you'd still have the original.'

'Try doing a figure of eight round those two buoys', he called to his pupil, who flashed an acknowledging smile, and changed course.

'But being produced in prints will only increase the sneers', Ben protested. 'Look at Jack Vettriano.'

'He has made millions though. Stuff the art establishment! Why does it matter what they think, if the public loves what you do?'

She might as well use this opportunity to pave the way for whatever the galleries' verdict was, Madge thought, and added lightly, 'Although Natasha wants to find a good London gallery that would exhibit your originals. We both think your paintings are brilliant.'

'*Natasha* does?' He was uncomprehending. 'But she's setting up a modern art gallery, for heaven's sake.'

'Yes, but she doesn't like the stuff – you should talk to her about it. Anyway, I really want to get limited edition prints made of some of your pictures. I've been looking into costs and the market, and they'd be very popular, I'm sure of it. Your mother thinks so too. We could sell them through firms that specialize in prints, and in the shop as well.' She smiled persuasively at him. 'Please say yes.'

She couldn't have picked a better moment. The tumble dryer in his head had started up again, and his bewildered brain was in no fit state for a further bashing. All certainty had gone and nothing was as it seemed. He stared at her, suddenly feeling outnumbered and outmanoevred.

'Are you two ganging up on me?'

Madge's eyes danced, and she chuckled, sensing capitulation. 'Yup. You don't stand a chance.'

The following day Madge had to go for an interview with the Arts Festival Organising Committee which in theory decided whether or not to offer her the part-time position of publicity officer.

'We've had to spend a lot more money than we first thought', Arabella told her, giving her a tour of the refurbished maltings, before the meeting. 'But we employed a first class architect, and the result is just a *triumph*. He's taken out a couple of the lower floors to give us this wonderful hall, with a stage at the end, which we can use for concerts and indoor sports.'

'And amateur dramatics', thought Madge as the doyenne of the Rundleston Players regarded her with the one eye that wasn't hidden by the sweep of purple hair, matched today with dangly earrings in the shape of grapes, and a calf length mauve cardigan over a pink dress.

'And in here', she opened a door, 'we've got a refreshment area. It'll be ideal for the Old People's Welfare Group, and the Young Wives Club.'

The contrast between the shiny newness, and that dusty, working building Madge had been in as a child was marked. Her sentimental side thought the transformation was a pity, but barley wasn't malted in the old way any more, so something had to be done with the place.

'The exhibition will mainly be in the mezzanine area around the hall, plus the floors above', Arabella was telling her. Although of course it's far more than an exhibition. We want to involve the local people. There'll be debates about the meaning of art, an installation called 'life as art', a sound...now what was the word Lyndon used..., well, thingy. Oh, it's going to be tremendous fun.'

'Lyndon?' queried Madge.

'Lyndon Scroby, who bought our house last year. He's one of the Young British Artists – you must have heard of him.'

'Oh, that Lyndon.'

Arabella beamed at her. It was such fun being on first name terms with a household name.

'And the gala opening party will be in the hall with the bar in here.'

'You won't expect me to be involved with that, will you?' enquired Madge anxiously. 'I'm, um, not very good at parties.' This was something of an understatement. She loathed the superficiality of the parties Luke had dragged her to, everyone out to impress, their eyes continually flicking over her shoulder in case there was someone more important to talk to. Generally she'd sought out a quiet corner where she could be unnoticed, or disappeared to tackle the washing up in the kitchen. It had been one of her failings as Luke's wife.

'Oh no, we've engaged an events organizer from Norwich, so that's all taken care of', Arabella assured her. And Lyndon has promised to try and get his friends along. He knows all the famous people in the art world – Tracey Emin, Damien Hirst, Tootsie Smalt, simply *everyone*. I'm sure they'll all come.' She clasped her heart at the joy of it. 'We want as much publicity as possible for the whole thing. It's *so* important for Rundleston that this is a tremendous success.' The emphasis jangled Arabella's several bracelets. 'And that's where we're relying on you.'

The official interview took place above the hall, the floor currently divided into rooms by folding partitions. Arabella Drail had found a local candidate she wanted to appoint, and the committee members knew their place. But each of them needed to be seen contributing. One wanted to know about Madge's background, and, it turned out, knew her mother slightly. Another asked about her IT skills, and she had to confess that they were a little out of date. However Arabella swept the problem aside by suggesting they would pay for her to attend a weekend refresher course, and after half an hour the committee had applied the necessary rubber stamp. Rundleston's art festival now had a Publicity Officer, although, as they explained, she would be expected to do whatever else proved necessary to the running of this tremendously exciting venture.

Arabella would have been mortified to know that she was missing out on a wonderful connection to the modern art world in the shape of Oliver Rabson's daughter, of whose presence in Rundleston she appeared blessedly unaware.

Since Natasha and Pauline had taken Chandlers' top floor for the whole summer, it felt like their own flat, and Natasha brought back from London various things to make the place more personal, which she was unpacking when Madge knocked on her door.

Seated on the sill of the dormer window overlooking the estuary, Madge told her about the interview. 'And Arabella's got me a cancellation place on an IT course this coming weekend.'

'Goodness, that was quick', Natasha placed a framed photo of her father on the chest of drawers.

'Well they've left it a bit late to get going on the publicity as it is, and I told her that was the best date because Luke is having Jamie then. You have to hand it to the woman, she doesn't hang about.'

'Can't wait to meet her. She sounds gruesome.'

'I won't be involved with the art side of things though, thank goodness', Madge went on. 'They realized they didn't know much about it, so they've delegated all that to something called Tomorrow's Art Today. Apparently it's a consortium of London art galleries who've got together to organize these sort of shows. Have you heard of them?'

'Pauline will know. She's coming down this weekend.' Natasha unzipped her clothes case. 'Or my mother might have worked with them, although she usually organizes gallery preview parties.'

She filled Madge in on the results of her visits to two London galleries with Ben's paintings. 'They both liked them very much', she reported, 'but they said there simply wasn't a market for that sort of art by someone unknown. It seems people with money will spend a fair amount if it's by a pop star or a household name like Rolf Harris, because that overrides the fact that it's not the 'in' style. Otherwise anything by a figurative painter, however good, is a dead duck. People are afraid of looking unfashionable.'

Somehow this didn't surprise Madge, whose course had covered crowd psychology. 'It's odd how sheeplike people are', she observed. 'Even the ones who get to the top feel they must follow the trend. What a shame.'

'They said paintings like those would only sell if you lowered the price right down to a couple of hundred', Natasha continued indignantly. 'But of course the galleries won't and neither would Ben, would he? It's a bummer.' She added nervously, 'We'll have to sneak them back into his studio'. The thought of facing his anger if he found her there was not one to be relished.

'No we won't.' Madge related how she'd cornered Ben and got his agreement to reproducing some of his paintings as prints. 'After that I'll go for the birthday cards permission', she declared determinedly. 'They'll really make a difference to the shop takings, and we should be able to sell them wholesale. It's a big market. Every card is an advertisement in itself too. It's a win, win situation.'

'He'd never agree, would he?'

'Just a question of working on him', Madge smiled confidently. 'And although I didn't say we both trespassed, I did tell him that you weren't a fervent admirer of contemporary art. In fact you love his paintings. So you should find him less hostile. Oh yes', she remembered, 'what did your mother say about her and Ben?'

Opening the wardrobe door, Natasha hesitated. 'Well, she simply said that she was a life model at the art school where he was a student. So that would explain why he has a portrait of her. She said they went out together a couple of times, but that was it.'

'How disappointingly unromantic.'

'Yes.' Natasha hung up a jacket. 'Except she was fobbing me off.'

'How do you know?'

'My esteemed mother juggles boyfriends like mad, so she has plenty of practice at stretching the truth, and she's pretty good at it. But I know all the signs.'

As Natasha closed the cupboard door she turned and looked at Madge. 'She was lying through her teeth. And what's more she was really bothered that I was asking about him. Is that intriguing, or what?'

Ben had much to occupy his mind. He'd grown fond of his roost in the foc'sle of the Hetty Jane. The faint slap of water against the hull was soothing, and the difference in feel as the barge floated and then settled back on her mud berth was a reassuring tidal rhythm that he'd incorporated into his life.

True, his temporary home would disappear downriver every so often, in the role of party venue, but he was usually crewing, which was a pleasure in itself. And if for some reason Flitch took Danny instead, Ben had an open invitation to make himself at home in Danny's converted tug.

After initial puzzlement, Bodger had adapted to his role of ship's dog, and evidently enjoyed patrolling the deck in the early morning, vainly trying to intimidate swans and seagulls, while his master cooked breakfast in the galley. Eating eggs and bacon while sitting on the sunny deck, looking across the estuary, the smell of salt water and mud wafting on the breeze, was a priceless privilege as far as Ben was concerned. It was an opportunity to absorb sunshine, beauty and fresh air whilst the mind rested. But in the last couple of days the tranquility he'd built into his daily routine had been shattered, and he felt like a driver faced with a blue traffic light. His everyday life was now dominated by what if's and what now's, everything else thrown out of focus.

Uppermost in Ben's mind was how to verify his suspicions about Natasha's parentage. His computer now lived in his mother's dining room, and warily he'd done an internet search on paternity tests, hoping Nora wouldn't see it listed as search history. She didn't use the computer much, but he had been encouraging her to learn. Paternity tests were expensive, he'd discovered, but not prohibitively so, and he could surely obtain a hair or two of Natasha's without difficulty. The real problem was that the result would come by post, and his mail was being delivered to Chandlers. He couldn't take the risk that his mother would see where it came from, or open it by mistake. Besides, it was a lot of money to spend, perhaps needlessly. Learning that she'd been a premature baby would settle it. If he could only talk to the girl and ask her some leading questions... But how? It needed to be a social situation, relaxed and chatty, he reckoned, failing to conjure up an idea of how this could be achieved. If she came for supper at Chandlers, Nora would be there too, so that was ruled out. And he couldn't invite her out on her own, it wouldn't look good. Better let it rest just for the moment, he concluded. Perhaps something will come up.

Meanwhile there was Madge's proposition to consider. It was hard to know what to think. For so many years what he painted had been private. Those first years in Rundleston after his father died he'd worked hard to hone his talent, studied the great artists and taught himself tricks and techniques until his own style became settled. Now his paintings were a reflection of him and how he saw the world. They were precious, and not to be sold for peanuts. Also at the back of his mind had been the belief that some day they would be ammunition in his fight against Oliver Rabson and all the obscene excesses of the modern art scene. Somehow, releasing them as prints detracted from that possibility, although he couldn't have argued coherently why.

On the other hand, Ben told himself, Vermeer, the painter he most admired, had died unsung and in debt because he kept his art largely private. It was the self-promoters in history who became successful artists in their own lifetime, he reflected ruefully. Maybe he was being too obstinate about his own.

Madge had felt so strongly about it that she'd raided his sanctuary and stolen some paintings. No, stolen wasn't the right word. She was trying to help after all. In fact she'd gone to a lot of trouble, fact-finding about getting prints done. It was good of her. Nora was always singing Madge's praises, perhaps she was right. But he remembered the amusement on her face as he tried to change the subject, and bristled. The girl was too sure of herself. He wasn't having it.

And then today, she'd cheerfully greeted him, 'Morning Vincent'. True, there was a twinkle in her eye, but it clinched his determination to get his own back. Now, as he framed some child's piano exam certificate for a customer, a plan was forming, bringing a smile to his face. Right, Madge my girl, he thought pleasurably. You've asked for it.

This was her last day helping in the shop. She was going on some computer course at the weekend, then starting the part-time job next week, doing the publicity for the art fiasco. So taking over from her this lunchtime would be the last opportunity for some time, he reckoned.

He walked round to the shop a few minutes before twelve, taking the completed customer orders. Having for years resisted doing framing as a service, he reluctantly had to admit that it was quite rewarding. There was satisfaction in using his artistic instincts to choose materials that complemented the subject, and he sometimes did double surrounds and drew fine coloured lines at no extra cost. The result flattered the framed subjects and drew exclamations of delight from their owners which pleased him.

When he and Bodger came in, Madge was serving a perennially crochety pensioner who was complaining that a bunch of noisy teenagers now congregated on the verge outside his house every evening.

'Why not collect dogs' mess, and make the area an unpleasant place to stand until they move elsewhere', was her sympathetic suggestion, and they laughed about this left-field solution while he handed over his money without the usual reluctance.

It wasn't the first time Ben had watched customers respond to Madge's warmth and vitality. There was a quiet charm about her that came from within, not your shallow, 'have a nice day' variety, he reflected. Takings had certainly gone up since she arrived, and he didn't think it was all down to the framing service and additional stock.

Even so, she wasn't going to take the mickey out of him and get away with it.

'We're going to miss you', he remarked as the customer left with a smile on his face. 'You've done wonders for the business, been a real breath of fresh air.' Before she could respond he added, 'And thinking over what you said about my paintings, you're absolutely right. I do need to be more commercially-minded.'

Madge, jotting down a reminder to herself, looked up, surprised.

'You talked about prints, but I was thinking there are several more ways we could reproduce the images. Calendars for instance. They're always a big seller at Christmas. I've contacted a local printer to ask about costs, and a calendar company is getting back to me.'

'Calendars?' she echoed uncertainly.

'Yes. And tea towels.'

'What!'

Ben nodded genially, enjoying the consternation on her face. 'We could sell those in the shop, even though they're not stationery. People always want them as gifts don't they.'

Madge eyed him suspiciously, but his expression was guileless. Maybe she'd pushed him too hard. But this change of mind was disastrous. Tasteful, and fairly expensive, limited edition prints to build up his profile and reputation were one thing. Tea towels and calendars were quite another.

'And then I thought mouse mats, and coffee mugs, maybe even T-shirts', continued Ben seriously.

'Oh. But... Look, when I said it was a shame nobody saw your paintings, I didn't exactly mean...'

'No, no, you're absolutely right', he interrupted, deadpan. 'I've been too prissy about it.'

Amid confusion, a light went on in Madge's head. 'So you're happy about birthday cards as well?'

Damn, should have seen that coming, thought Ben. He couldn't very well say no now. 'Well, okay.'

94

Madge was still fazed by his ruination of her marketing strategy, and in a totally unexpected way. 'You won't do anything about these ideas till I come back, will you?' she pleaded. 'Only I think some of them might not be, um.. well.. helpful to your reputation as an artist.'

'Oh'. Ben feigned hurt surprise. 'Don't you think so'.

Madge's mobile rang, and she searched her handbag beneath the counter. 'Sorry, this'll be Luke about what time he's coming to pick up Jamie.'

As she answered it, the door opened and Natasha came into the shop, saw Ben and explained, a trifle nervously, 'Just coming to see where Madge has got to – we're going to have a pub lunch.'

He looked at her with new eyes. He'd only ever seen Gaye in her face before, now he searched it for any hint of himself, and gave her a warm smile, just as Madge exclaimed, 'Oh no! You can't mean it! But you said this weekend was clear, and I was relying on you.'

Ben and Natasha exchanged awkward glances, unavoidably privy to the conversation.

'But Luke it's important for me, and especially for Jamie. He's been really looking forward to seeing you, and he's been talking about stock car racing for days. Please don't let him down. That matters far more than work.'

Natasha went over to see Bodger until the conversation finished, and Madge put the phone back in her bag, visibly upset.

'Luke's not coming', she said unnecessarily. 'Apparently something's turned up and they want him to work the weekend. I'll have to cancel the course, which is a bit of a nuisance.' 'But', there were tears in her voice, 'what I really mind is how disappointed Jamie will be.

'Why don't I look after him?' Natasha suggested impulsively. 'I could move down and sleep in your room.'

Ben had promised himself a day out in Norfolk on Sunday, but didn't hesitate. 'And I'll take him sailing', he volunteered, and smiled at Natasha. 'You go off on your course, Madge. Don't worry, we'll make sure he has a good weekend.'

Chapter Eight

Ben found Tricia giving Hetty Jane's saloon its weekly clean when he returned that afternoon, and consulted her about the practicalities of entertaining a nine year old boy.

'I feel sorry for the kid', he remarked. 'His parents have split up, and the poor little blighter's been yanked away from the place he's known all his life and set down in a strange place, in a new school. And now his dad's let him down.'

'He'll need cheering up, or at least distracting', she agreed, reaching under the central table with her broom.

'I wondered about perhaps having a barbecue at Woodshey Bay, but it would be a bit flat, with just me and Natasha for company.'

The broom stopped, mid-sweep. '*Natasha* and you?'

'Yes. We've undertaken to look after him between us while Madge is away.'

'What happened to the 'rich city bitch' thing then? You even moved out, for heaven's sake, so's not to be under the same roof as her.'

'Oh.' Ben sought in vain for a plausible explanation. 'She's... um, she's okay. Means well.'

'That's a change of tune I must say.' Tricia looked at him quizzically. 'You haven't taken a fancy to her, by any chance.?'

'*No!* Absolutely not!' Ben was anxious to hit that one on the head pronto.

Tricia remained unconvinced. Even Flitch, who'd never been known to notice anything unless it had a bow and a stern, had asked 'who's the stunner?' the day Natasha helped on the Hetty Jane. And Ben had been that bit too emphatic.

He wanted to talk about the boy, not Natasha. 'Part of the problem is that Jamie's lost all his old friends. I don't suppose your Stephen would like to join us, would he? He must be about that age.'

'They're in the same class at school, but when I suggested Madge's boy could do with being befriended it didn't go down very well. You know how cliquey kids are.'

Ben didn't, having had nothing to do with children. Helpfully he began lifting the bench seats so Tricia could sweep underneath, and she smiled her thanks, adding, 'So I don't think Stephen would want to be included in a beach barbecue. But', inspiration struck, ' I've got a better idea. Remember you said what a mess of litter there was on the bay – why don't we organize a clear up party, with something to eat afterwards?'

'A party?'

'In fact', she continued, the plan taking shape 'the tide'll be just right, so we could motor up there on the Hetty Jane and pick up a buoy. Row ashore in the dinghy. And we wouldn't have to stumble home in the dark through the woods.'

'Trish, you're a genius!'

'I know', she said modestly, inclining her head towards the dustpan and brush in the corner. Ben took the hint, and bent to sweep up the pile of dirt she'd accumulated.

'Come to think of it though, cooking food in the galley would be a better bet than a beach barbecue', she decided. 'Less chance of food poisoning for a start, and much easier to organize.'

'I'll buy the food', he offered.

'No, thank you all the same. Leave the catering side of it to me. I may not be good at many things, but feeding people is one of them. And we can use Hetty's plates, cutlery and glasses.' She was thinking aloud now. 'What shall we do about drink?'

They settled on beer, cider and soft drinks, and decided people would be asked to contribute towards the costs.

Now fired with the notion of helping Madge's son make friends and have a great weekend. Tricia was already reviewing which of her pals she would ring. 'We need a few boys, but not too many, otherwise Jamie will tend to get left out of things. It's pretty short notice, but I'm sure we could get together a nice crowd. Would Nora like to come?

Ben wasn't keen. The occasion would be useful for talking to Natasha. He didn't want any possibility of his mother overhearing, or getting the wrong idea about the two of them, as Tricia had.

'We can bring a comfortable fold-up chair', Tricia urged him, 'and she can help me with the food rather than pick up rubbish. Ask her. See what she thinks.'

Like a nestling about to fledge, Nora was torn between pleasure and apprehension at the prospect of a trip on the Hetty Jane, which would be her first active outing. Thankfully, the days of dragging pain were fading into the distance and she was almost back to her old routine, pleased to be in the shop again and plugged in to all Rundleston's happenings. The Bed and Breakfast side of things having been block-booked by Pauline and Natasha lessened work considerably, which was fortunate. It was that, too, which solved her main problem, of being unable to do the gardening. Ben had always cut the grass for her, but asking him to weed was like expecting a small child to tidy the toy cupboard. You'd come back an hour later and find him busily drawing bumble bees or studying light and shadow on dandelion petals. Pauline, however, was a keen gardener, and more than happy to do the things Nora's back made difficult. Getting her hands dirty made a relaxing contrast to hectic London life. 'I only have a few containers on my flat's balcony', she lamented. 'To be let loose in a beautiful walled garden like this is a real treat.'

She arrived from London that Friday evening, and immediately wanted to do a tour with Nora, seeing what had come out since she was last down.

The garden behind Chandlers was unexpectedly large for a town house, and was one of the reasons Nora would never consider living anywhere else, although even estate agents would have hesitated to describe the house as 'convenient'. Her roots there ran as deep as the huge fig tree which almost covered the south-facing wall, unfailingly producing a wonderful harvest. Although the Banding family had done well for themselves financially, with an eye to practicality past custodians of the garden had made sure that it was planted with apples, pears and a spreading plum in the centre, round whose leaning trunk was a circular wooden seat. Reminiscent of a temperamental great aunt, the tree veered between generous bounty and huffy meanness. This year promised a crop so large the tree was already shedding half-formed fruit onto the surrounding grass in alarm. Pauline bent to pick one up, and looked up into the branches.

'Oh, there'll be plenty more', Nora answered her unspoken question. 'In August you'll be going back to London laden down with the things.'

Each successive generation had added to the garden according to their interests, and Nora's was scented flowers. Now, in early June, the evening air was intoxicating as the perfume of the first roses wafted from the warm walls, competing with old-fashioned pinks, sweet peas and the peppery smell of lupins in the beds below.

'This is just my kind of garden', murmured Pauline contentedly, already shedding the tensions of work as they walked slowly along the brick paths, discussing various plants.

They'd discovered another interest in common – Rundleston Grange, where Pauline's son Tommy was now a resident. It was such a worthwhile charity, they agreed. Nora had been energetically fund-raising for it over many years, and Pauline promised to help next time she had a bric-a-bac stall in its aid.

Despite an almost twenty year age gap, the two of them felt comfortable together. For different reasons, both had had to cope with being alone which, they felt, made them stronger and more independent in mind. Their deepening liking was unexpected but, like a photographic negative, each perceived in the other someone they could have been, given a contrasting life experience. Pauline was keen to hear about the problems and rewards of running a shop in a small town. At forty-eight, she occasionally pondered taking early retirement and doing something similar herself. In turn, Nora found stories of Pauline's job in London fascinating. She was aware though that Ben hadn't hidden his feelings about a modern art gallery opening up next to the family shop, and felt she should apologise, explaining his dislike of Oliver Rabson.

'Don't worry', Pauline assured her. 'Rab puts lots of people's backs up. I think he quite enjoys it, to tell you the truth.'

'He's certainly got an irascible reputation, if the papers are anything to go by. How do you cope?'

'Well some of it's put on. It suits him to be famously bad-tempered, then people are flattered when he turns on the charm.' She bent to smell a rose. 'And the job's very well paid. I used to work for a gallery owner until Rab offered twice the salary to come and be his PA. That money was a godsend for looking after Tommy – paid for the special school and all the help he needed. Also', she smiled, 'I stand up to him. He's just bored and dissatisfied, and takes it out on the people around him. If you fight back though, he respects that.

'It's strange to think such a famous man's daughter is staying here', Nora remarked, picking off spent foxglove flowers to stop them seeding. 'And isn't she charming.'

'Yes, Natasha's a sweet girl, amazingly enough, given her background. She certainly softened Rab, but he's relapsed since he sent her down here,' Pauline reported ruefully, pulling out some groundsel and rolling it round in her hand to crush the yellow heads. 'He's just gone off to the opening of Art Basel, and he's got a big project on the go, so this week has been hectic. He was particularly impossible as soon as Natasha came back to Rundleston.'

'Why do you stay, now that Tommy's off your hands? There must be easier people to work for.'

'Been wondering myself lately', Pauline confessed. 'The Grange prefer you not to visit too often, it stops them meshing into their own community. So since he's been there I've had weekends to do what I want, which is wonderful – if that doesn't sound selfish. And coming down here has made me think that perhaps it's time to move out of London and unwind a bit.'

The tour done, they made their way to a bench against the wall by the fig tree, looking back at the house. At this time of year the seat was bathed in light before the evening sun disappeared behind neighbouring roofs, and they sat enjoying the invisible cloud of scent from the honeysuckle Nora had planted behind it.

The last few fine days were a treat in what had been a soggy summer so far, and Pauline took off her glasses, raising her face to the sun's warmth, and spoke with her eyes closed. 'But I enjoy the buzz, to tell you the truth. Journalists, collectors, publicists, galleryists, museum curators – they're an amazing crowd, although you wouldn't necessarily want them as friends. And it's fun reading the papers and knowing lots of people in the news. But that isn't what makes me stay. It's…', she paused, opening her eyes and analyzing it in her own mind. 'It's loyalty to Rab', she concluded, as if finding the missing puzzle piece under a cushion. 'He couldn't manage without me now. And it's always nice to be needed, isn't it, whether the person realizes or not.' Then she shrugged, 'Mind you I'll probably lose my temper with him one of these days, and he won't take that. I'll be out on my ear.'

They walked slowly back to the house, and Pauline asked, 'Where's Natasha? And what on earth does she want Rab's helicopter for?'

'Helicopter?'

'Yes. Rab told me just before he left that he'd given her permission to use it on Sunday. Apparently she wants to take a couple of passengers up for a ride. Who would that be?'

'Well she's helping to look after Madge's son for the weekend. Perhaps it's connected to that. They've taken him to the cinema this evening', Nora explained, and told her about the proposed beach clear-up party the following night, to which she'd been invited.

'I think you should definitely go, it sounds fun', was Pauline's verdict. 'In fact I'd like to join in as well, if that's okay. The weather's looking a bit iffey though, isn't it, with thunderstorms forecast. Still, if it rains perhaps they'll let us oldies pretend to help with the cooking on board.'

Natasha had found her few days in London unsettling. Apprehensively she'd wondered if her father would talk about Charles and the drugs thing, but he steered clear of the subject. There seemed no holding back on affection towards her though, which was reassuring, and despite preparing to go to Art Basel he'd made the time to discuss at length what sort of pieces she should stock at the gallery. She'd half hoped he would invite her to go to Basel with him, not daring to ask. But nothing was said, and she got the message. Missing out was part of her punishment. And Rab didn't want to be seen with a daughter who'd messed up.

That was hurtful. Although she deserved it, she told herself. She should have known what Charles was up to. Asked more questions about where his money was coming from. She also understood that her dad couldn't afford to be compromised. Not only was his standing in the art world at risk, but that autumn he was launching Rabsons as a lifestyle luxury brand, and the name and image must not be tainted in any way.

The visit increased her determination to regain her father's approval. She would make this gallery he'd entrusted her with into a real success, she thought, driving back to Rundleston. Show he could be justly proud of her. Yet she couldn't help picturing him at the glittering gatherings to which she might have been going, having bought some really special new dresses. It was a crying shame.

So when Madge's distress at Jamie's disappointment made it clear help was needed, Natasha was extra glad to offer. Looking after Jamie would be a welcome distraction, taking her mind off what she was missing out on. That Ben was sharing the responsibility was also useful, it would surely give her opportunities to talk to him and find out what her mother was hiding.

Fortunately a Disney film was showing in Ipswich on the Friday evening, and they had a Chinese meal afterwards. It was difficult to tell whether Jamie enjoyed the outing, but Natasha had to admit that sneakingly, she rather had. Maybe I'm not so long out of childhood, she reflected sheepishly. And she was glad that Ben had obviously warmed towards her. They were now team mates on a Keep Jamie Happy Weekend.

A very generous amount of money arrived for Jamie in the post next morning with an apology from his father, and he immediately wanted to go and buy a camera. So after consulting with Ben who was manning the shop, Natasha drove him into Ipswich again, this time accompanied by Pauline, and afterwards they treated him to lunch at

McDonalds. He was a nice kid and she empathized with his distress at the family situation.

'My parents split up when I was only a baby', she told him. 'And my mum made sure I didn't have any contact with my dad. Said he didn't want to see me. That was a rotten thing to do. At least your parents are still on good terms, and you know they both love you. Has to be a good thing.'

'Mm', he agreed. 'But I had lots of friends at Spentwood. And I don't fit in here. They call me Ginger, and Carrot Top. No-one wants to be friends with me.'

Natasha looked at him with sympathy. 'I might just be able to help there', she told him. 'Would you like to go up in a helicopter tomorrow?'

His eyes opened wide. 'A *helicopter*! Oh wow!'

'Well I've arranged for a trip, and you can take one other boy. If you make sure people know that this evening, I should think they'll be falling over themselves to be your friend.'

'Wicked!'

'That's just to get the ball rolling of course', she warned him. 'Bribery doesn't make real friends – after that you've got to show you're a nice person to be friends with as well'.

She was gratified to receive a smile of approval from Pauline over his head, and it was an excited and hopeful small boy who was handed over to Ben later.

It was low tide, and the fine weather of yesterday had given way to a sullen closeness, so the conditions were less than perfect for a first sailing lesson, but there was sufficient breeze out on the river to make it possible.

'I was going to take you out in our boat, Sound Lady', Ben told Jamie, as he fastened him into a life jacket. 'My father designed it himself, and I helped him build it. But the winds are too light today, so I've borrowed a friend's Mirror dinghy.'

He found the boy an intelligent and responsive learner, who grasped the basics quickly and thought ahead. By the end of the afternoon Jamie was fired with enthusiasm for the freedom and exhilaration of harnessing the wind, and the feeling of being in charge of a live thing as the boat responded to the tiller.

'That was great!' he exclaimed after they'd hauled the boat up the slip and left it on its trolley at the sailing club. His tutor had enjoyed the afternoon too. It was rewarding passing on skills to the younger generation, and he wondered if there was an outgrown Optimist class dinghy for sale at the club. It would be just right for Jamie to helm on his own.

Ben released him from his lifejacket, and took him back to tea with Natasha and Pauline. While they were being introduced to the excitements of the new video game, he went into the shop to see if Nora would like to be relieved before closing time.

'Tony rang', she told him. 'Says he's coming down this evening. I do wish he'd give me a bit more notice. I told him about the beach clear-up party and that we'd all be out, but it didn't seem to put him off. Said he'd like to come too.'

'Oh.' Ben's response didn't have quite the right nuance.

'So I rang Tricia, but she said sorry, they were up to their legal limit for passengers.'

Ben happened to know this wasn't true, and silently blessed her.

Tricia's decision to have the meal on board the Hetty Jane had been partly prompted by fears that a beach barbecue would be rained off, and indeed the early evening weather forecast of thunderstorms caused the participants to arrive clutching anoraks and oilies as well as spare shoes and jerseys. Besides Tricia's son Stephen, there were two other boys among the three families she'd invited. Including

Danny, who was crewing, the numbers totted up to twenty-one. Enough to clear the beach effectively, she'd thought, and provide a good mix as well. It had been decided that Nora and Pauline would stay aboard to help Tricia. Flitch wasn't willing to leave the barge unmanned, but everyone else was to be rowed ashore armed with plastic sacks and rubber gloves, and split up into teams of two.

The families already knew each other, but Tricia and Nora saw to it that Pauline didn't feel left out. And they were about to spend the evening doing good, so whether it rained or not, the glow of righteousness coupled with enjoyment was a winning combination, and the chattering was happy and relaxed. Ben noticed Danny staring at Natasha. With her striking beauty, even in jeans and grey fleece, she certainly stood out like a Fabergé egg in a car boot sale. As soon as Danny had cast off and they were out in open water, motoring up the river, Ben introduced them.

'Danny's an electrician, a real whiz. Lives on that old tug boat in the yard. But if you need help with electrics at the gallery you'll have to be nice to him', he teased. 'He only works his magic for people he approves of, don't you Danny.'

With a tall, angular body and hollow cheeked face, Danny Larber was reminiscent of a Meccano model. Everything worked, but aesthetics didn't come into it. He must have bought a job lot of short, navy smocks, at any rate he was never seen in anything else. In summer they were teamed with shorts that were not flattering to his bony knees, in other seasons baggy jeans hung off his spare frame. As if to emphasise indifference to conventional rules of appearance, his lank brown hair was drawn back in a pony-tail, bound with a red rubber band, and guesstimates of his age varied from twenty-five to forty-five. He'd just appeared up the estuary two years ago, at the wheel of a decrepit tug on its last chugs, which settled thankfully onto a soft mud berth at the yard and never left. His story was that he'd been summoned from Seattle to England by an uncle with terminal cancer and a beloved tug to bequeath. But he could have been a prisoner on the run for all anyone knew. He was soon assessed though by the regulars at the Spritty as odd but harmless, and earned the puzzled respect given to the resolutely self-contained. Hermit or not, the man was useful, prepared to do odd electrical jobs on a cash basis that busier sparks couldn't be bothered with, and having him at the yard was a godsend to Flitch, especially as he proved a competent barge crew. His reputation was also spreading as something of a computer geek, and nobody hesitated to invite him in to fix a computer problem. He was like a long-dead spider discovered under an armchair, hunched and still, and no threat at all.

'What fun to live on a boat', Natasha responded conventionally, bestowing her enchanting, gap-toothed smile on him, and Ben left them talking while he attempted to integrate Jamie into the knot of boys standing at the bow.

Tricia had firmly informed her son that he was to partner Jamie for the beach clearing exercise, but left everyone else to sort themselves into twos while the Hetty Jane was securely moored to a buoy, and the lee boards partly lowered. The shore party prepared to be rowed ashore in relays.

'I'll go with Ben', Natasha volunteered, with an eagerness that didn't go unnoticed.

They were in the first boatload, Bodger sniffing the wind and standing at the bow like a furry figurehead. He leapt into the shallow water as soon as they grounded, and was already bounding along the beach by the time Natasha and Ben had put on shoes and set off towards the far end, their agreed pitch, accompanied by Stephen and Jamie, who were to be the next pair up. The incoming tide had some way to travel, but the sand was damp and firm, wrinkled further out with ripple marks, interspersed with little rivulets meandering towards the water. Indicating the reaches of successive high waters, there were lines of seaweedy detritus, mostly brown, but green where the latest tide had dumped weed that was still alive, mossy and soft to the foot. In amongst the weed and crunchy cockle shells were bits of blue rope, plastic bottles, sandwich packets, shapeless lumps of polystyrene and endless gobs of plastic sheeting. But further up, where land and water battled at spring tides, the ugly blight of jetsam was worse.

'What a lovely place', Natasha looked about her with appreciation. 'A secret bay. Such a shame there's all this rubbish.'

'Come on', Stephen called to Jamie, running towards a lorry tyre that dangled invitingly on a rope from a large alder, leaning out over the sand.

Leaving the boys to catch up, they passed the tree root on which Ben had sat, memories bubbling to the surface like methane gas, and he wondered now how on earth he was going to find out if she was his child. After all asking whether someone was a premature baby wasn't the sort of conversation one naturally fell into. Perhaps he could introduce the subject of zodiac signs, although it would sound a bit odd.

When they reached the end of the bay where the land curved into a bank of shells, reeds and the grey leaves of sea purslane, Ben took a stick and drew a demarcation line up the beach.

'We'll clear this patch and you do from here to the next team. Okay?' He gave the boys their gloves and rubbish sacks. 'Any problems, just say. And watch out for broken glass.'

'We'll get this done quicker than them', Jamie was heard to remark, as they started work. 'And then we can go back to the tyre swing.'

The shore was now busy with people, and Ben reached for his camera.

'Must get a shot of all these figures on the bay, with the Hetty Jane in the background', he said. 'I could make something of it.'

'Is that what you do?' Natasha watched him framing the best view, as she put on gloves. 'Take photographs and turn them into paintings?'

'Well, not exactly. I prefer sketching, but there isn't time today. And both of them are only a base. You can improve on most compositions by putting in something that wasn't actually there. It's one of the things that makes Constable's work so satisfying.'

'I love your paintings', she told him. 'The ones I've seen in your mother's flat, and Madge's', she added hurriedly.

Putting the camera away, Ben remembered Madge's remark. *'Natasha doesn't actually like modern art. You should ask her about it.'*

'I'm flattered, but how can you say that?' he challenged her. 'You're going to be selling stuff in that gallery that's the complete opposite of everything I do.'

Natasha was having no success in opening a black plastic sack, torn off a roll. Probably never had to prise one open before, Ben thought wryly, taking it from her and pulling the sides apart. Comes from a different world.

'What we sell has got nothing to do with personal taste though', she defended herself. And as they picked up and bagged the litter she told him how Rab regarded the stuff he supposedly collected, but in fact quietly sold on, as just a commodity that rich, suggestible people could be persuaded to buy.

'Most of them do it to show off how wealthy they are', she said, 'and they generally think it's an investment as well. Some just see it as a ticket to art gatherings where they'll meet movers and shakers. Or there are various tax dodges it helps with.' She glanced at Ben. 'Whatever the reasons people buy, it doesn't do any harm.'

'Of course it does!' He was aghast that she could be so blinkered. 'To get them to spend millions, this load of trash has to be promoted by an army of vested interests. And they can only do it by holding in contempt anyone who has what used to be called artistic talent. We're just sneered at. I'd love to paint full time, but there's no way I can because people like Rab skew the market.'

This rather ignored the difficulty of making a living from work lying unseen in a studio drawer, but there was no mistaking his resentment towards her father.

'Oh. Well…I hadn't thought of it like that.'

The water had crept higher, playing Grandmother's Footsteps with them. There was a shout of laughter from the neighbouring stretch of beach where both boys were larking about with the dog, now returned from rabbit hunting in the woods. Not much litter picking going on there evidently, but at least their strategy for Jamie seemed to be working, and Natasha and Ben exchanged pleased smiles, lightening the atmosphere between them.

'You guys aren't going to beat us at that rate', he called across good humouredly. 'No chance.'

At the sound of Ben's voice Bodger ambled back to them, and Natasha threw a stick for him, glad of an interruption to the conversation. She was wondering whether to broach the subject of Gaye while she had the chance. Part of her warned against it, but something about her mother's discomfort had acted like yeast on her curiosity

'Apparently I look like my mother when she was young', she said lightly, disinterring a blue plastic comb and chucking it in the bag. 'Would you say that was true?'

Ben recognized the leading question and that she wanted to talk about Gaye. Okay. So did he, in a way.

'Seeing you that first time just knocked me for six', he told her. 'I couldn't believe it wasn't Gaye who'd suddenly appeared.

'You met at art school, didn't you? When she was a life model', she prompted.

If Natasha was his daughter, Ben thought, she deserved to know about her parents, and suddenly he wanted to tell her how much he'd loved her mother.

'I adored her', he said simply. 'She was so beautiful. And the sweetest, purest, most angelic girl in the world. She was my soul mate. I knew that from the very first moment.'

'My mother?' questioned Natasha disbelievingly. It was not a description of the sophisticated, fun-loving Gaye she knew.

But Ben was back in the happy-ever-after mindset of the romantic. 'We didn't have any money, but neither of us cared. We had each other, and we spent every moment we could together', he recalled, pausing and gazing unseeingly over the water. 'And then I managed to get a portrait commission, and wanted to use the fee for an engagement ring, but Gaye wouldn't let me. She'd taken a fancy to a tiger's eye stone on a silver chain in a jeweller's window near the art school. So I bought her that instead.' He smiled sentimentally at the recollection. 'It was our engagement necklace. I painted a portrait of her wearing it.'

Natasha almost said, 'I've seen it', but stopped herself. Best not to admit to the studio raid.

'She still has the necklace', she told him instead. 'But what happened to the portrait?'

'Gaye never saw it.'

'Why not? What went wrong?' She was half afraid to trample on his tender memories.

'Everything. It was awful. My father drowned in a sailing accident, so of course I rushed home. And when I got back to London a few weeks later Gaye had… She was…' He stopped.

Natasha looked up enquiringly and he shrugged. 'I'm sorry, there isn't any nice way to say this, but… she'd been seduced by your father and they were engaged to be married.'

A child's teddy bear lay half buried in the sand. Gingerly she picked it up and discovered most of its stuffing had gone. Almost apologetically she consigned it to the sack, its furry face gazing up at her reproachfully.

'That was rotten.' It seemed an inadequate thing to say.

'I never stopped loving her though. I thought about her constantly, and there couldn't have been anyone else.'

Bodger had been overseeing their litter picking efforts with boredom, and was now taking an interest in something thick, soft and translucent in the seaweed.

'Leave it', Ben instructed sharply. 'It's a dead jellyfish', he explained to Natasha, who peered at it with fascinated repugnance. 'I don't know if they're still capable of stinging, but best left alone.'

Natasha had now discovered the link between Ben and her mother, but there were things that still didn't fit. Why had Gaye been so uneasy about her daughter's questions if he was just a casual boyfriend to her? And if he'd been something more, surely they would have got together after the divorce?

'The marriage didn't last, as I'm sure you know', she said carefully, consigning a pot noodle container to the sack. 'Why didn't the two of you meet up again after the divorce?'

Ben didn't respond at first. It was a question he'd never allowed himself to dwell on, and he dodged it now. Pulling at an old sailing boot, he answered, 'To start with I had no idea they'd split up. And later...well, I didn't know where Gaye was.'

The sand released its grip on the boot with a sucking sound, as the obvious corollary remained unsaid. She had known where to find Ben. If she'd wanted.

Evidently Gaye didn't want. In any sense. As Rab's ex wife she was nicely set up financially. And Natasha was pretty sure she wouldn't have needed much seducing. Well none at all really. Certainly not when an eligible millionaire had crossed her path. From as long as she could remember, her mother had enjoyed chasing and being chased, playing boyfriends off against each other, never at a loss for a lover. Or two. And in the background had been Ben, sweet natured and sensitive, still hopelessly in love with the soul mate of his dreams. Led on and then dumped. No wonder Gaye hadn't liked her daughter asking questions about him. She was ashamed.

From across the water came the flight yodel of a redshank, followed, as if in answer, by a loud rumble of thunder. And it was getting darker by the minute.

'I think we're going to have to call it a day', decided Ben, and this was clearly the consensus all along the beach, as people gathered their full sacks together and began moving towards the landing point. In response a dinghy put out from the Hetty Jane, Flitch's broad frame unmistakably pulling at the oars, while another roll of thunder announced that the storm was closer.

The first few drops were falling heavily as the last boatload made it back to the barge, and the atmosphere on board was one of relief at escaping the rain, and animated chat about the weirder items of litter cleared.

'We haven't finished plating up yet, you're a bit earlier than I expected', Tricia told everyone as they crowded below deck, but no-one minded, and she had more offers of help than she could possibly use.

They ate cosily in the saloon, listening to rain thrumming fiercely on deck accompanied by rolls of thunder. It was pity the job wasn't quite finished, but anyone caught out in that would be a drowned rat, they agreed. And Ben offered to go by boat next day to collect the sacks that had been left high up the shore, safe from neap tides at least.

Afterwards, while willing volunteers tackled the clearing up, Danny got out his guitar and sang. With his long, spindly legs he may have been as gawky as an anorexic heron, but he sang like a blackbird, and soon had everyone happily joining in with favourite songs.

'I'll crew on the way back', Ben suggested quietly, seeing Flitch look at his watch. 'Pity to break up the party.'

'It's been a *lovely* evening,' Pauline remarked to Nora as they stood on deck later to watch Flitch's expert docking skills, the sky now brighter, although a mass of dark cloud and rain that was the thunderstorm lowered belligerently off to the east, heading out to sea. 'But didn't you say your younger son was going to walk along and join the shore party? I wonder why he didn't.'

'Oh he must have thought it wasn't worth it', Nora concluded. 'Probably find him ensconced in the bar at the Spritty when we get ashore.'

She couldn't have been more wrong.

It had been annoying not to get a place on the barge, but having thought about it, Tony decided he could turn the situation to his advantage. He'd offer Natasha a meal at that new Italian restaurant, he thought, and persuade her to walk back with him, instead of going with the others on the boat. So he'd get her on her own. And what could be more romantic than a walk through the woods beside the river on a June evening, with a sophisticated, good-looking man?

He'd taken the trouble to think through some conversation topics, including where to insert favourite anecdotes that pointed up his astuteness, spotting art and artists which an impressed director in charge of the bank's collection had then bought, to their advantage.

But the thought of picking up rubbish had less to recommend it. No-one would notice if he wasn't there for that part of the evening, he reckoned. He'd have a couple of drinks first, then walk along and find her. She wouldn't know he hadn't been on the beach all along.

He arrived in Rundleston to discover Chandlers empty of its inhabitants, who were at that moment boarding the Hetty

114

Jane. Tony let himself into the house and changed out of his work suit. Casual, but still smart enough for the restaurant afterwards, he thought, but footwear proved to be a problem. The intention was to borrow a pair of Ben's trainers, not wanting to mess up his own, but he'd forgotten that his brother's flat was temporarily occupied by someone else. He'd come only with a pair of expensive Oxford brogues, and he certainly wasn't prepared to ruin those. Ah well, it might prove a useful excuse if anyone asked why he hadn't been doing any actual beach clearing. Pausing to admire his image in the mirror that lightened the passage, just inside the yard door, he left the house and repaired to the wine bar opposite the maltings flats. The place was busy with people like him, just down from London for the weekend.

He set off towards Woodshey Bay a little later than intended, having schmoozed a blonde doris working behind the bar. She'd have been up for it if he'd had the time. Pity. Still, a far more important target to aim at this evening.

It was further than he remembered. He hadn't walked along this path for more than twenty years, he realised. The scenery was as beautiful as ever but, well, Rundleston had had no attraction for him since…what happened.

On Nora's mantelpiece was a framed photograph of him, aged about eleven, beaming triumphantly from the crook of a huge oak. It was such a good tree for climbing. Where exactly was it, he wondered, looking about him as the path left the far field. Couldn't be far into the wood. Then, with a shock of dismay, he recognized it. Instead of the broad, majestic tree he fondly recalled, what was left of its sinewy bare limbs pointed accusingly skywards. Clearly a bolt of lightning had riven it in two. Must have been some years ago too, time enough for the bark to fall off, leaving the branches weathered to a smooth silver. His life had been hit by lightning too, he reflected, looking at it. But it hadn't been able to destroy him, he'd made sure of that. He turned his back on the oak and continued walking. How might

115

things have been, he wondered, if the accident had never happened? Maybe he'd just have frittered his life away, like Ben. The fact is it'd made him stronger, more determined to succeed. So it could even have been a good thing, for him. But poor old Mum was left on her own, and now she had to go on working in the shop to make a living. He would make it up to her, he vowed. He'd marry this girl, and keep Nora in luxury in her old age.

The thought of money, always attractive, cheered him up. He could have a yacht, he mused pleasurably, imagining himself creating a stir as the luxurious craft creamed up the river to Rundleston. No, on reflection it would be too big for that. He'd want something substantial enough to make heads turn, even in Monaco.

He could see the sailing barge, moored upriver, and hear distant voices. But it was getting unusually dark for a June evening, the path difficult to see when it abandoned the shore and led up under the leaf canopy. And then there came a rumble of thunder.

Bugger! He couldn't ask Natasha to walk back if it rained, he thought, regretting not checking the weather forecast. On the other hand, they'd be bound to let him go back on the barge, whatever the licence said about passenger numbers. It wasn't as if anyone was checking.

Thunder was getting more frequent, and the rain started just as he reached the bay. He heard the drops first, hitting the leaves and plopping on the ground. And the beach was empty of people, occupied only by clusters of black sacks, like gossiping penguins. From a small boat out on the water barely discernible figures were clambering aboard the sailing barge. They'd gone without him! How could they! The bastards. And as he shouted and waved his arms, the rain clouds released their deluge. It was like standing under a waterfall. He retreated to the trees and took out his mobile. But Nora's phone was turned off, and he didn't know Ben's number – never had cause to ring his brother. Spitefully the leaves tipped their watery load down on him in streams, he was soaked through already. In fact he was so wet there was no point in staying there until the storm passed, he soon realized. He was going to have to walk back to bloody Rundleston anyway. Might as well start now.

Tony's mood was far from sunny as he set off into the dark woodland. In places the path had become a stream, and his expensive shoes soon filled with water, their smooth leather soles caused him to slide helplessly, imitating a drunk on an ice rink. With rain running down his face and hair plastered down, he could hardly see where he was going. Brambles scratched his cheek, and a branch jabbed him in the eye. Scrambling up one steep slope his feet slithered from under him and he fell, hitting his nose on the ground. Immediately it began to bleed, red mingling with the dirt on his clinging, muddy shirt. Holding a handkerchief up to stem the flow, he then had one less arm to balance with, and was soon down again.

In more superstitious times the inhabitants of Rundleston told tales of ogres in the woods. Had Tony stumbled into town then they'd have had all the proof they needed. But rain was still pelting the streets, gurgling downpipes spewing water on to the pavements, and the figure squelching his way back to Chandlers encountered no-one. Opening the door from the yard, he immediately stripped off, not caring whether he was alone in the house or not. But then he caught sight of his image in the mirror, and almost frightened himself. Nose bruised and swollen, one eye bloodshot, face scratched, muddy and red with blood, matted hair full of twigs. *Shit!* Suddenly he did care. Natasha mustn't see him like this! What if she came back right now! Galvanised into action he leapt up the stairs in his underpants, grabbed the case and suit off his bed, and a few minutes later was roaring away from Rundleston in the Z4.

When the others came in some time later, there was no sign that Tony had come down from London at all. But there was

117

a definite wet patch just inside the yard door, and Nora gazed at it, puzzled.

'Do you know that rain must have been so heavy it's somehow got in under the door', she remarked to Pauline. 'I'd better get Ben to look at it tomorrow.'

Chapter Nine

Madge soon found that the quality most required for her new role as part time publicity officer for Rundleston's art festival was tact. The problem was that each of the organizers viewed the whole extravaganza in different ways.

To the consortium of London galleries, Tomorrow's Art Today, it was an opportunity to showcase their wares and get paid for doing so. True, Rundleston was unsophisticated and provincial, but this whole thing could indicate an important breakthrough. Up to now the regions had proved tiresomely resistant to fashionable art. But if this insignificant place in East Anglia were to run a successful festival, it might signal that the provinces finally 'got' modern art. And the more the religion spread, the greater profit was in it for them, so the success of the festival mattered. It could open up a whole new market, both for their artists' work, and this new venture of organizing joint exhibitions. To maximize the chances of media attention though, it was important the event was run their way. T.A.T. already had control over what was displayed in the main exhibition, and how it was presented. But they also wanted a big say on publicity and, most importantly, the opening party. The way to get maximum media coverage was to have as many art world celebrities as could be persuaded to attend, and if possible some startling incident – stage-managed if necessary.

The Norwich-based event management company contracted by Rundleston's art festival committee to organize the opening party was, however, resisting any interference. They'd been told it was a local affair, for prominent East Anglians plus representatives of the various sponsors. Tomorrow's Art Today was insisting that art world stars must be invited, but then unhelpfully refused to divulge their contact lists. In return the party organizer declined to tell the galleries exactly what was planned. The stand-off seemed insoluble.

Exacerbating this hostility, was Arabella Drail, in whose eyes Rundleston's art festival presented a heaven-sent opportunity to play a starring role among the luminaries of the art world, in addition to promoting the town and attracting tourists. Also there should be local participation. She wanted to involve schools and the people of Rundleston, so they saw it as 'their' festival. (Even though it was actually her festival). She instructed Madge to emphasize this side of the event in the publicity, while T.A.T. was adamant that it be promoted as an art world happening. The sponsors meanwhile, simply wanted their names prominently featured.

Madge was reminded of pigeons flapping aggressively at each other in a tree, and realized that her task would be impossible unless it was sorted out.

Those who regard exams as essential would have considered her most unsuitable for the role of publicity officer, and to be honest she was unsure if she was up to it herself, but the lack of paper qualifications was more than made up for by common sense. With T.A.T seeking an art world splash, whereas Arabella wanted the emphasis on Rundleston, there was, it seemed to Madge, a useful link between the two, in the form of Lyndon Scroby, famous Young British Artist, and now living in Rundleston. Well, just outside to be precise, in Rundleston House, bought from the Drail's last year, and currently undergoing major refurbishment. She looked up his details on the internet.

'Lyndon Scroby's theme is intertwining', she learned. *'His initial pieces, which caused shock and outrage (and thereby made his name) featured the intertwining of inappropriate things, such as a butterfly and a penis, an angel and a penis, a fire-engine ladder and a penis. Many of these early works were bought for his collection by Oliver Rabson, and are now worth upwards of ten million pounds each. One of the first of the Young British Artists, Scroby gradually progressed to intertwining colours rather than recognizable objects, for example twisting psychedelic pink with scarlet, or orange and purple. He now employs assistants in a London studio to create the artworks, and the original intertwining has metamorphosed into two linked half circles, which is now his signature motif. These days his art works consist of this shape in various colours, sometimes very large, or thousands of them in one piece, used to create the suggestion of something else.*

There were many references to things of a more scurrilous nature on less official sites, 'scandalous parties' and 'swinging both ways' being among them, but also opinion that age and wealth were taming a rebellious spirit. Madge wondered if Arabella Drail was aware of his reputation. When referring to the buyer of Rundleston House, now a neighbour, she liked to make it sound as if they were great chums.

Arabella and Harvey Drail had finally given up the financial struggle of keeping their sprawling nineteenth century home in good repair after an architect had inspected the house with much sucking of teeth, and made the practical suggestion of converting, and moving into, the old barn flanking the road. Arabella told everyone they were downsizing because it was the sensible thing to do, but the loss of a prestigious address hit hard. ('Just put Rundleston House, Rundleston', she'd enjoyed instructing call centre operators). Then the buyer turned out to be a member of the BritArt pack, and that helped to take some of the sting out of losing her 'lady of the manor' status. The man was famous and now enormously rich, he was new to the area and he was their closest neighbour. She was assiduous in telling him everything she knew about the house, popped in for friendly chats to ensure he didn't feel isolated, and was generally welcoming.

Initially Lyndon Scroby had been polite, and helpful with advice on applying for grants and sponsorship for Rundleston's art festival. But his neighbour was unacquainted with the concept of moderation, and he now wouldn't answer the door without first checking the CCTV to see who it was. Staff also had strict instructions about who to admit, and latterly she'd found he was absent a surprising amount.

Arabella reacted to Madge's suggestion like a horse offered a sugar lump. 'Of course! What a good idea', she exclaimed. 'Lyndon has already agreed to come to the opening ceremony, and he sort of said there might be something of his available to exhibit. But you're right, if we linked the whole thing in with him more strongly, it would show Rundleston was the sort of place famous people choose to live, and it would please the Tomorrow's Art Today people as well. I'll go and see him.'

Several abortive visits and phone calls later, she managed to pounce as he walked his Great Dane past the barn. There was no escape, and the man's reluctant consent was duly obtained to opening the art festival, his artwork to be prominently featured. His preferred avoidance of the spotlight had nothing to do with Lyndon having a shy and retiring nature. Far from it. But he had been hoping to keep the whereabouts of his new home a secret, to get away from the paparazzi and enjoy a bit of privacy. The media were hardly going to be headlining a small town art fest though, and it now occurred to him that his planned house-warming bash could be tied in with the opening. Might bring the festival a few more art world celebrities, which would enhance his reputation in the locality.

Arabella was quick to convey the new emphasis to Julian Bisk, the man co-ordinating things at Tomorrow's Art Today's, only to discover there was a problem.

'We don't have any of Lyndon Scroby's work available to exhibit', she was told. 'Tate Modern has some, and the MOMA, but most of his work is in private collections.'

'What about new stuff? Surely he's still producing work?'

At the other end of the phone the T.A.T. man smiled at her naivety. She clearly wasn't aware of the hype and careful customer and media manipulation that went into launching new pieces by major artists. The idea of simply exhibiting them in some provincial art festival was laughable.

'I'm afraid the gallery that represents him isn't part of our consortium', he informed her. 'So they wouldn't allow any new work to be shown.'

But a couple of minutes later he rang back. 'I forgot', he said, in a rare admission of human weakness. 'One of the Festival's sponsors, Grashe's Bank, has a Scroby they might be willing to lend, in exchange for extra publicity. Would you like me to approach them?'

Madge found herself completely torn. On the one hand, she hoped Rundleston's art festival would be a success. It was what she'd been taken on to help bring about, and she wanted to prove, to herself as much as anything, that she was capable and businesslike. Having been immersed in looking after Jamie since university, she'd never had a proper job. Not that three mornings a week could really be called that, but it was a challenge nonetheless.

At the same time she empathized with Ben, to whom the art fiasco, as he called it, represented everything he hated. He and Natasha had gone to such trouble to give Jamie a good weekend when she'd been away. It was lovely to hear animation in the boy's voice when he told her about Ben's sailing lesson, the barge evening and the helicopter trip, and he was also thrilled that Stephen had invited him to be one of his crew for the regatta's raft race. They were going to dress up as vikings, for which Nora was kindly making the costumes, and he now disappeared to the boatyard for hours at a time, helping to construct the craft. Madge could feel the lifting of her son's spirits, and she was truly grateful.

One way for her to return Ben's kindness was to forge ahead with arrangements to have prints made of some of his paintings, and she was also getting quotes for a range of greeting cards. She suggested that they spend one of her free mornings in his studio, sorting out the best candidates for both, and he agreed without any of his previous reluctance.

Last time she'd been in the studio above the garage, it was as an interloper, guiltily filching paintings with Natasha. To accompany its owner was a very different feeling. And Ben was plainly so at home here amongst the things he understood. It was like seeing a cat relaxing in its own territory, loose and content.

A red check cloth covered a table in the middle of the crowded room which she didn't remember from before.

'Expecting visitors for tea?' she enquired, and in response Ben revealed its function as a dust sheet over a large map in the course of being framed.

'See what a slave you've made of me', he commented, indicating a pile of work still to be done . 'I can hardly keep up with customer orders.'

He insisted she had the only chair, while he sat on an old cardboard box which sagged ominously under the weight. Used to long, quiet sessions up here, Bodger made for his blanket nest and settled down with a sigh. Madge had brought some capacious plastic storage containers which she placed on top of the plan chests, and as they prepared to go through the drawers they decided on guidelines.

'Ones that are especially personal, or are of recognizable people, we'll put aside shall we?' she suggested. 'Then possibilities for prints in one container, card candidates in another. And anything that's second rate or unfinished over here.'

'Second rate? echoed Ben seemingly outraged. 'Are you suggesting that...'

'No, of course I didn't mean...' Madge interrupted hastily, then caught his eye and laughed. 'You know what I mean.'

It was an enjoyable session for them both. Ben had never sorted through past paintings before. They'd just been shoved into drawers and forgotten. Now, as each one was examined it was like reliving his life.

'That cutter used to come up here regularly', he remarked, looking at an estuary scene. 'Lovely lines she had.' He picked up another. 'And that's the old boy who used to run a ferry service over to the other side. You're too young, you probably won't remember.'

'Yes I do', she responded indignantly. 'If you met him in a shop he always smelt slightly of seaweed.'

She held up a winter street scene, figures dark against white pavements, and looked at the date. 'That was my last year at school. I remember it was a really cold January. We spent all our time having snowball fights, with the boys trying to stuff snow down the girls' necks.'

Beneath it in the drawer was a depiction of a group, muffled in scarves, gloves and hats, throwing snow at each other, the low winter sunshine slanting blue shadows across the whiteness.

'Oh! Could one of those be me, do you think? No, that can't be the recreation ground, I don't recognize those trees.'

'They're actually half a mile away', Ben informed her laconically. 'I used the snowballers and put them in a better background.' Amused at her expression, he added, 'All painting's a bit of a lie, you know.'

They decided she couldn't have been included though. 'You were doing holiday work in the shop by then, and I'd have recognized you.' He smiled. 'Well, the hair anyway.'

'A pity. I'd love to be in one of your paintings. They're magic. Really atmospheric.'

Her genuine appreciation in contrast to the art establishment's sneering and rejection was heart-warming.

There were several featuring the family maltings.

'Do you still feel sore about what's happened to it?' Madge asked him.

Ben held up a painting, considering both it and the question. 'No, I suppose not', he decided. 'Your grandfather and mine would have been horrified, wouldn't they. But it's no good for modern processes, and both Dad and I tried to find other uses to keep it going.'

'It some kind of animal feed place when I was at school', she recalled.

'Yes. I wasn't very good at pressing farmers to pay their bills though', he admitted. 'Not cut out to be a businessman, as you might have guessed. We tried using it as a furniture store. And then a dealer thought it would be perfect as an antiques centre. But it wasn't.' He smiled wryly. 'Didn't help that there was woodworm and the roof leaked. The upkeep of the place was like pouring sugar into a swimming pool.'

He added the painting to the reject pile. 'So although I was angry with Mum, giving it to the town was probably for the best. You can show me round some time. It'll be interesting to see what's been done.'

He'd come to a depiction of children crabbing on the quay. 'I told Jamie I'd show him how to do that', he remarked, putting it in the greetings card box.

'You and Nora have been so kind to us both', Madge paused in her task. 'But really we ought to vacate your flat, now that I'm not helping in the shop. The use of it was part of the bargain.'

'Nonsense, I'm very happy on the Hetty Jane for the rest of the summer. Anyway, where would you go?'

'Well, we could probably find somewhere to rent. At least until the money comes through from the house sale. And then I have to decide – Canada with my parents, or here.'

'Don't go. Jamie's just settling in', Ben advised. 'What do you think about this one?'

There were a good many studies of people. Madge loved a depiction of Nora, absorbed in a newspaper crossword, sitting in her favourite armchair, light streaming in the window, through which was a view of the estuary.

'And that's Jimmy to the life!' she exclaimed over a full length portrait of a swarthy street sweeper, leaning against a doorpost, smoking. 'Just how he used to stand. Never seen without a fag in his mouth.'

'Never seen to use that broom either, unless his supervisor was around', observed Ben drily. 'Great for gossip though, he didn't miss a thing. Mum used to say he knew more about what went on in this place than she did. And that's saying something.' Madge passed the painting to him, and he looked at it critically. 'He's dead now you know. Died a couple of years back.'

'Lung cancer?'

'No'. He flashed her a mischievous smile. 'Doctors reckoned it was overwork.'

They sifted their way through the chests, and after nearly two hours had chosen far more candidates for prints and cards than could possibly be used.

'Do you think the ones for calendars and mugs and mouse mats should be the same, or different from, the cards?' he asked her seriously. 'After all some people might like to buy birthday cards to send away, and a mouse mat to keep for themselves.'

Oh dear, he hadn't forgotten about it, thought Madge with dismay. Clearly she'd been too persuasive. This conversion to the wrong kind of commercialism though was going to have to be tackled head on.

'Look...um...I don't want to pontificate, but selling is all about identifying your market and tailoring the product accordingly. We want to appeal to a quality market, not...'

'You can buy images of the Mona Lisa though on just about everything, and she's still the most valuable painting ever.' Ben was enjoying himself.

'But in the real world no-one's going to spend good money on a print to go over their mantelpiece if the same image is on someone else's wall as a calendar.'

He looked pained. 'But I thought you wanted me to be more business-like.'

'Yes I did, but...'

There was the faintest twitch of his lips, as he struggled to keep a straight face.

'Ben? You're having me on?'

'Who, me?' But mirth got the better of him, and he gave himself up to deep, joyous laughter.

'You *toad*!'

'Oh! Oh your face was a picture', he managed to gasp, fending her off as Madge lunged at him in mock revenge.

Whereupon, with the slow inevitability of a folding parachute, his cardboard box seat collapsed. Instinctively clutching at the dustsheet as he went down, he succeeded only in pulling it to the floor on top of him,

'Get him, Bodger!' urged Madge, through helpless giggles.

The dog needed little encouragement to join in this new game. Padding over, tail wagging, he thrust a large, wet nose beneath the cloth, his front paws on the shaking heap of hilarity, prompting it to shout weakly, 'Gerrof!'

It was some time before they recovered their composure.

'You deserved that', Madge told Ben with satisfaction, when he'd fought off both tablecloth and dog and picked himself up.

'So did you', he insisted, dusting himself down and looking round for somewhere else to perch. 'But I will concede that you're right about being more commercially-minded. After all this modern art nonsense isn't going to change. It's in too many people's interests. I even read recently that the market is used to launder money, as well as a tax dodge, and I can well believe it.'

'Launder money? How would that work?'

'Well apparently some dealers and galleries don't question where the money comes from, they're just happy to sell something for a couple of million, or whatever. And then that piece is sold on pretty rapidly, sometimes even back to the same dealer, probably for quite a lot less. But everybody's happy. Hot money is now legit, the gallery is quids in, ditto the so-called artist, who probably took less than a day to create it in the first place. If that.'

'Nice work if you can get it', commented Madge.

'Suppose so. It stinks, but no good me hollering, is it. You're right, I should be more focused on what opportunities there are.'

'And just treat the whole thing as a joke', Madge suggested. 'If you can't change it, laugh, like most of the public do.'

They'd now reached the bottom drawer of the last chest. Knowing it contained the portrait of Gaye, Madge wondered what he would say.

'Nothing much in there', he concluded dismissively, indicating the drawer. 'And we've got more than enough, surely. Shall we take these down and see what Mum thinks about them before we make final choices?

In the next few days Madge found herself thinking about that morning in the studio far more than she wanted. It had been eye-opening, in more ways than one. Examining the stash of paintings closely and discussing them, as opposed to riffling through them at guilty speed with Natasha, had reinforced her conviction that Ben was an artist of thrilling talent. It was simply a crime for them to be hidden away, unseen. She owed it to the world, as well as to their creator, to try to change that. Even if the art establishment jeered, surely the public would be entranced.

Disconcertingly though, what occupied her thoughts even more was Ben himself. When they'd talked while Jamie was practising rowing, she'd seen the hurt and vulnerable side of him, and it had aroused her maternal instincts. She'd felt privileged then, but that morning in the studio showed something more. This relaxed, teasing man, assured in his own territory, had been a revelation. The picture of him throwing back his head and laughing was now fixed in her mind, like an image on photosensitive paper. And hell, it was attractive.

The last thing you need, Madge my girl, she told herself severely, is to fall for a man. And this wasn't just any man. Ye gods, it was Ben Banding, whom she'd known for ever. What was the matter with her? How could she be feeling like that about him? Bewildered, she decided it must be what was meant by falling for someone 'on the rebound'. So pull yourself together, girl, she ordered. Just forget it.

But she was failing. It was as if a switch had been thrown that couldn't be reversed. And her resolve wasn't helped by the fact that her friends seemed to want to talk about him.

Natasha suggested they had a pub lunch together the day after the studio session. They sat in the Spritsail Barge's saloon bar, dull skies and drizzle making a table outside unattractive. With its smoke-stained walls and low, beamed ceiling it was rather gloomy on dark summer days. The landlord had recently proposed a repaint, but backed down in the face of vehement opposition from the regulars. It was their pub, they reckoned, not his, and they liked it just the way it was. Today the tables by the windows, looking out over the water, were all taken and the place was crowded, several small children wandering round gazing at customers

129

with the grave interest adults reserve for museum exhibits. So after greeting Tricia behind the bar and ordering from the blackboard menu, they found a secluded place in the corner next to the unlit fire.

There hadn't been a chance for a good natter on their own since the weekend, and there was much to catch up on. Between mouthfuls of chicken salad, Madge reported on her residential computer course and the start of her work for the art festival. In turn she heard Natasha's version of the weekend, and was able to thank her properly, emphasising how it seemed to be a turning point for Jamie.

'Oh I couldn't have done it without Ben', Natasha acknowledged modestly. 'He was brilliant with Jamie. Pity he's never had children of his own. And you know what, I think my mother's largely to blame.'

'Your mother?'

'Yes.' Natasha related in detail their conversation on the beach. She was clearly intrigued by the discovery that Ben had adored Gaye and, seemingly, never recovered.

'Explains a lot, I reckon. She dumped on him, big time, I feel really bad about it. He's such a nice guy you could hug him couldn't you.'

Madge blinked. Clearly relations between the two had improved while she'd been away.

'I've been wondering how to make him see that Mum never was the sweet, innocent soulmate he imagined', Natasha confided. 'I don't want to be unkind about her, and she has lots of good qualities, but that just isn't her character Or..' she considered, 'perhaps there's some way I could try and make it up to him. What do you think?

Madge?'

Natasha was seated with her back to the bar, but for some time Madge had been aware that their table was an object of interest. Now she said in a low voice, 'There's a man at the bar who's been staring at us ever since he came in. In a smock, with a pony tail.'

'Oh that'll be Danny.' Natasha swiveled round and gave him a bright smile and a wave, which he took as an invitation to come over, and she introduced him to Madge.

'Danny's magic on the guitar, really made the party swing the other night. And he's promised to give me a guided tour of the tug he lives on', she said gaily.

There seemed no sign of him returning to the bar, and Madge looked at her watch before making her excuses. Just time to do some food shopping before collecting her son from school.

After a meal and some hurried homework, Jamie was keen to join Stephen and the other raft crew members at the boatyard.

'Have we got any old water containers?' he wanted to know. 'We're using them for floats and fenders, and we need lots. The rules are we can't buy stuff, so it all has to be made out of rubbish or things people don't want. Come and see what we're doing.'

The afternoon drizzle had faded to an overcast sky as Madge accompanied him past the Spritsail Barge and the sailing club to the boatyard beyond.

For the sailing fraternity of Rundleston the new marina might be okay for Londoners and weekenders, but Flitch's was exactly how a real boatyard should be.

Being summer, just a few yachts remained, held up by props, a couple with homemade For Sale signs, the others clearly being worked on. Parked boat trailers and cradles indicated where there would be winter occupants, and a pontoon, stretching out into a dredged channel, offered the only mooring places at low tide, with the Hetty Jane taking up most of one side. Flanking the channel were mud berths, with Danny's tug, wind turbine slack in the still air, the largest vessel. From the exposed mud came a faint whisper of popping bubbles. A rubber dinghy leant against one of several shipping containers, which may, or may not, have fallen off a lorry, now being used for storage. Folded tarpaulins, fenders, heaps of anchor chain, huge mooring posts, rusty oil drums, balks of timber, strops and old steel girders provided an obstacle course for a mobile crane. A digger on caterpillar tracks also patrolled, its current task tipping rubble into huge tractor tyres stacked on the mud against the wharf. Evidently Flitch was expanding the yard into the river. On trestles by a large shed the boys' raft was taking shape, with wooden pallets lashed together, the spaces infilled with blocks of polystyrene, and an assembly of plastic water containers beside it.

'We used some of the polystyrene out of the bags we got off the beach', Jamie informed her, indicating a quantity of black bags piled up in a corner. And we're going to have a mast', he added excitedly. 'It's over there. But we've got to make a hole for it, and find a way to keep it upright and still have room for all of us.

And that's Ben's boat I told you about', he indicated a clinker-built dayboat alongside the pontoon. When we went to fetch the bags of beach rubbish he let me helm some of the time. It was ace!'

Nothing going on in the yard was missed from the windows of the owner's red-brick, nineteenth century cottage at the back, and they were soon joined by Stephen. Not wishing to embarrass Jamie by her presence, Madge responded to Tricia's window tapping and beckoning gestures, and picked her way past piles of planks and an old tractor chassis half buried in weeds, up to the house.

'Might come in useful', was clearly Flitch's mantra for the yard, but their home was Tricia's domain, and was kept firmly free of clutter. All the rooms that side had an enviable view, as long as the yard was kept in soft focus. Today there was hardly a ripple on the estuary, the bluey-grey surface reflecting the sky like a mirror. A boat was languidly making its way up river, sails furled, the sound of its engine clear across the still water. A family of Canada geese contemptuously overtook it, cruising at head height before splashing down with varying degrees of skill. Regrettably, a view of the river was something that Ben's flat at Chandlers lacked, blocked by the garden wall. But then, Madge thought, she'd never get anything done if there was all this to distract her. Tricia's kitchen table had been placed beside the window, and she and Madge sat companionably, looking out over the river while keeping an eye on their respective sons, who'd now been joined by another of the raft's crew.

'That Natasha's causing quite a stir – everyone's smitten with her', remarked Tricia.

'Really? Who's everyone?'

'Well, Danny – you met him in the pub today. Lives on the tug over there. A hermit if ever I saw one. Besotted', she announced dramatically. 'When he was playing the other evening the way he looked at her she *was*'The Girl From Ipanema. Practically melting, he was.'

Danny's reluctance to leave Natasha's table at lunchtime was now explained. But it seemed likely the object of his affections was completely unaware of her effect.

'Trouble is', Tricia continued with relish, 'Ben's in love with her as well.'

Madge had been watching a swoop of seagulls squabbling over a piece of bread, now her attention snapped back.

'What? Oh surely not.'

Tricia nodded vigorously, pleased to be the bearer of such unlikely news. 'Who'd have thought it. All the times I've tried to get him off with someone suitable, and he just couldn't be bothered…'

Madge wondered whether to put Tricia right, by reminding her about Ben's link with Natasha's mother, his long lost love, but instead she said, 'They agreed to look after Jamie for me. I'm sure there wasn't anything else to it.'

'Natasha's keen on him too, believe it or not.' There was no dissuading Tricia from her romantic script. 'She made quite sure they teamed up together at Woodshey Bay. You should have seen them together.'

The best antidote to unsuitable feelings, Madge reckoned, was being busy, and she flung herself with energy into her publicity tasks. Formulating press releases describing the art festival though, she kept coming up against the opening party. It needed to be mentioned. But could it be promoted as a glittering affair, newsworthy because of the famous people in attendance, or would it simply be a jolly for East Anglian worthies, of interest only to the local press?

She consulted Arabella, who now rather regretted engaging a local events management company when she should have been thinking bigger. With Lyndon Scroby on board, there was no knowing what a media splash the art festival could make. She was already anticipating photographs of herself in the national press alongside the starry guests, and glowing tributes to her role as chief organizer of such a successful and popular event.

'Trouble is, a contract's a contract', she told Madge. 'There's no way we can get out of it. Of course if they threw in the towel, that would be different. But they're hardly likely to do that, are they.'

In one of her telephone conversations with Julian Bisk, of Tomorrow's Art Today, Madge conveyed Arabella's willingness to have a more sophisticated outfit organizing the party, were it not for the contract already signed.

'Do you know, it's quite possible they'll have a change of mind', he said, as if he was a psychic with access to privileged information. 'I need to speak to the man responsible anyway. Leave it to me'.

He rang back the following morning. 'I think you'll find their letter asking to be released from the contract will arrive in the next day or so', he reported casually. 'Now, we need to think about a replacement. Someone we've had good experience with in the past, who knows the art world...'

'What did you do?' Madge challenged him suspiciously. 'You didn't threaten them or anything?'

'How could you think such a thing? Nothing so crude. I just told them that I'd heard about some performance art that was being planned.' He paused. 'And, er, not to worry about it.'

'What performance art?'

'Well, some of the guests, artists you know, were going to simulate collapsing with food poisoning. It'd create quite a stir. Really good for publicity. Bound to get in the papers.'

'But couldn't the company sue for having its reputation ruined? And how can you call that performance art?'

'Simple. Anything an artist does is art, if he says it is.

'You mean, if I did it, I'd just be pretending to be ill, and they could sue me.' Madge had never been good at conundrums. 'But if an artist does something like that, it's art.'

'Spot on', Julian confirmed cheerily. 'Useful sometimes. Anyway, we need to sort out a replacement who can come up with a really spectacular opening party.'

'Don't tell me', Madge was wavering between admiration and dislike at the man's audacity, 'whoever takes it on won't experience people falling about clutching their stomachs.'

'Well, I think the artists concerned could be persuaded to do something else', he agreed with exaggerated lightness. 'Now the person I'd like to approach made an excellent job of our opening party when we formed Tomorrow's Art Today. None of us minds sharing our guest lists with Gaye Rabson, in fact she could probably add some contacts of her own   So I need to know the terms of the old contract.'

The ensuing silence made him think they'd been cut off.

'Hello?'

'I...I don't know what the terms are', muttered Madge indistinctly. 'You'll have to talk to Arabella.'

That morning in his studio with Madge had affected Ben too. It was a surprise to him how many paintings there were, a record, in a way, of his life over the past twenty-three years. Some of them should have been chucked out, he reflected up in his studio, as he framed a diploma for a customer. To his eyes now the technique was poor, or the subject matter ill chosen. Quite a number he'd meant to finish, and never had. Most though, were good, he knew that in the same way that a joiner or clockmaker takes quiet satisfaction in producing an outstanding example of his craft. And Madge's obvious admiration was heart-warming. If she felt that way about them, well maybe ordinary people would too. And she was right. There were more ways of showing his art than originals in galleries.

He polished a sheet of glass before inserting it into the frame. She was such a nice girl too, he reflected, lively and good company. He couldn't remember when he'd enjoyed a morning so much. And she obviously loved Rundleston. Shame she didn't marry someone local. It was good of her to try and help him too. But were prints and greeting cards the right way to go? And what were the paintings *for*?

Like a thread of cobweb tickling his eyelid, that was the question that persisted. If it had been, 'what am I for?' there'd have been no problem. He was on this earth to paint and draw. It was a compulsion, the one thing he was good at, he'd have said. And it gave him peace. But hiding the results away, what was the justification for that?

Answering would mean examining things he'd managed to avoid contemplating over the years. But maybe it was time to sort things out in his mind.

Into the frame he fitted a coloured surround, followed by the diploma and backing card, thinking back. When those first attempts at getting his work exhibited were snubbed, he'd been young and less certain of his talent, and coming up against the new art religion had been bruising. He still remembered the supercilious look on one gallery owner's

136

face, dismissing him with the words, 'Forget it. The world's moved on, son. My clients want fashionable art and this is old hat'. The smarting was only accentuated by all the praise and money heaped on a load of crud calling itself art. And Oliver Rabson, the louse who lured Gaye away, was largely responsible for orchestrating that whole masquerade. Somehow, Ben had promised himself, he'd get even with him. It wasn't in his easy-going nature to be angry though, and he didn't like the way it made him feel. So the answer was not to think about it, and to put away the paintings, his one ace, and forget about them, with the idea that some day he'd get back at the bastard.

But how, how were they going to achieve anything? That was what he had to focus on. He cut brown tape to seal the backing board into the frame, and frowned. Hadn't the game changed now, though? Perhaps his art were just a sideshow, and the way to get at him was through Natasha, Rabson's daughter.

Or his.

It was unfortunate that over the weekend, apart from the beach clearing episode cut short by the thunderstorm, there just hadn't been the right opportunity to steer the conversation in a useful direction. So he was no nearer finding out if she actually was his child. She was a daughter to be proud of too. He'd got over seeing Gaye when he looked at Natasha, and had found himself liking her a lot – sweet-natured, vivacious, intelligent and beautiful. Like her mother of course. But that some of those genes might have come from Oliver Rabson was something Ben didn't care to contemplate. He and Natasha got on so well together, surely she was his. And, he thought, threading the cord through the metal eyes and knotting it, that makes it right she should be my weapon.

First he had to have proof though. Gaye was the guardian of the secret, but he quailed at the idea of going to London to ask. Her betrayal, if he was the father, was a fence he

137

wasn't up to leaping at the moment. And Natasha would surely want to know the reason for the visit, she'd be bound to hear about it. No, it was going to have to be a paternity test, and he would need several of her hairs.

He gave the glass a final polish, then made out an invoice, wondering how he was going to obtain his evidence. Originally he'd imagined it would be easy, but now the thought of trespassing in her room seeking a hairbrush was repellant. And they had to be irrefutably Natasha's. Taking the finished task down to the shop, dog at his heels, a smile hovered as he pictured himself saying, 'Excuse me but would you mind if I had just a few hairs from your head', or surreptitiously yanking some out as she passed.

As he opened the door, Nora threw him a 'rescue me' look. Arabella Drail was in full spate.

Arabella prided herself on being a good organizer. But not, in her own eyes, autocratic. No, it was important to keep people informed as to what the team, under her leadership, would be doing. Although Nora Banding wasn't closely involved with the art festival, it was due to her gift of the family maltings that it was happening at all, and Arabella felt it only right to keep her up to date with how things were going. Having all the sensitivity to people's feelings of a beam engine, she was oblivious to Nora's original expectation that Ben's paintings would be featured, out of courtesy to the donor if nothing else. Now she was recounting with verve how Lyndon Scroby had agreed to star in the proceedings, and the difficulties she was having about arranging insurance for one of his paintings to be loaned by Grashe's bank from their collection.

'Apparently it's worth millions', she said breathlessly. 'We'll need to install extra security.'

Ben put the framed diploma on the counter. 'Are you going to have any art happenings?' he enquired innocently.

'Art what?'

138

'You know, happenings. Like someone running round the town backwards. Or wrapping all the street lights in string. Very cutting-edge', he told her earnestly. 'And gets lots of publicity. That bloke who destroyed all his belongings was a hot topic for weeks.'

'Oh. Well…' This was something that hadn't occurred to Arabella, but perhaps it should have. 'Yes, that's a possibility. We'll have to think about it. We could have something before it all starts off, to get the press interested.' She was warming to the idea. 'And then maybe some apparently unscheduled event at the opening party.'

She turned to Nora. 'That promises to be even better now. Tomorrow's Art Today are bringing in a London events manager', she reported happily. 'They say she's very good. Gaye Rabson – I think she's Oliver Rabson's ex. Apparently she's organized parties for them before.'

'Oh', Nora exclaimed, 'that must be Natasha's…'

'Gosh!' Ben interrupted urgently. 'There's a *huge* black spider on your back, Mum. Just crawling up to your neck. Hold still', he instructed, as Nora squeaked in alarm. 'Gotcha! No…Damn. Dropped him. Running towards you', he told Arabella, who suddenly remembered a whole host of pressing things to do.

'Balloons, blown up with farts – get everyone involved', Ben suggested helpfully as she stood, hand on the shop door, making leaving noises.

'*What?*'

'An art event for the opening party.'

'Oh. Yes. Well… something to think about perhaps.'

'Wherever can that have emerged from?' Nora shuddered as the door closed behind Arabella.

'Probably came in with me,' suggested Ben. 'The studio's a great place for spiders. Big, black, hairy ones.' He spread his arms and loomed towards her making a face.

'Well it's here now, and I shan't feel safe until we find it.' Nora looked round the shop nervously.

'Oh Bodger got it', he assured her blandly. 'Didn't you dog.'

This would have required an unusual athleticism given that the canine in question had headed straight for his basket behind the counter. Ben saw realization dawn on his mother's face, and twinkled at her.

'Ben, you are the limit.'

'Well you wanted to get rid of the woman.' He shrugged. 'Besides, I didn't think it was a good idea for her to know there's a Rabson here already. Poor Natasha would be roped in to the art fiasco, and get no peace.'

'I suppose you're right.' Nora's thoughts shifted from threatening spider to the news that had given rise to it. 'How intriguing. Looks as though we're going to meet Natasha's mother.'

'Yes.' Ben picked a Father's Day card out of the carousel, and studied it thoughtfully. 'Yes it does, doesn't it.'

Chapter Ten

In the twelve months spent with her father, Natasha's role had been indulged daughter, being inducted into his business and social life. (Although he mostly managed to keep his girlfriends away from her, on the grounds of good taste.) So finding herself suddenly transferred from the fast, fashionable London scene where she was known and admired as Rab's charming offspring, to quiet Rundleston, was like being turfed out of a bus on a cold winter's night, watching its warmth and light recede, leaving her alone and shivering at the roadside.

With no parties, nightclubs or gallery private views to go to, she had plenty of time to reflect on who she was and what she intended to contribute to the world. Trouble was, no easy answers had been forthcoming.

Blessed with a stable and sanguine personality, and a loving nanny, as a child she'd just accepted that she had a mother, but no father on the scene. Plenty of people at school had similar home lives. It hurt dully that her father apparently didn't even want to see his child, but as lovers processed through her mother's life, she came to view men as shallow, egotistical and easily manipulated appendages she could do well without. And that included fathers.

To find out from Rab that he'd wanted to be involved with her childhood but had been rebuffed, was akin to discovering the world was round, after being firmly taught that it was triangular. It seemed Gaye had lied to her, depriving her of a loving parent. How could she do that? The betrayal cut deep. When tackled, her mother's defence was that she hadn't wanted her daughter to be brought up a spoilt little rich kid. Given that, thanks to a very sizeable sum extracted from her ex-husband, Gaye could lavish money on luxury with the best of them, this was hardly convincing. Natasha reckoned it had been pure vindictiveness against Rab, and she couldn't forgive. As a reaction she immersed herself in the new relationship with her father, her previous conclusions about the male sex quietly forgotten. Well, other men might be like that, but Rab was strong and capable, clever, caring and warm. Her father was rich, famous and respected. She was Oliver Rabson's daughter and he loved her. No need to look further for an identity.

Now here she was, in a small, unsophisticated town, having to keep her presence quiet, and faced with a daunting task set by a displeased father. She needed to prove to him, and to herself, that she was worthy of his trust and not just a decorative hanger on.

Natasha was welcome to email Rab from the dining room, using the wi-fi which unfortunately didn't extend to the top floor. Painfully aware that she had let him down over the Charles thing, keeping in touch seemed all-important. She sent him emails most days, asking questions and seeking advice, but also describing who she met and what she was doing. She told self-deprecatory stories about herself, a city girl, encountering small town culture, and the tone was light-hearted and amusing. Rab soon looked forward to her missives, which started 'Hi Dad', and always finished, 'Miss you loads'. His replies contained endearments that he would have felt constrained about using face to face, and as a result his daughter's absence managed to strengthen the bond between them. She sent him pictures of Rundleston, her room at Chandlers, and the shop that she and Pauline had decided on for the gallery. He smiled as he pictured her being a waitress on the Hetty Jane, and was surprised, and pleased, to read about looking after Jamie. She related the success of the helicopter trip, and told him about the beach clearing event and the party on the barge afterwards.

But not everything. Rab knew about her landlady's son being an artist, whose paintings were 'just brilliant!', but Natasha felt it wasn't suitable for him to hear what she'd discovered that evening, about Gaye's treatment of Ben years ago. Relations between her parents were bad enough without giving extra ammunition to one side or the other.

It preyed on her own mind though. Clearly Ben had been led on, blinded by his adoration, only to be trampled underfoot, leaving him emotionally crippled. Her mother had behaved really badly towards him. And then, by an unhappy coincidence, Rab had not only 'stolen' his fiancée, but he'd fanned the mania for modern art which resulted in Ben's wonderful talent being rubbished. That her father couldn't know the effect of what he'd done only made it a little better. The fact was her family had blighted Ben's life.

Charles – the first serious boyfriend – had now confirmed her poor opinion of men, adding 'untrustworthy and devious' to their list of characteristics, but Ben, in common with her father, was clearly different. For a start, he hadn't liked her, despite her efforts to charm. That wasn't the usual male reaction, so it made him interesting. And now that relations between them had improved greatly, she warmed to this sincere, talented, but hurt man. He was a sweetie, and she wanted to help him, to somehow make amends on behalf of her family.

The wonderful oil painting of Rundleston wharf that Nora had managed to get reproduced as a card hung on the dining room wall. It dominated the room and drew the eye, and Natasha never tired of looking at it as she sat at the side table sending emails. Madge was going to use the images of his paintings for prints and greetings cards, but Natasha tried to think of people she could introduce him to who might further his career. Trouble was, the only ones of influence she knew were deeply involved in contemporary art. And with indignation she recalled the London galleries swift rejection when she'd taken samples of his work. No, the whole art scene was deliberately ranged against him, but somehow she would find a way to help him.

Meanwhile there was much work to be done. The old greengrocers that she and Pauline had chosen for the gallery could have been called picturesque, but not by anyone who valued descriptive accuracy. Nor was it helped by inevitable comparison to Chandlers' ancient, tiled roof, big chimneys and pleasingly proportioned first floor windows with dormers above. Separated by only a few feet from its handsome neighbour, her future gallery was built of white-washed brick, the bright blue door dead centre, with two good-sized windows on either side. Fancy brickwork formed stripes up to first floor level, where they met a pretentious horizontal relief, topped by two small windows. The pitch of the slate roof was shallow and unsatisfying to the eye. The whole effect was of a plain woman with an unfortunate dress sense. An unsavoury sink room and loo at the back led to a door opening onto a small yard, accessed from the narrow passage between the two buildings.

There were some good things about it. Not being of historic importance, it wasn't listed, so that cut out hassle with the local planning people, and to avoid any delay from that direction, Pauline advised that the upper storey should be left as storage rooms. Also, its location, facing the square, meant the gallery would not go unnoticed by even the most fleeting visitor, and benefitted from market shoppers on Wednesdays and Saturdays. Not that those browsing among market stalls were likely to feel the urge to purchase an expensive piece of modern art. To be honest, Natasha couldn't quite picture who the customers were likely to be, but her father obviously reckoned Rundleston had potential, so who was she to question his judgement.

Rab's legal and financial people had sorted out the renting of the premises with commendable speed. It was owned by Peter Jahney, whose family brewery had, a few years ago, been turned into flats. According to Nora, he owned half the shops in the town, and several terraced houses as well. Accompanied by Pauline, Natasha had gone to The Dutch House, his large, extravagantly-gabled country house hotel outside Rundleston, to talk about her plans for a smart gallery. Now she had to put those ideas into practice.

The main shop area, scruffy and still smelling faintly of cabbage and bananas, was a good size, with plenty of light. But there were suspiciously rat-sized holes at the base of the lean-to storage area at the back, and she surveyed the 1950's washing facilities with dismay. Her experience of any kind of building renovation and makeover was precisely nil. To begin with she'd felt like the put-upon girl in the fairy tale faced with sorting out a huge pile of mixed grains. Get a grip, she told herself firmly, you can do this. Rundleston's birds might not, as in the fairy story, be rushing to help, but Pauline was ever helpful with comments and suggestion, and Nora recommended an honest and capable builder, the choice endorsed by Peter Jahney. The workmen themselves were a source of knowledge, often adapting her ideas for the better, or pointing out impracticalities.

Gradually, Natasha began to enjoy the task. Every time some problem was uncovered, having to make the decision that solved it increased her self confidence. She was learning too. The way buildings worked had never impinged on her consciousness before. The importance of guttering and drains, how roof slates were fixed, weight-bearing walls, boilers, hot water systems and underfloor heating, now became things she thought about daily. She was in awe of the electricians' expertise and knowledge as they began rewiring the place, and admired the casual skills of the plumber, plasterer and carpenter. She mucked in and helped where she could, made them coffee and strong tea, and chatted to them, discovering lives far removed from her own. Knocked sideways by her looks and unaffected interest, they laughed with her about past jobs, peculiar buildings and impossible clients, and confided their worries and grumbles.

A frequent gripe was how the town was changing, and not for the better. Most of them had relations who'd worked at the brewery or in the maltings, and they had nothing but disdain for the young city types living in the flats the various buildings now contained. Whilst sympathizing with these opinions, they made Natasha slightly uncomfortable, as she realised that turning a family greengrocers shop into an upmarket art gallery was part of the change they were complaining about.

It hadn't been her choice though, and the supermarket was to blame for making the shop unviable. Better to look forward to what would be her own business, which was already making her think in a more entrepreneurial and grown up way. It was pleasing to use her brain and personal skills, and she warmed to the thought that her father's genes were showing through. The disappointing thing was that she wasn't selling something which appealed to her. Rab had taught her that contemporary art was simply a commodity, able to be sold like any other. Might need a bit more hype and promotion than, say, bicycles, but whether it appealed to you personally or not was irrelevant. He was right of course, Natasha concluded dutifully, shoving her private dislike under a cushion and sitting on it.

It was encouraging to show Pauline, Nora and Madge how progress was being made in transforming the premises, and Peter Jahney dropped by most days. She had to liaise with him closely over costs, since he'd agreed with Rab's lawyers to foot the bill for part of the work. A tall, greying man, with military bearing, he looked older than Ben, but in fact they'd been at school together, she discovered, and were the same age.

Danny took to knocking on the door too, and coming in to see how things were getting on. It was good to have a second opinion about the electrical work being done, and Natasha felt comforted that she would have someone with computer experience to call on in due course.

He seemed just to like being in her vicinity, and animated conversation, well, any chat at all, didn't come easily. He reminded her of a long-legged lurcher, following her every step with mournful adoration in his eyes. Her heart sank a little – she knew that look. One of the reasons she'd yet to fall heavily for someone herself was that dumb worship was such a turn-off. Why did men turn to mush at the sight of a pretty face, she'd asked herself from childhood, observing them enslaved by her mother. As if it was a spell cast on them. She determined to marry a man who loved her for who she was as a person. Someone she could look up to and respect. How could you look up to a puddle of devotion on the floor? Charles had been attractive mostly because he'd seemed impervious to the spell, and they'd got on well together. Also, as she now had to admit, she'd been rather overawed by his aristocratic family. But that formula still hadn't worked. What he'd done proved he hadn't loved her, she thought sadly.

'I don't suppose you'd like to come with me to a folk-singing evening on Saturday', Danny asked hesitantly one afternoon, tying up a sack of electrical rubbish for her, before carrying it out to the yard. 'It's just a get-together at a village pub, nothing grand. Me and a few friends meet up every month.'

A whole evening of stilted conversation was hardly appealing. On the other hand there'd be live music, and a convivial pub night would make a nice change. Besides Natasha didn't want to hurt his feelings.

'That sounds fun, Danny', she responded, bending to sweep up the pile of plaster dust the sack had been sitting on. She smiled up at him, 'Yes, I'd love to come.'

Tony's face had not been his best asset for the past ten days.

'The result of seeing off three muggers', he declared casually to his colleagues at Grashe's Bank, in explanation of his swollen nose, bloodshot eye and torn cheek. The number of assailants grew with the telling. 'They hadn't reckoned on someone who actually fought back.'

Every window passed was an opportunity to examine his reflection, though with less than the usual satisfaction, and he peered assessingly in the mirror night and morning. Now, although there was still bruising round the eye and a scratch scab on his cheek, they could be explained away. The important thing was that his nose no longer resembled an overripe plum. Experimentally he gave his slow, meaningful smile to the mirror. Oh yes, back in business.

So, time for action. The annoying thing was that he hadn't managed to obtain Natasha's mobile number or email address. And contacting her through his mother would look impossibly gauche. But at least now his invitation would seem casual, not planned, so perhaps it was all to the good.

He was confident she wouldn't be able to resist the opportunity to get out of Rundleston, and enjoy a bit of sophisticated company He pondered where they should go. The need for her to keep a low profile was a nuisance, since that cut out anywhere fashionable. The opening night of the Aldburgh Festival was coming up, but there might be photographers for that occasion too. In the end he settled for Heddisham Hall, a Suffolk stately home converted into an upmarket restaurant, and booked a table for Saturday night. Then rang Nora to inform her that he would be coming down on Saturday morning. No need to cater for an evening meal though, he told her with certainty, he'd be going out.

One of the things about Rundleston Tony found disconcerting was that, despite increasing colonization by yachties and Londoners, it still seemed a world wrapped up in itself. In its small town life people browsed round the market stalls on a Saturday morning, exchanging repartee with the traders, and chatting animatedly to each other. Children went with their fathers to choose new library books, and teenage girls paraded in groups, giggling self-consciously. Working mums did a weekly supermarket shop, people took their sorted rubbish to the recycling centre, and middle-aged ladies lingered in the two charity shops, 'just looking'. No-one took the slightest notice of him, and none of these activities was in tune with anything in his own life. Normally he didn't get up till midday on a Saturday.

He made an effort though, and arrived at Chandlers late morning. The yard was empty, and finding Nora in the shop, he kissed her and enquired casually where the Fiesta and the B & B guests' cars were.

'Ben's gone to Norfolk for the day, Madge is getting Jamie some new football boots, and I don't know where Natasha is', Nora told him. 'Goodness, you have been in the wars, what happened?'

'Some guys were harassing a couple of girls', he explained airily. 'Well, I couldn't let that happen without wading in to help, could I. That's why I didn't come down last time. I know I said it was because of something important at work, but I didn't want to worry you.'

He decided on lunch at a pizzaria that had opened next to the maltings flats. At least its clientele were young and trendier than Rundleston's old guard. But the day was not going to plan. He'd pictured himself calling in at Natasha's potential gallery, discussing art, and making helpful suggestions. She'd be delighted to have someone so charming and knowledgeable to talk to, and at the end he'd say, 'Look it's been great fun talking to you. So good to find someone who shares my interest. Why don't we go out for a meal tonight?' Unfortunately the gallery-to-be was locked up, and there was still no sign of her Mini.

The sun alternated with big, white clouds, and there was a little wind, which gained in confidence as the sun went in, like a schoolchild playing up when teacher wasn't looking. Morosely he walked past the Bandings family maltings, and stopped to look up at it. It'd be interesting to see what had been done inside, he thought. But a pity Nora and Ben hadn't given in to his pressure to convert it to flats years ago, when they stood a chance of getting planning permission – and a load of moolah. He was the only one of the family with commercial nous, that was the trouble.

He wandered down to the sailing club, where there was much activity in preparation for afternoon racing, the breeze creating a gentle clinking of halyards against masts. Part of him had a sudden yen for a couple of hours out on the water, using skill and tactics, judging the wind and current to swing round the cans ahead of the field. But he quickly suppressed it. Wouldn't be appropriate to his status now. He'd moved on. If he went sailing these days, it was on one of Grashe's forty footers, and he was a valued member of the bank's crew for Cowes Week.

Turning back towards the town, he paused to peruse a noticeboard where the good citizens of Rundleston announced forthcoming activities. Carpet Bowls for the over-fifties, he read derisively, Yoga classes, all abilities welcome. Digital photography course. Table top sale. Music Festival and Family Fun Day, in aid of the air ambulance. How could any of that be described as anything other than wince worthy? Good grief, what suffocatingly parochial lives they led. Annual Regatta. His expression changed. The regatta! Heavens, was it still going on. Nostalgia crept up on him, as he remembered with what enthusiasm he used to enter the various events. All silly of course, but great fun.

'Hello stranger!' a voice behind him interrupted his reminiscent thoughts. 'Tony? It is you isn't it?'

He turned to find a man holding a child by the hand, heavy shopping bags in the other, and experienced the time-shifting recognition of someone last seen as a teenager transformed into a jowly family man, complete with paunch and thinning hair.

'Rick!'

'Long time, no see! I was only telling Darren last week – this is my son – how we used to make balsa wood framed gliders and fly them up at the recreation ground. Do you remember?'

By the time they parted, after a long catch-up conversation, the boy tugging impatiently at his father's hand, Tony's mood had lifted. He poked his head round the shop door.

'Mum, what happened to all the stuff out of my bedroom, when you changed the place over to B & B?'

'I put everything into two tea chests in the under stairs cupboard, she told him. 'It'd be a really good idea if you went through it, I'm sure a lot could be chucked out now.'

Tony heaved the tea chests into the dining room, and the next three hours flew by unnoticed as he took everything out. Soft toys were set in a group on the table, the rest of the contents spread across the floor. The farm, Dinky cars, clockwork air sea rescue plane with the float that let in water, a wonderful spaceship set – cherished momentos of childhood, each one bringing back memories. His Hornby train set! Well, strictly speaking he and Ben had shared it. Unable to resist, he laid out some of the track on the dining room table, with engine and coaches. Absorbed in the past, he didn't hear Natasha return and go up to her room.

And there, down at the bottom, was his magic set, complete with wizard's hat! He'd been pretty damn good as a magician, he recalled, donning the conical black hat with silver stars, and striking a pose. He fanned out the trick pack and offered it to the assembled soft toys. 'Take a card, any card', he suggested confidently.

'Oh, sorry, I didn't know you were in here.'

He whirled round, causing the magician's hat to tilt over his ear. Natasha was standing in the doorway, laptop in hand.

'I was going to send an email, but it's…um, not urgent. It'll do later.' She eyed the magician's hat. 'If you're busy', she added, and Tony cringed at the amusement on her face.

He snatched the hat off and dropped it into the tea chest. 'I..I was just going through all the things out of my room', he stammered. 'My toys and stuff. From when I was young', he emphasized hurriedly, realizing that the situation was not improving. 'Nora asked me to.'

As if on cue, Nora appeared from the hallway. 'So this is where you've got to', she observed, and Tony seized on her presence with relief.

'Didn't you Mum', he appealed to her desperately. 'Ask me to go through the toys.'

'Yes. Although I'm not sure how helpful it is for them to be covering the floor', she commented, stepping carefully over them to the table. 'Oh you've found Muvvins!'

Nora picked up a dark coloured bear, dressed in waistcoat and trousers, one eye loose, giving it a rakish, slightly unhinged expression.

'You've no idea how important Muvvins was', she told Natasha, attempting to push the loose eye into place. When he was little Tony wouldn't be parted from him, took him everywhere. He was a great friend to me as well', she continued teasingly. 'I don't think we'd ever have achieved potty-training without him.'

Kindness dictated that Nora be deflected, but the situation was too enjoyable.

'Mum, I really don't think...' Tony began.

'Why not?' Natasha sounded politely interested

'Well, Tony got the hang of peeing, but he was such a mucky little pup, he never seemed to mind his pants being smelly.'

Her son was experiencing a car crash in slow motion.

'We had to pretend to potty-train Muvvins too, complete with lavish praise. And imitation turds of course.'

'Turds?' Natasha's voice was suspiciously high.

'Yes.' Nora laughed. 'I've never felt quite the same about those chocolate flake bars since.'

Natasha kept control with difficulty. Cruelty should only go so far. 'Well I must go', she said shakily, not daring to look at Tony, still clutching his magician's wand. 'Will there be enough hot water for a bath this early?'

'Yes, of course. Going somewhere nice? enquired Nora.

'Mm. A folk-song evening, with Danny. Should be fun.'

The key to Tony's golden future was halfway through the door before leaning back. 'Bye Muvvins', she waved naughtily, and escaped upstairs, overcome with mirth.

Chapter Eleven

The week before the town's regatta, as Ben walked down the steps of his studio, he found Madge taking her washing off the line in the yard, and chatting to Nora about the event.

'I'm going to show Jamie how to go crabbing on the quay', she was saying, 'so if you have any fish heads will you keep them for us?'

'Fish heads?' Ben joined in, obligingly unpegging a sheet for her. 'They're no good. What he needs is a nice bit of bacon. Preferably rather whiffy. Crabs simply can't resist.'

'Load of baloney', objected Madge cheerfully, taking one end from him. 'Fish heads get the big 'uns especially. I won the crabbing contest three times, so I should know.'

'Show off!' he teased her across the sheet, as they folded it.

'It sounds as if you'll have to settle this with a contest, children.' Nora was looking on amused.

'Right,' Ben challenged Madge with mock seriousness, chucking the pegs into a bag. 'You're on. How about tomorrow?'

It was supposed to rain the following evening, but Rundleston's inhabitants were united in their derision of the bods in the Met Office and their predictions. What did they know? Certainly not about conditions hereabouts. Didn't seem to stop everyone watching the weather forecast though. Far more important than the news. They just made their own adaptions.

The local interpretation was proved right as, in warm, early evening sunshine, the little group assembled on the quay, complete with buckets for the captives, and a folding chair for Nora. Jamie as apprentice crabber, had a variety of baits to try – sausage, ham, fish and bacon, while Nora and Natasha were there to ensure fair play. Madge bought some mackerel from the supermarket's fresh fish counter and thus had her preferred bait at the ready, but Ben failed in his quest for bacon well past its sell-by date.

'On the whole it's best if my B & B guests don't go down with food poisoning', Nora had told him dryly. 'Of course I don't have any smelly bacon hanging around – the stuff you used when you were a boy was kept specially. You'll have to make do with fresh.'

They'd selected the middle of the quay, away from the shade of the buildings, and Ben had brought bolts from the boatyard as weights. Jamie's string was tied on the end of a garden cane, so that he wouldn't have to be right on the quay edge. Ben used a paper clip to attach his strip of bacon, but Madge had brought for herself and Jamie two net pouches intended for washing machine tablets, in which to place the bait.

'What are those for? Ben asked, surprised.

'Secret weapon', she smiled at him mischievously.

'Right', declared Nora when they were all set up, 'whoever catches the most crabs in the next forty minutes is the winner. As we haven't anything to weigh them with, Natasha and I will judge when one big crab equals two small ones.'

'Foregone conclusion', Ben goaded Madge amicably, selecting a spot a few feet away where he could sit on a bollard, Bodger beside him.

'Nah, you don't stand a chance', she joshed back. 'And no cheating!'

The allotted forty minutes seemed more like ten. Young seagulls were testing their new flying skills, and formed a rowdy line on the roofs of the two converted maltings towering over the quay, the evening sun making the mellow brickwork glow. Residents now parked their cars at the base of the buildings, where once cargo would have been stacked, and people walking past stopped to chat. The crew of a visiting Dutch botta, moored against the quay, wandered over, attracted by the presence of Natasha and what was evidently a quaint English custom, and a fisherman left his rod to offer advice, so there was soon a small crowd surrounding them.

Ben was the first to score. Jamie was fascinated to see a little brown crab, determinedly clutching its tasty bacon meal, hauled out and deposited in a bucket of water, which the dog had to be discouraged from investigating closely. Almost immediately an experimental lifting of his own line revealed a diner, and he squealed with triumph and alarm as Nora helped him pull in the catch, clinging tenaciously to the net bag in its attempt to get at the bit of sausage inside. Natasha held out another bucket, and guided it in.

'I got one! I got one!'

His freckled face lit up with pleasure as he peered at the small, pincered creature, and Madge and Ben exchanged delighted smiles.

The smell of Madge's fish heads evidently affected crustaceans like frying onions does hungry humans, but, contrary to confident prediction, her captives were all small to middling in size. After his initial bite, Ben's bait was proving less effective, but just as Nora was about to call time on the contest, a large crab seized the dangling bacon in its pincers.

'Oh yes! This is the clincher', he called across to Madge triumphantly. 'You've had it now. This chummy's *huge!*'

He was too. So big that as soon as Ben tried to haul him in, the crab's weight tore the bacon and he plopped safely back into the water. Madge was officially declared the contest winner by Nora and Natasha, amid clapping from the spectators, and all the crabs were safely returned to the river.

'You should have had your bait in a bag like Jamie and me', suggested Madge as they all walked back to Chandlers. 'Then you'd have won.'

'Not sure that's allowed, you know', he responded good humouredly.

'Course it is', she smiled at him, and teased, 'You just don't like losing, that's what.'

There was a delicious savoury rice waiting for them, to be followed by strawberries and ice cream, and the mood round the dining room table was happy and relaxed.

Natasha told them about her pub evening with Danny, and how much she'd enjoyed it.

'I really didn't expect to', she said. 'But everyone took it in turns to sing or play whatever they fancied. It was magic. Just embarrassing that I didn't have anything to offer. I felt like a fraud.'

Ben watched her across the table. He saw her as herself now, no longer a Gaye lookalike. And she fascinated him – her face, her mannerisms. Was she? Wasn't she? The possibility that she might be his daughter loomed large in his mind these days, but now seeing her next to Nora a further thought dominated. If she was, then his mother was sitting beside her own granddaughter, unknowingly. The pity of it.

He would find out, he promised himself, studying the curve of her cheek, and the way the evening light from the window behind caught her hair. Get the truth out of Gaye somehow.

Nora surveyed the lively group with pleasure, noting approvingly that Jamie ate what was put before him without any of the fuss so many children got away with nowadays. It would be wonderful to have a daughter-in-law and grandchildren. No good looking to Ben of course, she was now resigned to the fact that he'd never provide them. But perhaps Tony might oblige soon. He'd rushed back to London so abruptly, she thought. Maybe the reason was some girl he was serious about at last.

Madge regaled them with stories about the preparations for the art festival, relaying some of the dafter bits of art pseud, as used by Tomorrow's Art Today, and enthusiastically parroted by Arabella Drail.

'We must have *suspended exhilaration*', Arabella's husky tone was imitated to perfection, as Madge peered up through hair pulled over one eye. 'People should feel they've touched base with truth', she gestured dramatically, 'yielding up the *full, multi-layered complexity* that expands the *parameters* of life'.

Natasha listened to her with admiration, laughing with the others. It would have been lovely to have had a sister, she reflected. To have been part of a proper family that sat round the table at mealtimes and enjoyed each other's company.

Today's ad hoc family made sure that Jamie didn't feel left out. Natasha asked him about the raft building. and he told them how it was nearly complete. Stephen had yet to decide though if they should launch it early and have trials. That would improve their paddling teamwork, but the danger was it might break up, and leave them without a craft at all. Besides, it was going to be a lot easier to launch than to heave back out of the water.

'It was a good thing we collected all that stuff off Woodshey Bay', he said. 'We used nearly all the polystyrene out of the sacks to give it buoyancy.'

'Buoyancy' was not a word he would have known a few weeks back, thought Madge, pleased to see him looking at ease and behaving so creditably, surrounded by adults. Concentrating on Jamie's well-being helped too with fighting her own unsuitable feelings for the man sitting next to him. She really had to stamp on this foolishness.

'Those sacks of rubbish', Ben was telling Nora now, 'You've no idea the problems we're having getting rid of them. Apparently we can't put them out for the weekly collection, because they're not household waste. And the tip won't take them unless we can describe the contents in detail.' He made a face. 'And of course we can't. The council told me it was the Environment Agency's responsibility. So I rang, and they said, "Nothing to do with us, pal", or words to that effect. Would you believe the council want to charge us two hundred pounds to collect and dispose of the sacks.'

157

'So what are you going to do with them?' asked Natasha, joining Madge in clearing away the plates.

He shrugged. 'For the moment they'll have to stay put. Flitch doesn't need the space in the boatyard in summer. We'll think of something.'

Jamie had been studying Ben's big painting of Rundleston wharf, above the mantelpiece. 'Were the maltings still working when you painted that?' he asked.

'No, unfortunately not', Ben told him. 'The quay was much busier than it is today though, because there was no marina for visiting boats to go to. But there were already more efficient ways of malting barley, which needed far fewer workers. The industry used to employ lots of men. In fact', he said, giving a 'thank you' glance up at Madge as she put a bowl of strawberries down in front of him, 'the regatta really started as tugs of war and contests between the men working for the different maltings, and the brewery. It included sailing races for the barges – there was a lot of friendly rivalry among the skippers. Between the barge owners too – our family, the Drails and the Jahneys. He smiled at Jamie. 'Your raft race is part of a long tradition.'

Rundleston's regatta bore about as much resemblance to the grand affairs staged by Cowes and Henley as a corner shop to London department stores. Divided into low tide and high tide sports and events, it was purely an in-house, or rather in-town, affair, a sort of water-based fete. For the old timers it was an opportunity to reminisce about exploits past – the year it hailed, the time that woman got so stuck in the mud the fire brigade had to be called out, and epic tugs of war between teams from the brewery and each of the maltings. Those were the days. For the youngsters it was licence to indulge in competitive fun on water, beach and mud, in front of cheering onlookers, with a chance of getting their photos in the local paper. In many people's minds it also marked a clear division between the 'real' inhabitants, and the yachties and flat dwellers who looked on bemused at these curious, and frankly risible, activities.

Natasha was determined not to be seen as one of the disparaged incomers, and somewhat apprehensively agreed with Madge that they would both go in for the women's mud race. Jamie's hopes and excitement centred on the raft race, but he was also keen to try everything else that could be fitted in, not least because, as the day drew near, who was going in for what was a hot topic at school.

The sailing club was responsible for organizing the day's events, and Ben was, as usual, roped in to help, while Nora had offered to do her bit in the refreshment marquee that had been set up in the dinghy park.

Madge wondered if her memories of regattas past were just recollections overlaid with the idealized haze of childhood. But when she, Jamie, Pauline and Natasha joined the gathering of spectators beside the sailing club on the Saturday morning, the sense of communal solidarity, expectation, and enjoyment of the place they were lucky enough to live in was just the same as she remembered. Jamie soon detached himself and melted into a group of children excitedly discussing the various events. This might have been a desire to blend in, or to distance himself from a mother who might embarrass him in the women's mud race.

The sky was overcast, with quite a strong wind blowing down the river. The sailing races later in the day promised to be lively, but it was far from warm, and the prospect of plunging into the grey mud exposed by the low tide was about as inviting as eating worms.

'You're nuts, both of you', was Pauline's opinion, and Madge was at that moment inclined to agree. She felt rather guilty at coercing Natasha into entering the race with her. Theirs was to be the first event of the day, and there were cheers from the crowd as she and Natasha stripped to shorts and tee shirts, bound their trainers on with duct tape, and joined six others at the start line.

How crazy is this, Natasha thought, aghast at what she was about to do. Only the English... Still, too late to back out of it now.

A man dressed unconvincingly as Neptune, clutching a cardboard trident in one hand and megaphone in the other, reminded the line up of shivering entrants about the course, before Ben sounded a portable yacht foghorn to start the race. Cheered on by the spectators, they ran down the solid, fairly sandy shore, but the further they went, the stickier the mud became, until they were running in shallow water, rounding a mooring post, and then heading back towards the shouting spectators. Panting for breath, slipping and sliding, Natasha could see Madge and two runners ahead of her, but the others were trailing. And then, toiling up the slope to the finish, Madge slowed down and held out her hand as Natasha caught up. They crossed the line together, laughing and triumphant, soaked and steaming, smelly gunge covering their legs, their faces black with splashed mud.

As the runners began hosing each other down in exhilarated camaradie, Ben came over.

'That's what I like to see around the place. Touch of glamour!' he greeted them, laughing. 'Fine pair of mudlarks you turned out to be – where's your competitive spirit?'

'Trumped by sisterly solidarity', Madge countered breathlessly, scraping the black goo off her legs. 'Anyway, what happened to "it's not the winning that matters, it's the taking part"?

'It was fun!' gasped Natasha, black smears across her cheek, her golden hair streaked with brown and hanging in rats tails. Her enjoyment seemed doubtful, but the feeling afterwards certainly was. Deciding not to join the queue for the sailing club facilities, on a high she and Madge walked back to Chandlers, had a shower and a quick change of clothes, and then returned to join the spectators just as a men's tug of war heat was about to start.

'Oh look who that is!'

The tall, gangling figure on the end of the line was unmistakable.

'He doesn't usually take part in anything', commented Tricia, coming up behind them. 'Can't think what's got into him all of a sudden.'

'Come on Danny!' Natasha joined in the cheering, as the teams strained and slithered until Ben judged that the rope's central knot had convincingly gone over the line marked at the end of the slipway. After Danny's team had lost two out of the three heaves, they squelched and slid their way up to the sailing club showers, family and friends clustering round, and Natasha congratulated the losing back man on a great effort. He seemed pleased, although expressions were difficult to read under the layers of black.

When all the sports that could be accomplished floundering about in mud had been exhausted, it was time for the children's beach activities, and the crowd moved expectantly across to the wall above. Rundleston's modest stretch of sand was hardly long enough for sustained running races, so they majored on a treasure hunt and other novelty events for the under fives, and sack, egg and spoon and three-legged contests for the older ones. Jamie had persuaded Sarah, a girl he sat next to in school, to be his partner for this, and they achieved fourth place, earning them both a medal on a green ribbon.

Then in the Parent and Child Wheelbarrow race, with Madge as the upright bit, steering Jamie, they came in first. 'The trick is to choose a place furthest down the beach', she confided to Pauline. 'The sand's firmer there. Discovered that when I was young.'

Pauline watched it all with a smile, tinged with sadness. These parents didn't know how lucky they were to have ordinary, active children. With limited speech and the uncontrolled emotions of a toddler, her son Tommy had no prospect of a normal life. But at least she could watch him sailing this afternoon, something she would never have predicted. Rundleston Grange had succeeded in getting him interested, and he'd been looking forward to helping to sail the home's specially adapted boat in the regatta.

In truth, with most sailing races there wasn't much for the spectators to see. Just a load of sails to-ing and fro-ing out on the water, with little indication who was in the lead. But the race of non-class boats that Tommy was involved in, did at least have the merit that they were all different, and so easily identifiable. The Grange boat didn't win, but as it docked at the marina, Pauline was thrilled to see the animation on her son's face. The place was doing wonders for his confidence, and he was joining in so much better.

Stephen and several of his friends were keenly competing in various sailing races, and Jamie was disappointed not to be able to try his hand. But although Ben could probably have borrowed a Topper dinghy for him, he was miles short of the experience needed.

'Couldn't we go in for the Novice and Father race?' he'd suggested hopefully. 'We could pretend you were my dad. No-one would know.'

To keep the interest of the non-participants during the sailing races, there were crabbing competitions on the quay, divided into different age groups, with a 'fish-off' between the winners. To Jamie's disappointment Madge's patent fish head bait attracted a few tiddlers, but nothing large enough to win his competition – though the chat and joshing amongst those taking part, and their supporters, made him feel less of an outsider.

The children's homemade raft race was the last event of the day. Much construction work had been put in in the previous weeks, with parental involvement in proportion to their attitude to the 'no adult help' rule. For safety reasons each craft had to pass the sailing club's assessment of seaworthiness. The course was over the shallow water that had crept up towards the beach, so anyone forced to take a dip wouldn't be out of their depth, and there were a couple of rescue boats on hand. Stephen's raft, confidently named 'The Conkerer', with Jamie and the other two crew members, all dressed as vikings, was the first of the five contenders to get stewards' approval, and they paddled up to the start area.

Beneath the decorative trimmings, theirs was basically two wooden pallets bound together, with added buoyancy, but other entrants had based their craft on slabs of polystyrene, plastic barrels, big logs, or fenders with planks over the top. Oars were the most popular paddles, but the all-girl team on their polystyrene raft had lashed table tennis bats to broom handles, and the big log affair was to be powered by garden shovels.

Just getting the field lined up fairly was a challenge, but eventually Ben sounded the foghorn and they were off, on a simple 'round the buoy' course and back, so that steering and manoevrability would be tested as well as speed.

Amidst loud support from the assembled watchers, it became clear that some ideas were better than others. The log raft was extremely heavy, and the shovels tiring to use, so although it set off at a lick, the crew were soon flagging, and found it almost impossible to turn at the buoy. The girls on the all-polystyrene craft, by contrast, found that their lightness meant it had a tendency to spin round and round, plus the wind blew them off course. The lashings on the plastic barrels were not as tight as they might have been, and under the strain of making way, the whole thing began to break up before reaching the turning point. Its disconsolate crew were soon decanted into a rescue boat, while what remained of their entry was towed back to shore. The main problem with The Conkerer was her square nose, which not only made the thing unwieldy, but tended to dig into the water as soon as they got up any speed. Nevertheless it looked as if the race was between her and the fenders-and-planks raft, paddled by a family team of two girls and two boys.

163

'That's your landlord's brood', Nora informed Natasha. The Jahneys are very competitive. In fact they usually win the raft race.'

Once both rafts had succeeded in rounding the halfway buoy and it was a straight race to the finish, the other two well behind, the cheering rose in volume. What price the Derby? This was much more important.

'Come on vikings!', the inhabitants of Chandlers shouted enthusiastically, while Madge proudly took photographs of her flame-haired son, who was surely the most likely looking viking, paddling valiantly towards the finishing line, with Conkerer awash from the bow wave she was creating. But she was slower than the Jahney's fender craft, and they also had the advantage of practiced teamwork, and soon forged ahead. It was looking a certain result, until one of the Jahney boys managed to lose his oar paddle, and it floated tantalizingly out of reach. Deciding that it would be best to pick it up, they lost time manoevring back to retrieve it, and by the time they had full power restored, Conkerer had overtaken them and was just a few feet from the finishing line. Crossing it first, Stephen and his crew waved their paddles in delight, soaked and exhausted, but triumphant.

To complete Rundleston's annual celebration, and help raise money for the following year, the sailing club hosted a jolly in the evening, with a local group playing in the marquee, tickets available to members, and over-eighteen event entrants and their partners. If there were any spares left over, they went on offer to the general public. There seldom were.

'You must both go', Nora urged Madge and Natasha. 'I'm looking after Bodger, and can easily keep an eye on Jamie. Pauline and I will just be having a quiet meal and a natter.

During the day Madge had come across several people she'd known from schooldays, and hoped this evening might prove a chance to catch up with them properly. Natasha was a little more hesitant, not knowing what to expect, and what you wore to such events anyway.

Madge decided on an olive green skirt and cream top, with an amber pendant and earrings, exactly complimenting her burnished colouring. Her normally tied-back hair hung loose and glorious round her shoulders. She might just have stepped from a Botticelli painting, Ben thought appraisingly, waiting for them both in Nora's sitting room. Natasha wore a white sleeveless linen dress, with a gold belt. The elegant simplicity of it, coupled with her lovely face framed by honey-coloured hair, would have made her stand out like a gardenia in a bunch of daffodils in any crowd, let alone a sailing club dance in a small, provincial town. The entirely unintentional effect was to draw every eye when they got there, and from the males, as she walked into the marquee and sat down at a table with Madge and Ben, she prompted a disbelieving 'Oh wow!'

The evening went with much bonhomie and implied self-congratulation that another regatta had been organized and enjoyed, plus public thanks for all the hard work put in by various officers and helpers. The same ones as usual. As she'd hoped, Madge got to talk in more depth with a couple of school contemporaries. Natasha was soon asked to dance, and Ben drifted away to the bar, keeping a desultory eye on her. Every time he checked, she seemed to be dancing with what appeared to be enjoyment, so as he was chatting to Flitch and Tricia at about nine-thirty, he was surprised to feel a touch on his elbow.

'Would you like to dance?' she enquired, looking up with those dark-lashed, grey eyes that were so like Gaye's.

'Oh, well...no, I don't think...' He really didn't want anyone getting the wrong idea.

'Only I could do with being rescued', she mouthed at him. 'Will you be going to fetch Bodger soon? Could I go back with you?'

'It won't look good, you know', Ben injected some joviality.

'Stuff that', she responded lightly.

Perhaps she wasn't feeling well. He was concerned. 'Yes, of course I'll take you back to Chandlers now, if you want. Did you have a coat?'

They left the marquee, and stood for a moment to savour the freshness of the evening air in contrast to the laden atmosphere inside. The tide was on the ebb again, leaving areas of glistening mud and that faint seaweedy smell that to Ben meant home. From across the other side came the quivering mourn of a curlew.

'You seemed to be on the floor a lot, so I thought you were having a good time, he told her, as they began walking up towards the High Street.

'I do like dancing of course. But... well, if you don't accept an invitation it looks stand-offish, and if you do it's taken as interest. When there really isn't any on my part. Thank goodness Danny wasn't there.'

They continued in silence for a moment.

This sounds awful', she volunteered hesitantly, 'but I really don't enjoy having all these guys...' she stopped, embarrassed.

'Fawning over you?' he suggested, with sudden understanding.

'That's it. They don't know anything about me – what sort of person I am, whether we've got anything in common, what's inside, basically. They just see the outer packaging and... Well, it's so shallow.'

She was also potentially very rich as well, it now struck Ben.

'It'd be even worse if they were aware of...' He didn't want to say "who your father is". 'That is, if they knew your background.'

'Yes. You won't tell anyone will you? I just want to be ordinary.'

166

She was 'ordinary' like a diamond in a sugar bowl was ordinary, thought Ben.

'Everyone's surely going to find out when the gallery name goes up', he pointed out.

'Yes I suppose so. But I'd hate people to think I was trading on the Rabson name, like my mother. Plus she milks her effect on men for all she's worth', Natasha confided, adding quietly, 'As you know.'

She glanced at him, but the implication clearly passed him by, and she marvelled at the persistence of Gaye as icon in his mind. Words had no effect. Might as well try to dislodge a barnacle with ping pong balls.

'I'm determined not to be like that', she went on. 'Alienating all the women, and leading men on. I want something honest and solid, someone to love who'll be my best friend as well.'

Ben felt honoured that she was at ease enough with him to voice such things. 'Bound to be a Mr Right out there', he assured her as they reached the house. 'And he's going to be one lucky sod.'

He left her telling Nora and Pauline about the evening, in lighter vein. To give Bodger a run, he set off through Market Square, up the hill to the recreation ground beyond, and let him off the lead. The strong breeze of the day had dropped, and the cloud was breaking up, the setting sun's rays escaping through gaps, tingeing the edges with gold. Light in all its manifestations was thrilling, Ben reflected, trying to memorize the effect. No wonder people thought heaven was in the sky. They looked up after a drab day on earth, and saw clouds tipped with a glorious light, as if there was a wonderful party going on to which no-one down here had been invited.

Twenty-third of June – they were past the longest day already, he thought, walking slowly round the perimeter, the sweet smell of cut grass hanging in the air. His family had bought the land and given it to the town, back in the nineteenth century. He was proud of that. As a result Rundleston had taken its cricket, and later football, seriously. And now there were two courts, and a thriving tennis club as well. A foursome were still playing, despite the fading light. Their voices mingled with the excited squeaks of low-flying swallows, which Bodger seemed to regard as a challenge, looking up as the birds swooped near the ground, chasing after them fruitlessly.

The area used to be bounded by fields, and today houses overlooked it on three sides, changes that had happened in his lifetime. Nothing stays the same, Ben thought with uncharacteristic moroseness.

Reaching the cricket pavilion on the far side, he sat down on a bench looking back at the crowded buildings that made up the centre of Rundleston, wide estuary glinting beyond, and the far shore now indistinct in the dusk. He'd often painted that view, with a cricket or football match in the foreground, or just children playing.

He remembered the snowballing scene in his studio that Madge had exclaimed over, and her words came back to him. 'I'd love to be in one of your paintings'. She'd looked most attractive tonight, he thought, picturing her in the flattering, colour-savvy outfit she'd chosen, and then smiled, comparing it with her mud-spattered self in the morning. She was a good sport. He must paint her some time. And Jamie.

'Evening', he greeted an elderly man accompanied by a daschund which, with its head-down waddle, seemed to echo his master's stooped resignation that there wasn't much left in life to look forward to. They were a familiar sight, and Ben had a bet with himself that one day he would get more than a grunted response out of the old boy.

This evening there wasn't even an acknowledgement, and he watched them shuffle slowly towards the town.

He called Bodger, who was bounding playfully over to them. Would that be him in twenty years' time? he wondered. Growing old and bitter in the place where he was born?

No. He rejected the image firmly, getting to his feet. He couldn't change the way of the art world, so he'd never make it as an artist. Except perhaps long after he was dead. But if nothing else, he'd got a daughter. There'd be grandchildren.

He felt certain now that Natasha was his. Especially after their intimate talk this evening. 'I want someone to love who'll be my best friend as well', she'd said. It reflected his own attitude entirely. Genes will out.

That this indicated less than goddess-like behaviour on Gaye's part, was something he refused to acknowledge. His mind simply blanked it out. He bent to stroke Bodger, and confided regretfully, 'I did find my soul mate. It's just that she was seduced by that bastard Oliver Rabson.'

Chapter Twelve

Rundleston got lasting value out of its regatta, with gossipy anticipation beforehand and good-humoured dissection afterwards of its events and participants. But this year a new happening was on the horizon, and with the regatta now past, talk in pubs and shops turned to the art festival.

Quite what this would mean for the town and its largely sceptical inhabitants was the subject of much discussion. For over a year they'd speculated about what was going on inside the big maltings building. First there was an invasion of important looking men in suits and, incongruously, hard hats. In due course scaffolding, builders' trucks and cement lorries caused traffic snarl-ups in the narrow streets. Local builders resented the fact that they hadn't been given a look in when it came to quoting for the major contracts involved, and muttered darkly about work being given to outsiders whose faces fitted. The fact that none of the local building firms was large, and all were fully stretched keeping up with new house building in the locality, plus refurbishment and conversions of existing property, was neither here nor there. As if they were cats catching a whiff of tasty rodent, they sensed public largesse on a very desirable scale, and should have been asked.

Their grumblings found no echo in the pubs and eating places benefiting from the extra trade. And those providing accommodation for the influx of strangers weren't complaining either. The Jahney's Dutch House hotel enjoyed a noticeable increase in custom, as the representatives of the various quangos involved came to inspect progress. The rather dingy Malsters' Arms Hotel in Market Square couldn't remember a time when they'd had such a good occupancy rate, and at least three households decided to offer bed and breakfast on the back of the increased demand. Before Nora's two rooms were congenially block-booked for the summer by Pauline and

Natasha, she'd had a procession of people staying who were involved with the conversion. Keeping quiet about the building having been gifted by her to the town, she asked interested questions about the work in progress, and was amazed at the amount of funding clearly being provided by the Arts Council and regional development bodies, in addition to a big dollop of lottery money.

To the newcomers – largely occupants of the flats in the former Jahney's brewery and other converted maltings – the fact that there was to be a modern art festival reinforced their decision to live in Rundleston. The place was waking up, and would undoubtedly be mentioned in the media as somewhere edgy and up-to-the-minute. 'You might like to come down for a weekend while the art festival is on', they would be able to suggest casually to friends and London colleagues, and no longer have to explain where Rundleston was. The whole thing would boost their standing. It would also do the value of their properties no harm at all, a fact seized on by local estate agents, who took to stressing to out-of-town enquirers that Rundleston was on the way to becoming a fashionable hot spot, advising them to leap in now before prices rose. At the same time, they delighted sellers by suggesting higher asking figures, thus ensuring their prediction was self-fulfilling.

The native inhabitants of the town had no great objection to the maltings building itself being regenerated, apart from the temporary nuisance it caused, but there was general discontent at its proposed use.

'A modern art festival?' people questioned. 'What, all those unmade beds and lights going on and off? That sort of stuff. Load of rubbish if you ask me. Complete waste of money.'

The tone of disapproval drifted up to the organizing committee, and they discussed how the community could be won over, or rather 'educated', the word that Arabella Drail was now inclined to use. Increasingly frequent dealings with Tomorrow's Art Today had made her feel proud that she was part of the modern art world, and she'd taken on board the line that those who thought it one huge con were simply dim, obstinate fuddy-duddies. But not unredeemable. And if Rundleston was to move into the spotlight and be celebrated as a fashionable, forward-thinking place, then its populace must be taught the new rules of art.

The way to do this, she and the committee decided, was to involve them. The schools would be invited to exhibit their pupils' work, and prizes offered. The problem was that children foolishly liked horses, boats and people to look recognizably like horses, boats and people, which didn't hit the right note at all.

'I'll talk to the teachers', Arabella decided, 'and make sure they know that nothing representational will be displayed. It's so old fashioned.'

But what was really needed, it was felt, was to get the whole town thinking positively.

'Why don't we invite people to perform some, er, performance art?' one of the committee suggested.

'Or part of the exhibition area could be set aside for stuff, you know, art, done by locals', was another idea. 'Could we get Grashe's bank to stump up for awards? Hefty ones, to tempt people to take part. And make the results newsworthy.'

'They're asking me to stress all this in the publicity', Madge told Nora, the Saturday following the regatta. She felt it was important to keep her informed about what was going on, partly out of friendship, but also to remind her kind benefactor that she was on the family's side, and not part of the art festival set up, despite working for it. She also wanted to suggest that Ben contribute something, just for a laugh.

The weekend was in marked contrast to the sociability of the previous one. Natasha had gone to a schoolfriend's hen party, and it was the turn of Madge's ex to have Jamie. She missed him, and felt vaguely at a loose end. Confiding as much to Nora that morning had immediately resulted in an invitation to come and have supper. There'd been a bond of affection between the two since the early days when, still at school, Madge had helped in the shop. It was hard, thought Nora, having no parents around to give support. She hadn't enquired directly about the cause of the marriage break up, but had gleaned enough from Natasha to get the picture. She admired Madge's dignity, and devotion to Jamie, but realized there was emotional turmoil beneath the calm and independent surface.

It was pleasing to see that the girl had taken the trouble to change out of jeans into slim-fitting, brown velvet trousers and ochre top. That wonderful auburn hair piled into a soft coil enhanced her graceful looks.

They ate companionably in Nora's sitting room, in comfortable armchairs, a small table between them, looking out over the estuary, the sun glinting gold on the water. Quite a few boats were still out, their sails differing shades of white, like a washing powder advert.

'It's lonely for you', Nora remarked sympathetically. 'Any thought of finding romance again yourself?'

'Heavens no', was the instant response. 'I've messed up Jamie's life enough. He deserves all my attention, and as much stability as possible, to try and make up for what's happened.'

Then her expression lightened. 'He's been much happier the past few weeks though', she reported. 'Rundleston's working its magic. I've asked for the details of a cottage in Quay Street that I heard is coming on the market. We really mustn't keep Ben out of his flat much longer.'

'Oh I don't think he's in a hurry to move back', Nora assured her. 'He likes his cosy cabin.'

As if on cue, the unmistakable outline of an East Coast sailing barge came into view, heading away from the quay.

173

'Looks as if the Hetty Jane's got a party hiring', Nora commented. 'Ben always enjoys those.'

'What do I enjoy?' enquired her son genially, entering the room unnoticed behind them, and holding the door open for the dog.

Madge jumped at the sound of his voice, and gasped audibly. Every time they met the pull of attraction was stronger, she felt like a swimmer struggling against the current. Was this what people meant by being in love? Because it had never been like this with Luke. The whole thing was just foolishness on her part, she told herself, an illness that had to be fought. And out of self-preservation she'd been doing her best to avoid Ben.

'Must you do that!' his mother admonished him mildly. 'Gave us both a fright. I assumed you were on the Hetty Jane. We've just seen her go out.'

'No, Danny's crewing tonight.' Ben settled himself on the sofa, while Bodger ambled over to greet Nora and Madge. 'And I thought I'd come and see my aged mother.'

'Nothing to do with the fact that your floating home has just disappeared down the river then.'

'Pure coincidence', her son grinned at her.

'Have you eaten?'

'Er, well, no. On my way to the Spritty...' he responded unconvincingly.

While he demolished the remaining shepherds pie, Nora told Madge how well the prints of Ben's paintings were selling.

'You've really done us a good turn. Not only reorganizing and modernising the shop – which badly needed doing, I have to admit – but we've already broken even on the prints, so from now on the sales will be pure profit. They bring in extra customers too, and people are delighted with them.' She looked at her son with fond exasperation and added, 'I've been on at Ben for years to do something commercial

174

with his work, and he wouldn't take a blind bit of notice. What did you do?'

'Blackmailed him', she replied promptly, and a smile hovered. 'Do you think it would work for what we were discussing earlier?'

'Which was?' Ben looked from one to the other.

Nora filled in the background. 'And Madge thinks you ought to contribute to the art festival', she finished.

'You can forget that', he said dismissively. 'Why would I want to have anything to do with that bunch of charlatans?'

'Well, I wondered if you couldn't do something ironic like, I don't know – a roll of lavatory paper with a face on every sheet', suggested Madge. 'Or there was that man who filled a piano with washing powder, and explained history to a dead hare.' She paused. 'Except I think he was deadly serious. Did he do both at the same time do you think?'

'Pity we haven't got a town statue, then you could tie it up with string, like someone did at the Tate Britain a couple of years ago', Nora commented. 'I remember reading about it.'

'Oh yes', Ben recalled with amusement. 'And didn't a member of the public take a knife to it? The 'artist' was furious and claimed that the thing was ruined. But the man said not a bit of it, cutting it off was a work of art as well. You couldn't argue with that.'

He was beginning to see that there might be possibilities for a little mischief making. 'I did suggest to Arabella Drail featuring balloons blown up by farts', he remembered. 'But I'm not sure that's anatomically possible. Besides you'd need an awful lot of beans.'

'And what about the man who scrunched up balls of paper?' Nora suggested, taking the empty plates towards the kitchen. 'Apparently they were worth a fortune afterwards. Even I could do that. Money for old bits of paper, that is.'

After a moment she poked her head round the kitchen door, and addressed Madge. 'We've got peach slices drizzled with ginger wine next. In two bowls.' She nodded towards their uninvited guest. 'Shall we feed him?'

Ben found himself regarded by two steady blue eyes, and then Madge's freckled face creased into her infectious smile.

'Yes', she decided, adding playfully, 'but he has to agree to do something for the art fiasco.'

Ben had envisaged calling in at Chandlers just on a short social visit, on his way to the Spritty. If he could cadge a meal so much the better, of course. But he was soon enjoying stimulating conversation between the three of them as they ranged over internet shopping and its effect on small businesses; the demise of several family firms in Rundleston; changes in the past hundred years compared to the previous century; art and fashion's link with herd instinct; and the likely effects of global warming and rising sea level. Darkness fell almost unnoticed, and it was Madge who finally rose, saying regretfully to Nora, 'Well, I must go. Thank you so much for a lovely evening. Oh, I almost forgot, have you got an empty jam jar to spare? I need to go moth hunting.'

'What, outside?'

'No, there seem to be an awful lot of little brown moths in the flat'. She turned to Ben, 'Did you notice them last summer? Only I think they might be breeding in the carpet or something.'

He affected indignation. 'Are you suggesting my flat is moth-eaten?'

She smiled. 'Well I'm not sure feeding is what they have in mind at the moment. More having a flutter and finding a mate.'

'If you've got a moth infestation downstairs, it might be best to have the flat fumigated', was Nora's comment. 'Don't want them spreading up here.'

'I'll come and have a look', Ben volunteered. 'See if Bodger's any good at scaring them off. Or eating them.'

176

It felt strange going into his familiar flat and finding other people's belongings in it, like looking at his reflection in the water and seeing someone else staring back. Under new management the place was cleaner than it used to be, although not much tidier, he was glad to see. Bodger headed straight for the corner where his basket always was, only to stop, looking puzzled at finding nothing there.

'They tend to lurk behind the sofa', explained Madge. She got hold of one end and Ben helped her drag it away from the wall. 'Look, there's one. No, three. Four! Where's that jar?'

'It's easier just to squash them, isn't it.' Ben had no qualms about using his thumb for the purpose. But Madge preferred to put a jar over each one as it perched on the wall, before sliding a piece of stiff paper underneath, then taking the captive to the window and letting it go.

'That's far too slow', he declared, stalking another hopeful, unsuspectingly displaying itself on the wall. 'I'll dispose of three in the time you get one.'

'That's what you think. But they'll see you coming and scarper.' Laughing, Madge made a face at him, as his intended victim flew away just in time. 'Not surprising when a dirty great thumb's about to squash you.'

A friendly rivalry soon developed as their tallies grew, each determined to top the other's score. Bodger proved less than helpful to his master in the quest, and retired to the kitchen doorway where he could observe, with patient incomprehension, the two of them enjoying their childish game.

But the numbers of prey grew less until after about fifteen minutes it seemed no more small members of the lepidoptera family lurked on the walls and skirting boards, or fluttered tantalizingly past their heads.

'We'll call it quits, shall we?' suggested Ben, who in truth had lost count of his score, and hoped Madge had also.

'Yes', she agreed. 'Thank you very much for...oh, look there's one right up there! On the ceiling, above the door. Can you get it?'

It was just too high.

'I'll lift you up', he decided, 'then you can reach.'

To be in the friendly clasp of a man she was fighting her feelings about seemed as advisable as throwing petrol on a fire.

'Oh, no it's all right', she demurred hastily. 'I'll get it later, when it flies off somewhere else.'

'Come on. I won't drop you, I promise.'

She could hardly refuse. 'Well, okay', Madge agreed hesitantly, fetching the jar while silently invoking the god of inner strength, whoever he was. She mustn't give any hint of what he was doing to her emotions.

'But it's a joint score, mind', he warned jovially, catching hold of her round the waist and raising her high enough to reach the ceiling, chivalrously trying not to show signs of effort. She might be slim, but she was almost as tall as he was.

Confidently Madge approached the little brown invader.

'Damn.'

Her quarry had fluttered off, and she was about to admit defeat when it unwisely returned to a spot a few inches away.

Trying again, more slowly, this time she succeeded in placing her jar over the offender. She then slid the paper between it and the ceiling, trapping the moth inside.

'Got it', she announced, adding after a pause, 'You can put me down now.'

But Ben hardly heard. Her softness and warmth against him, her faint perfume so close, had sent him back twenty-three years to the glorious sensation of holding Gaye in his arms. Oh God. He was suddenly overwhelmed by a wave of longing for the love he'd lost. If only...

'Ben?'

178

'Oh. Um, have you got it?'

Reluctantly he released his hold and she slid to the ground, placing the jar upside down on the table for later disposal of its inmate.

'What's the matter?' Madge had turned and caught sight of Ben's expression.

'Nothing! Must go. The Hetty Jane'll be back by now. Glad we got rid of the moths.' His speech was rushed and almost incoherent. 'Come on boy.'

And he turned and left, leaving Madge staring at the door as calm and collected as a flailed hedge.

The Hetty Jane had indeed returned to her berth, but Flitch and Danny might still be aboard, and Ben was in no fit state to encounter anyone just now. In a daze he walked through the town to the sailing club, and sat on one of the upturned dinghies. There was still a faint lightening of the sky in the west, and a half moon was playing hide and seek among the clouds. Little ripples lapped the shore, their gentle sound like the breathing of the river in the dark, accompanied by the insistent clinking of rigging against masts.

Damn. Damn! His shocked brain kept repeating. What price emotional self-sufficiency now? The art-is-all-I-need guff. Shot to bloody bits.

And how could just holding a girl have done this to him? He shook his head in confusion. I was okay, he told himself untruthfully. Been fine all this time. Got life worked out.

But his layers of self-deception were shifting, the reignited yearning to love and be loved too strong now to be denied.

Gaye and I would have been so happy, if that louse Oliver Rabson hadn't seduced her, he said slowly to himself. Because of him, my paintings are rubbished. And as if that weren't enough, he thought venomously, now I know he stole my daughter as well.

179

That the angelic Gaye might have had more than a little to do with two of those happenings was conveniently slid over, as his mind rearranged its obfuscations.

The bastard has crapped all over my life, he told Bodger bitterly, the dog reappearing out of the darkness after investigating an interesting scent. Maybe I can't use my art as a weapon. But he's not going to get away with it. Natasha is mine, not his.

Doubt about Natasha's parentage had now given way to certainty. After all, how could he have found her so sweet and likeable if she'd been Rab's? The bond between them had to be biological.

He picked up a stick and offered it, so they could play a tug of war game, but Bodger only went through the motions, out of good manners, and his master had no heart for it either. Rabson would be coming down to open Natasha's gallery, Ben remembered, throwing the stick into the darkness, the dog declining to go after it. And maybe to the art fiasco as well. Surely there'd be opportunities to confront him. He was thinking aloud now. And Gaye, she'd be here too. He must see her first. The thought of the encounter made him breathless. Maybe everything would come right. The meeting would rekindle their love, and when Natasha knew who her real father was, might they come together as a family?

As the idealist in him pictured this affecting scenario, the clouds parted and for a few moments Ben was enveloped in the pale, silvery light of moonshine.

Chapter Thirteen

As June turned to July, Madge found herself pulled more and more into the organisation of the art festival. Part of her relished the work, which called on all her skills, including some she hadn't known she had. Arabella Drail relied on her increasingly, delighted to discover that Madge would not only get things done quietly and efficiently, but had a way of ironing out personality problems. Arabella had always found that, unaccountably, people's feelings were easily ruffled.

Grashe's Bank was the main festival sponsor and, rather to her amusement, Madge found that the person she had to liaise with over the loan of the Lyndon Scroby painting was none other than Tony Banding, in his role as unofficial assistant to Bruce Spatchland, the director who was curator of the bank's art collection. Tony didn't seem to connect her with the woman currently residing in his brother's flat at Chandlers, and Madge took care not to mention it.

She found though that he was less than co-operative about facilitating the loan. Without fail he seemed to find some further impediment, as soon as the last one was sorted. It was almost as if he didn't want the painting to be exhibited in Rundleston, Madge thought, and then reproached herself for being unfair. He was probably just doing his job. This was his home town after all, he must surely be proud that his employer could enhance its art festival with an offering by one of the most lauded and talked about members of the contemporary art scene. Perhaps he just enjoyed exercising power over provincial people like her.

She had no way of knowing that Tony felt as if he were a cornered spider watching the inexorable approach of a vacuum cleaner. The prospect of the bank's Lyndon Scroby being exhibited in Rundleston filled him with panic. For one thing, Ben was bound to see it. Although Tony was preparing a defence against that. His brother could surely be leaned on, after all he'd hardly want to admit to being the creator of such a crude daub, as well as laying himself open to prosecution for forgery. Or it might be best to invoke family loyalty. He imagined himself saying reproachfully, 'You wouldn't want me to lose my job and go to prison'. Or the final, emotional, backstop, 'The disgrace of it would kill Nora'.

But it was learning that Lyndon Scroby himself now lived just outside Rundleston, and had been persuaded to open the art festival, that caused Tony to wake up in the night, sweating. He imagined the opening ceremony, with camera-wielding press and television bods filming the world-renowned artist as he came to his own work, the prized jewel in the bank's modern art collection. Bruce Spatchland would be there, and probably the Chairman as well. He was always up for a bit of media exposure. Scroby would stand in front of the painting, flashlights popping, and announce, with a face like a rancid raspberry, 'I've never seen this in my life before. It's an effing fake!'

There was a limit to the number of obstacles Tony could put in the way of the loan though, and he had just about come to the end of them. He was already afraid Spatchland might revise his recommendation that Tony should succeed him as curator, on the grounds that he now seemed to raise problems, instead of smoothing them out. It was beginning to seem odd too, that Tony was unenthusiastic about the painting being in the limelight. He was after all the one who'd tipped the wink to Grashe's about this Scroby being available on the quiet, as a result of its (imaginary) owner needing to realize some cash.

Wild ideas about kidnapping Scroby and getting someone to impersonate him, or simply disrupting the ceremony occupied Tony's thoughts. Could he perhaps start a small fire somewhere in the maltings building? But common sense prevailed. A fire that was soon put out would only postpone things, and if it became serious he would be found out. No, arson was not the answer, nor kidnapping. But suppose Scroby was ill, or put off carrying out the opening ceremony? That was surely all that was necessary.

He decided to do a little in depth research on the man, and began to build up a dossier on his background and career. There was plenty of stuff on the internet that presented him in a less than pleasant light, but then being shocking was part of his stock in trade. It was that which had got him much needed publicity in the first place. So blackmail was out. Besides, there was the little matter of gathering proof.

But it was at the renowned Black Art Gallery's evening preview of new Scroby work that Tony had his breakthrough. He'd quietly appropriated the prestigious invitation sent to Bruce Spatchland, and arrived a few minutes before the stated time to find a couple of the staff chatting before a depiction of two lurid yellow linked hands, with penises for fingers.

'Scroby hates frogs', one was saying. 'Don't know why.'

'Frogs?' Tony butted in. 'Did you say Lyndon Scroby has a thing about frogs?'

The young man turned, trying to assess whether this was a potential buyer, necessitating obsequiousness, or simply a hanger on, here for the networking, booze and birds. The latter, he decided. The rich never turned up early.

'That's an understatement. He can't stand them.' Then with deliberate rudeness he cold-shouldered the interloper, and resumed his conversation.

Normally Tony would have taken the slight hard, and made a point of stressing that he was there as a representative of Grashes Bank. But then in the usual run of things he wouldn't have arrived till halfway through the proceedings. Being prompt looked eager and decidedly uncool. Now he soothed his ego with the knowledge that the early arrival strategy had worked, and hugged this important scrap of information to himself.

A throng of admirers surrounded Lyndon Scroby as soon as he appeared, and several press photogaphers took snaps while their papers' arts correspondents gained quotes before filing copy for the next day's editions. Oliver Rabson arrived soon after, and Tony wondered if he couldn't wangle a conversation with the great man. He would mention casually that Natasha was staying in his Rundleston family home, and hint that she'd been grateful for his opinion about her new gallery. Establish a link. But he knew better than to try to muscle in on the gallery owner's carefully calculated social mix surrounding the famous art impresario. Besides, the invitation had been sent to Bruce Spatchland, not him, so a low profile was in order. Observing firsthand though, the almost god-like status in which Rab was held, only reinforced his ambition to become the multi-millionaire's son in law. It must be possible to repair his own image in Natasha's eyes, he thought watching enviously. The whole Rundleston's set up was such a peach, if it could just be played it right. Heaven sent.

The gallery was alive with interlinked swirls of neon lights, which lit progressively – and suggestively, since some of them appeared distinctly phallic. No expense had been spared on the champagne and canapés. Well they wouldn't. Tony was dazzled by the familiar faces among the guests – actors, film stars, politicians, as well as famous members of the Brit Art Pack. Tootsie Smalt was there, and Tracey Emin and Damien Hirst were expected apparently. Tony congratulated himself on his astute decision to show an interest in the bank's art collection. As a run of the mill analyst at Grashes he could make money, but becoming part of the entertaining, client-snaring apparatus was not only a fast track to a directorship, he reckoned, but promised mega-bucks. He didn't normally get to such important previews, but when he succeeded Bruce Spatchland as the collection's curator, he would get invited to gatherings like this all the time. And if he had Natasha on his arm...

Occupied by these pleasing thoughts, Tony was considering trying his luck with an attractive doris chatting to an ineffectual looking man, when he heard transatlantic accents behind him. A middle-aged couple were discussing the relative merits of the six million pound Scroby work in front of them, compared to the one they had back home. Should they buy it to make a pair, or would a Koons be a better investment?

HNWI alert! If there was one thing Tony was rigorously trained in, it was how to schmooze and land High-Net-Worth Individuals at art events, previews and fairs. And what's more this couple were temporarily without a minder from the gallery. Careless. But then the place was swimming in money this evening. Go for it lad, he spurred himself on, moving in on them with practiced charm.

He spent the next hour talking art and finance, giving the wife lots of appreciative attention, talking man-to-man with her husband about investment opportunities, monopolizing their company and deterring rivals with the determination of a fox making off with a plump chicken. When they left, holding Tony's card, it was with an invitation to come and view Grashe's art collection (a particular privilege that he, as curator, could wangle for two such knowledgeable art aficionados) and he would also arrange for special investment advice. Not something many people were accorded, they were given to understand. They departed without purchasing another Scroby, but pleased at having made an influential Grashe's bank contact. This trip was turning out well.

Glowing with triumph, Tony searched the crowd for a bit of skirt to round off the evening, but his former target must have left. So had Oliver Rabson. Shit, no hope of making contact now. But as his eyes roamed the room he was attracted by a petite blonde chatting to the gallery owner. Her scarlet dress showed a teasing expanse of tanned back, and large diamond drop earrings hung beneath short, sleek hair that was tinted and shingled in an expensively top-salon style. The slim hand clasping a champagne flute was heavy with impressive rings, but not on the fourth finger. And there was something familiar about the curve of her cheek and the way she stood. A famous actress maybe?

As he watched she took out her BlackBerry and turned away to answer the call, so that more of her face was visible. *Natasha!* No. Christ almighty, her mother then! Had to be. Of course. She was an event organizer, this preview had probably been her work. Extraordinary that they could be so alike – those big grey eyes, perfect nose and that striking bone structure.

Talking on her phone the woman glanced across and saw him staring, fascinated by that provocative, worldly air coupled with the resemblance to her daughter. Shock must have been showing on his face, and she met his gaze questioningly, and held it, where most women would have looked away, embarrassed by the eye contact. Recovering, Tony gave her his bedroomy smile, and received in return an assessing flicker of interest before she turned that sexy, strokable back.

He went back to his flat alone, having failed to score, but then a lot of time had been spent on netting something more important.

A good evening's work, he congratulated himself, stepping into the lift after paying off the taxi. When he handed the Wealth Management guys that seriously loaded couple on a plate his stock was going to soar. Not least with Bruce Spatchland. Might have a bit of explaining to do as to why the gallery preview invite hadn't actually reached its intended recipient, but he could spin some story.

And he'd clocked eyes on Natasha's mother. He recalled the reception to his undressing smile. Well, maybe a bit more than that. He was unsure how to play her yet, but she had to be another card to strengthen his hand.

He punched in the front door's security code exultantly. It takes a lot to beat you, Tony old son, he told himself. No-one had managed it yet, and they weren't going to. Probably the best scoop of the evening was that scrap of information about Scroby. All he had to do now was find a way of acquiring a load of frogs, and letting them loose at the opening ceremony. Yess! He smiled as he opened the door, pleasurably imagining the scene. Lyndon Scroby would run a mile.

Natasha had hoped her gallery would be ready for opening by mid July, but she'd never before had anything to do with either the construction trade or officialdom. The building inspector evidently considered he wasn't doing his job properly if he couldn't find enough faults to cause the hold up of at least one project per visit. Then Natasha had chosen wildly expensive cream-coloured floor tiles, only to discover when they arrived that about a quarter were broken. For replacements, the supplier reported, she would have to await a new shipment from the Far East. There was a hold-up with the cabling for the underfloor heating, and an area of damp on one wall was taking forever to dry out after treatment – if it ever did. To add to her frustration, the firm supplying the centerpiece of the gallery, a huge wrought iron chandelier, was being decidedly evasive about when they would actually be able to deliver it.

Fortunately Rab didn't seem bothered that she kept having to report delays. It never occurred to Natasha that the setting up of a provincial gallery was merely a ploy to keep her occupied and out of the way. But she did privately question who on earth was going to buy the relentlessly contemporary art it would be purveying, after the Rundleston festival had been and gone. In fact if she was going to sell anything at all it seemed vital to have the gallery up and running in time for it. Then she could cash in on the media circus as well as all the potential buyers descending on Rundleston.

She discussed with Pauline how best to work in tandem with the art festival.

'Well, you could have your father officially open the gallery the day the whole shebang starts', she suggested. 'That'll ensure maximum publicity, both for the gallery and the festival, so the organizers will feel well disposed towards you, instead of seeing you as some sort of rival.'

Having suggested the whole idea of an out-of-town business in the first place, Pauline was torn between satisfaction at seeing Natasha knuckle down to the task in a mature and capable way, and anxiety that she would become depressed when all her efforts resulted in no sales at all. Both she and Rab were perfectly well aware that the project had zero likelihood of commercial success.

'You know', she remarked, inspecting progress, or rather lack of it, on the first Friday evening in July, 'you don't have to offer modern art exclusively. There's nothing stopping you reserving a bit of space for stuff more in tune with Rundleston. Things that appeal to you personally. And you can price those to suit more modest pockets.'

'What a great idea!' Natasha responded enthusiastically. 'I'd like the place to have an East Anglian flavour. In fact...are you busy tomorrow and Sunday? Could you come with me round a few studios? Nora and Ben will know where to go, and there's a pottery up in Norfolk I've heard about.'

They had a happy weekend, touring with a purpose, but at the end of it Natasha felt vaguely dissatisfied. They'd seen plenty of pleasant paintings, and pottery that was well made and decorated, but nothing inspiring. If the gallery's main wares had to be ugly contemporary art with which she had no affinity, then it was important the stock she could actually choose really pleased her. She wanted to be proud to offer it for sale, and genuinely able to enthuse about it to prospective customers.

After Pauline had driven back to London on the Sunday night, Natasha went downstairs for a coffee and a chat with Madge. 'The trouble is', she remarked, 'Ben's paintings have spoilt me. I look at other people's work and find it dull or chocolate boxy. Just not very good. I wouldn't want it myself, so what's the point of selling it? I mean look at that.' She indicated his depiction on the wall of the busy boatyard scene. 'You just want to gaze and gaze at it. People, boats, movement – and *light*. He captures light and it makes everything he does just magical.'

'Yes', agreed Madge, adding with no hint of self-congratulation, 'Nora's very pleased with the print sales. She says people love them.'

'It would have been ideal to sell reproductions of Ben's paintings in my gallery, as the non-modern art stuff', Natasha said, 'but of course I can't. It would take sales away from the family shop.

Do you think', she asked hesitantly, 'that he would let me sell some of his originals?'

'You'd have a job persuading him', was Madge's opinion. Ben seemed to regard his paintings like the children he'd never had. Plus there was some other element she couldn't quite fathom. It was almost as if, at the back of his mind, he felt there would be a use for them in the future. 'I thought perhaps my time would come', he'd confessed to her. She'd had to use all her powers of persuasion to get his okay for the prints and cards, and, quite apart from how she now felt about him, Madge prided herself that she was much closer to Ben than Natasha was. So it seemed an idea doomed to failure.

'You can always ask him', she said doubtfully. 'but I think you'd have about as much chance as persuading a small child to part with his comfort blanket.'

Ben was now rather taken with the idea of making a mocking contribution to the art fiasco. The trouble was that it had to be taken as a joke by the general public yet seriously by the organizers, and it wasn't clear where, if anywhere, the line was. In search of inspiration, he introduced the subject to the regulars at The Spritty, and somewhat to his surprise found an enthusiastic response.

'There's money in them modern art stunts', was Flitch's opinion. 'You could get a grant.'

'I think that's only if it costs money to stage in the first place', Ben told him.

'No. Trish bought a load of china at a jumble sale the other day, all wrapped up in old newspaper. There was this bit about a bloke who kicked a curry box down the street, to bring attention to...', memory failed him. 'I dunno. Anyway, it said he got a twelve thousand pound grant for it.' Flitch paused in disbelief. 'I could do with that.'

'How about holding a curry box kicking competition in the Square? Danny suggested. 'Then we could get twelve thousand each.'

'Like as not in Rundleston you'd just get had up for causing litter', someone remarked from the window seat. 'What about that man who nails planks of wood to his feet.' Looking pointedly at Flitch's bulging, hardworked trainers, he added, 'Might be an improvement.'

'We could arrange for all the street lights to go on and off', Trish contributed, washing glasses, 'with someone walking round the town backwards. Or', she glanced teasingly at the tall, gawky figure leaning on the bar, 'get Danny to destroy all his possessions like whatsisname did.'

'Wouldn't take very long though, would it', Ben joshed. 'But if he cut off his hair and added it to the pile of smocks we could call it Lock, Smock and Barrel.'

Danny might look earnest, but he could take a bit of banter with good humour. 'Better to pretend to do it, then it would be Mock Lock, Smock and Barrel', he responded mildly. 'I was sorting out a computer problem for the art festival office this week. And it seems they're going to offer a prize for the

190

best local entry.' He put down his pint. 'How about constructing a figure, a sort of Rundleston Man. Like an outsize scarecrow, but made up of things that are special to Rundleston – lifebelts and barley sheaves and things.'

There were nodding heads in approval at this idea, and Tricia added, 'Could we use some of the stuff off Woodshey Bay to build him. I can see those bags of rubbish growing roots if someone doesn't do something with them.'

'The only problem with building a figure is that it really would be a work of art, sort of', was Ben's comment. 'I want to do something that anyone with half a brain cell can see is rubbish, but the festival bods take really seriously. So we can all have a laugh.'

He decided to consult Natasha. Having discovered that she was a non-believer where contemporary art was concerned, he felt her inside knowledge might be useful. He found her in the little yard behind the gallery, painting the outhouse door a subtle grey-green, hair tied back, wearing faded jeans and a stripey rugby shirt.

'Do you like my charity shop outfit?' she pirouetted for him with a smile. Ben did. Seeing her in scruff mode made her so much more approachable. More him. Less Rabson.

Pleased by her unexpected visitor, she eagerly took him round the gallery, telling him what had been done so far, and how it would eventually be, and Ben was impressed in spite of himself. The girl had taste, and an artistic flair for colour combinations. As you would expect, with the genes she'd inherited, he thought with ego-boosting satisfaction. Her father's daughter, even if she didn't know it. And one day she will, he promised himself.

'I'm hoping you'll be able to give me some advice', he said, as she showed him the opened packs of floor tiles, with their damaged contents. He told her about his plan for an ironic contribution to the art festival. 'What sort of stunt is fashionable at the moment? I'm looking for something that has a connection to Rundleston, and we can easily stage in the maltings building – not daubing words on sheep or whatever.'

'Chickening out from posting yourself to it, then,' she teased him, 'or photographing your nether regions on an Intercity train? Well, let's think. The buzz words now seem to be 'found objects'.

'What, sort of lost and found?'

'No, everyday things, made into an installation. What you and I would call, well, rubbish. Only trouble is', she smiled up at him, 'the gallery has to make sure the cleaners know, otherwise they just clear it away.'

'Found objects', he repeated thoughtfully, a plan beginning to form. 'Hey, that's a great idea. Thank you. I'll work on it.'

'Got a favour to ask in return though', Natasha warned him, as they made their way out to the back yard. 'This is Dad's gallery, so it has to display contemporary stuff, but Pauline's suggested having an area for art I really like, at a price ordinary people can afford.'

'Oh yes', he remembered, 'you went haring all over the place at the weekend didn't you, looking at potential stock.'

'But we didn't see anything half as good as your paintings.'

'Flatterer', he accused her, pleased.

She moved the tin of paint out of the way, and looked up at him appealingly, 'And I was wondering if you would let me to sell some of your originals? Just a few', she added nervously.

Holy cow! His daughter wanted to sell his paintings in her Dad's gallery. The proliferation of paternity passed him by as he tried to grasp the ramifications.

'Ah. Have to think about that. Thing is, I don't really sell them.' Ben was hoping she wouldn't ask him why.

They were standing in front of the half-finished shed door. Grey-green, she'd chosen his favourite colour. He imagined his work next to the gunk that passed for art in the main gallery. There'd be no contest. But the price tags on his would be considerably lower, he realised. And that would be insulting.

'No, I … well, I think not', he concluded, adding gently, 'Apart from anything else, you want to entice people who can't afford the rest of the stock. And I'm afraid I couldn't let them go so cheaply.'

'Oh.' Natasha sounded crushed. There was a smear of paint on her cheek, and the man's shirt only emphasized her youth and vulnerability. She was his child, and he'd just refused to help her. Ben couldn't bear it.

'Look, I tell you what. How about if I paint some small ones specially? Eight inches by five, say. I'll frame them nicely, and you can sell those.'

The smile she shone on him was pure Gaye. 'Oh thank you Ben!' She squeezed his arm. 'I know your paintings will make all the difference.'

Chapter Fourteen

Danny's gleanings proved correct. A week later the art festival organising committee announced that entries were invited for a modern art competition, with a cash prize of one thousand pounds, courtesy of the main sponsors, Grashes Bank. Only those living in Rundleston would be eligible, but the display area was limited, so not all entrants could be granted a space, and to determine the lucky ones, hopefuls were asked to submit a rough outline of what was envisaged, and its dimensions. Having had the advantage of time to think about it, Ben wanted to be one of the first to put in an application.

The description of his installation had to be just right – serious-sounding but mocking at the same time – and hearing voices from the ground floor flat as he passed one evening, he knocked on the open door and went in.

193

Relations between him and Madge had not been quite the same since the moth hunt. It was as if some invisible barrier had now replaced their former easy, bantering relationship. She seemed wary of him. Madge was a great girl, clever, lively and sweet-natured, and also sensitive, he reasoned. She must have realised the emotional upheaval she had inadvertently caused him, and felt as awkward and embarrassed as he did. Although he refused to admit it, on his side the apprehension also lingered that just her physical proximity might have power over him again. As a result he now avoided being on his own with her. But clearly Natasha was there as well this evening, so he felt safe to visit.

He found them chatting in the kitchen while Madge cooked the family supper, and asked their advice about titling his proposed art installation.

'You need to use the right language', Natasha told him.

'Let's see. Juxtaposition, conceptual and metaphorical are all good. Oh, and polemic. The more buzz words you put in, preferably long, the more seriously the work will be taken. What is it anyway?'

'Ah, that would be telling', was all Ben would say, enjoying being secretive. 'You'll find out. The thing's a load of codswallop anyway. But it is going to have a local flavour.'

'If you make the description sound as if people have to be intelligent to 'get' it', suggested Madge, turning the gas down under the potatoes, 'I think that would find favour.' She added impishly, 'Especially if Arabella doesn't.'

'But there's nothing to 'get'', Ben objected. 'That's the whole point.'

'She won't know that. Anyway, as far as I can see all these so-called art things are a confidence trick, based on people being afraid of looking thick. Aren't they?' Madge looked at Natasha for confirmation.

'Mmm', she agreed. 'Well partly. At the top end where Dad operates, there are ranks of gallerists and art advisers

194

telling potential buyers what a good investment the stuff is, in fact the higher the price, the better.' Natasha smiled as an interesting notion occurred. 'Are you going to offer your installation for sale afterwards?'

'Certainly', declared Ben, who hadn't thought of that.

'What shall we say? Ten thousand pounds?'

'No, that wouldn't be any good at all', Natasha laughed at his naivety. 'It has to be at least a hundred thousand pounds to attract interest. And preferably a quarter of a million. Although, as you haven't got a gallery hyping you up I'm afraid it doesn't stand much chance of a sale.'

Having abandoned his homework, Jamie had been listening in the doorway, commiserating with Bodger who'd been ordered to stay out of the kitchen.

'This art thing – can I help you make it? And Stephen?' he asked eagerly.

'It's a very skilled job you know', Ben told him seriously. 'Yes of course you can. On condition that you don't tell your mother what it is. Otherwise we could be said to have influence in high places.' He gave Madge a guarded smile, and ventured, 'How are the moths?'

After a session on the computer, tackling his and the shop accounts for the tax man, he went in to see Nora, and told her about his plan to give Rundleston's inhabitants a good laugh.

'Sounds fun. This art festival might not be what I intended at all', she confessed, 'but I do think it will be good for the town. And holding it in August, which seemed crazy, could be a sensible idea after all. It promises to bring in lots of visitors who are on holiday with nothing much to do.'

'Apparently there are going to be all sorts of stalls and things going on in the market square', Ben reported, 'which should be a boost for the shops and eating places. Do you think we should get in extra stock, and if so, what?'

They talked shop for a while, until Ben felt the call of a pint at the Spritty.

'Pauline and I have been wondering', his mother remarked, as he made to go, 'how we could use the occasion to raise funds for Rundleston Grange's new swimming pool. We're going to try and arrange a street collection, but we want it to be a bit different. Remember all those costumes stored in the garage', she added with suspicious lightness, 'perhaps we could have collectors in the square dressed as woodland animals. Attract attention, if nothing else.'

'And just who do you envisage doing that?' enquired Ben heavily, already anticipating the answer.

Nora looked innocent. 'Well I thought perhaps you and your friends...'

'Mum, Rundleston Grange does a great job, and there are many things I would do for you', he interrupted. 'But trogging round the town dressed as a supersized squirrel is not one of them.'

'Doesn't have to be a squirrel.' Her eyes were laughing as she deliberately missed the point. 'There are a couple of fox outfits, and a badger. And lots of mice. No they might be a bit small.

How about a rabbit?' she called after him as he closed the door.

How about a rabbit, Ben repeated humorously to himself as he and Bodger walked down to the Spritty. Yeah, right. A breeze was blowing across the river, carrying a hint of rain on the air, and in the lowering light waves were slapping out an impatient rhythm. Those sitting at the tables outside had now migrated to the shelter of the pub, and there was a satisfying warmth and buzz of conversation as he pushed open the door.

Not unusually, Danny was propping up the bar. He was more eager to talk these days when they met in the boatyard and the pub, especially about Natasha.

'Do you know if she has a boyfriend? In London?' he asked now, as Ben waited for his beer.

'Well, yes, I think she was unofficially engaged before being sent down here.' This seemed a good way out for Natasha, and had the merit of truth.

'It's like an illness, isn't it, being stir crazy about someone. You can't stop thinking about them. Man but she's something.' His sunken face didn't do animation, but was making an attempt.

Danny might have very little, but his sturdy independence had been his strength. Now he was like a wounded animal, Ben thought. Knowing that Natasha's only response was not to hurt her admirer's feelings, he felt sympathy for them both.

'I've written a song about her', Danny confided. 'If I play it to her, perhaps she'll get the message.' Then he shrugged and added mournfully. 'But I'm just a boat bum. I can't expect her to...'

'This modern art competition' Ben changed the subject constructively, 'Why not go in for it? Thousand pound prize is not to be sniffed at.'

'But I'm not artistic'.

'Absolutely no talent necessary', Ben assured him airily. 'Any old stuff will do. In fact', he laughed thinking of his own entry, 'the more rubbishy it is, the better. Trust me.'

Producing a number of small paintings for Natasha's gallery was occupying Ben's time and thoughts rather more than the competition entry. He'd always painted just what inspired him, now he wanted to find subjects that would suit this unusual format, show off his skills and, most importantly, delight Natasha. He considered cutting down paintings stored in the plan chest, but rejected the idea. No, that wouldn't be good enough for her. She deserved the very best he could do, he thought, and went out seeking subjects, before spending considerably more time than usual in his studio.

As commissions, to be sold, the possessiveness he felt about his past paintings didn't apply. These really were weapons, he reflected with satisfaction, putting the finishing touches to a cyclist sitting eating a sandwich in sunshine, his back to a gate over which two horses were looking at him curiously, a gathering rainstorm in the background. His work would be hanging in a gallery owned by Oliver Rabson. The thought was immensely pleasing. It was putting one over on him, and no mistake.

Learning from Natasha that Rab dealt in contemporary stuff purely to make money, and not out of personal preference, was an inconvenient piece of information that Ben preferred not to dwell on. The man had encouraged the ridiculous excesses of the modern art world, he told himself, and all that'd meant for himself as an artist. And the bastard had stolen his fiancée, and his daughter. He knew that now. Well he could fight. And he would. He'd get them back.

He imagined meeting up with Gaye again at the art festival. The thought left him shaky with anticipation, and his mind shied away from the encounter in favour of more practical questions. Gaye would confirm Natasha was his child. No doubt about it. What then?

A vision of Natasha's face came to mind, with her innocent, lovely smile. He'd tell her, and prise her away, he promised himself. She was his daughter, not Rabson's.

Despite Natasha's frequent emails to her father, Pauline found herself closely questioned every time she came back from a weekend in Rundleston. Rab still very much missed Natasha's company, her youth, beauty and chatty joie de vivre. She was simply heart warming. He didn't in the least mind about delays to the gallery opening from the point of view of trading, the whole thing was always envisaged as a tax loss anyway. But he was beginning to question the necessity of sending her away for so long. His publicist had been in action, and Rab was confident that any media interest in Natasha would be muted now, especially as that louse of a boyfriend was pleading guilty, meaning no high-profile trial.

'She should have come with me to Art Basel, he complained, hovering in Pauline's office, as she checked her emails on Monday morning, 'she'd have learned a lot – and had a good time. And if she's going to come into the business seriously the sooner she makes contacts the better. Several people asked after her,' he added with fatherly pride.

Having observed Natasha both as Rab's protégée in London, and determinedly tackling problems in Rundleston, Pauline had her own ideas about which was better for the girl's development.

'The launch of the Rabson brand's only a few months away now', her boss continued, walking over to the window. 'It's important for her to know what's involved. Perhaps it's time to pull the plug on the whole gallery enterprise. Cut my losses and bring Natasha back.'

He looked at Pauline, but her expected approval was not forthcoming.

'She wouldn't be in the foreground, of course', he added. 'It's too soon after the drugs thing. But she could be helping me and being part of the venture. I'd insist she kept a low profile socially.'

'Natasha's not miserable, you know', his PA informed him with secret amusement, shrewdly assessing that this was actually more about Rab's wellbeing than his daughter's. In Pauline's opinion a display of unselfishness by men had much in common with the Indian rope trick.

'She's settled in well and made friends – bought a secondhand bicycle last week, and she and Madge went out for a day's bike ride yesterday. They had a great time, I'm sure you'll hear all about it.'

'Yes, she usually emails on a Monday evening.'

'Over the past couple of months she's really got stuck in to setting up this gallery', Pauline continued, looking at him over her glasses, 'and I think the whole thing's helped her to grow up. Besides, she wants to prove herself, and regain your approval by her own efforts. Summarily axing it would be a huge disappoint to her.'

'Oh. Well perhaps you're right.' There was genuine regret in Rab's voice. 'I just wanted to signal that she'd been forgiven. I might have been a bit hard on her', he concluded magnanimously.

One of the reasons she stayed in the job was that her boss listened to her, Pauline reflected. Now his parents were dead, nobody else could talk to him the way she did. It must be strange to be so wealthy and commanding that no-one dared criticise. Disorientating. I'm a very necessary anchor, she thought, with a certain satisfaction.

'Of course there's nothing stopping you going down to visit her', she suggested encouragingly. 'I know you've been kept in the picture, but I'm sure she'd be delighted to show you exactly what she's doing.' With a faint smile she added, 'as long as it's low key.'

He looked at her questioningly, taken aback. 'My daughter's ashamed of me?'

'No, of course not. You hardly need me to tell you Natasha adores you.'

Her reassurance was welcome. Love was not something Rab was used to.

'But she could have traded on you being her father and all that that implies, and she doesn't', his PA continued. 'And good for her, I say. She'd rather appear ordinary and have people accept her for her personality, not whose daughter she is.'

'What's that got to do with it?'

'Well most people's fathers don't descend from the sky in helicopters or turn up in a chauffeur-driven Bentley', answered Pauline drily.

'Is that so.'

Rab turned his taut, concentrated gaze on her, unnerving as a raptor tracking prey. But she'd learned to look for a hint of humour about the mouth, and it was there now.

'Shame the yacht's in the Med.'

Natasha was thrilled at the news that her father would be coming down on a visit, although he wouldn't say exactly when. She was dying for him to see the fruits of her labours, as if she was a school child with cherished work displayed in the class room. The replacement floor tiles for the gallery were unfortunately still on the high seas, but she succeeded in getting the elaborate wrought iron chandelier finished and delivered by using his name, something she didn't normally do. Oliver Rabson would be coming to see it, she told the forge. If he was impressed by their creation, it could well lead to future commissions. She somehow neglected to mention that he would be officially opening the gallery the following month anyway. The electrician was away on holiday when the completed chandelier arrived, so Danny did the wiring for her. It now dominated the room, its decorative tracery casting complicated shadows on the walls and ceiling, and Natasha was delighted.

The area behind the gallery was still full of stuff the builders intended taking away when their job was finally finished. Well, probably. So she hired a skip for a day, and her lanky admirer energetically helped her fill it, and sweep the yard clean.

She located a place selling pots from Tuscany, and chose two huge ones, each containing a standard bay tree, to be placed on the pavement either side of the shop door. They looked imposingly classy, but she had no idea how to keep the things alive, and was grateful for Pauline's advice. Madge came with her to the local garden centre for some smaller terracotta pots, which they planted up with white geraniums and yellow pansies, to go in the yard. The result was a smart, continental air. At their landlady's suggestion, Natasha searched for some dark green material in Ipswich, and Nora expertly ran up fashionable-looking scalloped curtains for the upstairs windows, even though they were not going to be anything but store rooms. 'They'll echo the colour of the bay trees', she said. 'Make the place look better from the street.' And she was right.

The awning, with the Rabson name emblazoned across it, wasn't ready, and in any case Natasha preferred Rundleston not to know yet what sort of gallery was about to open. But as she polished the brass door handles and cleaned the windows like an obsessive housewife, she felt proud of the transformation she'd organised and worked for in the past couple of months.

Of course it wouldn't be possible, until just before the opening, to install the art she and Rab had discussed as stock. As a result the empty premises could have been any kind of upmarket emporium in waiting. However there was one part of the gallery's wares which she could temporarily display, just to give Rab an idea of how things would be. Ben's collection of little pictures.

She hadn't been allowed to view their progress. Painting had always been a personal and private activity, and Ben wanted her to see only the finished perfection, not works in progress. It had been odd, confining himself to cameos, and the subjects had been chosen with the small format in mind. Also saleability, not something that normally crossed his mind.

He'd often been amused to notice the boatyard's cat dozing in the sun on top of a huge disused buoy. Now the tortoise-shell was there for posterity, its soft, feline relaxation contrasting with the hardness of the rust-streaked and salt-faded starboard buoy, plus a few bits of marine detritus round the base. He'd drawn Jamie out rowing again, and turned that into a picture which, with artistic licence, depicted Bodger in the bow like a figurehead, looking down into the water, dancing light reflected back. His sketchbook had been raided for a study of an old man, leaning on his fork beside a smouldering bonfire, a tongue of flame just escaping, lending the faintest orange glow to his nose. You could almost smell the smoke as it wreathed and curled upwards. In another, a small child, face only just visible beneath a floppy sun hat, sat absorbed on a beach, trickling water from a bucket, the plump little legs gritty with sand, toes curling in concentration.

Ben had poured himself into each tiny painting, striving for perfection. They were for Natasha. If he couldn't yet tell her the truth, he could at least make the paint speak for him, the best way he knew of expressing himself. She'd commissioned six, and he was still working on the last one, a simple orange marigold that Nora had put in a jar on her windowsill. The rays from the evening sun picked out some petals, which cast shadows on others, making it a breathtaking study of light and beauty. To add some animation, he was going to add a bumblebee, which entailed sitting in Chandlers' garden, observing and sketching the buzzing visitors. It's a hard old life, he reflected, luxuriating in the sun, while bees worked the flowers in front of him. He felt a certain affinity with the furry, unthreatening, clumsy creatures. Bit like me, he thought. Just bumbling along.

Natasha's news that Rab was coming to inspect the gallery, and that she wanted to have Ben's work on show, meant that he would have to frame those that were completed, rather than finish painting the last one. But he changed tasks with a glad heart. They were good, these little studies, he knew it. There could be no comparison with the hyped up dross that would fill the rest of the gallery. Not to anyone with an honest eye.

The day before Rab was expected, Ben brought the five framed paintings into the gallery and showed them to Natasha, who was bowled over by them.

'Oh Ben, they're just awesome!' she enthused. 'I'm going to put them here, in this little side room. 'Who's the old boy with the bonfire? I love him. And that's Jamie in the boat, isn't it. Have you showed it to Madge?'

Her obvious admiration pleased Ben immensely. That his creations were weapons against Oliver Rabson immediately went to the back of his mind. No, they were gifts to this lovely girl, his daughter.

The decision about how to arrive in Rundleston without embarrassing Natasha was the start of Rab's enjoyment. He went down to the Hampshire house and got out of the garage his treasured Triumph Bonneville, untouched and unthought of for goodness knows how many years. And why was that? he wondered, as he spent the next couple of days checking the bike over and getting it back into top order, dredging up his old skills, and asking advice online from other Bonnie owners. He'd loved this machine. Riding down to see Natasha was going to be a treat.

Used to getting over problems by simply throwing money at them, he found the bureaucracy needed for getting the bike back on the road frustrating. Then the day the new tax disc arrived he had a lunch scheduled with an important Russian collector who was interested in acquiring a Tootsie Smalt installation that Rab 'no longer had room for, and was thinking of letting go.' Regretfully, of course.

But the enforced delay served to enhance his pleasure as he roared down the A12 towards Suffolk next day, and beneath the new helmet his face was smiling. Weaving through London traffic before opening up and relishing the power surge, the rush of air and feeling of perfect harmony with the bike, took him back twenty-five years. Nothing now gave him a thrill like this, he thought regretfully, glancing behind before overtaking. Not even relieving that supposedly sharp Russian of eight million for the Smalt. A pity. Perhaps it was just age.

Rundleston appeared to have little to recommend it, but at least it wasn't difficult to locate the Rabson premises. He cruised past slowly, then returned and negotiated the narrow entrance to the yard, where he parked the bike. He was just removing his gloves when Natasha opened the door at the back of the building, preparing to instruct the intruder politely but firmly that this was private property.

He took off his helmet as she approached, and he saw her face change from annoyance to unalloyed delight as she flung herself into his arms.

'Dad!'

'Whatever are you doing on a motorbike!' she wanted to know, recovering from this wonderful surprise.

'Been stored away for years. I lusted after a Triumph Bonneville when I was young', her father explained. 'But I couldn't justify buying one when every penny was ploughed back into the business.' He gave the machine a fond caress. 'The day I finally bought this, was the day I knew I was going places. Now, I need somewhere to take off these leathers.'

It was a thoroughly enjoyable day. Natasha showed him round the premises, and he praised her generously for what she'd achieved. It might be a good idea to hire a few people as 'customers', he thought, realising, like Pauline, that it would be thoroughly demoralising to have worked so hard only to reap no sales. In a side room she'd hung a few small paintings, to take away some of the emptiness.

'I put them up just to show you', Natasha bubbled enthusiastically. 'They're by my landlady's son. I told you he was an artist. Aren't they wonderful! I'll introduce you to Nora – she runs the shop next door.'

'First things first', he said firmly, after every inch of the place had been inspected. 'I'll take you out to lunch. I brought a helmet for you. Ever ridden pillion before?'

They had an excellent and relaxed meal at the Dutch House Hotel, a mile out of town.

Natasha introduced Peter Jahney as the gallery's landlord. She wanted Rab to meet all her new friends, but after they'd got back, and he'd inspected her room and been shown the town, only Nora was to be found. Madge was watching Jamie play football, and Ben had apparently gone to see a supplier.

'I owe you a big thank you', Rab told Nora courteously, 'for making my daughter so welcome. I know how kind you've been to her.'

He glanced round the shop, noting the prints of her son's paintings on one wall. They certainly displayed an amazing talent – overtones of Monet crossed with Constable, plus a nod to Edward Seago. Natasha must have borrowed the originals on display in the side room.

'Who represents her son? And what sort of price do the originals fetch?' he asked Natasha, nodding towards the side room, after they'd returned to the gallery.

'Well I was going to ask your advice on that. For some reason Ben's very possessive about his art', she explained, filling the kettle in the little kitchen area at the back, while her father perched on a chair. 'I had to really bully him into painting those for me.'

'For you?'

'Yes. I'm going to sell them. Have that little room with nothing but his paintings.'

Rab absorbed the full import of this in silence, and Natasha saw displeasure darken his face like clouds over deep water.

'I thought it would be a good idea to have one area that was a bit different', she rushed to explain. 'With prices Rundleston people could more easily afford.'

'No.'

'Sorry?' Natasha paused, while getting out two mugs.

'Not in my gallery', he told her decisively.

'But you said I should have a go at opening a place in the provinces. And most of the people round here don't like the sort of stuff that sells in London. I thought...'

'Maybe I haven't made things clear. I assumed you understood about the different markets.' Rab was trying to let her down gently. 'Look, down at the bottom are people who want to buy an original painting for their walls, because they like it. Price limit about five thousand, and usually much lower. Quite a small market, because the public mostly put up posters and photographs, or Van Gogh's sunflowers. Kettle's boiling.'

A crestfallen Natasha got out teabags and poured the water, trying to remember if her father took sugar.

'Then there are people who are buying in a small way for investment. Or so they think.' A note of contempt crept in. 'They can be persuaded to spend on all sorts of trash, as long as they're told it's fashionable and will increase in value.' He watched her fish the teabags out and, unasked, stood up and fetched a plate for them. 'That's the market I want to expand into, what this gallery's all about.'

It wasn't true. He had no intention of bothering with the middle market. But Natasha shouldn't know this venture was just a front.

'And finally there's the top end. Nothing less than a million. You know all about that, you've seen how we operate.' He took care to be inclusive.

Taking the mug she offered, he went on, 'So tell me, are those paintings in there fashionable? Cutting edge?'

'No. But they are brilliant', Natasha said stoutly.

'I quite agree. They're remarkable. But it's irrelevant. The Rabson name is synonymous with modernist, contemporary art. What kind of message would it send if there was that sort of figurative stuff on the premises? And, remember I'm launching the Rabson brand in the autumn.'

Already he'd forgotten the 'we'.

'That's going to be really important. Just a fashion, cosmetics and perfume concession at first, but I'm negotiating to extend into jewellery and watches. It has the potential to be granted to high quality electricals, maybe

207

even cars – I'm in talks at the moment with a Formula One team. Anything with the Rabson name on it will be seen as cool, all over the world. A luxury, lifestyle brand.'

Rab put down his tea. 'So, my fault if you didn't understand. But we've got that straight now.' He looked her in the eye. 'Haven't we.'

Chapter Fifteen

From bubbling with anticipation, in the days after Rab's visit Natasha became quiet, and as forlorn as a February rose. At first Nora thought seeing him must have unsettled the girl and created hankerings to get back to London. But such a sudden change of heart seemed unlikely, and, she told herself, Natasha surely wouldn't want to leave before the art festival. She'd put so much hard work into opening this gallery. Now her enthusiasm just seemed to have died.

Normally Nora kept a polite distance from the paying guests. It was the best way of dealing with a succession of people who touched one's life so briefly. However, not only had the two rooms been taken for the whole summer, but she and Pauline had struck up a real friendship, and she took a kindly interest in Natasha. With good manners, beauty and innocent charm, she'd been a delight to have around the place. Now the set expression in contrast to her former smiling self was troubling. Nora questioned Madge, who herself seemed somewhat strained these days, but it appeared Natasha was keeping her troubles to herself.

Relations with her mother were not wonderful, by all accounts, and it seemed probable that now she'd had some sort of row with her father. Pauline would surely have been the best confidant, but she hadn't been down for a couple of weekends. Perhaps the poor girl would benefit from a grandmotherly figure to talk things over with, thought Nora sympathetically, and one evening, a week after Rab's visit, she knocked softly on Natasha's bedroom door.

When she and Ben had first discussed dividing Chandlers, Nora was surprised that he hadn't chosen the top floor as his flat. With the dormer windows overlooking the street on one side and the estuary on the other, the two bedrooms were light, and always warm from the sun on the roof tiles and in winter heat drifting up from the rooms below. In her dreams they still were occupied by Ben and Tony as children, each making a distinctive territory, reflecting their very different personalities.

Natasha was in Ben's old room, decorated in a subtle, willow green, with curtains and armchair cover in material that echoed it satisfyingly. Seated at a table by the riverside window, sketch book in front of her, she was evidently drawing an image of the Hetty Jane that was displayed on the open laptop. Music was playing on some piece of equipment Nora couldn't have put a name to, part of the personal stuff Natasha had now brought down from London. A photograph of her father took pride of place on the mahogany chest of drawers, but an equivalent image of her mother was telling by its absence. And flanking the photograph, leaning against the wall were the six paintings commissioned from Ben. They drew the eye like a Bolshoi Ballet performance on a station platform.

'I'm just messing about with a pencil', Natasha explained in embarrassment, getting up. 'I loved art at school, but I haven't done any since then. It's very bad though.'

Nora was reminded of finding the room's former occupant, as a boy, doing exactly the same thing.

'Ben had to teach himself you know', she said encouragingly, after apologising for the disturbance. 'He used to spend hours and hours practising, finding what worked and what didn't. And he'd take himself up to London galleries and study the great artists.'

She perched on the arm of the chair, while Natasha sat herself down on the bed, bare feet tucked underneath her.

'It's absolutely none of my business, Nora began hesitantly, 'but I can't help noticing things seem to be amiss, my dear. Is there anything I can help with perhaps?'

'Oh.. well..' Twisting a strand of hair anxiously,Natasha seemed divided about whether to tell, before finally making up her mind. 'It's Ben's paintings, you see.' She waved her hand towards them.

'Ben's paintings? Those?'

'Yes. You probably know I persuaded him to do little ones, specially for the gallery? Aren't they lovely?'

His mother smiled. 'I marvelled at your powers of persuasion.'

'That's half the trouble. I did have to twist his arm. And now...' she hesitated. 'My father says I can't have them in the gallery, and I don't know how to tell Ben. I feel awful about it. You've both been so kind.'

'Was that why you wanted to sell them? As a sort of thank you?'

'No! He's got such an amazing talent.' Her face lit up. 'It's a privilege to live with these. I look and look at them.'

'I shouldn't worry', Nora comforted her. 'For two decades my peculiar son has steadfastly hidden his light under a bushel and refused to sell any of his work. It's hardly going to be a great blow for that to continue.'

'There's something else though', Natasha confessed. It was good to have a sympathetic listener. 'Partly I wanted to have his paintings on display because they were what I'd chosen myself. Things I really liked. Instead of all the other stock... which will be the usual fashionable tosh.'

'Can't say I particularly bond with some of the lines we sell', commented Nora encouragingly. 'But people seem to want them, and having a shop is about pleasing the customer as well as oneself.'

'Yes, but no-one round here is going to like what's in the gallery', stated Natasha with certainty. 'And nor do I.' After a moment she confided, 'The thing is Dad wants me to join him in the business when this is up and running. I'd love to be with him – it's been so wonderful finding I really did have a father after all.'

Aware that this sounded odd, she hastened to explain. 'Well, of course I always knew who he was, but my mum said he didn't want anything to do with me, so I never even met him.'

The awful things people did to their children, Nora reflected, appalled.

'Perhaps she wanted to keep you all to herself. Some mothers can be very possessive.'

'No, I think perhaps she isn't capable of loving.' Natasha shrugged. 'It's not her fault, just the way she is.' Her face softened. 'I had a Nanny I adored though – she was like a mum to me, and we're still in touch. But then I was sent off to boarding school at eleven.' She noted Nora's shocked expression, and added. 'I did mind terribly at first. But there were other girls there in the same situation, and it taught me to be strong. I just got used to the idea that neither of my parents was interested in me.'

'You poor little soul.'

Natasha looked up and smiled, full beam. 'So finding Dad has made all the difference. We get on so well. And going in with him would be fun – lots of socialising of course. Lovely clothes, mixing with famous people, parties and art gallery events just about every night...'

'Dear me, how awful', Nora teased lightly, failing to see a problem. 'We country bumpkins can only imagine that sort of sophistication.'

Natasha's smile had faded. 'But this place has made me see it in another light. The people I've met in the last few weeks are different. Decent and genuine. There's no side to them.'

'Rundleston's not paradise, you know', Nora assured her. 'Don't get the wrong idea. There's plenty of back-biting and bad behaviour here, just like everywhere else.'

'But it's not all about who you know and displaying what oodles of money you've got, is it. Coming to Rundleston, and seeing Ben's lovely paintings, has made me realise how shallow all that is.'

'Oh.' Voices drifted up from the street through the open window as Nora considered how to respond. 'You said once your father...' she struggled for tactful wording, 'that he rather enjoyed taking money off wealthy people who were just showing off. Couldn't you just regard it in the same way?'

'He's totally cynical about the whole thing', Natasha agreed. 'But it's okay for him. When he was young he worked his socks off for something he believed in. He can be really proud of what he achieved. So now he doesn't give a stuff about what's basically taking advantage of gullible people.' She glanced up, eyes big and appealing as a child. 'But I don't want to look back at my life and say that's what I did with it. It just isn't me anyway. So I don't know what to do.'

Oh dear, this was a difficult one. It wasn't her place to encourage problems between father and daughter, thought Nora, one a cynic and the other with ideals unsullied by life.

She considered for a moment, then advised, 'When faced with difficult choices, I've always found time sorts things out and shows the way forward. And afterwards it seems so obvious you wonder why on earth you hesitated', she added, entirely forgetting her own sleepless nights worrying if it had been right to give away the maltings. 'You don't have to decide immediately about going into your father's business, do you?'

'No, I suppose not.'

'Well I suggest you concentrate on that gallery, and getting it ready in time for the art festival – only another three weeks. Put everything else to the back of your mind. By the time it opens you'll probably have come to a decision, almost without knowing it. And', she offered kindly, 'I'll tell Ben about you not being able to display his paintings, if you like.'

'No. Thank you. I have to tell him', Natasha said stoutly. 'I need to explain things.'

Her landlady's advice might have been wise, but the more Natasha thought about things, the more it seemed that Ben's art was pivotal to her situation, and she sought him out next day. Knowing that when he'd done his stint in the shop at lunchtime he often took Bodger for a short walk, she locked the gallery when she saw him pass, and ran after them.

'Can I come with you?' she asked breathlessly, catching up. 'Only I want to talk to you about something.'

About half an hour later Madge was queuing at the supermarket checkout when she saw them walk past, looking relaxed and at ease in each other's company, and icy fingers clutched at her heart. Was it possible Tricia was right, and Ben was falling for the daughter of his lost love? she wondered with dismay, reaching for the 'Next Customer' sign. Surely he couldn't be that deluded. She might look just like her mother, but Natasha would merely feel sorry for him if she realised, as she did with Danny. Still, you can't help who you fall for, Madge concluded, laying her purchases on the counter. As she had reason to know. Ben was very susceptible to beauty, and he'd been in thrall to Gaye's memory all these years. She added the empty basket to a stack under the counter. Staying in Rundleston and watching him in love with Natasha, would be difficult, she thought unhappily. Really hard to bear. She managed a smile and exchange of pleasantries with the checkout operator, but as she loaded her shopping into a carrier bag a new thought struck. Hold on, the art festival was bringing Gaye to Rundleston, she told herself. And she and Ben were bound to meet. That'd sort things out, one way or the other. Wouldn't it?

In the next two weeks the replacement floor tiles were laid and the shop fitters finished their work. Telephone and credit card systems were installed, the electricians and builders finished off, cheerily wishing her good luck, and proudly Natasha looked at what she'd created. With her father's finance certainly, but remembering what a shabby wreck of a place it had been before, her self-confidence blossomed. The evening the final workman left she did a tour of inspection, like a cat patrolling its territory. She'd planned and organised all this, she thought with pride. But what was the use of Dad putting her in charge of a business if she couldn't use her own taste and judgement? Ben had been so understanding too about the rejection of his work. He was a lovely man, as well as an inspiring artist, and he deserved better. Now as she stood in the small side room looking at the empty walls, things became clear.

Pauline always said Dad only respected people who stood up to him, she thought, and she needed to show him she wasn't a pushover. This was her gallery, and she would hang those lovely paintings. After all, who was to know? It's not as if it was going to be plastered all over the press. Media bods wouldn't even be coming in here. She'd price them high too, which was only right for Ben. And if Dad kicked up a fuss, then he'd have a fight on his hands. She was a chip off the old block, after all. She nodded to herself, feeling happy with the decision. Yes, that was the answer.

Danny had given much thought to Ben's suggestion about going in for the art competition, and duly put in a request for a space inside the maltings, with an outline of what was envisaged. But a week after the expiry date for applications came news that he had not been successful, at the same time as Ben received the go ahead for his. The Banding family had given the building for the art festival, so Arabella could hardly refuse to give the town's benefactor exhibition space, but in fact she very much liked the sound of the planned installation. It appealed to her as exactly the sort of sophisticated, thought-provoking work she wanted the festival to project. What was surprising was that it should come from Ben Banding, but perhaps he'd finally seen the light.

The competition entries were to be installed in the four days leading up to the opening of the art festival, and the Tuesday before, Ben, Jamie and Stephen raided the sacks containing the rubbish collected off Woodshey Bay that still cluttered a corner of the boatyard. Some of the contents were a little whiffy by now, after nearly two months.

'We'll spread out the contents of the bags and then we can each choose what we're going to use', Ben decided, giving them both a borrowed pair of Nora's gardening gloves. 'And watch out for anything sharp.'

Tricia was unloading supplies from the boot of her car in preparation for an evening hire of the Hetty Jane, and came over to see what they were doing.

'Found objects', Ben explained. 'Apparently that's the in thing in contemporary art. The council won't take this stuff away, so we'll turn it into an art installation. Then with a bit of luck someone will pay silly money for it.' He laughed. 'I'd like that. I'd like that a lot.'

She eyed the jetsam already removed with distaste. 'What's it supposed to represent?'

'It's called...' Ben stood up straight and proclaimed earnestly, 'Getting Around Reality By Almost Glimpsing Eternity'. That should be dense enough for them.'

He was rewarded by total blankness.

'What on earth does that mean?

'Zero, zilch, nada.' He picked out a flip-flop and looked in the sack to see if there was another. 'It's just the kind of pretentious drivel the art world likes.'

'So you're just going to make a pile of this stuff, and that's an art work?'

'Yup. Arabella Drail will love it.' Ben paused, and added mischievously, 'although it's probably best she doesn't dwell on the acronym.'

'What's an acronym?' Stephen looked up from disentangling a length of blue rope.

'A word made by the initial capitals.'

'Getting Around Reality By...' Tricia tried, 'what did you say?'

'Almost Glimpsing Eternity. GARBAGE', Ben added happily. 'Spread the word, won't you Trish. It's important we all have a good laugh.'

Jamie wrinkled his nose. 'Isn't some of this going to pong?'

'Probably. But we'll just say it's designed to speak to all the senses. They fall for that sort of tosh.'

After an hour they'd emptied the sacks and amassed several piles of stuff, although deciding what they were going to use was quite difficult, since just about everything had potential. Progress wasn't helped by the boys seeing if Bodger would play 'Fetch' with various items as they were encountered. (He would). Also Danny came over to chat, and kept picking out objects that 'might come in useful'.

'Shame about my entry being given the brush off', he lamented. 'I was going to ask you guys to help me run it.'

'Run it?' Ben paused, extracting a broken boat hook from a length of fishing line.

'Yeah. It was a human fruit machine.'

'Come again?'

'Three guys in a booth, separated by partitions from each other. And a window in the front', Danny explained. 'They each have an apple, orange, pear and banana in front of them, and when someone out front gives the word they hold up a piece of fruit. If they all hold up the same sort...bingo.'

Ben stared at him. 'Danny, you're a genius. It'd have been a sure fire winner. And they wouldn't give you space to do the thing?'

Danny shook his head mournfully, and confessed. 'It's not original though. I saw it used to raise money at a street fair a few years ago.'

'Now that is one great idea', said Ben slowly. 'There's nothing to stop you doing it on the Market Square, is there?'

'What's the point?'

'It'd be a great attraction. And we could use it to raise money for Rundleston Grange.' He told Danny about Nora wanting to use the occasion for a collection, although she still hadn't got permission. 'But this would be much better. Stephen and Jamie and I will all help. Won't we fellers?

Nora didn't need much persuading to adopt this promising idea. You couldn't just have a street collection, she discovered rather late in the day. Each one needed official sanction, and it was now looking as if permission would come through too late for the opening of the art festival. But a human fruit machine sounded great fun.

The next days were a scrabble to find a tent which could be adapted as a booth, complete with internal partitions. The Grange already had a space on the Market Square allocated to them, and readily agreed to make their bric-a-brac stall smaller to make room for the human fruit machine, and all looked set fair until Pauline rang from London.

'Won't it be regarded as gambling?' she warned Nora. 'You'll need to apply for a licence.'

She was right. People would be handing over money with a chance of winning more, if three identical fruits were held up. And there was no time to obtain a licence. The problem seemed insuperable, until Ben came up with the answer.

'We'll say it's an art happening', he decided cheerfully. 'If a man kicking a curry box round the streets is art, and publicly-funded at that, then three people in a booth holding up pieces of fruit certainly qualifies. Who's to say it isn't.'

The pace of Rundleston life was quickening as the town prepared for its big moment, and the maltings building was humming with activity. Hitches were found and put right, windows cleaned, floors polished, fire extinguishers installed and safety inspections made. The job title of publicity officer no longer covered the myriad things that fell to Madge, as she manned the telephone and helped Arabella field the last minute problems, hindered by frequent visits from members of the various art and development agencies who felt the need to inspect the results of their funding.

Three days before the opening, on the top floor the artwork entries from local people and schools were being hung, installed, and in one case, contained, amid the inevitable arguments about allocated space, which called on all Madge's reserves of tact and common sense to settle. Fortunately there were no disputes concerning the patch of floor marked out for Ben's installation, otherwise, with Jamie helping to assemble it, she'd have been open to charges of favouritism.

The Tomorrow's Art Today consortium were responsible for all the official exhibits, and seemed to know what they were doing. But their large pantechnicon managed to scrape an overhanging building, and sections of what looked sewer pipes proved too wide to be taken up to the first floor.

'You didn't tell me the stairs were narrow', Julian Bisk complained, after several attempts by his overalled shifters had made it clear they might as well try squeezing a hippopotamus into a taxi.

'Well how was I to know you were going to bring dirty great sewer pipes in here', protested Madge.

'They're not. Well, might have been once', he conceded. 'But they're now an artwork. "Infinite Love" by Bart Cloamer. Worth a fortune. But not if it's damaged', he added ruefully, surveying the impasse.

Luckily Madge came up with the solution – hoisting the sections up through outside doors on the first floor, like the sacks of barley that were once unloaded from carts. It involved lengthy traffic hold ups, but fuming local drivers would surely have been mollified had they known it was in the cause of Infinite Love.

Entrusted with overseeing the safe delivery of Lyndon Scroby's artwork, Tony was caught up in the congestion as the security van containing them both was delayed in the queue of vehicles.

'What dickhead thought that was a clever idea!' he fumed at Madge when they finally arrived. 'Been sitting in traffic for hours.'

He oversaw its unloading, and annoyed the T.A.T. staff who carried it up to the first floor by fussing and chivvying, as if they'd never handled such things before.

'This building belonged to my family', he informed Madge grandly, as they stood watching the painting being carefully unpacked. 'We gave it to the town.'

She liked the 'we'. 'Yes, I know. It's changed out of all recognition since my grandfather worked here, hasn't it.'

He looked at her with mild curiosity. 'Haven't I seen you in my mother's shop?'

It might have been a reference to her schoolgirl Saturday shifts, but she told him how she'd helped while Nora was off this summer, in exchange for staying temporarily in his brother's flat, an arrangement that Ben seemed happy to extend.

'He's up on the top floor now, she remarked. 'Guess what. Putting together an art installation!'

Tony shifted uneasily like a fugitive hearing the sound of hounds baying in the distance.

'Ben? In the building? I didn't reckon he'd set foot in the place. He was dead against the whole idea.'

'Oh he's really going with the spirit of the thing now', Madge lied, laughing inwardly. 'You must go and see what he's doing.'

The Scroby painting had now been positioned by T.A.T. staff, and Tony dismissed them without proper thanks.

'Is there a cover we can put over it until the opening ceremony?' he asked anxiously.

Considering the borrowed work was the prestigious jewel of the art fair, the world famous artist himself would be gracing the opening ceremony, and its generous loan from Grashes Bank reflected well on his employer, this seemed an odd request.

'To minimise the chance of theft. Especially as it hasn't been wired by Security yet', Tony added, sensing her puzzlement. 'It's enormously valuable you know. And, um, probably best if Ben doesn't see it as well. This sort of minimalist stuff annoys him, doesn't it.'

Unlike Tony to be so solicitous of his brother's feelings, thought Madge, going off to retrieve one of the sheets of bubble wrap it'd been packed in.

Arabella had spent the past hour entertaining a couple of representatives from the Lottery Fund, ensuring they departed for a well-earned lunch, satisfied that their money had been spent in a good cause. Now she joined Tony, excited as a helium-sniffing parakeet. Her efforts were all coming together. A Lyndon Scroby painting worth millions, was actually here in Rundleston!

'That's so powerful!' she exclaimed dramatically, gazing at a psychedelic yellow line intertwined with another the colour of spilled guts. 'You can just feel that tension in the narrative, it's profoundly resonant.'

She was unsure how to treat Tony. On the one hand he was simply Nora Banding's son, but he was also representing Grashes Bank, the art festival's major sponsor.

'Do you know Lyndon Scroby?' she enquired. This satisfied both counts, since if he did, it would give him a chance to talk knowledgeably about the famous man, but otherwise...

'Not personally,' Tony admitted. It seemed safest to stick to the truth in this instance.

'He's my neighbour now, you know. Bought Rundleston House last year.' Arabella looked up at him through her hair, its uncompromising colour in sympathy with the painting.. 'We get on *so* well.'

She might have picked up elements of art jargon, but she stood no chance at name dropping.

'Rundleston is becoming quite sophisticated isn't it', he observed casually. 'A friend of mine, Oliver Rabson's daughter, asked my advice before she came here to set up a gallery.'

'Oliver Rabson's daughter! Here, in Rundleston?' exclaimed Arabella, just as Madge returned with the sheet of bubblewrap.

'Oh didn't you know?' Tony rubbed in his victory. 'Yes, she's turning the old greengrocers into a gallery. Staying at Chandlers. I assumed you'd be asking her to the opening party.'

'But how extraordinary', Arabella was trying to take all this in. 'It's Gaye Rabson who's our event organiser. In fact I'm expecting her to arrive any moment. Would that be her mother?'

To Gaye Rabson the opening party of an art festival in some hick East Anglian town was a commission not even worth considering. Normally. But the Tomorrow's Art Today consortium had some important clients amongst its member galleries, and it wouldn't do to let someone else get a foot in their doors. Also Grashes Bank were a major sponsor, and for some time she'd been frustrated in her efforts to get the contract for their lavish client receptions. Most of them came under the aegis of the director who oversaw the bank's art collection, Bruce Spatchland, and he favoured another event organiser. His sister-in-law, coincidentally. But rumour had it that he was about to retire, so this would be an opportunity to put on a good show and find out who was likely to succeed as art curator. With luck whoever it was would be at the art festival's opening party, and a little schmoozing could be productive. Plus there would surely be an opportunity to mend fences with Natasha.

Why had Rab sent their daughter to Rundleston of all obscure places? Gaye now regretted engineering a rapprochement between the two of them. The idea had been for Rab to take Natasha off her hands financially, give her plenty of useful contacts among the super-rich and, especially, to act as a distraction, dissuading her from setting off round the world with Charles. Gaye had long suspected he was into drugs, and foresaw her beautiful daughter returning hooked. Charles was no longer in the frame, so that was good, but clearly Rab had been exerting his influence, poisoning relations between mother and daughter. In her mind she was the noble mother figure, selflessly bringing up her daughter alone, only to have her alienated once the hard work was done. Trust him to make a fuss of Natasha now she was a business asset, Gaye thought angrily. He never took any notice of her as a child.

So determination to visit and counter Rab's influence with Natasha was added to business reasons for accepting the art festival party commission. Against it was one very big one. Rundleston was where Ben Banding apparently still lived. Indeed, unbelievably, his mother was Natasha's landlady. He would have got on with his life, as she had hers. Nevertheless, best avoided. Weighing things up, Gaye finally decided to take on the job and just make sure she didn't come face to face with him. It wouldn't be difficult, she thought as she researched where to stay and decided on a country house hotel just outside the town. Her staff would be doing most of the work, and with a bit of luck he wouldn't even know she was involved.

Organising such events was pretty routine and, once accepted and planned, the art festival commission caused no worry. But if it was to go well the premises needed to be checked out, now that building work was complete, and she decided to go down a couple of days before.

Seeing the small town for herself was strange. Ben had described it with such affection, but somehow she'd pictured it more village-like. Unmistakable though was his family house on the High Street, with the shop. Next to it two workmen were erecting a dark green awning. 'Rabson' she read, and nearly drove the Maserati into a van ahead. So that was Rab's new gallery, the task he'd set Natasha. She'd just walk in and surprise her, thought Gaye, after finishing at the art festival building.

The maltings too was not as she'd imagined. Although Ben had spoken about it with pride, she hadn't realised how large it was, and what a fine building. But when she went in, it was to encounter only workmen, contractors and cleaning staff.

A man in a brown overall, lugging what looked like a six foot tin of sardines, paused at the sight of an immaculately made-up blonde wearing a chrome yellow jacket, figure-hugging black trousers and mirrored sun glasses, carrying a laptop. Not from round about, he astutely surmised. 'Boss lady's up on the first floor', he informed her.

Gaye made her way up there, high heels leaving little dents in the pine stairs. All was shiny and fresh, from varnished doors to the recently-plastered walls and dark blue banister rail. Numerous grey-painted cast-iron columns marched the length of the building, each with clusters of spotlights, like blackfly on plant stalks. Mellow brickwork arches gladdened the eye, and everywhere was the smell of newness. A large crate of multi-coloured milk bottles and a plastic sheep on a treadmill had been unpacked, but most of the exhibits were still in their protective packaging, or being brought in. Drawn by voices, at the far end of the first floor she approached a tall redhead, a small, plump woman with a purple sweep of hair, and a man who, as she grew closer, looked rather like Ben. Too late to retreat, they'd seen her. No, it wasn't Ben she realised with relief, yet she recognised this man from somewhere.

Arabella Drail introduced herself and the freckle-faced publicity woman, who was staring, obviously impressed.

'And Tony Banding. He's just brought this Lyndon Scroby from London, on loan from Grashes Bank.'

Well, well. So this was Ben's brother, the likeness made sense now. And he worked for Grashes did he. Bound to have the low down on who was taking over as curator. Attractive too.

She summed him up with a connoisseur's cool appreciation, remembering now where she'd encountered that fascinated look before. Hmm. Useful.

'We need to talk about arrangements for the opening party', she addressed Arabella, getting down to business. 'I'd like to see the kitchen facilities for a start.'

Tony reckoned he would just have time to call in to Natasha's gallery while the security people were wiring up the antitheft devices on Grashes' painting. His instructions were not to leave the Scroby until the job was complete, but he was expediently taking that to mean leaving the town, not the building. He pictured Natasha all of a flap, arranging her gallery wares, and delighted to accept advice from him. The humiliation over the toys, which he still cringed to think about, was far enough in the past now for her to have forgotten about it, he judged. Time to renew his campaign to join the Rabson empire.

He popped into the shop first, to say hello to Nora and make sure she knew who Grashes had entrusted with escorting their prized painting. Her younger son, the one with the starry career. Then he left, citing pressure of time, walked round the back of the newly declared Rabson's Gallery, and called through the open door, anticipating giving its young proprietor the benefit of his knowledgeable opinion on which works should be grouped together.

'I've come to see if I can help', he informed Natasha genially, after explaining why he was briefly in Rundleston.

'Wonderful. And just at the right time', she smiled at him gratefully. 'The dustmen will be coming any minute, and I meant to get the cardboard packaging put out for them. It's mostly in the store rooms upstairs, and some in the outhouse. Could you very kindly collect it all and tie it up in bundles. Thank you, that'd be really useful.'

Thus it was that a few minutes later, approaching the gallery now bearing her name, Gaye came upon Tony stacking large bundles of cardboard against the big bay tree containers on the pavement outside.

'Well, you do get about', she observed languidly, studying him over her sunglasses. 'Is Natasha around?'

Seeing mother and daughter together was like a 'before' and 'after' advertisement for some revolutionary cosmetic cream. Except that their differences were accentuated by Natasha in jeans and T-shirt, with unadorned face and tousled hair, while at a guess the price of Gaye's outfit would have purchased several of the prints in the gallery, not to mention the cost of her make-up and sleek, tinted hairdo. But Natasha's face was smiley with a childlike sweetness, while there was a knowing, determined air about the older woman. Others might have been wary of the discontented mouth, but Tony saw only a desirably sophisticated woman who still had the kind of beauty to cause any man pleasurable imaginings.

After surprised greetings, Natasha took her mother to see all she'd been doing, leaving Tony to finish putting out the rubbish, somewhat put out himself. This attempt at increasing his chances with Natasha was now clearly stymied. On the other hand, he thought, hefting the last bundle of cardboard, this could be a heaven-sent chance to get in with Gaye Rabson. Who knew what sort of art world and social doors that might open, as well as maybe helping his designs on Natasha? She might also have useful details on the opening ceremony, to be attended by the frog-phobic Lyndon Scroby. Unfortunately time was not on his side.

'I'd better go', he declared unwillingly, as they all stood chatting in the gallery, tour of the premises over.

'That's a pity', Gaye fixed her attention on him. 'I was wondering if you'd be kind enough to show me where this hotel is that I'm booked into for the party night. My sat nav seems to have broken', she added blandly.

He explained about having come down in the security van, which would be returning shortly.

'That's no problem. Is it.' She swung her sunglasses slowly. 'Why don't you show me, and then I'll give you a lift back to London. The maltings used to belong to your family I believe. I'd like to hear all about it.'

Her large grey eyes gazed into Tony's for just that bit too long, the beginnings of a sultry smile curving her glossy lips. She might as well have fired a ray gun.

Tony felt the breath go out of him. Christ almighty! This stunning woman, Oliver Rabson's ex, no less, was giving him the come on.

'Er, yes.. perhaps I could arrange...'

'Well that's settled then', she interrupted smoothly. 'As soon as you've got things sorted, we'll go and suss out this place and sample a bit of lunch.'

Natasha viewed the performance with weary disapproval. Why must her mother regard the opposite sex as a challenge. It was as if she needed to prove she could have any man. Then she just played with them, in all senses, and discarded the poor saps as soon as she had another target lined up. Why couldn't men see it?

Well, doubtless Tony could look after himself, she reflected, waving as the Maserati roared off down the street a short while later. Unlike poor Ben, who still seemed imprisoned by worship of the girl he fell in love with when young. Let's hope he doesn't discover this angel is busy seducing his brother, thought Natasha, going back to arranging a group of cushions made to look like giant eyes. Not that Tony seemed likely to need much encouragement. She smiled to herself, then paused, cushion in hand. Hang on. This might be just the jolt Ben needed. Maybe he should be told, and she could make sure he and Gaye met in the next few days. Perhaps that would finally break the spell she seemed to have cast on him, and set the poor man free.

In the run up to the art festival, Madge had found herself relying more and more on friends to look after Jamie, now that school had broken up. Sometimes he came to the maltings with her, but generally he found it boring as she sent out press packs, liaised with the tourist authority, and fielded calls from the local media, as well as all the unscheduled things Arabella asked her to do. Natasha kindly co-opted him into helping unpack the stock for her gallery, and paid him into the bargain. Nora let him serve in the shop a couple of mornings, and kept an eye on him if he was in the flat on his own. He hung around the boat yard with Stephen, who was mending, under Flitch's supervision, an old abandoned dinghy. And Ben took him sailing, which Jamie adored, and gave him drawing lessons, taking pleasure in passing on skills that were second nature to him. The unhappiness that had given her son that distressingly closed look was now in the past, and he talked enthusiastically about the school football team and maybe getting a sailing dinghy of his own. With the art festival almost here, it was also fun that both mother and son were involved, as Jamie joined in making the booth for the human fruit machine, which he would help to man, and laid out the GARBAGE art work.

After the Lyndon Scroby had been safely installed and she had a few moments to herself, Madge went up to the top floor to see how this great work was coming on. There was a mixture of attitudes amongst those setting up their exhibits, ranging from earnest dedication to light-hearted irony, but even those doing it tongue-in-cheek were getting into the swing of things now and enjoying themselves, and there was happy chattering and laughter. In the last couple of weeks Nora had been doing a roaring trade in plasticine, sticky tape, rubber bands and highlighter pens as the citizens of Rundleston put together their offerings to the god of modern art. Ben's framing skills too had been much in demand for those who reckoned art still had to be hung on a wall, even if it was just all one colour, a la Rothko, or dribbled paint in homage to Jackson Pollack. Someone had fashioned a sheet of thin Perspex to resemble a three foot high food tin, but filled it with brown compost in which earthworms could be seen disporting themselves. At least the ones that hadn't found their way out of gaps in the base, and were setting off to explore their new surroundings. 'Can of Worms' was the title. Another exhibit was cotton wool balls threaded together to form a giant exclamation mark. 'It's All Balls', the card above it undeniably proclaimed. Grey-painted, wooden plinths had been erected in rows for the smaller exhibits, and on the nearest ones plasticine animals, a bandaged doll, some unidentifiable creature made of toilet roll centres, and works featuring cling film, egg boxes and CDs were taking shape.

Arabella had allocated quite a big space against the end wall for Ben's effort, the arched windows above suitably looking out over the estuary. Madge knew what she was seeing was just a pile of jetsam collected from Woodshey Bay, yet she had to admit that, even not quite finished, it was impressive. Despite it being mocking, Ben's artistic instincts clearly wouldn't be denied. Bodger was sitting on a corner of the base mat, as if part of the artwork, being petted and spoken to by everyone who passed.

Jamie explained that the notice proclaiming 'Plot 93' was an estate agent's sign that must have fallen in the river, and showed her the small crab discovered, incredibly still alive, in a rusty tin.

'We've called him Christopher', he informed her animatedly. 'We're going to put him back in the water this afternoon. And how many plastic bottles do you think we found in those sacks? Seventy-eight!' He rejoined Stephen in their task of painting the letters proclaiming the work to be Getting Around Reality By Almost Glimpsing Eternity. Engaged in fluffing out a rope end, Ben winked at the boy's mother.

'Arabella will love this', she assured him, adding quietly, 'and thank you for being so good to Jamie. I don't think I've said that enough this past week or so.'

'Pleasure'. He clearly meant it too, intensifying the heartache she was trying so hard to suppress.

'Your brother's been here this morning', she informed him. 'I suggested he should come up and see what you were doing, but he didn't have time. Gone back to London now.'

'Tony? Here? And I missed him!' He put on a stricken expression, hand to heart, and Madge smiled.

'He was escorting the Lyndon Scroby painting. Asked me to cover it up so you wouldn't see it.' She laughed. 'I think he was afraid you'd throw a strop.'

'Let's have a butchers at it then. I could do with a bit of amusement.' He put down the rope. 'Back in a minute, fellers.'

They made their way down to the first floor, Bodger behind them finding the polished stairs difficult to negotiate.

'I can feel a tantrum coming on', he warned her jovially, as they stood in front of the tray-sized object, shrouded in bubblewrap, the pride of Grashes' art collection. 'Scroby's stuff is so mind-bogglingly awful. Just the pits.'

'Mustn't touch the painting – about five dozen alarms will go off.' Gingerly she reached up to grasp the cover. 'Ready? And 'ere we 'ave', Madge proclaimed in a cod French accent, whipping off the bubblewrap dramatically, 'Voila! Le masterpiece!

You have to guess what it's called.'

He was standing still in horror, as if staring at a cobra poised to strike.

'Bloody hell!'

'Nice try. But the title is actually Transformation.' She added mockingly, 'Worth several million apparently.'

'No. No it isn't.' Ben's voice was almost inaudible. He turned to her desperately. 'Madge, I painted that!'

Chapter Sixteen

What did the gods have against him? That was the question that churned round Ben's brain as he did a stint in the shop later that day. His special talent was rubbished by an uncaring world, the only girl he'd ever loved had been stolen by a rich and influential man, along with his daughter, who'd now been ordered not to hang the paintings he'd done for her with such devotion. And he could shortly expect to be arrested for fraud. Great. Just great.

There seemed no way out either. If he explained how he'd painted the lookalike Scroby in complete innocence it made things worse for Tony, and for all their lack of affection, family loyalty forbade that. It would hurt Nora too, for her sons to be actively fighting. She would feel the disgrace deeply as it was.

He must have a poisoned touch, he concluded morosely, punching the till keys with unnecessary force. Poor Madge had been dragged into it now as well. Why hadn't he kept his big mouth shut?

Wait a minute. There was something positive to be done, and he grasped at it. Tell Madge she must, for her own sake, forget what happened, and pretend she had absolutely no reason to doubt the Scroby's validity. Keep her well out of it. He must emphasise that as soon as possible too, he realised, before she let on to Arabella or anyone else.

He could hardly wait to shut up shop now that he had at least some action in mind. He went straight to the boatyard seeking Tricia's permission to invite a friend for a meal in the Hetty Jane's saloon. A few minutes later he was knocking on the door of the ground floor flat to ask Madge round for supper that evening.

'I'm sure Nora would keep an eye on Jamie', he suggested.

'Well actually I was just about to take him to football practice. Tricia could collect him though, and I'll see if she'll have him afterwards.'

'Ben's invited me for a Chinese', she said on the phone a few minutes later, by way of explanation.

'You're wasting your time there, girl', was Tricia's sceptical response, after agreeing to the arrangement. 'Told you, he's got the hots for that Natasha.'

'No it's not like that at all', Madge insisted. 'We just have to talk about something.'

And indeed his effect on her emotions needed to be put aside in the light of the day's news. Madge had been turning things over in her mind all afternoon, and had come to conclusions she was anxious to share. For his part Ben felt relief at the prospect of talking to someone about the whole bizarre situation. And there couldn't be anyone better, he realised, waiting in the Chinese takeaway. Madge was so intelligent and level-headed, and she knew the family well.

The last time she'd been in the Hetty Jane's saloon, it had been crowded with people enjoying a birthday celebration. Now as Madge climbed carefully down the steep steps the

231

space seemed cavernous. A faint smell of wet mud wafted in from the estuary, combining interestingly with the appetising aroma of Chinese food from the containers Ben was placing on the long central table. Submitting to an enthusiastic greeting from Bodger, she put her bag and jersey on the bench.

While she got plates and cutlery from the galley and he opened a bottle of wine, Ben related in more detail how he and Tony had disagreed about the lack of skill in contemporary art, and he'd clinched the argument by producing the imitation Scroby that had now turned up as Transformation.

'Do you suppose Tony set out to get something he could pass off as an authentic artwork?' he asked, pouring the wine. 'I keep thinking about it.'

'Does it really matter whether it was deliberate or he just succumbed to the temptation afterwards?' she responded diplomatically. No point in exacerbating family warfare. 'Let's just deal with the situation as is.'

'Two minutes it took. Two bloody minutes!' Prising off the lids he shook his head in disbelief at the consequences. 'He's dumped me in it good and proper.'

'Us', corrected Madge, as Ben began doling rice onto the plates. 'Now Rundleston's art festival has a fake as its prize exhibit. And I'm helping to promote the whole shebang, Lyndon Scroby painting and all. We've sent out loads of press releases about it.'

'No. I mean yes, you're right. But that's just what I wanted to talk about. It's really important to me that you don't get dragged into this. You've got to promise to forget what I said about producing it. You haven't told Arabella, have you?'

'Of course not.'

'No-one saw us talking by it, so you can just pretend you didn't know. Please.' He waved the serving spoon. 'I can't have you on my conscience as well.'

'Food's getting cold', she pointed out good humouredly. 'Look, I've been trying to analyse the situation. The public aren't going to notice anything wrong are they? And Grashe's are obviously happy to own a two-minute daub, with no plans to sell it.'

'So?'

'Well the only person who'll know the truth as soon as he claps eyes on it is the illustrious artist himself.'

'But Scroby's opening the damn festival, he's bound to be taken round', objected Ben. 'Arabella must have got that all planned.'

Madge looked innocent. 'Plans can go wrong, can't they.'

They spent the next hour, friends and conspirators, discussing tactics and possible diversions while they ate, and by the end Ben's mood had lifted. There was still little chance of escaping jail for fraud, but he'd made Madge promise to pretend she knew nothing, for Jamie's sake as well as her own, so that was one burden of guilt eased away. She'd given him hope too, and they'd even managed to joke about the situation. Her loyalty and help, in contrast to how his own brother had behaved was stark.

In the galley she dried the dishes while he washed up

'You could sell your services for settling wars, you know', he looked at her playfully over his shoulder. 'Have you thought of that?'

'Probably end up getting shot at by both sides', she batted back, resisting the urge to reach out and caress his face. And worse. The evening's easy intimacy and Ben's tantalising nearness were not helping the intensity of her feelings for him. How could he not be aware of it? Telepathy was bunk. Probably just as well. He'd recoil in embarrassment and the relationship they did have would be ruined.

As she waited on deck while he locked up, an onshore breeze felt cool on her face, the low sun reflecting richly on the water. An aeroplane sparked purposefully across the darkening sky like a firefly, and the incoming tide had taken the Hetty Jane in its arms, causing the gentlest of motions.

It'd be such a wrench to leave this lovely place, she thought, leaning on the guard rail, but perhaps it would be for the best. She couldn't keep on pretending she didn't love him, and the illness wasn't going to get better, seeing him every day. She had carefully not mentioned Gaye's visit, but the sight of his icon today had come as a surprise. How could he still be in thrall to that creature? Madge wondered now. Beautiful, yes, but so hard. It was as if the young Ben had been imprinted with her image, like a gosling following its human carer devotedly. Imprinting defied all logic too, so he'd never be cured.

'I'll walk with you as far as Chandlers, after you've collected Jamie from Tricia's', Ben said, joining her. 'Bodger needs his evening constitutional. Thank you for your wonderful support, I really appreciate it. You're so steady and sensible. Just what I needed.'

She smiled in response, but inside it hurt. That's all I am to him, she thought sadly. Good old Madge.

Arabella Drail couldn't get over her luck in discovering that a member of Oliver Rabson's family was opening a gallery in Rundleston. Unfortunate to learn it only at the last minute of course, too late to link it in with much of the festival's publicity, but it was surely an excellent thing for the town.

She approached the old greengrocer's shop with anticipation. That it was being renovated had certainly been noticed, but she hadn't questioned what kind of business was coming. Now, sure enough, there were new awnings above the windows with the word Rabson's emblazoned across them in gold. Rabson! A revered name in the modern art world, together with Charles Saatchi. She pictured his daughter as a way out individual with rings in her nose, or perhaps uptight and spectacled, every inch the businesswoman. Instead the door was opened by a beautiful, fresh-faced young girl in jeans and T-shirt, honey-coloured hair untidily styled.

Arabella introduced herself. Needlessly, since Natasha had enjoyed Madge's many amusing stories about the art festival's doyenne, complete with a take-off of her voice and mannerisms. Here on the doorstep was a bustling little woman in an aubergine-coloured skirt, orange blouse and black and white checked poncho, heavy gold earrings and a sweep of Mary Quant style purple hair. It could be no other.

Politely, Natasha showed her the gallery, which was now just about ready, almost all the stock having been unpacked and displayed. It had been decided there should be nothing extreme, mostly prints, with the odd piece of sculpture, if that was the appropriate word for a cat's claw sharpener made of spiral rope decorated with dead bumble bees, and a collection of multicoloured nails glued together.

'It's so important to celebrate the visual vernacular', Arabella commented knowledgably, her poncho catching on one of the protruding nails and almost pulling the edifice off the table. 'Oh isn't that a Tootsie Smalt!' she exclaimed, pointing to a print of red and yellow splodges. 'It pulls you into the present moment, there's such a symbiotic relationship between the images and the metaphorical spaces.'

Where did she learn all this guff, wondered Natasha, kindly refraining from telling her it was actually a Morwenna Lipping reproduction.

In a side room were six small figurative paintings, which Natasha Rabson was clearly in the process of hanging. They didn't fit somehow with the gallery's ambience, but Arabella was too eager to get her message across to ask about them.

'Now you *will* come to the festival's opening party, won't you', she turned to the girl. 'I'm only sorry we didn't know you were here before now.'

'Well, the thing is my father will be here to open the gallery, and I'm not sure what his plans...'

'Your father? Oliver Rabson! Oh, but will he not come as well. We would be *honoured* for him to attend.' Arabella laid on the event's attractions. 'Lyndon Scroby's asked lots of his friends – he's combining it with a house-warming that evening, so they're all going to stay with him for the weekend. Many of them are artists your father made famous. I do hope he'll join us in celebrating our little art festival.'

The promise to attend his daughter's gallery opening was not at the forefront of Oliver Rabson's mind. Abandoning guests, he'd abruptly left the yacht in Cannes, and flown to New York, to talk to a Wall Street banker who'd enquired if Rab would be willing to buy back a recently-acquired Lyndon Scroby artwork. Such a request was unprecedented. The movers and shakers that Rab 'allowed' to buy the art he was de-accessioning did so precisely to demonstrate how wealthy they were, and that they hobnobbed with high profile kings of the art world like him. The bigger the price and the more newsworthy and desirable the object, the more willing they were to buy. Some were astute enough to sell on quietly, or they gave the things to their national museums thus gaining a philanthropic reputation and the all-important tax breaks. What they did not do was intimate the purchase was something they now rather regretted and could ill afford. And this guy was hinting at a cashflow problem. Short term of course. But could Rab perhaps see his way to taking the work back?

It was antennae for money-making business opportunities that had propelled an otherwise unremarkable schoolboy to youthful millionaire. Now that same instinct was giving out warning signals. He'd been observing share prices this summer with unease, as mineral and metal commodities joined in a hectic upward spiral. It was reminiscent of the dot com boom, in which he'd burned his fingers. And here was just a hint, from one of its big players, that all was not well on Wall Street. Time to investigate, to make use of his personal connections and act accordingly.

The reminder from Pauline about his agreement to open the gallery came the same day as a light-hearted email from Natasha, conveying this fantastic opportunity to party the night away in Rundleston.

Unfortunately the trip to America meant he would now have to cry off the gallery opening. It was clearly less important, and Pauline was asked to give his apologies in person. He'd send an email and Natasha would understand.

'She'll be *very* disappointed', Pauline told him, her how-could-you-do-that? tone unmistakable down the phone, and he imagined his daughter's appealing, childlike face, her grey eyes gazing at him reproachfully. He'd asked her to set up this gallery, and made a promise that he would open it. What if she turned to Gaye instead for parental support? That did it. Pauline was right. He would come back specially.

One of the many advantages of being able to fly around the world in your own private jet, was that it gave you thinking time without distraction. As his Citation Ten cruised smoothly through the air, Rab reflected on what he'd gleaned so far from his American contacts. Everything – art, property, shares – apparently roaring ahead. So far, so reassuring. Yet that banker's request, the snapping twig in the distance, was troubling. For some time it had seemed to Rab that the art market had gone into a hype-driven spin. It was just too easy now to persuade the super rich to part with megabucks for, well just about anything, as long as it had the right name attached. The situation reminded him of a whirlpool – as a child he'd been fascinated by the bath water as it gathered into a swirl, faster and faster, until...

If the art market was about to go down the plug hole, well he'd had a damned good run. And, he reflected, perhaps it was time for a change of direction anyway. He could

237

concentrate more on launching the Rabson brand. That was going to be big. He gazed out of the window at the cloud beneath, so substantial looking when actually it was just vapour.

He'd deflected the banker's request to take back the Scroby, pulling on all the strings that worked with his sort. The best contemporary art was a fantastic investment which could only soar in value, he'd been assured. Rab laid on the flattery. Precisely because he'd appreciate it and knew a good deal when he saw one, he'd been chosen out of the many people who would have loved to buy the artwork. Owning a Scroby was a privilege few could aspire to, and would increase the confidence people had in its owner's standing. But, should the banker still decide to sell, Rab had offered to whip up some extra publicity about the artist. Get him and his work talked about in the press even more than usual, ensuring the maximum price for any Scroby put up for sale. That would give a very nice profit. Far better than simply passing it back to Rab.

Dammit he'd almost persuaded himself, he thought now, wryly. Have to watch that.

The idea of attending Rundleston's art festival party had at first seemed simply risible. But in the light of his offer to the banker, he decided it could just be helpful for publicity. Apparently, Lyndon Scroby had been roping in various stars of the art world for that and a house-warming party in the evening, to which Rab had been invited, although he hadn't intended going. And this was August, when nothing much happened, and editors struggled to fill their pages. They would be sending their art correspondents, or the ones not on holiday at any rate, and Rab's PR guru would be asked to do his stuff. A story about Oliver Rabson gracing some out of town art festival and partying with some of the big names of the art world could be useful. He would make sure that Lyndon Scroby was talked about, and it wouldn't be entirely for the American's benefit either. A couple of his own

Scroby's, and at least half of his collection, he decided, would now be finding their way quietly to grateful buyers, while the price was still buoyant. In a recession, cash is king.

Another good thing to be said for attending the art festival lunch occurred to Rab as he was being driven back to Berkeley Square from the airport. With art correspondents homing in on Rundleston, Natasha's gallery there was hardly going to go unnoticed. If there was nothing much else to say there'd be a temptation to regurgitate all that stuff about her getting mixed up in a drugs scandal. But with the emphasis on the art festival and its party, Natasha's gallery would be likely to go unremarked, or mentioned only in passing.

On arrival, he told Pauline of his decision.

'That place outside Rundleston, where I took Natasha for a meal – book me a room, will you. And tell her to accept the art festival invitation on my behalf.'

Tony's ego, never weighed down by self-doubt, was now on course for the stratosphere. Gaye Rabson had clearly fallen for him from the moment they met. And Gaye was a beautiful and sophisticated woman, who could have had her pick of the main players on London's social scene. Some would have said she already had, but Tony took the fact that she seemed to know everyone as a reflected compliment. It appealed to his vanity that she was on friendly terms with all these rich and influential people, yet she preferred his company. Clearly she didn't just regard him as a stud either, although he congratulated himself that she certainly hadn't been disappointed there. She was interested in him, wanting to know about his life and role at Grashes. He told her about his enthusiasm for contemporary art, and that he was in line to be curator of the bank's collection as soon as Bruce Spatchland retired. She seemed impressed, and asked how he had come to know Natasha.

'When I found she was starting up a gallery in Rundleston, of course I offered my advice, it being my home town', he told her, neglecting to mention that she was staying in his family's bed and breakfast premises. Such a mundane background would have trouble competing with a prestigious Richmond house and the sort of sophisticated lifestyle that Gaye clearly enjoyed.

Tony had never been in a relationship with an older woman before, it had always been he who splashed the cash, showing off to impress younger girls. Now it was his turn to be taken into a world previously only glimpsed with envy. The pursuit of Natasha could wait for the moment, he decided, basking in the glory of having a beautiful, worldly-wise woman demanding his attentions.

But although he tried not to think about it, he was uneasily aware that everything could all come crashing down, career, money and now high profile partner, if he was denounced as a forger in a few days' time.

Tony's idea of releasing frogs at the opening ceremony to put the wind up Lyndon Scroby and deter him from viewing Grashes' painting, seemed a great idea, but acting on it had proved far from simple in reality. He'd thought it would be easy to import a load of the things from France, but discovered that those intended for Gallic diners were almost all bred in the Far East, and imported frozen. Our native variety flourished in the countryside of course, but although he briefly considered a frog-hunting sortie, common sense soon dismissed the notion. How would you set about finding the sodding things, let alone catching them? And he'd need lots.

Research on the internet had offered a glimmer of hope, however. An entrepreneur in America was selling all the equipment required to set up a frog farm. Tony expressed interest, hoping merely to import the livestock, but soon realised he would have to pretend to be going in for it seriously, and buy cages, feeding machines, pellets, the whole paraphernalia. It was going to cost. But not compared to what he stood to lose if Lyndon Scroby clapped eyes on that lousy artwork.

The whole expensive consignment had duly been shipped, and arrived a few days before the art festival's opening ceremony. Keeping up the frog-farming story, Tony bribed a reptile fancying trader at the bank to take delivery and look after the loathsome creatures for the intervening days, at his place in Essex. Now all that was needed was to hire a van and... well actually he wasn't sure quite what he was going to do. Play it by ear was the answer. He would succeed, he thought to himself, self-regard overcoming unease. Tony Banding always did. Failure wasn't an option.

An apprehensive Ben was grateful for the distraction offered by constructing the booth for the Human Fruit Machine. One of Nora's friends had donated a square canvas tent that must once have been smart, proudly erected on camp sites. But in the intervening years it had lain folded up in a shed, dusty and unused except by some large black spiders and trundles of woodlice. Gingerly, he and Danny put it up in the boatyard, in the process evicting its indignant inhabitants, who then suffered the additional trauma of being delightedly pursued by a large, hairy canine. Once erected, the tent immediately proved irresistible to Stephen, Jamie and a couple of friends, who saw it as ideal for war games.

'You guys can make yourselves useful', Ben told them, ignoring what were evidently assault rifles poking out of the entrance. 'We're going to build a wooden frame, and partitions, but because we can't use tent pegs on the day, the thing'll have to be weighed down. So see how many heavy things you can collect – stones, old bolts, bits of chain... And then it'll need painting, jazzing up a bit. Any volunteers?'

He and Danny worked well together. Though a nerdy oddity, as a boat bum and sort-of electrician, the lanky American had a practical side, while Ben's labouring experience when converting Chandlers into flats had given him confidence in construction skills. They hoped to have the job completed by late afternoon, when rain was forecast, but the sun was playing 'come and find me' with the breeze, and every time it disappeared behind a cloud powerful gusts threatened the tent.

'Man, whose crazy idea was this?' was Danny's muffled complaint, as it partially collapsed with him inside.

Coming to the boatyard in search of Jamie at teatime, Madge admired their progress. A window had been cut in one side, and the wooden struts were in place, and sheets of hardboard were being nailed to the front part, creating separate compartments, so that the three occupants couldn't see what fruit the others were choosing. Ben explained how it was ostensibly an artwork, to get round any objections about gambling, especially with Stephen and Jamie helping. They and Danny would be holding up the pieces of fruit, while Ben was out front, exhorting the public to spend their money and try their luck in getting three matching fruits in a row.

'You do realise that'll disqualify your GARBAGE entry from the art festival competition', Madge warned him. 'The rules state that contenders can only be involved in one artwork.'

'But this is going to be out in the square, it's not part of the competition', he objected.

'Doesn't matter. Arabella's already threatened to disqualify someone else who was planning an 'event' in the town.'

'Who was that?'

'The old boy who runs the junk stall in the market. He was going to deck out a mobility scooter as a boat and 'row' round the town dressed as a pirate, treasure chest and all.

242

'With a parrot, and going "Ho, Ho, Ho and a bottle of rum", I hope.'

She smiled. 'Probably.'

So that was that. It looked as if he would have to ditch The Grange's fund-raising effort, Ben concluded, because he certainly wasn't going to give up on GARBAGE. Making the art establishment look foolish was too dear to his heart, all the more now that his two-minute 'Scroby' was apparently worth millions. But Nora would be disappointed, The Grange was her pet charity. Ben conveyed the bad news, but undaunted she had a constructive suggestion.

'If you wear some kind of disguise, no-one will know it's you, will they. Actually a colourful character is much more likely to attract public attention. And money.'

Well perhaps I could wear a mask or something', he conceded. 'Although young children find them frightening. I know I always did.'

'There are all those animal costumes out in the...'

'No. Absolutely not', her son told her categorically. But lying on his bunk that night, unable to sleep, he imagined how the art festival opening was going to go, and the disastrous consequences for him. There was only a slim chance of Lyndon Scroby being distracted by the various schemes he and Madge had hopefully outlined. No, he must be prepared for the painting to be declared a fake in the full glare of publicity. There would be an investigation, with the trail leading straight to him, via Tony. He would be charged with forgery and tried. And all the newspapers would carry pictures of him. The local paper would be happy to provide them from among its many art festival images. There he'd be, Ben Banding, forger, soliciting money from the public for gambling purposes. Faced with this unwelcome scenario, Nora's idea of the animal costumes began to take on a certain merit.

First thing next morning he unlocked the garage and investigated the Rundleston Players' props at the back, together with costumes in a mound of black plastic bags. Nora had been soft to say no about storing them, typically. Each sack was labelled with the name of the production, and some also had details of the character costumes inside. Several were labelled 'Jack and the Beanstalk'. A pity the pantomime hadn't been Dick Whittington last time, he thought, the cat costume would have carried a certain elan. 'Private Lives' – they were useless. Ah yes, 'Reginald Rabbit and the Woodlanders'. He remembered Nora slaving over the outfits. 'So many of them', she'd complained, 'I don't think Arabella gave a thought to the costumes, just the number of people she could cram into the production. Mice, squirrels, weasels – how am I going to make a weasel look like a weasel and not a rat, for heaven's sake?'

Clearly the mice costumes had been worn by children, so they were no good. But what about a squirrel? No, too small.

He opened the bag labelled 'Reginald Rabbit' and Bodger pushed his nose in interestedly. Ben pulled out a light brown, man-sized furry costume with a concealed zip up the back, ending in a large fluffy white tail, which Bodger clearly found fascinating. 'Leave it', Ben told him, reaching for the creature's head at the bottom of the bag. Prominent front teeth, long ears, one with a bend halfway giving the creature a quizzical air. Unmistakably a rabbit. Attention grabbing, unthreatening to small children – and wonderfully anonymous.

'How would you feel about being owned by a giant rabbit', Ben enquired of the dog, putting the costume over his arm and shutting the garage door. 'Be fitting revenge for all the small furry creatures you've chased over the years.'

Nora was feeling decidedly schizophrenic about the art festival, now that it was upon them. She tried to imagine how things would be if, as she'd intended, the occasion was a celebration of what she still insisted on calling 'proper art'. The trouble was she had to admit that the buzz and trade the town was currently enjoying would probably have been less. The shop was satisfactorily busy, she could have let her rooms several times over, had they not already been occupied, and those she knew who also offered accommodation were experiencing the same demand. Pauline recounted with amusement how she'd had to ensure the Jahneys suddenly 'found' a room for her employer, when they'd at first stated they were fully booked. Only the commercially illiterate would turn down the opportunity of having someone like Oliver Rabson staying.

'It's one of the reasons the rich and famous have a different take on the world from us ordinary mortals', she remarked dryly to Nora. 'Everyone falls over themselves to be obliging.'

She'd arrived on the Wednesday evening, with the idea of offering any help and support that might be needed before the gallery opening on Friday. Natasha was delighted to see her, and like an eager child wanted to grab her by the hand and show her immediately everything that had been done since her last visit.

'I'll admire it all tomorrow, in full daylight', Pauline said firmly. 'Then I'll see it with a customer's eye. Your father's instructed me to take you out for a good dinner – he thinks you don't eat properly, so there's a table booked for us at The Dutch House. I managed to get him a room there, so we'll go and inspect it, shall we.'

Natasha liked Peter Jahney, who, as the gallery's landlord, had gone out of his way to be helpful whenever she'd consulted him about improvements to the building. He'd clearly inherited the family's business gene, but had an air of old world courtesy that contributed to the success of the hotel, with himself as mine host, while his hard-working wife Camilla oversaw the catering.

'Would you like to see the room Oliver Rabson will be having?' he asked Pauline when she'd introduced herself, and took them up to a high-ceilinged bedroom looking out over the estuary. The room's proportions were just right for a large four-poster bed with red and gold brocade curtains, placed so that its incumbent could lie, propped up on pillows, admiring the view. A red plush-covered rococo style sofa and armchairs clustered round an imposing Victorian fireplace, with ornate mirror above, and the impression was one of lord of the manor opulence coupled with bordello overtones.

'The Americans always coo over it, especially the circular whirlpool bath in the en suite', he remarked proudly, opening the adjoining door to show them. 'It's our best room, and I hope Mr. Rabson will be happy with it.'

'It's fine', Pauline assured him, adding mischievously, 'Who did you have to evict to free it up?'

Peter Jahney smiled, but skirted the pitfall. 'Ah well, people's plans change.'

'There is another Rabson booked in for Friday night', he said carefully, as they went downstairs. 'A Gaye Rabson. Would that be any relation?'

He already knew exactly who Gaye Rabson was, having typed her name into an internet search engine, but it seemed diplomatic to ensure at least one of the ex-partners realised they would be under the same roof.

'That's my mother', confirmed Natasha. 'Holy moly. She said she was staying locally but...' she turned to Pauline anxiously. 'Do you think we should tell Dad?'

'I shouldn't worry', Pauline reassured her. 'Rab's an early riser, and I would guess Gaye is, er, not. So he'll probably have already checked out by the time she comes down to breakfast.' Her eyes twinkled behind her glasses. 'And it's not as if they'll be throwing plates at each other. In any case, it seems they're both going to be at the art festival party.'

Over their meal in the wood-panelled dining room, Pauline encouraged Natasha to talk about all the triumphs and difficulties of getting the gallery up and running, smiling at

246

the girl's youthful enthusiasm. As a plain woman working in a sophisticated art world dominated by buyers who worshipped the twin gods of money and appearance, she'd developed a scepticism towards outward beauty. But you felt Natasha was lovely all through, she reflected. That Gaye and Rab between them should have produced such sweetness was about as likely as discovering a gold torque in a muck heap.

'Have you done anything about finding someone to help you?' she enquired, as their main course arrived. 'You won't want to be tied to the place all day and every day.'

'Well I talked to Dad about that, and he said best to have limited opening hours to begin with, and then see how things were going.'

Knowing that he wanted his daughter back in London, Rab's PA rather thought it'd be the gallery that would be going.

Natasha related how Rab had arrived unexpectedly on his motorbike, Pauline having already heard his version of the day's visit.

'Gave me such a surprise. And he was very pleased with what I'd done', she reported proudly, then her expression clouded. 'Well, not everything. Dad said I wasn't to include Ben's paintings. They were specially commissioned, so that was a real bummer, and I felt bad telling Ben they weren't going to be shown after all. They're just awesome too', her face became animated again. 'Really brilliant. You'll see them tomorrow. Because I've thought about it', she confided, 'and decided to hang them after all'.

Ah, so there was a bit of the old Rabson steel in there. Who'd have guessed. But while Pauline cheered the girl on in spirit, alarm bells began to ring. Standing up to Rab was something she frequently did herself. But she knew where the line was, and you crossed it at your peril.

'Is that wise?'

'It's my gallery isn't it', Natasha defended herself stoutly. 'He said I should use my own taste and initiative.'

'I quite agree that Ben is an outstanding artist', said Pauline lightly. 'But perhaps it might be tactful not to have his work on display when your father comes to open the place on Saturday. You can always put them up after he's gone', she added with a smile.

'What the eye don't see, the heart don't grieve over? You taught me that when I first came to help in Berkeley Square', recalled Natasha warmly. 'But one of the reasons I want to do it is to show Dad I'm not a patsy.' She leant forward earnestly. 'He needs to take me seriously. I'm grown up now, and I know I've got a lot to learn, but my opinions matter. They do to me anyway. And then there's loyalty to Ben – selling those paintings will help his career as well as the business. And the gallery being a success will make Dad see I was right.'

'Hmm.' Pauline had her doubts about that. 'All the same, I don't advise it.'

But Natasha's mind was made up. 'He'll respect me more', she asserted confidently. 'I'm sure of it.'

Next day was the busiest Thursday Madge had ever known. All the entries for the art competition were supposed to have been finished by the previous evening, but inevitably a few people were sneakily making amendments to their efforts. In between incessant phone calls, she had to deal with Gaye Rabson's party staff, who were decking the place out with an underwater theme for the next day's buffet lunch, to which VIPs, selected media representatives, sponsors, local dignitaries and stars of the art world had been invited. Julian Bisk was fussing over the main exhibition pieces, some of which had apparently been damaged either in transit or when they were being set up. Or so he said. Madge didn't see that it mattered for the visual exhibits, since any anomaly would surely be taken as deliberate. But the machine running a film in a loop, featuring a bald man threading laces through his shoes, before tying them, kept breaking down. Also it was proving impossible to adjust the volume on a sound installation, so that every few seconds a female voice rang loudly through the exhibition floor, announcing, '*Cashier Number Five, please*', or '*The train now leaving from Platform Thirteen is the twelve forty-nine for Birmingham New Street, calling at...*'

'How could anyone stand to have that in their own home?' she asked Julian, trying to block out '*You are being held in a queue. Your call is important to us, please wait while we try to connect you.*'

'Well you don't play it. Obviously', he retorted with irritation. 'It's owning the thing that's the privilege. This is a Crispin Rankle. People are falling over themselves to buy his work at the moment. It's shooting up in value.'

Madge would have asked what, if any, meaning the thing was supposed to have, but he'd only tell her it was a 'challenging' piece. At that moment Arabella came down from the top floor in a tizz. Apparently the lights up there, which had been flickering all morning, had now failed completely. It was tempting to enquire facetiously if that wasn't actually one of the artworks, but getting Arabella to see the humorous aspects of contemporary art was a lost cause. Might as well try explaining curtain rails to a goldfish.

'I'll get someone to sort it out, Madge assured her, but the contractors who'd wired the building were based in Worcestershire, and it transpired none of the local firms had an electrician who could come at such short notice. Maybe Danny could fix it – although strictly speaking not qualified. Arabella agreed it was worth a try, but a call to his mobile revealed he was on the Hetty Jane. Of course, he was crewing. Madge should have known, since Jamie was on board too. Flitch and Tricia had kindly allowed him to come along as part of the 'crew' on the barge, which had been hired for a day trip. Her son was thrilled.

'Sure, I'll be there. As soon as we get in', Danny promised obligingly.

Gaye's staff left, their preparation work complete. Arabella went into Ipswich to have her hair done, (*So important to look one's best on the great day*), and Julian departed after altering or mending exhibits to his satisfaction, with the exception of the sound installation's volume, which resisted adjustment and had mercifully been switched off. The phone calls lessened, and Madge found herself alone in the silent building. It was a strange feeling. She ran a finger over an irregular-shaped lump of plastic, imaginatively entitled 'Blob', wondering what her grandfather, and Ben's, would say if they could see the place now. And smiled. Probably be unrepeatable. But the thought of tomorrow was giving her the heebie jeebies, now that she had time to contemplate the likely events. She paused by the supposedly multi-million Lyndon Scroby, and the temptation to set fire to it was strong. One little match would do it... No evidence, no forgery charge for poor Ben. I just *have* to save him, she thought, as the sound of Danny ringing the bell came faintly from the administrator's office. She let him in, carrying his toolkit, and what looked like a lunch box.

'Left over sausages and buns', he explained. 'Trish put them by for me. You don't mind if I eat on the job do you? Got a gig tonight.'

Madge took him up to the top floor, pausing on the way by the errant sound installation. 'Any chance you could work some magic on this as well?' she asked. 'It's sending me up the wall.'

Chapter Seventeen

Nora had cleared the spare room in the expectation that her younger son would want to sleep there after the art festival opening. Especially as he'd apparently been invited to Lyndon Scroby's house warming party that evening. But it appeared he had other plans. Might have to dash back to London, he muttered mysteriously. Probably have something vital on at work next day.

On a Saturday?

Actually Tony wasn't at all sure where he was going to end up that night. If things worked out right, then pleasurably shagging Gaye at The Dutch House, but if they didn't...

He went over in his mind how the event would go. Lyndon Scroby was opening the festival, after attending the lunch for press, local VIP's and sponsors. Until then he was unlikely to go round the exhibition, thereby discovering that the artwork supposedly by him was no such thing. So the frogs needed to be released at the opening ceremony. Or, better, just as Scroby set out to view the exhibits. Quite how he was going to do that wasn't clear in his mind. But once they'd been set free, infesting the exhibition floor and giving the frog-phobic artist the screaming hab dabs, he would surely abandon the tour, amid flustered apologies from the organisers. But if that didn't work, and the worst happened, Scroby was going to stand in front of the painting, jewel of Grashes' contemporary art collection, and declare the thing an effing fake. Tony went cold at the thought. Best to have quietly disappeared. He'd drive the van back to London, dumping the cages and other paraphernalia on the way. And then what? Wait for the law to come knocking? Or jump on a plane somewhere? Concern for the trouble Ben would be in as well hardly featured. Banished, along with imagining the anguish caused to their mother. Such pictures didn't sit easily with the cherished image of himself as the family go-getter.

In any case Tony didn't see that he'd done anything seriously wrong. Grashes were pleased to have the work in their collection, what did it matter who really painted Transformation? The great man probably wouldn't have touched the thing even if it had been a genuine Scroby. As the art world well knew, in the background was an array of assistants who actually did the work. Ben had just been an unofficial assistant.

But the frogs would do the trick. They had to. Just hold your nerve, old son, Tony told himself, and you'll come out on top. As usual.

Bruce Spatchland was going to be there, and the Chairman had now decided to attend, reaping good publicity from being a major sponsor. So it would be a heaven sent opportunity to hobnob with the Chairman, making sure he knew it was Tony's family that had given this impressive building to the town. Could be a major career booster.

As organiser, Gaye would be overseeing the whole thing, but she'd surely have time to mingle with the guests, giving Tony the chance to indicate that they were an item. He'd made sure as many people as possible knew about his latest conquest, which reflected so well on him. Such a stunning, worldly wise woman demanding his company, and much else, was a thrill he still couldn't get over. She dazzled him with her frank sexuality, contacts and lifestyle. In the last three days she'd taken him to two parties and a high profile gallery private view, attended by more celebrities and art world big hitters than he'd ever been close to before. And now he was going to escort her to Lyndon Scroby's house warming bash. It was as if he'd gone to the cinema only to find he was starring in the film. This glittering world was where he belonged, he now realised, and Gaye had seen that, recognising his outstanding qualities.

Tony's aim of marrying Natasha and becoming Oliver Rabson's son-in-law was now somewhat blurred. Moved down the 'To Do' list, the idea remained as a vague ambition, for the future. He would still do it though, he promised himself, glossing over the small matter of how he, as Gaye's former lover, might be viewed by Natasha. She'd probably enjoy making her mother jealous, he reckoned confidently. It was what he'd do in her place. Tony always judged people's likely reactions using that yardstick, and found it pretty accurate. At work, anyway. But going after Natasha could wait, the unexpected status quo was too enjoyable to pass up for the time being.

Guided by Pauline, Natasha had sent invitations to selected art correspondents, the local newspaper and Suffolk Radio, in the knowledge that they would be attending the official art festival lunch anyway. As a result she needed to lay on drinks, but only token eats. Pauline had suggested the emphasis be on Oliver Rabson's presence to cut the ribbon. This would ensure the invitations were accepted – 'Art Supremo Comes to Rundleston', etc – but would avoid highlighting Natasha herself. Rab wanted his daughter to feel appreciated for her efforts, but it was only a few months since she'd featured in drug scandal headlines, so best for her still to keep a reasonably low profile.

Natasha would also have liked the people who'd helped and supported her to be there. Madge was unfortunately too involved with the art festival's buffet lunch, but Peter Jahney agreed to come. Danny was invited too, to show appreciation for his help, although Natasha was a little concerned it might be seen as encouragement. After that first sing along in the pub, his invitations to go out had been gently declined, and she hoped the message of merely platonic friendship had now been taken on board. But he continued to regard her with mournful adoration, like an emaciated bloodhound puppy. Ben apologetically declined, on the grounds that he'd be setting up the Human Fruit Machine in the Square. He could surely have spared just a few minutes, especially as his work was on display. But

Natasha remembered his antipathy to her father – increased since Rab wanted to exclude Ben's paintings – and realised it was an excuse.

She agonised over whether Gaye should be asked. After all she would already be in Rundleston, and might be able to slip away from her party organising duties for a few minutes. But Pauline, when consulted, reminded her that the gallery, although all Natasha's work, was actually Rab's, financially speaking. And his ex-wife's presence would be a discourtesy to him.

'Yes, you're right', Natasha agreed gratefully. 'What would I do without you to give me sound advice.'

Nora was of course invited. 'I wouldn't miss it for anything – you've worked so hard on that place', she declared. 'Betty's kindly agreed to mind the shop while I'm at the art festival lunch and opening ceremony, so I'll just ask her to come a bit earlier. And the old glad rags will do for both', she added cheerfully.

She was the earliest guest to arrive, in a floral printed dress, with smart white jacket, pearl earrings and a touch of makeup, which made her look years younger. Natasha and Pauline were tussling with the first bottle of champagne, the cork flying out just as Nora opened the door, causing her to duck theatrically.

'Repelling invaders! Your father's going to be so proud of you', she declared encouragingly, looking round at the expensive white stone floor and intricate, wrought iron chandelier that dominated the main room. 'The place just oozes class and atmosphere. A pity he didn't see the state it was in before.'

'Oh thank you. But I couldn't have done it without everyone's help. Your curtains were such a good idea. And don't Ben's paintings look wonderful!' Natasha responded enthusiastically, leading her into the small side room, before the sound of the street door indicated the arrival of another guest.

Natasha hoped it was Rab, but found Peter Jahney and an incongruously smartened Danny being greeted by Pauline, shortly followed by a reporter and photographer from the local paper. Soon she was answering questions about the gallery from him and the art correspondents of three national newspapers, as well as being asked to pose for shots. The photographers couldn't believe their luck. Assigned to cover some boring modern art festival, their aesthetic sensibilities were delighted by this gorgeous honey blonde in a fetching cream blouse, and black lace jacket. With those appealing eyes and amazing bone structure, any shot of her was going to be the star of their portfolios. Such easy-on-the-eye subjects were usually the perk of their fashion colleagues, but they were the ones in luck today.

Rab had decided a little ostentation was in keeping with the official opening of his daughter's gallery, and that on this occasion Natasha wouldn't be mortified by him arriving in the Bentley. But powerful cars are no help in traffic jams, and he sat fuming as the dual carriageway from London became a five mile snake of crawling vehicles. He should have come in the chopper. Or on the Bonnie,which could simply weave through the congestion. If he didn't get to Rundleston in time, the media would have moved on to cover the art festival jamboree, and Natasha wouldn't get the fanfare opening he'd promised. That might in fact work to his own advantage in strengthening the case for closing the gallery, but he owed it to Natasha to keep his word, and phoned to tell her he was still hoping to make it.

Two of the art correspondents had clearly come just for the drinks, and confined themselves to a quick look round the main gallery, but The Informer's man ventured as far as the small side room. And immediately took out his notebook, with quickening interest.

'Who's the figurative artist whose work you're hanging in the other room?' he asked Natasha quietly a few minutes later, as his photographer was lining her up for a shot. 'Bit

255

old fashioned isn't it, for Oliver Rabson? Surely he isn't turning his back on the contemporary world?'

'Ben Banding lives in Rundleston', she told him. 'I thought people round here would love the chance to buy them – give the gallery a local flavour. Isn't his work brilliant!'

She was right. Hopelessly traditional of course, but very striking. Why hadn't he heard of this artist? Better look him up on the internet as soon as possible – bound to be lots of stuff.

'But the Rabson name is synonymous with cutting edge art...'

'Those paintings are *my* choice', interrupted Natasha. 'Have you got all the shots you wanted?' She'd been holding still for the camera, hand draped elegantly across a swirl of metal on a stand, entitled Fresh Start.

The journalist now scented a different story. Family strife. And his rivals were missing it, chuntering away to each other, enjoying the free booze.

'This is a new venture for your father, isn't it. His first provincial gallery. Is he happy for it to be selling representational art?' he enquired lightly.

Whoops. Natasha could see the way this was going.

'Well, he hasn't actually been to the gallery yet', she lied hesitantly. 'But he said I should choose some things that I liked personally... oh, here he is!'

Getting the media on board was key to any new enterprise, and in the couple of minutes before they had to leave for the art festival lunch, Oliver Rabson stood in the main room, feeding them the necessary quotes, praising his daughter for the creation of the gallery, before declaring it officially open, and posing for the paps.

Natasha's pleasure at Rab's praise, and her adoration, were obvious. Knowing now about that bleak childhood made it all the more heart-warming seeing father and daughter together, Nora thought, watching them. The poor girl was clearly flourishing in the love and approval of the father she'd been kept away from, like a plant brought out into the light.

By coincidence Gaye was apparently here in Rundleston at the moment, as party organiser at the maltings. Nora decided to try and get into conversation with her. What kind of mother wouldn't have doted on such a lovely, sweet-natured creature as Natasha?

Leaving Pauline in charge of Rabson's Gallery, duly open for business should Rundleston's citizens feel the urge to acquire some cutting edge art, Nora set off with father and daughter to walk to the maltings. Although warm, cloud was covering the sky with just a hint, now and again, that the sun was fighting to come through, and the forecast was for a wet afternoon.

'My son's running a fund-raising stand this afternoon', she told Rab, as they passed stall holders busy erecting trestles and tables, surrounded by boxes of stuff. 'I do hope it doesn't rain. But it's usually later than they say.' She was suddenly self-consciously aware that she was walking through her homely little town chatting in relaxed fashion to a famous man she normally only read about in newspapers. And, oh dear, she was talking about the weather! Switching tack, she told him about the town's history and the maltings' background, and Rab seemed interested, although whether that was real or mere politeness wasn't discernible. Perhaps his reputation for brusqueness and short temper was exaggerated.

The whole thing was so odd. She still thought of the maltings as her family's building, even though it had been given away. But stepping into the midst of a crowd of noisily chatting strangers in the old sack weighing room, she immediately felt as out of place as a camel on an ice floe. The place was unrecognisable for a start. Presumably the idea had been to turn it into some sort of sea grotto, or simply to celebrate water. Polystyrene shapes that may have represented dolphins disported themselves on the walls and hung from the ceiling, skilfully avoiding blue glass balls, to the accompaniment of the unearthly sounds of whales calling across the deep. Lights in revolving cylinders caused a flickering on the walls that was probably meant to imitate the shimmer of light through water, and an unseen pump drove a noisy trickle from a big glass tank into the one above, through a drooping tap that looked suspiciously phallic. The sound would soon have everyone heading for the loos, thought Nora, practically, just as a large green bubble welled up from the bottom of the lower tank, and rose like a helium filled jellyfish to burst on the surface with a satisfied *blurp!*

Gaye chose her serving staff for their looks, and attractive girls in slinky silver dresses, covered in shiny scales, were plying the guests with drinks and sexy smiles. Dressing them as mermaids would have been far too literal for a contemporary art festival, but their suggestive air banished any idea that they might be fish.

Arabella, resplendent in a long red and orange striped skirt with matching waistcoat and jacket, her hair newly-purpled, sailed across the room to the newcomers.

'We're so *honoured* you could attend our little art festival', she breathed huskily. 'In fact', she turned to Rab, 'I wondered if you would deign to co-judge our competition for local people, on the top floor. Lyndon Scroby has agreed to do it, but it would be wonderful for such a famous art collector to give an opinion. Who knows', she gave a coquettish little laugh, 'you might find something that took your fancy!'

Rab would have avoided the task anyway, but now he was trying to get extra promotion for Scroby.

'Thank you, but no. Lyndon Scroby is a world famous artist, you could have no-one better to be the sole judge.'

Arabella was in her element. This was the culmination of her hard work. Around her was a throng of sophisticated people, many of them famous, who would never normally set foot in Rundleston. Probably never even heard of it. And it was all due to her inspiration and dedication. She had every right to feel proud.

Ensuring Nora was parked with a representative of the Lottery Fund and a member of the East of England Assembly, she returned to monopolise Oliver Rabson and Natasha, only to find that he was being dragged off by his daughter.,

'You must come and meet Madge', she urged him, taking his arm. 'She's been such a good friend.'

Progress across the room was slowed by the necessity of greeting and acknowledging people. It was pleasing to be seen with his beautiful, vivacious daughter again. There was something about a lovely young woman that was utterly delightful. That was the main reason Gaye had managed to bewitch him, Rab had long since realised, and he'd made sure it never happened again. Natasha was different though. Special, a part of him. She might owe her appearance to her mother, but his genes had created a wholly different character, thank God. His wise decision to send her here had proved that. Instead of sulking and protesting when banished to the sticks to undertake the task he'd set her, she'd knuckled down and done it well. And she'd made friends with local people, no trace of London rich girl snobbery about her, he thought, looking down at her with love and pride. She would have been such an adorable little girl too. It hurt to think how he'd missed out on all those years because of her mother's lies. But at least she was his now, as Gaye, whom he'd already spotted, must realise, seeing them arrive together.

Madge was duly introduced, and found Rab knew quite a bit about her.

'Natasha tells me everything', he informed her teasingly, 'I could set up as a gossip columnist for the local paper on the basis of her emails.'

259

Julian Bisk was astonished that Arabella really had managed to get Oliver Rabson to come. He hadn't believed her. And his daughter too. What a knockout! He extracted himself from a conversation with the Arts Council representative, and eased his way over to see if he could join the group, just as Tony made the same decision.

Tony had managed to convey to the chairman that this whole art festival was courtesy of his family's philanthropy, in giving the building to the town. Making clear that they were more than just friends, he'd also brought over Gaye, resplendent in a clinging dress covered in iridescent butterflies, to be introduced. That she immediately went into charm mode with the chairman put him on the back foot, not knowing whether to be proud or jealous. He told himself she was doing it for him, as well as increasing her all-important contacts list. Nevertheless, it nettled him, and he felt fully justified now in paying noticeable attention to Natasha. Two could play at the flirting game, and a bit of jealousy from Gaye would add spice to their relationship.

Rab observed Natasha's magnetic effect on young males with amused possessiveness. Any prospective son-in-law of his would have to jump through so many bloody hoops his legs would be worn down to the knees, he reflected grimly.

Lyndon Scroby was holding court in a corner, unmissable with his dyed blonde hair, nose and eyebrow rings and stubbly beard. Not so much an enfant terrible though now, not with that paunch and increasing jowl. More an old goat. There was surely something not quite right with the world, thought Rab, when such an unprepossessing individual became rich and celebrated whilst having no discernible talent. That he himself had had more than a little to do with the process by deliberately creating hype in the first place was best not dwelt on. Rab kept an eye out for an opportunity to speak to the famous artist alone. When it came he moved swiftly.

'A word in your ear, Lyndon', he said quietly. 'You should know that a high profile American is about to sell one of your early works.'

'Oh. Which one?'

'Up For It. I de-accessioned the thing last year. This banker needs to retrench apparently. Between ourselves, I think he won't be the last. I've just come back from The States, and there's a whiff of something not quite right over there. With you following Damien's example and talking to an auction house about selling direct...'

'Who told you that?' Scroby interrupted, but Rab, his suspicion just confirmed, remained inscrutable.

'Give me a little credit for knowing what's going on. The point is it's in both our interests for that forced New York sale to go well.'

'So?'

'So, a boost to your public image is in order – acres of newsprint and internet chat, if possible. That's why I'm here, to give your local art festival extra publicity. And I'll see to as much promotion as possible. Your party this evening will help. Anything else you can think of?'

Rab had ensured he kept a good distance between himself and Gaye. Now he was uncomfortably aware that she'd joined an adjacent group.

'The more column inches, the better', he concluded, preparing to remove himself from possible contamination. 'Preferably not for humping that Great Dane of yours', he added dead pan. 'But if you must...'

He'd been surveying the guests. A surprising number of art world people were there, enticed by Tomorrow's Art Today's promise of publicity, as well as already being invited to Lyndon's house-warming bash in the evening. An assurance that people like Bart Cloamer and Tootsie Smalt would be in attendance helped too. Everyone liked to be seen with the in crowd. Rab's eye had alighted on a sleek, well-dressed figure at the far end of the room. Grashes' chairman. Talking to the director in charge of their art collection. Pauline had told him about the loan of the bank's Scroby to Rundleston's art festival. This could be a useful opportunity to offload a couple of his own, as well as bigging up the artist to inflate the American banker's sale.

He now moved to join them, and was immediately welcomed into the conversation. As one of the world's most renowned art collectors, his opinion on trends was respected and influential, and it certainly did the two of them no harm to be seen chatting to him. The Grashes duo were gratified to learn from him that the bank's Transformation was now worth double its current book value because of increased Russian interest in the artist's work. But also, Rab confided, glancing across the room at the man in question, he was in a position to know that Scroby was watching Damien Hirst's venture into direct selling at auction with interest. If that went well, Scroby was proposing to do the same, which would mean the end of being able to pick up his new work at less than the top price. Of course his existing pieces would soar as a result. He let that information sink in, pausing to select a savoury from a tray proffered by a simpering fish/mermaid. Regretfully though, Rab went on, he was contemplating letting a couple of his go.

City people always fell for inside information, so he baited the hook. In strict confidence of course, he told them, he needed to liquidate some cash prior to the launch of a new project, the Rabson brand, the start up costs of which were going over budget. They nodded understandingly. Temporary financial embarrassment among the super-rich was something they were used to. Mentally the Chairman tossed up whether Grashes should offer a loan, or grab the chance of a couple of Scroby's complete with the Rabson caché at an advantageous price. He caught Bruce Spatchland's eye. There could be no better investment.

'Er, Grashes are currently looking to add to weight to our collection...' he said casually. 'Perhaps we could come to some arrangement.'

That was the beauty of dealing with people at the top, the seller reflected with cynical satisfaction. Their self belief was so strong it never occurred to them they were being manipulated.

The Informer's art correspondent was hovering, clearly waiting to catch Rabson's attention. Perhaps he wanted to check something for his write up of the gallery. The press were an invaluable weapon, important to keep on side, so, leaving his marks congratulating themselves on the fortuitous meeting, Rab obligingly eased himself away.

The journalist began with harmless and largely unnecessary questions, then remarked innocently, 'The Rabson name is synonymous with discovering the latest sensation, contemporary art that tests the boundaries – do you think the traditional paintings showing in your daughter's gallery will damage that reputation?'

Although taken by surprise, Rab was too old a hand to give him an unguarded quote.

'I didn't have time to look round, but there's plenty of work there by well known contemporary artists – like Morwenna Lipping and Ray Vessey. Prints and limited edition pieces, obviously. It's intended to be accessible art for the provinces.' He was flicking his little finger, which Pauline would have known was not a good sign.

'So you don't mind if your daughter is representing a local figurative artist? His work's in a small side room', the journalist explained helpfully.

Rab sipped his drink with apparent unconcern. 'As you know, a business has to appeal to its likely clientele. If Natasha thought that kind of art would sell, then that's her judgement. It is after all, her gallery.' He sought to head him off at the pass, as well as turn the encounter to his own advantage. 'Have you been invited to the Scroby party this evening? Now that will be a story worth splashing. I'm told he's spending almost as much on the party as he has on doing up the house.' (Wholly untrue, but it would make an excellent quote.) 'Everyone who's anyone in the art world will be there.' He fixed the man with his laser gaze. 'I could probably have a word with Lyndon and get you invited.' There was no need to add, 'I'll do you a favour on condition you don't make life difficult for me'. It was perfectly understood. Nor did the journalist hesitate. Getting on the wrong side of Oliver Rabson was not to be recommended. With his contacts and influence, he was perfectly capable of blighting a career. And an inside account of an art world extravaganza at the home of one of the most talked about Young British Artists was a much better story, pumped up big time. Best of all none of his press rivals would be there.

'I'll see what I can do', Rab promised. 'Now if you'll excuse me...'

Tony sneaked away from the buffet lunch unnoticed, and made his way to the first floor cleaner's cupboard where he'd earlier secreted what were going to be show stoppers. Or so he fervently hoped. 'Mad as a box of frogs' was a common expression, but must have been coined by someone unfamiliar with the repulsive little buggers. Because those in his container appeared perfectly content with their quarters. Perhaps he'd been feeding the damn things too well, or maybe those bred for the table were particularly docile. He carried the large plastic box along to where Transformation was taking pride of place on the wall, and opened the lid.

'Hop it!' he commanded the inmates. 'Your job is to scare the crap out of Scroby.' Three of them made the leap and squatted silently, their throats working. Frogs being somewhat deficient in facial muscles their emotions remained unknown, but he sensed a lack of exuberance. 'Go on.' He kicked the box. 'My balls are on the line.'

From below came the sound of applause as speeches were made. Shit! If the art festival had been declared officially open the tour would begin any minute. In a panic, Tony tipped up the plastic box, ejecting its remaining inhabitants on to the floor, and, avoiding stepping on his live deterrents, hastily deposited it back in the cleaner's cupboard.

'*Mind the doors!*' a bland female voice warned him, and he jumped guiltily. Bloody sound installation. He cast an anxious glance back at the frogs, which were now beginning to explore satisfactorily, and hurried downstairs.

Madge had been unable to eat any lunch, she was rigid with nerves. Oh God, it was going to be a nightmare. The cream dress she was wearing had been chosen specifically for its unobtrusive pocket, into which she'd slipped a stink bomb purloined from Jamie's joke box. She fingered the small glass phial, wondering if she dare drop it just as the official party approached Transformation. She and Ben had agreed on ringing the fire alarm too, but now the day had come, how was she going to get away and activate it? And when? And what if it just delayed the awful moment when Scroby declared he'd never seen the sodding painting before? She looked round for Tony, the cause of all their troubles, and saw him slip back into the room while Arabella was speaking. Must have been in the loo, probably feeling sick with fear. Serve him right too, for involving poor Ben.

Arabella finished her speech, into which, inevitably, every high profile name had been dropped, and Lyndon Scroby was standing up to declare the art festival officially open, when a loud insistent ringing made everyone jump. They looked at each other. Was it the fire alarm? Or an art happening? You could never tell nowadays.

'I never touched it!' Madge wanted to protest, like a child caught eyeing the sweet jar. It was quite the wrong moment anyway.

In the ensuing confusion, with guests, flirtatious fish and kitchen staff shepherded towards the fire exits, two things became clear. It was a false alarm – one of the guests in embarrassment confessed to inadvertently setting it off while having a quiet fag. And the fire brigade were already on their way.

Madge was tasked by Arabella with finding some way of turning it off, and then meeting the firemen, who, their controller insisted, needed to come and check for themselves that all was well. It was their duty. (They welcomed a trip out from the station, was Madge's interpretation). Meanwhile the judging and tour of the exhibition would go ahead as planned.

Hunting for the fire alarm instructions in the office, she pictured the VIPs on the floor above approaching Transformation, probably at this moment, and closed her eyes despairingly. There was nothing, absolutely nothing she could do about the impending disaster for Ben now.

The false alarm had got people chatting animatedly, social restraint broken as, over the insistent ringing of the bell, similar experiences were recounted.

'Some guy put a match to one of my pieces at an exhibition in Paris a few years ago', Lyndon Scroby remarked to Rab as they went up the stairs, the media and other guests in a straggle behind them. 'Whole place went mad.'

'Oh yes, I remember. And wasn't there a row about the compensation?'

'Yeah. I never got a penny. Their insurance company disputed the value, and then refused to pay out anyway, on the grounds that it was arson. Typical. Bloody Frogs! Can't stand 'em.'

'We're so delighted to have one of your artworks on display', Arabella fell into step beside them. 'We gave it pride of place, of course. And I do hope you'll approve of the setting.'

A movement caught Rab's eye as they reached the top step, and he paused, interested.

'That's a very lifelike frog. What's it made of?'

Arabella gave a little scream. Another had just leapt across in front of her. And three more were lying in wait further on.

'Live frogs – well it's orginal, I'll give you that.' Rab bent towards the nearest, which jumped athletically onto Arabella's foot, then hastily away again as she shrieked. 'Something to do with you, Lyndon?'

They were certainly noticeably clustered in front of the offering that announced it was Transformation by Lyndon Scroby, on loan from Grashes Bank – whose chairman just happened to be now standing beside the artist.

The press photographers were delighted, and there was a chorus of shouted comments.

'Can we have Lyndon kissing a frog in front of Transformation?'

'Yeah! Snog a Frog!'

'When's it going to be transformed into a princess then?'

'What if it turns into a prince?' The Informer's art correspondent couldn't resist enquiring, and his camera-wielding colleague gave a snort of laughter and muttered, 'He'll be easy either way.

They're under starter's orders, a woman's voice informed them, over the ringing fire alarm. The volume control had defied adjustment, which was probably just as well under the circumstances.

'Is it a frog race then?' one of the journalists enquired hopefully.

'Can you turn towards the painting, Lyndon. Hold it!'

As Scroby obligingly examined the masterpiece in front of him, coherent thought was fighting four glasses of champagne. When did he do this one? His mind was a blank. He couldn't recall even putting finishing touches to it, which was his only contribution these days. The studio did everything else. And this was owned by Grashes. Odd. Surely it couldn't be... the possibility suddenly occurred – a fake? Could it? He peered closer, frowning.

Fault! First service, the sound installation announced.

Why hadn't the frogs caused Scroby to gibber with loathing? Seeing him completely unfazed by the deterrents he'd had such trust in, Tony felt cold fear clutch at his stomach. He'd left Natasha's side, and was uncharacteristically hanging back behind most of the assembled guests. Might need to make a quick getaway. Now seeing Scroby staring intently at the artwork, Tony felt as if he was in a tunnel with a train bearing down on him at speed.

Damien had had three wrong uns turn up recently, Scroby recalled. But they were spot painting prints. This was an original. Could it have come from that village in China where they churn out lookalike paintings? No, more likely one of his assistants had craftily slipped out one on the side.

'Why's it called Transformation? the press wanted to know, impatient at the great man's silence.

How the bloody hell should I know? Scroby felt like snapping back. It was a crap title, he'd have conjured up a much better one. Hold on, better think things through. Denouncing this as a fake would get acres of publicity all right. Grashes would go ape for a start. But everyone discussing how easy it was to fake a Scroby was hardly going to boost that New York sale. Or the credibility of his own direct selling venture. Especially if people began to wonder how many others might be out there.

This vehicle is reversing. Beep, beep, beep. This vehicle is reversing.

'Well', he turned away from the painting, 'the intensity comes from deep experience, making powerful use of traumatic spoken memories.' Art jargon could be so useful. 'It's a door into another kind of reality' he added authoritatively, 'the ability to rethink space.'

'And the frogs? Where do they come in?' The Informer's art correspondent wanted to know.

Most of the freed amphibians had wisely retreated from the human invasion and by now found secluded nooks in which to lurk, but one chose this moment to bound back towards Scroby. For a moment they stared at each other, a peach of a pose that sent all the photographers into action.

Presumably the escaped livestock were from some artwork, thought Rab, but no picture editors would be able to resist using that image. Better give them some blurb to go with it.

'The frogs represent a great leap forward in art over the past few years', he informed them smoothly.   'Symbolised by famous artists like Lyndon Scroby.'

Great Leap Forward. He was pleased with that. They'd all run it.

Tony was almost wetting himself with relief. The train had thundered past and somehow, miraculously, left him unscathed.   And suddenly the jangle of the alarm bell ceased, the blessed silence broken only by the sound installation.

Game over.

During lunch Nora had felt diffident about introducing herself to Gaye, although there'd been no difficulty identifying her. In that silky dress covered with iridescent butterflies, carefully made up face and immaculate, highlighted hair, she seemed a caricature of Natasha, giving off concentrated sex appeal as if she was some exotic jungle plant attracting pollinators. Now, as the lead party moved on, Nora found herself standing next to her.

'What do you make of all this way out stuff?' she enquired conversationally.   'I have to confess to being a little sceptical.'

'Oh you get used to it', replied Gaye. 'When I modelled at an art college I'd be quite upset at the way some of the life-class apparently saw me. Picasso wasn't in it!'

'A life model? What fun. Where was that?'

269

'At Queen's Art Academy in London.'

'Oh', Nora responded surprised, 'my son was a student there. Well, briefly anyway. Perhaps you knew him? Ben Banding.'

The glamorous jungle plant paused. 'No', she said matter of factly. 'No, I'm afraid fraternising with the students was definitely discouraged.'

It was a mistake ever to come here. Gaye was now regretting her blasé assumption that she could just organise the party in Rundleston and disappear without consequences. This kind-faced, diminutive woman was Ben's mother. And Tony's. An end to the conversation was advisable, and she put on her It's Been Nice Meeting You expression.

'Well we do have a link', Nora informed her, as the crowd around them passed knowledgeable comment on a pair of binoculars constructed from Thermos flasks. 'Your daughter Natasha has been staying with me since the spring, and she's utterly delightful. You must be very proud.'

Most mothers would have basked in the compliment, but Gaye only nodded acknowledgement. Hell's teeth, was there no end to the entanglements. The sooner she got out of this damn place, the better.

'It's been like having a surrogate grandchild in the house. Lovely for me', Nora continued as they moved on with everyone else. She gave a wistful little smile, 'My sons not having seen fit to provide any.'

Gaye seemed to freeze. 'Oh God there's one of those frogs! Julian, were they some crackpot idea of yours', she demanded, seeing him chatting in a nearby group of guests.

He came over. 'Nothing to do with T.A.T. Although I wish we'd thought of it. Great launch party, by the way. We must talk about an important preview bash my gallery are organising in the autumn.'

Gaye showed no signs of introducing her, and the business conversation that was about to ensue was clearly exclusive, so Nora gave up and hung back, seeing Madge coming up the stairs.

'What happened?' her lodger enquired anxiously.

'About what?'

'Er, when Lyndon Scroby saw his painting...'

'Nothing.' Nora was puzzled. 'Oh you mean the frogs. Someone's let loose a whole load of frogs in the place. The photographers snapped him and a frog gazing at each other.'

'And that was...all?'

'Yes. Come on, let's catch up with everyone or we'll miss the judging of the competition. Ben and Jamie will be so pleased if their GARBAGE wins, won't they.'

Madge pictured an apprehensive Ben out in the Square with Jamie, and resisted the urge to rush out and tell him that somehow, incredibly, he'd already won the greatest prize he could have hoped for.

Arabella had guided the Great and the Good round the displays on the rest of the first floor, eager to show her integration into their world. Tomorrow's Art Today might have been responsible for the exhibits, but the important thing was that she understood them.

'It's so vital that there's no constraint on the expectations of the viewer, don't you think', she remarked to Oliver Rabson, as they stood in front of the outsize crate of coloured milk bottles. 'They're objects with such a powerful metaphorical resonance.'

Natasha's entertaining emails hadn't spared the multi-coloured doyenne of Rundleston's art festival, and Rab was aware of his daughter's suppressed giggle behind him.

'Yes, it's a utilitarian aesthetic, is it not', he replied gravely.

'Hope you know your stuff, Lyndon', he murmured in an aside to the famous artist. 'Big responsibility, judging the local competition upstairs. The nation awaits.'

The following crowd of guests had thinned out by the time they reached the top floor, networking and art world gossip proving more engrossing than the exhibits. Or some, among them the chairman and Bruce Spatchland, to Tony's disappointment, had taken the opportunity to depart altogether. Nora and Madge made sure they caught up, and the press stayed with the judging party. Modern art was always good for stirring controversy and enlivening the letters page, and they might glean something useful to go with that frog pic.

Blissfully unaware many of the entries were intended to mock, Arabella was proud that the people of Rundleston had come up with such a sophisticated and eclectic display. The larger entries were ranged around the outside, with the rest on the grey-painted plinths in lines down the long room. Trouble was, there had been fewer smaller submissions than expected, so some of the plinths were empty. Anxious to dispel the impression that this might have been due to a lack of enthusiasm among the local populace, she explained that numbers needed to be limited, such had been the rush to take part.

'What criteria am I supposed to use?' the putative judge enquired cautiously.

Lyndon Scroby, neighbour, world famous artist and friend, was publicly asking her opinion! She'd arrived. 'Well, she told him earnestly, 'engagement with the social and cultural context of course. The symbiotic relationships and layers of interpretation. Exhibits which take your mind on a journey.'

'So now you know, Lyndon.' Rab was congratulating himself on dodging the task.

Scroby was beginning to regret ever introducing his eager neighbour to the language of art. Slowly they walked round the room, examining the entries. To Nora and Madge's eyes there was nothing to touch Ben's and Jamie's GARBAGE. As well as fulfilling its ironic purpose, it actually looked good. Perhaps that was its undoing, anything attractive to the eye being suspect. Too derivative.

'Right, I've made my decision', Scroby announced, tour complete, adding as a necessary preliminary, 'The standard of entries is excellent. But third prize goes to 'Spring Clean'.' He pointed to an old dishwasher filled with large, artificial daffodils. Second prize to, er, 'Tache Cache.'

False moustaches stuck on a collection of wall tiles, the art correspondents scribbled in their notebooks, while their photographer colleagues moved to snap these successful entries.

'And first prize', he intoned sententiously, 'goes to this one on the plinth', he indicated a blue plastic box. 'Doesn't seem to have a name, but the winning artwork works on several levels. Celebrating the visual vernacular with telling minimalism, it effectively pulls you into the present moment, and challenges the viewer to speculate about what's inside.'

Madge hugged herself. She knew exactly what was in the plastic container. Leftover sausages and buns that Danny hadn't had time to eat yesterday, and must have forgotten about. Oh the joy of it. But Arabella would surely spoil everything by revealing that it wasn't a real contender. Unless...

Gathering her wits together, Madge stepped forward. 'My fault, I'm afraid', she confessed self-deprecatingly, 'it should have had a title card. It's called...' she screwed her face up as if trying to recall what should have been typed on a card, 'um, The Importance of Not Forgetting, and the entrant is Danny Larber.'

'And what's the prize?' one of the journalists wanted to know, as the photographers did their stuff.

'First prize, £1000, Second prize £200, and Third £50', Arabella told him. She couldn't remember this entry at all, although the creator's name was vaguely familiar. Madge clearly knew all the necessary though.

The judging process complete, Lyndon was effusively thanked, and the media and remaining guests began to disperse.

'Well, I'll go and have a word with Tony – keep seeing him and then he disappears before I have time to say hello. Pity GARBAGE didn't win', Nora commented regretfully. 'Ben would have liked that.' She exchanged smiles with Natasha, who had taken her father's arm and was evidently telling him about the artwork's origins as jetsam from Woodshey Bay. 'Then', she said to Madge, 'I must sample the delights of Rundleston en fete – can't miss this Human Fruit Machine.'

They joined the guests slowly making their way down to ground level. 'Glad it's all over?' enquired Nora, becoming aware that Madge had a grin on her like a woman who's just learned that it's twins, not sextuplets after all.

'Oh yes! I was dreading today. And everything's turned out...' Madge wanted to hug Nora with relief, to tell her how the family had been saved from disgrace by some miracle. But she mustn't know.

'Tell Danny he's just won a thousand pound prize', she suggested instead, and laughed. 'The best bit is he won't know he was in the competition anyway.' Delightedly she let Nora in on the secret of the food box. 'That'll tickle Ben no end, won't it', she added. 'Please tell him about Lyndon Scroby's comments on that awful Transformation daub, as well. He'll be...well, just tell him. He'll love it.'

And how.

Frogs were still infesting the first floor, one gave them both a fright, leaping out as they walked past the prized artwork.

'Whose mad idea was that, releasing frogs? And what's going to happen to them?' Nora wanted to know, but Madge only shrugged. Who cared?

'You can be sure of one thing though', she said lightheartedly. 'Arabella is going to reckon rounding up the damn things is part of my job description. She just forgot to mention it at the interview.'

Chapter Eighteen

Nora called in at the shop to find that Betty, though busy, had no need of extra help for the moment.

On his bed behind the counter, Bodger was looking disconsolate. 'We'll go and see what your master's up to then', she suggested, finding his lead. 'You might get a bit of a surprise though!'

The Square was bustling with activity, as if it was a particularly busy market day. Instead of parked cars, it was filled with stalls offering home-made cakes and jams, bric-a-brac, secondhand books, plants and jewellery. Reluctantly acknowledging that they were supposed to be in sympathy with an art festival, room had been made for a stand selling artwork by students at the local college. A good proportion of Rundleston's inhabitants were either involved in the organisation and manning of stalls, or knew someone who was, and there was a festive atmosphere as people sauntered round in the warm afternoon sunshine, browsing, buying things they didn't need, greeting friends, treating themselves to tea and scones at the tables in the centre provided by the Women's Institute, and giving in to their children's pestering for ice creams. Hell, they might have one themselves, without guilt, it being a special day. Holidaymakers compared their humdrum existence with the clearly exotic lives of Rundleston natives, and thought wistfully about moving. Those maltings flat dwellers who happened to be down on a Friday congratulated themselves on their choice of weekend retreat, while foreigners took photographs of this peculiar English celebration.

The primary school had put out a call for comics and discarded toys, and pupils were busy selling the resulting wares with a cheeky confidence that suggested profitable careers awaited as City traders. Several stalls had been set up to promote good causes, and next to the RNLI stand was The Grange's, featuring fruit, flowers and vegetables grown by the residents, plus donated clothes and some of their handiwork from the various workshops. Beside it a blue and white striped booth announced Reginald Rabbit's Human Fruit Machine, and from a window cut in the front, Jamie, Stephen, and Danny peered out at the public beneath cardboard hats declaring them to be respectively Fruit Cake, Fruit Case and Old Fruit. In order to help with the height difference, Nora had been asked to provide a low stool for Danny, while the boys were sitting on, unseen, two of her dining room chairs, plus cushions, to bring them up to the level of a shelf in the front, on which they each had a selection of fruit – orange, lemon, apple and pear.

Outside a giant, sandy-coloured rabbit with pink-lined ears was drumming up business.

'Come on ladies and gentlemen,' Ben's voice, slightly muffled, emanated from the costume. 'See if you can beat the Human Fruit Machine and win five pounds.'

He was getting plenty of takers. Judging by the crowd thronging round the stall, people found the whole thing fascinating. A father helped his toddler son give the rabbit a pound coin, whereupon it instructed the booth occupants, 'Okay, Spin!' Obediently Jamie held up an apple, as did Danny, but Stephen chose an orange.

'Oooh!' The crowd reacted to the result.

'Sorry, not this time', Reginald Rabbit apologised kindly to his young punter, putting the pound into the money bag slung in front of him. 'Who else wants to try their luck? Three matching fruits to win five pounds', he called. 'All it needs is a bit of mind manipulation. See if you can bend the Human Fruit Machine to your will.'

Stephen and Jamie laughed. They were obviously enjoying their role hugely, and even Danny's long, mournful face creased into something approaching a smile.

Ben had got into the swing of things now, and if it hadn't been for the leaden dread of what must surely have been going on at the official art festival opening, would even have been enjoying himself. Vision was somewhat limited in his costume, but catching sight of his mother with Bodger among the crowd, he beckoned to her.

'How did it go?' he demanded quietly, his note of urgency at variance with the furry face.

'Okay. Quite fun really.'

'No, I mean... well, did nothing...happen?'

Nora thought it a strange question.

'Someone released a whole load of frogs', she told him. 'Poor Madge is having to round them up. And Danny's won the competition.' Bodger was straining at the lead, and she was having trouble holding him. Normally well behaved, he must be unsettled by the crowds of people. And of course this bizarre creature spoke with his master's voice. 'Madge said to tell you...' The dog gave an extra strong pull. 'Look I'd better go.'

'No, hang on. Jamie wants to video this', he indicated the booth. 'Could you possibly replace him for a few minutes?'

'Oh!' She was taken aback. 'Yes, I suppose so.' It was turning into a very odd afternoon.

A teenage girl approached the pink-eared master of ceremonies. 'How much is it for a go?'

'A pound. For a chance to win five', he told her, brought back to his duties.

'(Thanks Mum. After this go, then.)

Right, spin!'

The Fruit Machine went into action. A pear, an apple and a lemon held up this time. Another gain for The Grange.

'Who wants to try their luck with the Human Fruit Machine? We're just going to change one of the cogs', Reginald Rabbit announced breezily. Ben could hardly believe what he'd just heard. By some miracle he hadn't been denounced as a forger! How had Madge pulled that off? It was as if the firing squad had lowered their rifles and announced, 'Only joking'. He felt like hollering and dancing with relief, and his voice lifted with joy.

'Come on now, ladies and gentlemen, see if you can outwit the Human Fruit Machine. Try your luck!'

Nora found herself squeezed into the right hand cubicle, wearing the Fruit Cake hat. It was hot in there, and she felt more than a little self-conscious, with so many pairs of eyes fastened on her. But it was nice to sit down. And all she had to do, on cue, was choose a piece of fruit and hold it up. Outside, Jamie was struggling to hold on to Bodger while at the same time videoing Reginald Rabbit and The Human Fruit Machine. Straining at the lead and giving little yelps of excitement, the dog seemed riveted by the large-eared, furry creature in front of the booth, and his tugs were becoming frantic. How to use a camera with a big, hairy sheepdog causing it to bob up and down had somehow been omitted from the instructions. A bystander kindly offered to hold the lead while the boy took his shots.

Perhaps it should have been someone stronger.

'It wasn't my fault. Honest', Jamie recounted to his mother in the flat at the end of the afternoon, as they caught up with each other's happenings. 'He must have let go of the lead. Or something. And Bodger...' laughter broke through as he pictured the scene again. 'He just hurled himself at Ben, knocked him over and stood on top with his tail wagging, and a grin all over his face. You should have seen him. Everyone was cheering and laughing. It was ace!'

'Was Ben okay? Madge called anxiously from her room, hanging her dress in the wardrobe after changing thankfully into comfortable jeans.

'Yeah, he was fine. He couldn't get up though until we hauled Bodger off him.' Jamie laughed again. 'I got everything on my camera. Come and have a look. I'm uploading it onto YouTube.'

'Well you'll have to hurry', she headed for the kitchen. 'We've got to leave. Are you sure Ben's up to sailing all the food and barbecue stuff to Woodshey Bay? He didn't hit his head or anything?'

'Course he is. We'll probably be using the engine anyway. But I could sail the Sound Lady myself now', her son added proudly, closing the laptop, 'You should come with us and see.'

'Love to another time, I really would. But this evening I've arranged to walk there with Nora and Pauline.' She looked at her watch. Come on, got to go, or we'll be keeping Ben waiting.'

They'd taken wet weather clothing, just in case the Met Office was right. But Nora's firm opinion that rain either petered out before reaching Rundleston, or made much slower progress than forecast, was born out by the beautiful mackerel sky. A front was coming in, but their beach barbecue was still likely to be safe from rain. In fact the evening was perfect, the ground reflecting back warmth absorbed during the day, light from a milky sun glinting on the estuary, with an occasional breeze darkening the water and stirring the topmost branches of the trees. It was low water, but coming in, so Ben and Jamie chose a dry spot fairly high up the beach, and had unloaded the boat by the time the walking party arrived.

'Oh this is heaven', declared Pauline with satisfaction, sitting on a rug, glass in hand, with the smell of sausages proving an effective appetiser, as Ben, assisted by Jamie, did the cooking. 'Such a good idea of yours, Nora. That glitzy party of Lyndon Scroby's has nothing on this.'

'Can't wait to hear all about it from Natasha, though', Nora confessed. 'Don't expect she'll get back till the small hours. Tony's going as well apparently.' She gave an answering wave to the crew of a yacht motoring up the river.

'What was Natasha wearing?' Madge enquired, interested. 'I wouldn't have a clue how to dress for a celebrity party like that.'

279

But Pauline couldn't help. 'I think she must have been in the shower when I left. There was no answer when I knocked on her door anyway.'

A cormorant flew straight down the river, wings just a few inches from the water, while along the beach, a safe distance from Bodger, a little egret was slowly patrolling the shallows that were silently creeping up the sand.

'Isn't it strange', Nora nodded teasingly towards the chefs, 'how men always take charge of outdoor cooking, but show them a kitchen and they run a mile.'

There was no lack of things to talk about, each of them wanting to recount their experiences of the art festival day opening day, and there was much laughter. Madge was bursting to tell Ben the details of their miraculous escape, and he to hear all about it, but they needed privacy.

'Race you to the end of the beach!' he challenged her when they'd all finished eating, the cooks had been duly praised, no scrap of the raspberries and cream remained, and Jamie had gone exploring in the woods with Bodger, who could be heard barking at rabbits, real or imagined.

'I don't know how they have the energy', Nora remarked, watching Ben and Madge tear off down the sand, laughingly competitive. Reaching the end, they began walking slowly back. Very slowly.

'They make a nice couple', observed Pauline casually.

'Oh,' Nora looked at them with new interest, then shook her head in mock despair. 'No, I've given up with Ben. It's never going to happen. Art's the passion in his life, and that's all there is to it.'

The breeze freshened with the gradual fading of the light, and reluctantly they began packing up.

'Pity it isn't June with the really long evenings', Nora commented, as the women set off homewards along the shore path, having helped to stow everything into the boat.

'I think we could sail back, don't you', Ben suggested, shoving off and stepping in at the last moment, wet to the knees, while Jamie pushed on an oar to take them further out. 'The tide's against us, but that breeze is dead downriver. Should be a nice easy run.'

They set just the mainsail. There was no hurry, and the lack of a jib gave Bodger more room for his favourite role as canine figurehead, snuffing the air and menacing any water birds they passed, unabashed by their indifference.

'Here, you take the tiller', Ben offered, 'but any gybes and you'll be keel-hauled.'

'Doesn't have a keel', Jamie responded cheekily.

'Well, there is that', Ben conceded, smiling to himself at the beatific expression on his helmsman's freckled face. When you were young there wasn't much you were in charge of. The boy reminded him so much of himself at the same age, now that suffering look had gone. It would be good to paint him properly some time, Ben reflected. Madge would like that.

Water chuckled beneath the bow as they made steady progress downriver in companionable silence, broken by Jamie after a few minutes.

'I need to ask you something...'

'Is there a prize for the right answer?'

'Um...well... Could you marry my Mum?'

'*What!*' Ben had been expecting a sailing question.

'It would be great. We wouldn't have to go to Canada, and you could be my second Dad, and I could have a boat of my own, and... stuff.'

He looked at Ben appealingly. 'You like Mum, don't you.'

'Yes, of course I do. I've known her since she was a schoolgirl, helping in the shop on Saturdays.'

A large motor sailer passed, creaming purposefully down the river, owner standing proudly at the wheel. Ben kept an eye on its wash as he sought to tackle this without any hurt feelings.

'I'm honoured that you would have me as a second Dad, of course', he said gently. 'But when people get married it's because they love each other. Liking isn't enough.'

'That didn't work with her and Dad though, did it? Couldn't you just be friends, the way you are now?'

Ben had successfully fielded the matrimonial ambitions of several Rundleton girls, but this was like being ambushed by a red squirrel cub. And he was assailed by an unsettling thought – could Madge have put her son up to this? If so, he'd read things entirely wrong.

'What does your mum think about this idea?'

'Oh please don't tell her I said anything!' Jamie was alarmed. 'She'd totally rinse me!'

'Watch that burgee', warned Ben, relieved, sensing the wind's slight change of direction. 'Look, it's really nice of you to suggest it. But I don't think you need to worry about the Canada thing. And people don't usually rush into another marriage. We'll carry on as we are, shall we. Just good friends.'

'Natasha's left her light on', Nora noticed, looking up at Chandlers' dormer windows, as she, Pauline and Madge walked up Rundleston High Street.

'I'll turn it off', Pauline offered. 'She won't have locked the door.'

But as she came up the stairs to the top floor an hour later, having stayed chatting in Nora's sitting room, the crack of light visible under the door suddenly went out. Not right. Not right at all. Natasha should have been enjoying herself at Lyndon Scroby's exotic house-warming party.

'Natasha?' Pauline knocked on the door. 'Natasha! Are you all right?'

No response. 'I know you're in there, my dear.'

She didn't. Might have been an intruder, but it was an odd kind of burglar who spent more than an hour in one room, she reasoned.

The crack of light reappeared, and after a moment, with obvious reluctance, Natasha slowly opened the door. Pauline took in the shirt and leggings, unbrushed hair and puffy eyes, and sensed the fluttering distress of a torn-winged butterfly.

'You probably don't want me to, but I'm coming in to talk to you', she said decisively. 'Now', she walked over to the bed and sat down, 'what's the matter?'

'Nothing.'

'Are you feeling ill?'

'No.' Natasha still stood by the open door. If she thought that would effectively curtail the visit, she was wrong. 'I just didn't want to go to the party', she added dully.

'Oh. You should have said,' Pauline commented lightly. 'And come on our beach barbecue instead. Have you eaten?'

Natasha closed the door and shrugged as she went to shut down the computer. 'I didn't want anything.'

'Well I've got some very yummy looking chocolate brownies next door. They were on The Grange stall, Tommy helped to bake them. Utterly sinful. Why don't you make us both a cup of coffee', Pauline suggested firmly, noticing Ben's paintings back on top of the chest of drawers, 'and I'll go and get them.'

No point in resisting. She was going to find out anyway, thought Natasha tiredly. And perhaps it would help to talk to someone.

But Pauline didn't press. Instead she commented on Danny inadvertently winning the competition with his lunch box, told Natasha about Madge having to call in the RSPCA to deal with the frogs, and Bodger stealing the show outside by leaping on Ben in his giant rabbit costume. Relating the happenings with amusement and a bit of embroidering, she succeeded in lightening the atmosphere and even getting a laugh.

'Now', she said, judging the moment, 'tell me what the problem is.'

Propped up on one elbow on the bed, Natasha regarded her with affection. 'Oh... all right. No-one can keep secrets from you. Even Dad.'

'*Especially* your father', Pauline emphasised humorously. 'I presume it involves him. And those?' she nodded towards Ben's art, lined up like icons on an altar.

It was a relief to pour everything out to the one person who would really understand what it had taken, confronted by a curt and angry Rab, to stick up for herself.

'So you had a row this afternoon after I left. He ordered you to remove Ben's paintings. And he wants to close the place', Pauline summed up, when she'd heard the story, generously refraining from saying 'I did warn you.' 'Rab doesn't do gentle hints. We both know that. So you must surely have realised how he would react when he found the paintings still there. At the end of the day that is his gallery, sweetheart. His name on the door.'

'Mine too', Natasha pointed out quietly. 'And I thought he loved me.'

Pauline put down her cup. 'Of course he loves you. He's just...autocratic. Likes to be in control of everything.'

'I'm not a thing.' Natasha's voice strengthened defiantly. 'I thought he would respect me for having my own opinion and standing up to him. I knew he'd be cross and I'd have to fight my corner, but he didn't need to say...' her face was crumpling, 'what he did.'

'What things?'

'He said he expected more from his daughter. That this brand launch was very important, and I was undermining him.' She hesitated, tears welling. 'Disobedient and disloyal, he called me.'

'Oh my dear.' Pauline left the chair and gave her a comforting hug, then sat beside her on the bed. 'He had no right to say that. It was unforgiveable.'

Clearly Natasha had spent the evening dwelling on the whole thing, and Pauline sought to turn her thoughts.

'So what are you going to do now? I see you've removed the source of contention.'

'Well he's probably right about closing the gallery', its creator admitted unwillingly, reaching for a tissue and blowing her nose. 'Even I could see it wasn't going to attract many buyers. Not with that sort of stock – which was one of the reasons for wanting to include Ben's paintings.' She glanced at them and brightened. 'They're so special. There ought to be a good market for them, surely. In fact I wondered... well, if that's what I could do. Publicise his art and promote his career. He's so hopelessly uncommercial isn't he.'

'Act as his agent, you mean?'

'Mm, but more than that. Open a gallery to exhibit his work. And there must be others like him – not as inspirational – but really good artists who are just regarded with contempt, because they're unfashionable. Maybe I could change things.'

Oh the innocence of youth. Imagining that reason might triumph over hype.

'Your father would never allow it.'

'No, he'd be furious.'

Pauline was doing a quick assessment of the idea. Did the concept have any commercial chance? Well just possibly.

'There's no way you could turn the market. People have tried, but too much money's being made from the way things are.' She smiled. 'You must know that, your father being one of the big players. But it might be possible to make a specialist niche for Ben. The only way you could do it would be to make him into a story', she said, thinking aloud, 'and get the media interested.'

'He's got hundreds of paintings up in his studio', Natasha told her eagerly

'That's a good start, the newspapers could make something of it. "Reclusive genius with treasure trove of art!." "Modern Van Gogh refuses to sell his work!"' Pauline parodied the headers. 'You'd have to get his agreement of course, and you might not. He's a sensitive and private person.

And where would you get the finance from? It costs a lot to run a gallery in London – I know, I used to work for one.'

'I thought perhaps I could persuade one of Dad's clients to put up the money. They've all got zillions, and that fat guy who owns half of Greece – the one with the unpronounceable name – said to let him know if he could ever be of help.'

You bet he did. Pauline was appalled at the idea of this beautiful, trusting child woman seeking business backing among the super-rich. As vulnerable and unknowing as a kitten on a motorway, and with about the same chance of surviving unscathed.

'If that's what you want to do, you'd have to go into it carefully', she cautioned kindly. 'Take lots of advice. And use your contacts shamelessly for promotion. But Rab should be the one putting up the money'

'He wouldn't. He doesn't love me. I just thought he did'. Natasha's voice trembled. 'So I'm better off on my own. Like I was before.'

Pauline regarded her with motherly compassion, and growing indignation. How could her employer alienate his daughter like this, such a lovely girl, and with strength of spirit too – it took courage to stand up to Rab. He was due a piece of her mind. If he wouldn't take it, she suddenly decided, then that was the end.

'No', she put a supportive arm round Natasha and gave her a squeeze, 'you're not alone. If Rab doesn't back you, then I'll come in as your business partner. We'd make a great team. Me as admin and finance wallah, you as front of house.' Pauline smiled at her, 'How would that be?'

Chapter Nineteen

Natasha's absence from the party did not go unnoticed by either Gaye or Tony.

Tony was well aware that he risked Gaye's displeasure if too much attention was paid to her daughter, but he very much wanted to be seen with two beautiful women at his side. His own adoring harem. 'That's one lucky dude', he imagined men muttering enviously. 'Must pack some trouser-punch. Who is he?' He also knew that Gaye avoided Rab, whereas Natasha would almost certainly introduce them. So it was disappointing to find her absent, but there'd surely be other occasions, now he was in with the glitterati of the art world, his talents and charisma appreciated at last. That this fantastic gathering was taking place in his home town, and he was the only inhabitant attending just put candles on the cake. If only all those people who'd bad mouthed him about his father's death could see how far he'd come, he thought, fingering his mental scar. And Mum. He must go and see her in the morning and tell her about the exotic occasion to which her younger, successful, son had been invited, citing some of the famous people he'd rubbed shoulders with.

The arrangement was that he would share Gaye's room at the hotel, but he made out that the bank had summoned him in on Saturday morning, and he'd have to leave first thing. They needed him urgently, he told her, making sure she knew how highly regarded her new lover was. The truth was that he had to return the hire van, and dispose of the incriminating cages and frog paraphernalia as soon as possible. It was unlikely the police had been informed, but he couldn't risk some scuzzy tabloid journo nosing around.

He took care not to drink himself to incoherence. Or non performance. It was too early in their relationship to give Gaye a night of anything less than a thousand per cent.

Gaye, besides networking with the cream of the art world, poaching some event ideas and thoroughly enjoying herself, had intended using the party to attempt a rapprochement with Natasha. There'd been no chance at the art festival lunch, and afterwards Rab had gone off with her to the gallery. But surely during the evening there would be an opportunity to take a breather in the garden away from everyone else, and play the hurt, rejected mother. Rab had no right to alienate their daughter, the child she'd struggled to bring up on her own.

Lyndon Scroby confirmed that he'd been expecting Natasha, but finding out from Rab why their daughter wasn't there was out of the question, and her phone was switched off. So Gaye had to be content with leaving Natasha a message saying because of a pop star's birthday bash the following night, she would have to go back to London early. Why not come and have breakfast with her next morning at The Dutch House?

After dropping off Jamie and the barbecue stuff at Chandlers, Ben repaired contentedly to the Spritty for the rest of the evening. The place was crowded, and a cluster of regulars at the bar greeted his entrance with a cheer and a chorus of ribbing.

'Well if it isn't a thirsty rabbit!'

'And a dog who knows what he's about. Why didn't you eat him, Bodger, when you had the chance?'

'Come in for a nibble? Thass a shame. Carrots is all gone.'

Ben grinned, and was soon joining in the general chewing over of the art festival, afternoon events in the square, celebrities seen in the town, plus the lavish art party taking place up at Rundleston House, to which quite a few of the guests seemed to be arriving by helicopter.

'And don't forget we have a great artist here tonight', he reminded them jovially, putting his pint down on the bar. 'The winner of the art competition. What are you going to do with the money, Danny? Buy some sticking plaster for that hulk of yours?'

Ben's aim of making the competition judges look foolish by giving first prize to a load of jetsam had been entirely trumped by a simple lunch box, which was a slight disappointment personally. A beautiful illustration of the whole nonsense though. It was just a pity no-one could point this out, or Danny would lose the prize money.

But his heart was singing as he and Bodger made their way back to the Hetty Jane after a convivial evening, the first few drops of rain now beginning to fall. Truth to tell he'd rather enjoyed his role as Reginald Rabbit, and they'd raised over four hundred pounds for The Grange. The barbecue had turned into a pleasant evening, and best of all the threat of disgrace, notoriety and prison that awaited him if his painting had been denounced as a fake had fizzled out, like a forest fire succumbing to a downpour. It was a miracle. Or more likely Scroby simply didn't have anything to do with the stuff that went out under his name.

His cosy foc'sle cabin awaited him, warmed by the afternoon's sun on the barge's dark hull. September next month though, he thought, hearing the rain gather confidence, thrumming insistently on the deck above. He'd need to reclaim his flat when the weather got colder. Surely Jamie's anxiety about going off to Canada was wrong, they would probably rent somewhere in the town. Lying in his bunk, with Bodger comfortably settled on his own bed, Ben smiled drowsily, remembering the boy's extraordinary suggestion. It was a touching compliment, and he and Madge certainly got on very well. She'd be amused, if Jamie's confidence didn't forbid him sharing it with her What a child couldn't be expected to understand – maybe no-one could – was that Gaye was his only love. There could never be anybody else.

Gaye! He was suddenly wide awake. My God, how could he have forgotten! He'd been too preoccupied by the impending havoc to remember that she was here, in Rundleston! Or had been today at least, organising the art festival opening lunch. Would she have gone back to London already, and he'd missed his chance to speak to her? Or might she have gone to Scroby's party, and still be here tomorrow morning?

If so, she would hardly have an early night. Or, therefore, get up before, oh about ten – a louchly late hour in Ben's eyes. But he was due to mind the shop till lunchtime. Hell's teeth. How would he get to see her? He lay thinking, and decided that first thing in the morning he would go and ask Nora to swap shifts. She'd want to know why, and he'd have to lie. And then he'd quiz Natasha about where her mother was staying. Probably at The Dutch House, but maybe further afield.

Natasha. He pictured her face. So uncannily like Gaye when she was young. And he was certain now, his daughter, wishful thinking having banished all doubts. Quite apart from the question of dates, how could that louse Oliver Rabson have had anything to do with producing such a honey of a girl. Tomorrow Gaye would surely confirm it, and then he would have the great satisfaction of snatching something away from Rabson. The man had stolen the love of his life, and his child, and then completed the kicking by ensuring his art was rejected. Now at least he would take back his daughter.

There was a certain disparity in this rosy scenario, which his mind conveniently overlooked. It made Oliver Rabson an injured party, and meant Gaye, his angelic icon, had deliberately deprived the man she loved of fatherhood, and passed another man's child off on her husband. Neither was an acceptable thought.

Defensively he painted them out, figures that just didn't work in a landscape. Drifting off, he envisaged Gaye coming back to him, their inspiring love rekindled. She must have a lonely life now, divorced and on her own. And

Natasha would greet her new found father with joy. All things were possible. Today's miracle had just proved that.

When sleep came, his dreams were a jumbled succession of sails and sausages, spinning apples and Gaye, laughing, looking up at him with those big grey eyes, beckoning him to follow her. They were both young and carefree, and she loved him. He reached towards her, but somehow he was now a giant rabbit. He could feel her breath soft on his face, and she was licking his ear...

Reality dawned.

'Gerr off, dog!'

He lay for a moment, listening to the familiar sound of water lapping against the hull. Today... Oh God, he was going to see Gaye!

He found Nora eating toast at the dining room table, light streaming in the big sash windows. Newspaper propped up in front of her, she was, as usual of a morning, doing the crossword.

'Ah, just the job, a fresh mind', she commented, after greeting him. 'What's another word for infatuated? Natasha and I reckoned it was obsessed, but nothing else fits so I'm beginning to think that's not right.'

'Natasha?' He walked over to release a bumblebee that was scrabbling uncomprehendingly at its invisible glass prison. 'She's already had breakfast? Surely she must have got in very late last night.'

'No she didn't go to the party in the end. Said she was just too tired. She's gone to The Dutch House to see her mother before she goes back to London.'

He closed the window. This was good news and bad news. He now knew where Gaye was staying, but pointless trying to talk to her if Natasha was there. Mind you the Mini was still in the yard.

'The clue is 'inspired with a compulsive and unreasoning passion'. Nora was rubbing out the old answer. 'Finishes with 'd'. Pity, obsessed seemed just right.'

Ben couldn't resist getting a rise out of her. 'How about looking that up then', he suggested artlessly, making as if to get the dictionary out of the bookshelf under the windowsill.

'Certainly not. The whole point of doing the crossword is to stop me going ga-ga in my old age', his mother retorted firmly. 'No good if I cheat, is it.'

Nora's insistence that looking in the dictionary was cheating, but consulting other people somehow wasn't, always amused her son. How could she not see the lack of logic? 'Fixated', he offered helpfully.

'No, that's only seven letters. Needs to have eight.'

'Um...what about besotted? Mum, I've come to ask a favour. Could you possibly do the shop this morning instead of me? I'll do next Saturday. The next two Saturdays if you like.'

'Besotted it is!' she exclaimed with satisfaction, 'no wonder nothing else would come right.' She pencilled it in and glanced up, noting that her son seemed rather smarter than usual, sporting a clean pair of jeans and the blue shirt she'd given him last Christmas. And his curly hair looked newly brushed. 'Yes, if you want. Any particular reason?'

'I think Bodger needs to go to the vet', Ben had prepared his excuse, and taken the precaution of leaving the canine in question out in the yard, looking as hangdog as a lamb in May. 'He seems a bit off colour.'

'Nothing wrong with his energy yesterday', commented Nora with a twinkle. 'But yes, that's fine. I'd better get a move on then.'

Lying sleepless in bed the previous night, Natasha had come to a conclusion that was helping her feel better about the row with her father, optimism being the natural ally of adoration. Maybe the problem was that she simply couldn't work for him. That was the cause of friction. And the talk with Pauline, culminating in her heart-warming offer of support, had increased Natasha's resolve to try and market

Ben as an artist. The move would show Rab she had strength of character and the ability to make her own mark on the world, just as he had. The past few months doing up the gallery in Rundleston had given her much needed confidence in her own judgement and abilities. She would use her and Pauline's contacts, help a family she'd grown fond of, and above all it would be something she believed in. As someone to whom cynicism was entirely alien, that really appealed.

Trouble was, the biggest obstacle to all this wasn't money. Natasha might come across as a sweet innocent, but she was well aware that beauty and well-aimed charm, if she chose to use them, would have a magical effect on the purse strings of potential backers. She'd watched her mother manipulate dazzled men often enough, and promised herself she would never do the same. But if it was for a cause as good as this...

No, the main obstacle was going to be Ben. He would need to allow himself to be made into a story – written about, interviewed and promoted. And as Pauline had pointed out, he would be a very reluctant celebrity. Emotionally frozen, any shrink worth his fee would have concluded, in thrall all these years to an ideal of love and femininity. That was a joke, given that Gaye was the object of his worship – akin to a gardener venerating an artificial rose. If he could just see her as she was, instead of this soft focus image in his mind, maybe he'd be cured. That would not only set him free, which the poor man deserved, but it would be a tremendous help for her gallery project.

Gaye had left a message asking her to come and see her at The Dutch House. Was there any way, Natasha wondered, that she could bring Ben along too?

As she opened the passage door to the yard, she'd come up with no better idea than driving down to the Hetty Jane and suggesting it, out of the blue. Only to find Bodger bounding up to her with the enthusiasm of a prisoner long held in solitary confinement.

'Does this mean your master's here?' She fondled his shaggy head. Probably in the studio... No, the door was locked, but standing at the top of the steps reminded her of what she and Madge had discovered inside, the day they borrowed the key.

She found Ben in the dining room, talking to Nora.

'Slight problem', she declared. 'How do I avoid letting Bodger into the street when I open the gate to drive out?'

'Oh sorry. I'll come.'

As she and Ben went down the stairs, Natasha decided now was as good a moment as any.

'My mother would love to see your portrait of her', she said casually. 'I'm on my way to see her at The Dutch House. Why don't you come with me, and bring the painting?'

In the square the usual Saturday market stalls were already up and doing business, no trace of the previous day's usurpers remaining. It was going to be a lovely day, and a queue was already forming in the sunshine for the fruit and veg man who charged a bit more, but made a point of greeting his customers like old friends.

'I've got something to tell you.' Natasha told Ben, keeping her voice non-commital as she drove through the town, Bodger taking up most of the Mini's back seat. 'I'm closing the gallery. Well, my father is.'

'But you only opened yesterday. And you've spent months doing the place up.'

'We, um, we've had a bit of a disagreement. Over your paintings. I don't want to run the place if I can't choose what I sell. And he won't have anything in it that conflicts with the Rabson image.'

'I'm sorry to have been a bone of contention.' It was politeness only. In reality, to have acted as a wedge between Rab and his supposed daughter, even inadvertently, gave Ben quiet satisfaction.

'It's better to close straight away rather than complicate things by trading', she went on. 'So after I've seen my mother I've got to talk to Peter Jahney, and tell him. But there are two things I need to ask you. The first is easy. Please don't breathe a word to Gaye. It's better she doesn't know about the closure, and the row with Dad.' She attempted a smile but it didn't spread to her eyes. 'I'm sure you wouldn't have said anything anyway, you'll have lots of other things to talk about.'

They were turning in the hotel's drive, and sensibly Natasha parked beneath a huge horse chestnut tree, so that the car was in the shade.

'And the second thing?' Ben queried, as she off turned the engine, and they sat companionably in the ensuing silence.

'That's something for you to think about. I want to market you as an artist and set up a gallery selling your paintings.'

Peter Jahney had given Gaye Rabson a room at the back of the hotel, on the top storey, making a chance meeting with her ex-husband less likely. He'd also instructed his staff that they should be seated as far away from each other as possible in the morning. But as Pauline predicted, Oliver Rabson had finished a sparse breakfast by the time Gaye appeared, disappearing upstairs with a couple of newspapers to peruse before checking out.

His PA's assumption that Gaye was unable to get up early in the morning was not in fact right. When it mattered, she could, and it was important that, should she meet her ex, it was not in the company of Tony. Also when her daughter arrived, the role of hurt, neglected mother would hardly be helped by having a smirking lover in tow. She had accordingly chivvied him into rising when the alarm went, and made sure he was off the premises by the time she came down to breakfast. He could hardly object, what with the bank supposedly needing him urgently.

Shown to a table in an alcove looking out over the lawn and woodland beyond, Gaye's progress across the dining room prompted a succession of turning heads, of which she was satisfyingly aware.   To match her striking looks, she had an aura of condescending sophistication combined with a challenging sexuality.   It was an unbeatable man pheromone.   Other people might be blessed with artistic flair, selling abilities or a soaring soprano voice, and woven their lives around those gifts.   Gaye Rabson's talent lay in being beautiful, and fascinating men, and she had accordingly made the most of it.   But, uneasily aware that her power over the opposite sex had a shortening time limit, her self-esteem now required the trophy of a new lover with ever more frequency.   At Lyndon Scroby's party last night she had identified a desirable new target, but the prospect of jettisoning Tony was giving her pause.   Not because of his hurt feelings.   They didn't come into it, and in any case he'd been lucky to be picked in the first place.   The problem was that Gaye knew, with certainty, he would then immediately go after her daughter.   And that could not be tolerated.

From the doorway, Natasha glanced apprehensively round the diners, hoping not to see or be seen by Rab, and spotted her mother immediately.   Well it wasn't difficult.   Perfectly made up, in a snakeskin pattern bolero jacket with large gold buttons, Gaye stood out like a bird of paradise in a pheasant run.

Natasha was well aware that Gaye would want to know why she hadn't been at Scroby's party, and had no intention of telling her.

'You'll never believe this', she volunteered gaily, sitting down opposite, 'but I fell asleep!   Reckoned I'd have half an hour on my bed before getting ready.   And next thing I knew it was past ten, and I just thought, oh stuff it.   Party was good, was it?'

Not many people could outmanoeuvre Gaye, but her daughter had had many years of experience, and this was only going to be a token visit. In addition to the unwelcome possibility of encountering her father, Ben was waiting in Reception for the planned handover. Gaye had only just begun her description of the evening when a waitress came to enquire what the extra guest would like.

'No, nothing thank you,' Natasha apologised, looking at her watch, 'I'm just leaving.' She turned to her mother. 'We'll have to catch up another time I'm afraid. Have to rush. I need to speak to Peter Jahney about something, and then there's the gallery...'

She stood up, and gave her mother a peck on the cheek. 'I brought a friend along who's got something to show you', she announced, smiling sweetly. 'I'll get him. Must go.'

Chapter Twenty

Preoccupied though he was, apprehensively waiting in the lobby for Natasha to give the word, Ben couldn't help observing that the hotel had been hauled up several notches since Peter Jahney had taken the place over from his parents. The dingy interior had had a makeover, there were fresh flowers everywhere, and comfortable armchairs invited guests to linger, chatting. Good for him.

Passing through, Peter greeted him with surprise.

'Hello Ben. What brings you here at breakfast time? Come to see Tony?'

'Er, yes.' Where his brother had spent the night was now confirmed. And he was certainly due a few home truths. His misuse of the mock Scroby had so nearly done for them both. He'd catch him after speaking to Gaye, and have it out with him, Ben decided. Best to have a row away from Chandlers.

But it must seem odd that his brother hadn't stayed in the family home.

'He said he didn't want to disturb Nora, coming in after the party', he explained.

'Oh I think there might have been more to it than that.' Peter Jahney laughed. 'He was sharing a room with Oliver Rabson's ex, would you believe. Always was one for the highlife, your Tony.

Sorry, must go.' The receptionist was calling him over.

It was probably just as well. Ben reeled into the nearest armchair, as if someone had hurled a brick at his head. Gaye and Tony! It couldn't be true. Could it?

When Natasha came to say she'd prepared the way for him, he was still dazed and disbelieving. He had to go through with this, he told himself firmly. It'd come out all right. Somehow.

She might not have seen him for twenty-three years, but there was no mistaking the attractive, curly-headed man, carrier bag in hand, making his way hesitantly across the dining room towards her table. Mentally Gaye cursed the gods, whilst rising with an automatic smile, presenting her cheek to be semblance-kissed.

'Ben! I'd have known you anywhere. You haven't changed a bit!'

Good manners decreed that he return the compliment, but he was just staring at her as if she'd come out worst in a paint-balling shootout.

'I'd have looked you up, but things were so hectic', she gushed. 'Sit down and tell me how life's been treating you.

Endlessly he'd imagined this encounter, usually in some picturesque setting. Never had the envisaged meeting been in a busy hotel dining room at breakfast time. Nor with the revelation that his feminine ideal was sleeping with his brother. How could it all be so wrong.

The conversation was hardly romantic either. She was speaking to him like a stranger at a cocktail party. Ben pulled himself together. If this wasn't played right there might never be another chance.

'Gaye', he interrupted her glossed up account of how she had started an events organising business, 'I have something to show you. And a question to ask. Can we go out in the garden?'

This was surely a good idea. Whatever Ben had come for, it was best not played out for the entertainment of the other guests, most of whom had been at the party last night.

Round the back of the hotel they found a gravelled courtyard, occupied today with overspill parking, and at one side, warmed by the morning sun, a convenient, white-painted bench. They sat down, overlooking a round ornamental pond where goldfish led quiet, contemplative lives among the water lilies.

'You said you had something to show me.' Gaye wanted to get this over as quickly as possible. 'Is it in that carrier bag? I'm dying of curiosity.'

Reaching into it and unwinding a protective swathe of bubble wrap, Ben handed the painting over without a word.

He couldn't have found a better way of breaking through to her. Gaye stared at the portrait, the innocent beauty of its subject thrillingly captured, the sweet, childlike smile, eyes sparkling with light and fun. Herself when young.

'It's brilliant!' The false mannerism had vanished. 'Ben it's just wonderful. When did you do this?'

'At the college, as a surprise for you. And then my father...well, you know what happened. So it was finished in Rundleston. I was going to give it to you, but... when I came back to London you didn't want to speak to me.'

'Yes. That was, unfortunate.' Gaye sounded sincere. 'I'd met Oliver Rabson by then and things were a bit...well, rushed.'

It was a good cue.

'Was that because', Ben said slowly, looking straight at her, 'you were pregnant? Gaye, is Natasha my child? That's the question I want to ask you. Because I think she is.'

A couple who'd been on the same table at the party emerged from the hotel dragging suitcases and walked over to a silver Mercedes a few feet away.

'That's ridiculous!' There was a note of alarm in Gaye's voice, causing the woman to glance at them with interest before searching her handbag for the car key. 'I don't know what you're talking about.'

'I think you do. I'm not going to be fobbed off about this', Ben warned her, beginning to feel reassuringly in control. 'If you won't tell me the truth, then it'll have to be a DNA test. Natasha's living in our house, don't forget. I've already got everything I'd need.'

The nearby guests were beginning a tetchy discussion about who last had the car key, as Gaye quickly assessed her options. There was no arguing with a DNA test. And when Rab got to know about it, as he was bound to, Oh God, he'd grind her into the ground. On the other hand, there was just a chance Rab would never know if she confessed to Ben and appealed to his better nature. She put the painting down on the bench and turned to him.

'Yes', she said in a low voice. 'You're right. I'm sorry.'

Faced with the truth at last, he felt dizzy, hardly knowing how to react. Anticipation had been coupled with slight dread, in the way that a lottery winner realises things will never be the same again, reassuringly familiar life gone for ever. But uppermost in Ben's mind was incomprehension at what she'd done.

'Why? Why didn't you tell me? Gaye, how *could* you!'

The nearby couple had ceased arguing, and the wife was now returning to search their hotel room, leaving husband guarding the cases. He probably wouldn't bother to eavesdrop, nevertheless Gaye kept her voice warily quiet.

'I found out I was pregnant just after your father's accident, when you'd rushed back to Rundleston. I didn't know your address or telephone number. Or even if you'd be coming back.' This helplessness did rather depend on there being no telephone directory available, so she added, 'In any case, you were devastated about your father drowning, I couldn't add to the bad news.'

'What about your parents? Did they know?'

'No. They thoroughly disapproved of me leaving my boring old job in Nottingham to try and get into acting. How could I have gone back to them with a baby? Neither of us had a penny, did we.'

Relations with her mother were problematical, Ben remembered.

'And I was only able to come to London because my cousin let me live in her flat while she and her husband were in America for a year. They were due back in a couple of months, so I wouldn't have had anywhere to live.'

'But...' Ben was still trying to take it all in. 'If only I'd known. My mother would have helped.'

'To be honest, I was seriously thinking about an abortion.' Gaye paused for that thought to sink in. 'I'd made the appointment. And then I met Rab at an art party.' She shrugged in justification. 'He was so loaded the money didn't make any difference to him. Marrying him was the ideal answer.'

Ideal in lots of ways. Ben's sympathy and goodwill were very necessary now. She must get him on side...

'It meant Natasha would have a secure childhood', she continued, 'lovely holidays, the best education...'

'And no father', he interrupted bluntly.

'Well, after we split I kept her away from Rab for your sake.' This was a good angle. 'It was better that she had no father in her life than the wrong father.'

'But why didn't you tell me after the divorce. If you and I couldn't make things work together, at least I'd have got to know my daughter. After all she was my child, as well as yours. And Nora's granddaughter.'

This was a difficult one.

The staccato sound of a car being unlocked encroached on their conversation. The key had finally been located in last night's jacket pocket, and the man began to load cases into the boot.

'It was for Natasha', insisted Gaye righteously. Having lived with the lie so long, she almost believed it. 'Stability was the best thing for her. And she's turned out so well', she added persuasively, 'that must have been right.'

Where the mind is willing, logic is weak, and this explanation might have worked up until a few minutes ago. Now it was perfectly clear to Ben that Rabson's money had far more to do with it than the child's well-being. The part of him that had worshipped his lovely icon for so long was being painfully crushed, sentence by sentence.

'But she needs to know the truth now. She's my daughter, for heaven's sake. It's no wonder we get on really well.'

'No! We must both think of Natasha', Gaye countered with alarm, a winning strategy taking shape. Ben had been deeply smitten once. Her future depended on getting him onside, and that hotel room was wonderfully convenient. A charm offensive should do the trick.

'I understand how you must feel', her tone was sympathetic nurse. 'And of course you're right. Natasha should be told. But now is not the time, just when she needs to concentrate on her gallery. Which, don't forget, Rab is funding.'

She was conscious that the wife had returned, and, cases now stowed, husband was calmly explaining how the key must have fallen out of her handbag, as he'd found it on the ground.

'Best to wait a while. I'll choose a moment when she's visiting me in London.' Gaye paused. 'Look, it's not the ideal place here, is it. Why don't you come up to my room and we can talk about this, and... old times?' She gave him a slow, full-on smile, and put her hand on his thigh, giving it a subtle caress. 'It's wonderful seeing you again.'

'No!' Ben pushed her hand away as if it was covered in rat droppings, and stood up abruptly. 'Were you going to turf Tony out for half an hour then?' he demanded harshly.

Gaye had never inspired revulsion before, and for a moment gazed up at him in shock. And who could have told him about Tony?

'It's not how you think', she protested, 'there's a very good reason.'

His stare was disbelieving.

'He was going after Natasha.'

'What?'

'I couldn't let that happen, could I. Knowing he's her uncle.'

Ben closed his eyes tiredly. It was as if he'd gone seven rounds with a road drill, and his brain couldn't take any more. 'I've got to go.'

'Promise me you won't tell Natasha and upset her', pleaded Gaye.

Ben wasn't at all sure how to handle the revelation. But he wanted his daughter to know who he was. Who she was. The whole story.

'The last thing I'd do is upset Natasha', was his careful response. 'I'm going back now. There's a lot to think about. Thank you for telling me', he concluded over his shoulder, adding with edge, 'In the end.'

He'd reached the Mercedes, wife now observing them both interestedly through the windscreen, when Gaye remembered the painting on the bench beside her.

'You've forgotten the portrait!' she called after him.

Ben stopped, and turned to look at her. 'Keep it', he said. 'I don't need it any more.'

If he'd been in a fit state to register anything, as he began the walk back to Rundleston, he'd have noticed Pauline's car parked under the horse chestnut tree, in the space left, only a few minutes before, by Natasha's departing Mini, complete with large, hairy sheepdog on the back seat.

Pauline had done a good deal of thinking since her last night's talk with Natasha. She told herself that the girl's envisaged venture had zero chance of success, and it would be nonsensical to throw up her own prestigious position to help her. True, with Tommy now off her hands, she had been thinking of jacking in the high-powered life – the idea of a small plant nursery somewhere near Rundleston appealed. But, her head told her, joining a no-hope enterprise in the art world was just crazy.

Like a wasp in August though, the impulse to do it kept coming back at her. Emotion was to blame, and she was unused to it, having spent her life being solid, cerebral and sensible. It was, after all, what made her so good at her job. Now affection for Natasha was governing her thoughts, but even more, anger at Rab. How was it, she seethed, that such an intelligent, perspicacious man could be so *stupid*. So bone-headed. She couldn't any longer work for him, feeling like this, she rationalised. Better say so now, and get it over with. Whether she then grew a little business herself, or went in with Natasha would remain to be seen.

She knocked on the door of her employer's room, and found him dressed in an open-necked shirt and casual trousers, packing his clothes from last night. There was a special stand by the window for guests' suitcases so they wouldn't damage the red and gold bedcover, but Rab liked to do things his way and the case had been plonked on the four poster bed. His BlackBerry and open laptop occupied the table in front of the sofa and armchairs, beside which The Times and Financial Times lay, crumpled and read, on the floor. A wide screen television was tuned to the BBC News Channel.

He greeted her with pleased surprise.

'Ah Pauline, you must have read my thoughts, I was just about to ring you.' He reached for the remote and turned the sound down. 'Two things. Connected really. A galleryist at the party last night let slip that an Indian industrialist I met at the Venice Biennale last year is now looking to buy a Scroby. He's in Switzerland at the moment, so I'm going to fly to Geneva first thing tomorrow morning. To see if I can't offload one of mine. Two, if possible. Back in the evening.'

He indicated the screen. 'And I don't like the way things are going. At all. As well as de-accessioning as much art as possible, I'm going into cash. So I've put my broker on standby for major selling, and I want an emergency meeting in Berkeley Square with my accountant and financial advisers first thing on Monday morning. I've emailed them, but have a feeling old Jowly Jetton is on holiday. Could you chase them up, and if he can't get back in time make sure they send their next most senior man. And notify the skipper that I won't be joining the yacht at Monte-Carlo. More likely Corfu, although I may not make it at all. Please apologise to the guests on my behalf and...'

'I won't be able to do that', Pauline managed to interrupt the flow. 'I won't be in the office on Monday.'

Rab stopped in mid fold of his pyjamas. 'Why ever not?'

'I've come to give you my resignation.'

A fresh breeze stirred the curtains, carrying the harsh machine-gun chatter of a magpie. Impassively Rab studied the dumpy, bespectacled figure of his PA, as essential and unconsidered as a comfortable pair of shoes.

'What have you done?'

'It's what I'm about to do that's the problem.'

'Sorry?'

'I'm going to give you a piece of my mind. I can't do that under the constraint of being your employee. So it's better this way.'

'I'll be the judge of that, shall I.' He indicated the armchairs, but she shook her head and remained standing. 'Which particular piece of your mind did you want to part with?'

Rab thought he knew what this was about. Pauline must have been involved in, or at least known about, the figurative paintings Natasha had put in the gallery. It was a lapse, but he had no intention of allowing her to resign over it.

'It's about money. And Natasha', she responded enigmatically. 'And you.'

No, there must be more to this, he realised, it wasn't just the gallery. But if Pauline left, it would be disastrous, especially now. Whatever was bothering her it was vital he fix the problem.

'Look Pauline', Rab kept his voice light, 'we've been together so many years, I couldn't manage without you. Sit down and let's sort this out.' He walked over to the side table, set with a tray of cups.. 'Something from the mini-bar, or coffee?'

She sat herself down on the red velveteen sofa, bending down to pick up the newspapers from the floor. As she folded The Times, a photograph caught her attention, and she stared at it.

'Have you seen this?' she began, but Rab, filling the kettle and switching it on, wasn't listening.

'What's changed?' he demanded.

'You have', was her unexpected response from across the room. 'When I first came to work for you, you were ramping up unknown artists, making them famous and then quietly selling on, as a kind of joke. Just playing on wealthy people's gullibility. Not something you took seriously.'

He was puzzled. 'Things might have got a bit more complex, but essentially I still do. What's different now?'

'Your priorities.'

'And what does that mean?'

'When you saw those paintings in the gallery yesterday you told Natasha she was disloyal and undermining your brand launch. How could you?' Pauline reproached him.

'Well, that might have been a bit strong', Rab admitted unwillingly, tearing open the coffee sachets. 'But this brand is all about image. You know that as well as I do. And the press would have a field day if they found out my daughter was selling traditional art. The Rabson brand will be aimed at the cool and fashionable.'

'There you are, you see. Business matters more than Natasha.'

'No, of course it doesn't.' He was carrying his PA's coffee over to her. It didn't escape either of them that this was a reverse of the normal order of things. Putting it on the table beside her, she continued the assault as he settled into one of the matching armchairs. 'Her mother is...well, what she is. Perhaps you don't know how betrayed Natasha felt when she discovered Gaye had lied about you wanting no contact during her childhood. She longed for a father to love her, a strong figure to counterbalance her flibberty gibbert mother.

So when she learned the truth she hero-worshipped you. And now... I couldn't bear to see her so miserable last night.'
'Oh...well...I didn't mean to upset her.' He sounded genuinely remorseful.

So unexpected for her to mind, thought his PA tartly.

'I'll go and see her and make my peace. The gallery's not going ahead now anyway, so what she wanted to sell in it doesn't matter. But she has to understand the importance of image and promotion. Personal liking doesn't come into it. And I can't have her jeopardizing the Rabson brand.'

Brand still more important than daughter, it seemed to Pauline, as she determined to get something else off her chest before delivering the explosive gallery news. Something she'd been wanting to say for years.

'Perhaps Natasha instinctively shies away from the falseness of it all', she ventured carefully. 'She sees you cultivating people you don't like and mostly hold in contempt, playing on their vanity and insecurity. What kind of life is that to look forward to? And you surely don't need any more money. Why not do something else? More worthwhile.'

His mother might have spoken to him like that once, but since she died no-one had dared. Yet it was a fair question, one he occasionally asked himself. The truth, when faced, was that he enjoyed his influence and celebrity status. There were plenty of successful entrepreneurs, which was all he used to be. But only one Oliver Rabson, art impresario, a name known by the rich and famous all over the world.

Rab fidgeted with his ear lobe. 'If I found something to be really enthusiastic about, then perhaps. He looked up. 'But none of this is a resigning matter. So what's happened?'

'There's something you don't know.' Pauline put down her cup, deciding it would be best for her to convey the news and bear the brunt of his anger. Mentally grabbing her shield, she said, 'Natasha wants to start up a gallery on her own, showcasing Ben Banding's art.'

'*What!*'

'And I've said I'll help her.'

If she'd whipped off her skirt and blouse and performed the dance of the seven veils, he could not have been more taken aback. It was out and out betrayal.

'You...would leave me...for Natasha!'

'That's only necessary if you refuse to help her yourself. I'll guide her through finding financial backing. And be her mentor.' Pauline looked at him, 'But it should be you, her father.'

'You expect me to finance a gallery selling art that's the exact opposite of what I've made my name promoting! I'd be a laughing stock in the art world. As would the Rabson brand.'

'So you'd prefer to alienate your daughter, the one person who loves you unconditionally, for fear of what the art world you profess to despise, might think! And for a brand launch to make more money. Which you don't need.' Pauline's round face was pink with indignation. 'It's your priorities that are so wrong.'

'I'm not prepared to listen to a lecture on my personal relations', Rab stood up, glowering at her.

'But it's time someone told you a few home truths, retorted Pauline, taking her undrunk coffee back to the tray. 'What was the profit from de-accessioning that early Tootsie Smalt artwork last month? Eight million wasn't it. And how much ransom money would you pay if Natasha was ever kidnapped?

'I don't play silly games', he snapped.

'What is silly – sad more like – is that you don't value what matters. The love and happiness of your only child. Is it because she's Gaye's daughter?

She didn't wait for him to answer. 'Because I'll tell you something. Gaye didn't take half your money. Well, she may have done, but what you got in return was priceless. A beautiful, intelligent, spirited daughter. Who adores you. Gaye didn't steal. She gave.'

He was staring at her as if he couldn't believe what he was hearing.

'And one more thing before I go.' Pauline walked back to the sofa to pick up her handbag. 'When the modern art bubble bursts – as it will, we all know it will – Oliver Rabson'll go down in history as just as gullible as everyone else. Worse in fact.'

The thunderstorm of his anger was about to break over her head.

'I'll go in tomorrow and clear my desk.' She reached the door, and then paused. 'By the way, that photo in today's Times, of the dog attacking a man in a rabbit suit, that's Ben Banding, the artist in question. I'll tell Natasha. Should make a wonderful hook for publicity.'

Chapter Twenty-One

Bugger, bugger, *bugger*! Oliver Rabson smashed his fist against the wall, anger and dismay intertwined with incredulity. God, not now. Not *now!* He felt like a farmer whose trusted working dog had gone savage, leaving his flock exposed on the hill with a blizzard brewing.

How could she! Pauline, his solid, indispensable assistant, had turned against him. It was treachery. And it hurt.

Nursing his hand, he walked to the window and gazed across the fields to the estuary, the little white triangles traversing the blue water reminding him of circling sharks. How to get her back? Increase her salary? By a lot. No, he told himself, turning away, this wasn't about money.

Yes it was. She thought so anyway. But his, not hers. 'Alienating your daughter for a brand launch, to make more money. Which you don't need.' Pauline's scathing words hung painfully in his mind.

Not fair, he fumed, going to the wardrobe. The Rabson brand would be something for Natasha to inherit, more solid than art. Nobody knew better than he did that a big financial crash could send the art market tits up.

The screen was showing a commentator with a background of large pound notes, and Rab searched for the remote to flick the sound on, listened for a few moments, then pressed the mute button again. The tone had been reassuring, but every business instinct was telling him that the financial world was about to plunge into a serious crisis. Not the ideal time to launch a celebrity lifestyle brand, he mused. It would be unthinkable for it to flop – Oliver Rabson didn't fail, any more than glass went rusty. Perhaps it might be best to pull the plug, for the moment anyway, however much that would cost at this late stage. He could tell Pauline she'd influenced his decision about it, which would please her.

She must be tempted back. How could she think of leaving him for some mad-cap idea of Natasha's?

Thoughtfully, he laid last night's suit on the bed. Natasha. She hadn't been at the party last night. And now he knew why. She was sobbing her heart out because of what he'd said to her. He pictured the scene, and winced. He could hardly bear to think about his lovely girl alone in her room and desperately unhappy.

'It's the wrong priorities that are so alienating', Pauline had reproached him. She hero-worships you.'

Had he failed her as a parent? Self doubt was not a condition Rab usually entertained, but his PA's desertion had rocked him. He thought back to his youth. Where would he have been without his own father's help and encouragement when he was starting out? And his mum's steadying influence, as the bicycle business became successful. 'Never lose sight of what's important, Ollie. Don't let big money change you.'

He folded the jacket. If his mother had still been alive, there would have been someone for the girl to run to, not just Pauline. And she'd have taken her granddaughter's side too. A ghost of a smile touched his lips as he pictured his mother, who'd never liked his venture into the art world. 'Manipulating people to buy rubbish – not what you should be using your talents for,' was her view, even though he assured her he was just doing it as a mocking outsider. It was simply parting suggestible mugs from their money. He imagined her forthright comment on the present situation.

'I warned you, Ollie. Money doesn't matter. Natasha's happiness does.'

With no mother around to say it, Pauline had. And was willing to leave him and help his daughter. 'But it should be you, her father.' Putting his jacket in the case, her words echoed in his mind as reluctantly he came to the conclusion. Bloody hell, the woman was right!

But there was more to it than simply agreeing to back Natasha's gallery, ramifications which seemed to have passed Pauline by. Championing a figurative artist would ruin his reputation in the contemporary art world. They'd laugh like drains, or more likely a pack of hyenas, and the press would seize on it with glee. Surviving all that would be tough. Along with his credibility would go the ability to make artists famous and sought after simply by buying their work. And then quietly selling on. So it'd mean a complete change. He'd have to reinvent his whole way of life. But would that be such a bad thing? He considered when he had last been positively happy – as opposed to triumphant or quietly pleased. Roaring down the road on the Bonny was the nearest he'd come to it, he had to conclude.

There'd been two distinct phases to his business life so far. Maybe it was time for a third, something he could build with Natasha, that she could take over eventually. They could start working together now, over this. It wouldn't make any money, but that in itself would be good experience for her, and they could move on to something else in due course. He nodded to himself as the idea appealed. It'd be enjoyable, building up a business again. Perhaps Pauline had been clear sighted about that too. And her accusation that he cared more about the art world's opinion than his daughter's welfare had hit home. Plus the jibe about him going down in history as just as gullible as everyone else. God forbid. His buying and apparent collecting had been ironic, maybe it was time the world knew that. Before it was too late.

The BlackBerry on the table beeped to signal an incoming email, and he went to read it. Life was going to be hectic in the next few days. Relations with Natasha must be put right now, at once, and Pauline won over.

Walking back to finish packing, he noticed the television picture, of a man dressed as a giant rabbit. He grabbed the remote, as what looked like an Old English Sheepdog launched itself at the costumed creature, and stood triumphantly on its chest, tail wagging joyously.

'...at an Art Festival in Rundleston, Suffolk', the commentator informed him when the sound came on. 'The footage on You Tube has already been viewed over twenty million times. And now for the weather, we go over to...'

The man inside the suit was apparently Ben Banding, Natasha's artist. Pauline was on the button there, it was a great start for publicity.

Positivity was beginning to take over from dilemma. Financing and mentoring his daughter would ensure Pauline wouldn't leave. Two problems solved in one. And if anyone could make a success of promoting a traditional artist, he could. Well, Natasha, with his help, influence and contacts.

Checking that nothing had been left in the bathroom, he caught sight of himself in the mirror. His face was now a better match for that prematurely grey hair which had prompted the nervously admiring 'Grey Wolf' soubriquet when he was young. The hazel eyes were just beginning to

313

have that aging, hollow look, and frown lines had been accentuated by his habitual scowl. There would be pictures in the media tomorrow of himself at Scroby's party, playing to the image he encouraged – astute hard man, rich, powerful and bad-tempered. Not to be messed with. Now, gazing at his reflection, he asked himself an uncomfortable question. Had he segued inside to the character he'd projected all these years?

It was not something he was prepared to admit.

But he'd said harsh things to his daughter and reduced her to tears, he thought with shame, and was suddenly overwhelmed by a rush of tenderness. As soon as he'd checked out he would go and find Natasha and apologise. Give her a huge hug. Tell her that he loved her, and would always look after her. He'd guide and protect. Make up for lost time and be a proper father to her. His little girl.

From now on, he resolved, she would be the centre of his life. He was a father, before everything else.

A few minutes later, crossing the foyer to check out of the hotel, he spied his ex-wife coming away from the reception desk. Normally he would have turned aside to avoid a meeting, but Pauline's words still resonated, acting as cooling rain on his still seething resentment. 'Gaye didn't steal. She gave you a wonderful daughter.' As their eyes met, Rab nodded to her.

'That was a good show you put on for the art festival opening yesterday.'

'Oh.' Taken aback, she only managed, 'Thank you.'

Settling himself into the Bentley, their brief encounter was still causing him some amusement. It was pleasing to be unpredictable. As he drove towards Rundleston, he passed a man sitting, his back against a gatepost, apparently watching a combine harvester at work in the field. Rural life was lived at a different pace, Rab reflected. Maybe, besides a new enterprise, he should buy himself a proper estate and take an interest in country matters. Give Pauline a nice weekend cottage too. His mood now matched the sunny day. He was about to mend the rift with her, and embrace his daughter. There might be a financial crash, but they'd be all right. He'd see to it. It would be them against the world.

Ben had walked unseeingly away from the hotel, down the drive, his mind in turmoil. He needed to come to terms with so many things.

Confused and angry, he turned towards Rundleston. Just seeing Gaye had been a shock. Older of course,and still beautiful, but everything about her jarred, from the studied, sophisticated outfit and elaborate make-up to the provocative expression and gushing insincerity. The difference between Natasha and her mother had been as stark as freshly fallen snow compared with stuff that lingered for weeks, trampled, soiled and frozen hard. And this had been his icon, the goddess he'd worshipped all these years!

There was a good deal of Saturday morning traffic, as people headed towards shops and the market, and some might even have been intending to visit the art festival. Preoccupied with his thoughts, an unnoticed car overtaking a tractor and trailer nearly struck him, and he retreated to the verge. What an idiot! he thought, applying it to present and past.

How could his young self have been so wrong? Had she changed radically, or was it simply that he'd been too naive to judge her character, blinded by those enchanting looks?

Probably a bit of both, he concluded, trying to order his thoughts. Being able to mesmerise men must have a corrosive effect, and then she'd married a very rich man. My God, he stood still as the realisation struck home. She'd really used Oliver Rabson. Palmed someone else's child off on him, and married him for security and money. For the first time Ben felt a scintilla of sympathy for his enemy, but quickly swept it aside. That man had wielded a malign influence over his life, now the tables were turned, and with this new knowledge, he had power over Rab's. He was about to take something precious away from him, and it was a satisfying feeling.

The verge nearest the road was a strip of fresh green, where the council had mown a few weeks ago and young grass was growing again. Further towards the hedges the thin stalks were tall and straw-coloured, interwoven with late summer flowers, yellow snapdragon, coarse hogweed, yarrow and the thick, fluffy heads of thistles gone to seed. Ben's artist's eye automatically took in the soft colours, as he considered what to do now.

He was a family man! Gaye's confession had changed everything. He wanted to rush and tell Natasha she was his daughter. And after that? What?

The tractor had turned into the gateway of a wheat field just ahead. There was a lovely view from there across the water to the fields and woods on the other side, one he'd painted several times. Today the river was busy with a sailing club race, and, amid a cloud of dust a large, red combine harvester was noisily working its way round the ripe corn, accompanied now by the tractor and trailer, the two drivers skilfully keeping pace as the grain was transferred in a golden arc. Ben sat down against the gatepost and watched. The foreground activity contrasting with that crowd of dinghies would make a great composition, and he reached for his pocket sketch book and began drawing. As always he felt it relax him, as soothing as a cigarette to a stressed smoker.

It was odd not to have Bodger sitting by his side, but the dog would have gone mad at the numerous rabbits making a dash for safety, their tall corn sanctuary growing smaller by the minute. Ben smiled as his pencil deftly recreated the scene. Yesterday a giant rabbit, today a father. For someone living a quiet, uneventful existence it was all a bit much.

Could this be the beginning of a new life? he wondered, an unrealistic picture of Natasha moving permanently to Rundleston to be with her father and grandmother forming pleasurably in his mind as he drew. Was he moving from a dull and shadowed past to happy sunshine?

As if in answer a white, woolly cloud moving inexorably on the westerly breeze, obscured the sun, and he shook himself back to reality. No good trying to plan for the unknowable. And on a practical note, he must go and retrieve Bodger from Natasha. She'd kindly undertaken to look after him so that the vet story wouldn't be rumbled. Perhaps it would prove to be the moment for breaking the news he was dying to give her. Instinct would tell him.

Getting to his feet, he noticed a mass of field bindweed, its pretty pink trumpet flowers appealing in their loveliness, heartlessly smothering the life out of a young oak sapling beside the hedge. In a spirit of comradeship with the struggling tree, he bent down and yanked off the bindweed's main stalks at ground level, before setting off again towards Rundleston. He rather liked the analogy with himself, now released from Gaye's smothering influence, conveniently ignoring the fact that his own imprisonment had been self-inflicted.

Gaye had got her tendrils round Tony now, Ben thought. But his former shock and anger had been replaced by a detachment bordering on satisfaction. Hell they deserved each other. After all, Tony hadn't known about the past, and if Gaye was to be believed, he'd previously been chasing after Natasha. That was a revolting thought.

As he approached the centre of town, he regretted not confronting his brother at The Dutch House. Tony must be made aware in no uncertain terms that his misuse of Ben's innocent daubs was known, and unforgiven. And be warned off Natasha. Probably gone back to London by now though.

But when Ben reached Chandlers, the yard gates were open, and his brother was just getting into the driving seat of a large hire van, preparing to back out.

It was the sounds of argument a few minutes later that made Madge, carrying some rubbish to the dustbin, hesitate in the act of opening the back door. She'd never heard mild, easy-going Ben raise his voice before, but this was clearly a serious row with Tony, who she'd already encountered this morning. No prizes for guessing it was about the fake Scroby. Good manners dictated that she retreat out of earshot, but the temptation to listen was too strong. Holding the door slightly ajar, she could see Tony, standing beside the van.

'No need to get your knickers in a twist. Scroby doesn't do his stuff himself anyway. Lighten up.' He shrugged dismissively. 'Forget it.'

'No. I won't forget what you did,' his brother told him tersely. 'And you'd better remember how nearly you caused a disaster for the family.'

Madge would have added 'again', but Ben generously refrained.

'And that's not all.'

'Oh I get it. You're after your share of the money.'

'I wouldn't touch a poisoned penny of it.' Ben almost spat the words. 'And how you can...'

'I don't have to stand and listen to you pontificating', Tony cut in impatiently, opening the driver's door.

'You will if you know what's good for you. Because there's something else you need to know. Stay clear of Natasha. Do you hear. Keep away from her.'

'Fancy her yourself, do you', sneered Tony. 'Imagine a high class piece of skirt like her would even glance in your direction? In your dreams!'

'If I ever find you chasing after her, you'll be out of Grashes and into a prison cell so fast your feet won't touch the ground.' There was no mistaking the menace in Ben's voice. 'I'll tell them everything they need to know about that Scroby.'

'You wouldn't do that.' But some of Tony's bluster had gone. 'You're the one who produced it. Had you forgotten that. You'd be in it up to your neck as well.'

'Just try me. Or rather don't. Stick to the mother.'

It took Tony a beat to catch up.

'You just can't bear for me to be successful with money and women can you. Because no female in her right mind would fall for a no-hope dork like you, you're eaten up with jealousy.'

'I think you'd better go', Ben responded with restrained anger. 'But din it into that sick brain – *leave Natasha alone.* Or else. Got it?'

Madge heard the van start up and manoeuvre out into the road with a furious gunning of the engine. Shakily she leant back against the wall, as if it was a lift that had just fallen forty floors.

Before the van had disappeared down the High Street, Ben was already reproaching himself. It was hurtful for Nora to have her sons quarrelling, and he shouldn't let Tony get to him. Jealousy over women didn't come into it, but he couldn't deny that Tony *was* a success in the eyes of the world, whereas his older brother...? Might there be a sliver of truth about his own sensitivity to the comparison? No, they simply had different values, Ben told himself defensively. And natures. Stuff it anyway. He must calm down and go and retrieve the dog. Talking to Natasha would make him feel better, especially hugging to himself his new knowledge.

As he shut the yard gates, he pictured her packing up the stock, chastened and alone, preparing to close down the business before it had even started because of Rabson's bullying, uncompromising attitude over the gallery. And Natasha, bless her, had sided with him! Her announcement this morning that she wanted to set up on her own selling his work had been like the first day of spring after a long, cold winter. She believed in him and valued what he did, in defiance of Rabson.

Crossing the square, so Nora wouldn't see him pass the shop window, his heart swelled with love for his loyal, spirited daughter. Right now she'd be feeling a bit raw though, in need of cheering up – and a loving, supportive father. As he was going to be. In fact this was probably the perfect time to tell her who she really was.

He walked round the back of the gallery where the Mini was parked, and knocked.

Natasha flung open the door, that heart-stopping face aglow with pleasure at seeing him, and Ben was swept with loving pride.

'*Ben!*' She seized his arm with delight. 'You're here! Isn't it wonderful!'

He stared at her, puzzled.

'Didn't you know? Haven't you spoken to Nora? She's been fending off the media and no-one knew where you were.' Natasha lowered her voice. 'Well I did of course, but...' she looked meaningfully at him and put her finger to her lips. 'My father's here. You must come and meet him. I've told him all about you.'

There was something very wrong with this script.

Ben followed her through the kitchen area into the main gallery. Sitting on one of the edgy but uncomfortable tube chairs was unmistakably Oliver Rabson, the man he'd hated from afar all his adult life, the man to blame for his art being spurned and ridiculed, who'd seduced his fiancée and stolen his daughter. And now he was making a fuss of his dog!

But seeing his master, Bodger sprang towards him, and Ben was subjected to a paroxysm of welcome, as Natasha laughingly made the introductions.

'Dad, this is Ben. Reginald Rabbit, no less! Complete now with dog.'

Unwillingly Ben held out his hand which was shaken firmly, the hazel eyes coolly assessing him.

'Ah, the man of the moment. My daughter's a great fan of yours. She's been telling me all about you. And your work.' Rab nodded towards the far wall, on which now hung two of Ben's small paintings, the other four on the floor beneath, leaning against the skirting board.

'You're a celebrity, Ben! And Bodger.' Natasha picked up a copy of The Times and showed him the photograph. 'Apparently several newspapers are carrying it. Someone posted what happened on YouTube, and it's gone viral. Didn't you know?'

Ben was bewildered. He was aware of YouTube, but had never bothered with it himself. 'What does it mean?'

'Reginald Rabbit is now a global image, an internet sensation. We've got to link that with you and use it to market you as an artist', Rabson told him. 'I'm getting my publicist on to it, and organising a press conference on Monday in Berkeley Square, to fan interest in the media. A website is an urgent priority – I'll organise that – and we'll work out a campaign.'

We? Who was this 'we'?

'Dad and I are going to pack this into boxes,' Natasha waved at the stock, 'and have a van take it back to London tomorrow, together with all those paintings in your studio. Can we take the framed ones from your flat – and do you think Nora would let us borrow hers? They'd be a real wow.'

Ben looked from one to the other of what was apparently his new promotional team. 'You want me to go up to London for a press conference? About my art?' he queried incredulously.

Natasha bestowed on him her delicious smile. 'Oh yes. With Bodger of course.' Her eyes danced mischievously. 'And you're going to need that Reginald Rabbit suit...'

Oliver Rabson, celebrity and multi-millionaire, launched into the task of packing up the gallery with a willingness to muck in so at variance with Ben's image of the enemy it was akin to discovering a bad-tempered rhino giving beach rides to children. He himself undertook to sort out all the saleable work in his studio, as well as raiding Chandlers for pictures, after obtaining Nora's agreement. Apologising to Madge about denuding her flat's walls, he said, 'Can I come and explain this evening. There's so much to tell you.'

Nora invited him to supper, and he found Pauline there as well, which was useful. Quietly pleased at the turn of events, she was able to reassure him that his coming few days in the spotlight would be handled well.

'I'll be organising most of it, so I can make sure Rab doesn't push you too hard', she assured him. 'You've been booked into a central London hotel, but if you and Bodger would rather stay with me you'd be very welcome.'

Her presence also meant his mother couldn't pursue him about the morning's disappearance, complete with turned off mobile. Nora had to be content with letting the matter ride for the moment. It was a small town though, if her son declined to tell her she knew she'd find out eventually.

As soon as they'd finished eating, with the excuse that he owed Madge an explanation for whipping the art off her sitting room walls, Ben left the two women chatting, and knocked on the door of the ground floor flat. He found her in a calf-length skirt and soft jersey, auburn hair loosely tied back, iron in hand whilst watching TV. Graceful Botticelli model, even doing the ironing, he thought, soothed to come upon such a blessedly mundane activity after the most abnormal of days.

As she turned off the television, he looked round the sitting room, walls starkly bare of their familiar paintings, while Bodger padded round his old home in exploratory fashion.

'Apologies for the raid on the flat', he nodded towards the empty spaces, faint outlines showing where the pictures had hung. You'll have them back soon, I've insisted on that. But there's going to be a press conference at Rabson's place in London, with a background of framed work. To showcase me, would you believe', he said wonderingly.

'So I heard.' She was moving the pile of ironed clothes from the armchair. 'I popped in to see Natasha at the gallery while her father was taking Pauline out to lunch today. Mending fences apparently. Did you know Pauline told him where to stick his job this morning?'

'Really? Why?' He took over folding the ironing board, and leant it against the wall.

Natasha didn't know what it was about, but it's my guess she told him to treat his daughter better, or else. So that's why he's changed his mind and is backing you.'

'I've just had a meal with her upstairs, and she never said a word.' He sank down thankfully on the sofa. 'You're probably right though, that would certainly explain it. I can hardly believe what's happening, Madge, and it would be a real help to discuss things with you.'

'Ben!' Excitedly Jamie rushed into the room in his pyjamas. 'Isn't it ace! That clip of you and Bodger – it's *massive*, everyone's watching it! And I uploaded it!'

'Oh it's you I've got to thank is it Jamie.' Ben clapped his hand to his head in mock despair. 'Forty-two years of blameless life and I end up as a bl... ruddy rabbit', he lamented, raising his voice for the benefit of the boy's mother, taking the iron to cool in the kitchen.

Through the doorway she could see her son sitting happily on the sofa, as he played the now famous clip for Ben on the computer. This was how it ought to be, the man she loved as part of the family. And after Jamie's bed time, just the two of them. She fought a sudden wave of longing to kiss him and melt into him.... Stupid besom! she checked herself.

You mean nothing to him. And judging by this morning, she thought with desolation, never will.

'This whole thing gets weirder', Ben commented, as Jamie did a search to show him the references to Reginald Rabbit now proliferating across the internet. 'The local paper and BBC Look East insisted on doing an interview today, and I'm just not suited to people wanting to know all the sort of stuff you see in articles and on TV. It was as if I was a newly discovered species. "Traditional artist, found living in obscurity on British coast."'

'With a penchant for dressing up as a giant rabbit', she added mischievously. 'Would you like a coffee? Or a carrot?'

'I'd prefer a glass of wine – let's celebrate the great escape.'

'White or red?'

'You mean you're entertaining the great Reginald Rabbit and you haven't got in dandelion!'

It was the first time there'd been an opportunity to talk properly since their brief walk back along the beach at Woodshey Bay the previous evening. After Jamie had gone to bed – with surprisingly little resistance, and an odd glance at Ben – Madge curled herself up on the armchair opposite him and they chewed over their narrow escape from disaster at the art festival opening, and what could have prompted Scroby to validate Transformation. Each for their own reasons avoided mentioning Tony's culpability in the forgery. Better to surmise who was responsible for the frogs, and relish the delicious irony of Danny winning the competition.

There were also commercial implications for the shop of Ben's sudden, and decidedly eccentric, fame.

'I think Nora ought to order more prints', was Madge's opinion. 'All this publicity should push up sales. Our very own Monet', she said, making mock obeisance to him, 'tourists will be flocking to Rundleston like they do to Giverny.'

She ducked, laughing, as Ben threw a cushion at her.

'This whole thing's just going to be a nine-day wonder', he stated. 'If that. What I can't decide though, is how to handle it. Do I meekly let Rabson present me as his latest protégé, take the money from selling paintings at inflated prices, and run? Or do I use the press interviews etc to sound off about contemporary stuff being a complete confidence trick?'

'Rab won't like you doing that. That's what he's made oodles of money from.'

'All the more tempting. I've always hated the man', he confessed, 'and what he stood for... Picking on some crap student and making out he's a new Leonardo. With prices to match.'

'Now he's sprinkling his stardust over you!' Madge got up to refill his wine. 'Only this time he's picked a real talent.'

'Can feel my head swelling already.'

'Here's to Reginald da Vinci', she raised her glass to him teasingly.

Ben laughed. 'There's more to it than just selling my paintings though. He apparently thinks this whole Reginald Rabbit thing has commercial possibilities. In fact Natasha's been instructed to go and see Arabella Drail tomorrow and make an offer for the copyright of her play, giving Rab full rights to the character. It's not something I want to get mixed up in. I'm me, not Reginald Rabbit.

What do you think? And I also have a favour to ask you.'

'That'll cost you', she informed him. 'Especially if you're going to be Mr. Moneybags now. What is it?'

'Well, could you possibly cover for me in the shop while I'm in London? It's not fair for it all to fall on Nora. Your job at the art festival was only up until the launch, wasn't it?'

'Mm. Arabella might ask me to go in for a few hours this week, but basically that's it. I shall have to think what to do now. So of course I'll help, it'll be a pleasure. But', her voice was stern, 'you have to promise to report back to us yokels on the great metropolis.'

'Done. And thank you, it's much appreciated. Now, I really would value your advice on this. Do I have fun? Or concentrate on making money? Probably the only chance I'll ever have.'

Fingering her glass, Madge looked across at him. The curly hair, greying slightly at the sides, soft brown eyes with that slightly wistful expression, and the mouth she desperately wanted to kiss. A deep and unspoilt man, whose amazing art had been ignored by the world. Well it didn't help that his paintings had been stashed away unseen. But now was his moment. Publicity and promotion by the Rabson machine was just the boost his talent needed. If he played along. She pictured him feted and flattered, latched on to by the art-partying crowd.

'I think', she said slowly, 'that you should be yourself. Marketing is all about glossing and shaping a product, and making it desirable in the public's eyes. Rab will try to do that with you and your art, and the result will certainly be more money. But that's not as important as...'

On impulse she reached across and lightly put her hand on his. 'Don't let them change you.' She smiled up at him. 'You're lovely as you are.'

It was with reluctance that some time later Ben tore himself away from the homely atmosphere and Madge's relaxing company, to give Bodger his late night run before returning to the barge. Now as he walked back to the boatyard, thoughts and images from the day swirled and merged as if his mind was a kaleidoscope. Gaye at the Dutch House and that life-changing confirmation about Natasha, the caustic row with Tony, meeting Oliver Rabson, such a bogeyman all these years, and packing up his paintings for transport to

London tomorrow. But it was the flat where he'd just spent the last couple of hours that kept coming to the fore. Boarding the Hetty Jane in the half dark, sniffing the familiar scent of wet mud and seaweed, he found himself comparing the natural grace and elegance of Madge, even doing the ironing, with Gaye that morning, all dolled up, brittle and self-aware. The contrast was stark.

He could have married someone like Madge, he reflected, helping Bodger down the steep stairs to the focs'le. Had a proper family life. Hell, he could have married Madge, after all he'd known her since she was a schoolgirl. Why hadn't he seen what a pearl she was? Instead he'd had his eyes fixed on a mirage all these years. Fool! *Fool!* The ache of what could have been was hard to bear.

But was it too late to put right? Jamie had done him the honour of asking him to be his second father. Lying in his bunk, wide awake, he saw anew that conspiratorial look before going off to bed, and realised now the boy had been egging him on to pop the question. Madge as his wife. The thought was suddenly thrilling.

Capable, intelligent, lively and fun, she would make a wonderful companion. He recalled how the customers responded to her warmth and friendly interest. And Nora already treated her like a daughter. He pictured life with her, and could find nothing that wasn't delightful. Living in a place that meant so much to both of them, giving Jamie a secure and happy homelife. Loving each other. Cautiously he unlocked the memory of Madge in his arms the night they'd been catching moths. Oh yes. Oh God yes. Loving her was not a problem.

But why would she want to have anything to do with him?

'No female in her right mind would look at a no-hope dork like you.'

Tony was right. He'd made a complete mess of his life. This gleam of fame and success was just that, a spark that would fizzle out. No, the whole thing didn't stack up. It was yet another fantasy, he reproached himself. Thirteen years younger, there was not a chance that Madge would feel the same way. She probably just felt sorry for him.

But then he remembered the touch of her hand, and that gentle encouragement, 'You're lovely as you are.'

And a seedling of hope grew in the darkness.

Chapter Twenty-Two

The next five days were the most surreal of Ben's life. He felt as if he'd been drawn into a tide race, with no steering way – buffeted, banged and tipped every which way. He and Bodger spent only one night in the hotel, before thankfully accepting Pauline's kind offer of sanctuary. Her West Kensington flat at least represented some semblance of normality, and he was able to email Madge and Nora every evening. He missed the beauty of the river and the reassuring familiarity of Rundleston, but above all he found his thoughts, at night, when at last he was on his own, turning to Madge. He pictured that effortless stride, her freckled face and blue eyes, her smile. He went over the times they'd laughed together, the good-natured teasing, her supportive loyalty, and that hand over his. Could it have been a caress? The memory of it now caused him to tingle with suppressed excitement. She was the woman he'd waited all his life for – the certainty grew. That he hadn't been able to see it, and for the moment could do nothing, made him feel as helpless as a hostage held against his will. But soon the ransom would be paid, and he would be free to rush back to Rundleston and tell her he loved her.

Two things must be got over first. It was now especially important to make the most of this extraordinary publicity that was promising sales of his paintings at figures he could only gasp at. No longer would he be some penniless nobody, they would be able to buy a house in Rundleston. Nothing grand of course, but better than the flat. One of the old bargee's cottages, perhaps.

He was also waiting for a moment that was exactly right to tell Natasha the momentous news that Rabson wasn't really her father. *He* was. Now there'd been time to absorb Gaye's confirmation about her parentage, the need to tell Natasha gnawed at his mind. When she'd driven him up to London, shadowing the van containing his paintings, she'd wanted to know about his conversation with Gaye, and it should have been the perfect time to reveal the truth. But seeing her bubbling with enthusiasm and pleasure at the rapprochement with Rabson, he couldn't bring himself to do it. Instead he just made up some guff about giving Gaye the portrait, and consigning her now to the past. It seemed to please their daughter.

He'd thought that there would be lots of opportunities to tell Natasha when they got to London. But he hadn't reckoned on being so much in demand. Oliver Rabson and Natasha, aided by Pauline, were both his lifeline and chief tormentors, filtering out the hundreds of commercial opportunities and requests for comments, commissions and personal appearances, but organising every hour of his day.

To date the YouTube clip had been viewed over two hundred million times, and a Reginald Rabbit fan club sprang up on the net. An American film producer approached Rab about creating a cartoon character. The brewery which had taken over Jahneys beer were proposing to bring out a special Reginald Rabbit ale, and several other companies wanted to use him in advertising campaigns. And Bodger too. Ben wasn't at all sure about that.

But true to his promise, Oliver Rabson had ensured this mania was harnessed and linked to the man inside the suit. Ben Banding was an artist of rare talent, was the word he put out. This was a modern John Constable, ignored and derided and reduced to dressing up as a giant rabbit. His talent though had been recognised by Rabson's daughter, who would be setting up a London gallery to showcase his work. With the stock market and financial world in a worryingly wobbly state, Rab intimated that, as an investment, Ben's traditional style and outstanding talent might turn out to have more substance than a lot of other things the rich had put their faith in. Who wouldn't have been glad they'd bought an early Constable?

A special party was being thrown at Berkeley Square for those who might like to meet this artist that everyone was talking about. It would of course be an invitation for the select few, and an early opportunity to purchase his work, since Rab, employing his legendary instinct for the next big artist, had tight control of all the originals. People wishing to buy a Ben Banding now had to negotiate through Natasha nominally, although no-one was under any illusion about who was standing behind her.

But the media sensed a story behind the story. At the Berkeley Square press call on that first Monday afternoon Rab had batted away their questions. Did his enthusiasm for this realist artist mean he was turning his back on the contemporary stuff he'd previously bought, the collection of art he was known for? Had he had a change of heart?

'Not at all. I'm inspired by talent, wherever I find it', he intoned unctuously. 'Whether it's Lyndon Scroby or Ben Banding. This division between art expressions is entirely artificial.'

It wasn't in Rab's interest to repudiate his 'collection'. That all had to be sold on quietly first. And he wanted the focus to be on Ben Banding, newly discovered artist, championed by his daughter.

The art correspondents especially had other ideas. This stood a chance of getting in the news pages. The papers' editors reckoned public unease usefully boosted circulation, and so many impossible things were happening, with banks swaying like woollen skyscrapers, it seemed the world as everyone knew it was coming to an end. A challenge to modern art increased that iconoclastic feeling, and was also popular with the general public, so several papers came out with unhelpful headers to their stories.

Rabson champions traditional art! *Rab sees the light! Daughter opens Rab's eyes.*

Ben did a number of interviews where the questions were obviously influenced by this take on things, and didn't hold back on his opinions.

'What do I think of most modern art? Unrepeatable. The whole thing's a confidence trick designed to make money', he stated enjoyably. 'If we leave dirty plates in a bowl, we're just not bothering to wash up.   But if a so-called 'artist' does the same thing, well, suddenly it's worth thousands of pounds. Never mind logic and reason. Isn't it time we all laughed at it.'

The art establishment was quickly up in arms. There was already nervousness about the wobbling financial world and the consequences for wealthy buyers on whom galleries, art dealers and fair organisers, investment specialists and art advisors depended. They fought back with snide references to Ben Banding as a failed artist who'd never sold a painting in his life, champion of a deeply old-fashioned, derivative style. The thinking world had long since moved on.   They also turned on Rab with fury. What did he think he was doing, breaking ranks, challenging the whole construct and belief system! You simply couldn't extol the genius of a canvas consisting of just one colour, at the same time as admiring a recent representation of a mother and child walking beneath sunlit trees. It was about as tenable as a woman maintaining she was partly a virgin. You either got modern art, or you didn't. No half measures.

Natasha reckoned the public fighting was helpful, resulting in more publicity. But having been one of the art world's leading figures for so long, Rab was finding the whole thing thoroughly uncomfortable.   When challenged face to face, he weaselled out of it by intimating that his daughter was determined to champion this artist, and he was backing her to prevent a family split. Meanwhile Natasha was instructed to tell Ben to tone down his comments. Most of the potential buyers invited to the party on Friday would have substantial collections of modern art, she told him dutifully. It wasn't in his interest to make them out as mugs. Not if he wanted them to be encouraged to buy at the highest prices.

In his emails home, Ben relayed the fact that Natasha had asked him to pull his punches, and he'd reluctantly agreed. He omitted to mention his new eagerness to make as much money as possible, a basis for the married life he now joyfully envisaged.

He was seeing a side of Natasha now that surprised him. She seemed so at home in London, confident and assured, in contrast to his own feeling of being lost and out of his depth. When she wasn't helping to organise the launch party, fielding commercial possibilities, or setting up and escorting him to interviews, Natasha scooted round looking at various premises for her gallery. Although supportive, Rab warned her that she would have to find other artists to represent, in addition to Ben Banding. And he insisted that she only arrange to rent, not buy. The main trouble with traditional art, he advised, was that quality work took time, so you had a problem of supply. No such difficulty of course with contemporary stuff. That had been the beauty of it.

Ben viewed Friday evening's event at Berkeley Square with some apprehension.

'I'm just not a party animal', he confessed to Pauline, who'd somehow divined as much.

'Don't worry', she reassured him. 'Most of the A-listers will be there to mingle and network with each other. They know of course that their invitations rest on the requirement to buy, or at least go through the motions, so there'll be a lot of insincere cooing. But you're only the excuse for the gathering, not the main event.'

Ben didn't know whether to be insulted or relieved at this information. For two decades his talent had been scorned by the world, even his drawing ability summarily dismissed by the college tutors. Resentful and defiant, he'd seen public recognition for his art as just an impossible dream. Now, unbelievably, a swish party had been organised in his honour, and the rich and famous invited. And they were only coming to meet each other.

You have to laugh, he emailed Madge and Nora, just before leaving for Berkeley Square. *Think I'll just regard them as a different species, with curiosity value. Which is probably just how they'll view me. Can't wait to get back to the real world, I tell you.*

The real world was very much absent from the evening, which passed in a whirl of people many of whose faces he seemed to know from somewhere, and only afterwards did Ben realise he'd been speaking to a high-profile industrialist, celebrated actress, newspaper editor or member of the government. Or rather they had been speaking to him. The paintings from Chandlers, interspersed with many others from the studio that Natasha had now had framed, looked wonderful on the walls of the beautifully proportioned rooms. Both the Government Art Collection and the Arts Council were expressing interest in buying, a Whitehall mandarin informed him, and two of the most important British ambassadors had requested originals for their embassies. Ben was heartened to have quite a few people exclaim, with apparent sincerity, that they loved his work. How refreshing it was to see paintings that gladdened the eye, they said, and stayed with you. 'Real' art, instead of hideous creations that had to be 'explained', and you wouldn't know which way up to hang anyway. That was if you could bear to live with the stuff.

He was asked about Rundleston, his art philosophy (what did that mean?), how many paintings did he have for sale, what was his connection with Natasha Rabson (if they only knew!), would he be willing to do portraits, and how had he come to be dressed up as a rabbit last week? (First Friday in the month, he told them. Always did.) And most frequently about Bodger, who sat quietly at his side, submitting to being petted and fussed over by complete strangers, peering out from his fringe with a patiently amused expression, occasionally looking up at his master as if to say, I'll stick with you, but what have you brought me to now?

Ben observed Rab working the room, and slowly realised this was the sort of party that only those who'd made it had a hope of being invited to. No wonder the guests relished the opportunity to network, as well as to see and be seen. If the price of the invitation was merely buying a piece of high-priced art from Rab's daughter, that was as good as done. It would be regarded as an excellent investment socially as well as, in all likelihood, financially.

Natasha was not exactly a disincentive to buy either. She was wearing a deceptively simple black dress with a scalloped neckline, the curves echoed on the silver belt. Even Ben's untutored eye could tell this was not a dress you could go into any old shop and buy, and it enhanced her childish attraction by adding a hint of latent sophistication. She was simply delicious, with a correspondingly mesmerising effect on all the men, partnered or not. But she declined to flirt back, and spent just as much time and attention on the women, bringing people over to introduce to Ben, and generally acting as a charming hostess. He was torn between pride at having produced this lovely girl, and pain that she didn't know it. Also another man was getting the credit. Not just anyone either, but his bête noire, Oliver Rabson. To crown everything, the paintings Ben had stored away all these years, promising himself would one day be used as weapons against Rabson, were now displayed in the man's house, or at least the modern art gallery he ostensibly lived in. Apparently he'd even earmarked one for his own office, an unheard of compliment, according to Natasha.

These past few days Ben's antipathy had changed to a grudging respect, but there was never likely to be any warmth between them. Not even liking. He accepted Natasha's explanation that the stuff Rab supposedly collected, but in fact made a great deal of money from, was simply regarded as a commodity like any other. But the calculating falseness of it all was beyond Ben's comprehension. How could you live life like that? Pretending to espouse something you actually despised? If Natasha had truly been fathered by Rabson, he told himself, she could never have been blessed with that sincere and open nature. Those were clearly *his* genes.

That the party was going well was something of a relief to Rab. As an acknowledged colossus of the art world, up to now his parties had consisted of stars from that sphere leavened with other celebrities. But with its present hostility, no-one from the art world had been invited tonight. Instead, working with his publicist, he'd sent invitations to A-listers from across the spectrum. And gratifyingly, most of them had come, perhaps prompted by the Reginald Rabbit publicity phenomenon. His own name might have been made in the world of art, Rab reflected, looking round with satisfaction at the many famous faces animatedly enjoying each other's company, but if he was going to leave that behind, with these sort of connections he was not short of choices for the future. This oddball artist of Natasha's might have come at just the right time. He caught her eye, and she moved towards him, a vision of feminine sweetness. Pauline was right. She was worth everything to him, no sacrifice too great.

'Everyone's enjoying themselves, he told her unnecessarily, 'and you're a wonderful hostess.' He touched her cheek affectionately, 'I'm so proud of you, Tash.'

Her answering smile of love lit up his heart like a flashbulb.

Between conversations, unwillingly Ben had noticed the natural partnership of the two Rabsons, overseeing the party together. Now as he watched from across the room, he saw Natasha look up at Rab and smile, and felt his stomach lurch.

It was the same adoration that he'd seen on the face of the little girl on the beach, looking up at her father.

He couldn't bear it. Suddenly the desire to get away overwhelmed him, away from all these people, the babble, noise and shallowness. Finding Pauline he told her, almost incoherently, that he wasn't feeling too good, and needed to go back to the flat. Anxiously she got him a taxi, and promised to get home herself as soon as she could. Probably thought he'd had too much to drink, Ben realised, leaning back in the seat as shaky as if he'd been grazed by a speeding lorry. To shield himself from the memory of that smile, he turned on his phone and found a text message had been sent earlier in the evening.

Mayday! Mum's taking us to Canada, the words on the screen burnt into his bruised brain. *Please help! Jamie.*

Chapter Twenty-Three

That Saturday evening visit to the flat had changed things for Madge too. Ben's face, his voice, the image of him and Jamie relaxing happily on the sofa, just wouldn't leave her. She thought about him every minute of the day, and now realised what people meant by being deeply in love. It was like an illness, somehow affecting everything from breathing to brain. Especially the brain. But the row with Tony had also burnt into her mind, and reading Ben's daily emails from London in which Natasha featured prominently, her feeling of hopelessness was reinforced. If she stayed in Rundleston she'd see this man just about every day, the equivalent of being an alcoholic with glass of wine permanently set in front of her.

'You were right and I was wrong', she admitted sadly to Tricia, as they waited while their respective sons confidently completed a midweek cycling proficiency course. 'Ben seems to have got over Gaye, but transferred his fixation to Natasha. Leaves no room for me.' Her freckled face was pale and set. 'I can't help the way I feel about him, so I've decided to go away.'

'No!' This unwelcome news was out of the blue. 'You can't mean it girl! It's been great having you back.'

'And I've loved being here. But... well I think a clean break in Canada might be best. For everyone.'

'Not for Jamie', Tricia observed, watching the helmeted small boy in question energetically weaving through the slalom, a gleeful smile on his face. 'He's happy here now. And what about your ex? Hardly a good idea from his point of view, surely.'

'I'm going to talk to him about it', Madge told her, with the guilty discomfort of one trying to justify damaging other people. 'See what we can sort out.'

'Well I think it's a daft idea. Why can't you and Ben get together? – you'd make a great couple.' Tricia's matchmaking skills were now challenged. 'He should be flattered that you're nuts about him. What did he say?'

'He doesn't know.'

'You haven't told him!' Then how can you be sure he's only got eyes for Natasha? You could be wrong.'

'I found out by accident', Madge said carefully, 'something I overheard. Believe me, it's true.'

Stephen was now about to tackle the slalom, and Tricia gave him an encouraging wave.

'Well I'll give Ben an earful when he gets back', she decided, 'tell him he'd be mad to let you disappear across the world just because he's mooning after some girl who's young enough to be his daughter. Needs his head examined.'

'Oh no, please don't say anything', pleaded Madge. 'You can't make someone love you. He doesn't have a clue how I feel, and it's better that way. Truly.'

Nora was very glad of her help in the shop, where they were noticeably busier. Partly this was because increasing numbers of holiday makers were putting Rundleston's art festival on their agenda (something to do, and they could have lunch and look round the town at the same time), but also curiosity sparked by Reginald Rabbit mania was bringing visitors. This little place was where the famous YouTube clip was shot, and through the shop window tourists could be seen already posing for each other in the exact spot where the giant rabbit had been leapt on by an exuberantly shaggy dog.

At Chandlers Nora and Madge had been amazed by the extraordinary power of the internet, and discussed the things Ben was getting up to in London, as relayed by him in humorous emails to them both. They searched the newspapers for mentions and listened as far as possible to his interviews. Yet Madge's sparkle had gone and her face was strained. Nora sensed her distress, but also that she didn't want to talk about the cause, whatever it was. Jamie was to spend the weekend with his father, and there seemed to be increased tension between Madge and her former husband. The cause of that, and evidently her general unhappiness, was revealed when Madge came up to Nora's flat on Saturday morning and announced she had decided to leave for a new life in Canada.

'Are you really set on this?' asked Nora. 'Why not give it more time.'

'No, I'll need to get Jamie into a school by the start of the term, and...' her voice trailed away.

'You'll be so much missed, my dear, that hardly needs saying', Nora gave her a comforting hug. 'I'm really sorry, and if there's anything I can do to help just tell me. Are you sure you're still happy to do this afternoon's shift in the shop?'

'Yes of course. It's good to keep busy, takes my mind off Jamie being away.'

Ben found it more difficult than he had anticipated to escape from London. He'd forgotten there was a photo shoot and interview scheduled for Saturday morning, which couldn't be got out of. He also had to field Natasha's anxious enquiries as to what had prompted this sudden desire to leave, and pleaded exhaustion.

'But I can always come back if needed', he assured her, 'it just isn't fair to leave Nora struggling with the shop. Especially as things are picking up, she says.'

Rab offered to have him driven back, but Ben hastily declined, cringing at the thought of arriving home in a chauffeur-driven Bentley. He'd never live it down. So the car took him and Bodger to Liverpool Street station.

There were engineering works on the line, which caused delays. This was frustrating when he was willing himself back to Rundleston with all speed, but it did give extra time to get his thoughts and turbulent emotions in order.

With one adoring look, Natasha had smashed the dream of reclaiming his daughter. He'd instinctively known it at that moment, but now he had to think things through. Brought up effectively without a father, the girl now clearly loved, and was loved by, the parent she thought she'd found. For the past five days Ben, her biological father, had been able to observe her on her home territory of London, a place that felt so alien to him. And there was no denying that she was at last happy and secure – materially as well as emotionally.

'Do no harm', Ben had always been struck by the simplicity of those words, part of the Hippocratic oath. By revealing the truth of her parentage he would do immense harm to his own daughter. And for what?

The train crawled past a harvested field, a twenty-acre scraper mat of golden stubble, as he dissected his motives, and ruefully had to admit that it was purely for himself. He wanted this lovely girl acknowledged as his child, and if he was honest, a driving force behind the quest had been taking revenge against Oliver Rabson. The weapon to hurt and humiliate the man he'd always hated was now in his hands. It was just that generosity and genuine love for his daughter forbade the use of it. You have to like yourself.

So, Natasha must never know. Gaye's secret was, against the odds, safe with him. He pictured his first love sitting on that bench by the lily pond and marveled at the magical power of good looks. She probably hadn't been at all the right character for him, even when young. He'd just been dazzled by her beauty. Oh the foolishness of youth. Well his own youth anyway.

But if the dream of a daughter was dead, there was still hope of happiness. He was heading, albeit with exasperating slowness, towards a partner for his future life. Ben imagined Madge, and a smile hovered. He would do it right this time, take things slowly. He'd never wooed anyone before – old fashioned word – Gaye hadn't needed any such encouragement. He'd take Madge to the theatre, for meals and long walks, they'd go away for romantic weekends and josh and laugh together. With time she would surely come to return his love and forget this nonsense about going abroad.

Bodger always melted hearts, and accepted pattings and admiration from strangers with admirable tolerance. Ben's thoughts now were broken by a young woman across the aisle from them, who'd been especially taken.

'Doesn't he look like that dog on YouTube. You know, the one with the rabbit.'

'Yes', agreed Ben blandly. Well he did.

The dog had good instincts where people were concerned, his master thought, remembering his evident partiality to both Madge and Natasha. Jamie too.

The afternoon was largely gone by the time the train reached Ipswich station, and it was five-thirty as a taxi left him and Bodger outside Chandlers.

'Late customer', he announced, pushing open the shop door at the moment Madge approached it from inside, preparing to put up the closed sign. 'Just the sort you don't want.'

She looked tired and strained, he thought, as he lugged his case down the step, Bodger heading delightedly for his bed behind the counter. This was far from an ideal situation, but better make use of the opportunity of being able to talk to Madge on her own.

'What's this I hear about you going to Canada?' he demanded, locking the door for her and turning the sign round, as she prepared to cash up, greetings over.

'I... I've decided it's for the best.' Madge seemed to be concentrating on the credit card machine's buttons. Nora must have told him.

'It absolutely isn't.' He was aware that he sounded hectoring, and added lightly, 'I thought you liked it here in Rundleston. When were you planning on going?'

'Wednesday.'

'*Wednesday!*'

She put in a code and the machine spewed out the day's information.

'There's nothing to keep me here now that the art festival's launched', she added tonelessly.

Ben felt like a condemned man watching the sun rise on his last day. How could this be happening? In four days' time she'd be gone, there'd be no chance of persuading her to love him. And he could hardly come straight out and tell her how he felt. She'd just be alienated. But he did have one card that might save the situation, the small boy who'd like him as a second Dad.

'Madge', he said quietly, 'There's something you should know. I promised I wouldn't tell you, but... Jamie has asked me to marry you.'

She was caught off guard. 'Jamie did! When?'

'After our picnic on the beach. While we were sailing back.'

She tore off the roll of paper from the credit card machine and appeared to examine it.

'And what did you say?'

'That people needed to love each other. Friendships and good intentions weren't enough. But', he added hastily, 'that was before the scales fell from my eyes. Madge I've been a fool. I've had time to think in London, and I need you. I love you. It would work. Please don't go.'

She opened the till drawer, and began taking out the cash. 'No', she said at last, not looking at him. 'What you said was right. It's no good if only one person is in love.'

Ben couldn't understand how everything had turned to ash. For so many years he'd wanted his art to be recognised and appreciated, telling himself some day it would happen. Now, amazingly, that was coming right. But it hardly seemed to matter any more. What was the use of his talent bringing praise and a bit more money, if Madge wasn't there to enjoy it with him? He'd lived for the time he could get even with Oliver Rabson, and instead had given his daughter to the old enemy. And the woman he loved, the girl he should have married years ago if he hadn't been such a blind idiot, just thought of him as a friend. She was leaving his life for ever. In the past he'd regarded himself as independent and self-sufficient. Now, with the wonderful prospect of life with Madge first glimpsed, then snatched away, he knew it for an illusion, and was left envisaging years of loneliness stretching ahead.

There was no chance to talk to her again, even if he'd had the nerve, since next day she was away, thrashing things out with her ex, and bringing Jamie back in the evening. The day was overcast and drizzly, a thick blanket of grey cloud matching Ben's mood. There was pressure on him now to complete lots of unfinished paintings still up in the studio, and to start on new ones, but he had no heart for either.

Morose and with all the energy of a wet bonfire, Ben repaired to the Spritty at lunchtime on Sunday. The bad weather was keeping visitors away, but Ben's long face was hardly likely to persuade them of the delights of drinking in Rundleston, Tricia thought, seeing him come through the door.

'Well, what's up with you? Touch of myxomatosis?' was her jovial enquiry, as he approached the bar.

But it didn't even raise a smile.

'What have they been doing to him up in London then?' she enquired of Bodger, leaning over the counter. 'If this is what a bit of fame and fortune does to you, I must instruct my agent to cancel that world tour.'

'It's not London that's done it. I'm just bloody miserable, that's what.'

'Oh dear', she began drawing his pint. 'Tell your Auntie Trish', she suggested solicitously. 'Maybe I can help.'

'No. Nobody can. Well only one person. And she won't have me. Can't blame her,' Ben stated gloomily. 'I'm nothing, am I. Who'd want to team up with me?'

So Madge was right. This was delicate ground too, with the age difference and all. Tricia slid his beer across the counter.

'Well Natasha's a good deal younger, and used to living in...'

'*Natasha!* Whatever gave you that idea!' Ben interrupted incredulously. 'It's Madge of course. I asked her to marry me yesterday, and she said no.'

Tricia paused in the middle of putting money in the till.

'Madge? Turned you down!' She pushed the drawer shut.

'It's not because of Jamie, I know that. He very sweetly asked me to be his second Dad, a while back. I told her yesterday. Fact is I love her, Trish.' Ben ran his finger round the tankard rim, then looked up. 'And she's going. I'll never see her again,' he concluded with desolation.

'Perhaps you didn't make things clear. Would it help if I had a word?'

'No, you can't make someone love you if they don't feel the same way.'

Tricia stared at him. 'Well now I've heard everything.'

'What?'

But cogs were turning in her brain.

'I meant to ask you', she said, as if casually changing the subject, 'now you're back. Would you be free to crew the Hetty Jane tomorrow evening?' She smiled at him reassuringly. 'It'll help take your mind off things.'

After breakfast next day Stephen was despatched by his mother to ask Jamie round to play at the boatyard, and Tricia took the unwilling emigrant on one side to reveal her plan.

'Oh, wicked!' was his enthusiastic response.

'Would you be able to do it – you'll need to be convincing. You can row, can't you. Well enough for that?'

'Course I can. Ben says I'm strong for my age.'

'Tell your Mum we're taking the Hetty Jane out anyway, testing an engine repair or something. And that you'd really like to go along – with her of course – as a last treat. Oh and she doesn't need to bother with an evening meal, we'll fix up something. Just don't tell her Ben's going to be on board, okay.'

'I'll make sure she knows Danny's crewing, shall I?'

'Yes. Actually we do need him as well. And I'll keep Ben out of sight until we're under way.'

'Do you think it'll work?' asked Jamie anxiously.

Tricia didn't want to raise his hopes too high. 'We'll give it our best shot, shall we', she encouraged him, adding under her breath, 'behaving like a couple of tiresome toddlers, the pair of them.'

Ben had insisted on manning the shop all afternoon, to give Nora a break, and was so busy he didn't have time to brood on his troubles. Madge had been right, there was increased demand for the Ben Banding prints, so it was a good thing she'd gone ahead and ordered more. Local customers welcomed him back with obvious pleasure, which was heart-warming, and congratulated him on being 'discovered' by Oliver Rabson. If strangers spotted Bodger snoozing in his bed, they excitedly got out their cameras. One or two then connected him with the man behind the counter, and Ben found himself being photographed too. Cashing up at the end of the day, he was pleasantly surprised at the totals. Trade had certainly picked up. It hurt though, to know that he and Nora had Madge to thank for her ideas on revamping the shop, yet she wouldn't be around to see the long term results. It just pointed up the bleakness of the future.

After closing, and putting the takings in the bank's safe deposit, he went upstairs with the till float.

'Must rush', he told Nora. 'Got to give Bodger a quick run, and then I'm crewing on the Hetty Jane tonight.

'Oh yes', Nora said as if this was old news. 'Nice evening for it too. I'll give them a wave when they go past.'

Who was 'they'? Ben wondered belatedly, as he took the dog up to the recreation ground.

When he and Bodger arrived at the boatyard a short while later, they found Tricia loitering, almost as if she'd been waiting for him.

'Flitch and I were at cross purposes', she announced matter of factly, 'so I'm afraid both you and Danny have been asked to crew this evening. But it would be good to have the two of you because Flitch wants someone to check out the engine while we're under way – it's making a funny noise. Worn bearing or something.' She had no idea if that would cause a noise, and hoped Ben wouldn't either. 'Oh and could you kindly come and help me change the gas bottle in the galley. I've got a slight problem with it.'

Madge had mixed feelings about her son's request for their penultimate evening. There was no refusing it of course, but the pleasure of a trip on the Hetty Jane would emphasise all that she was leaving behind. Resolutely, she put such regrets aside, and once aboard, gave herself up to enjoying the next couple of hours. Jamie seemed to be especially excited about it.

They were lucky with the weather. Yesterday's clammy drizzle had passed on, and the day had progressively brightened, so that as Danny cast off and Flitch expertly nosed the big vessel away from the pontoon, the sun twinkled on the water, casting bright, squiggly reflections on the hulls of boats at their moorings.

Madge was standing at the rail watching Jamie and Stephen coiling mooring ropes for Danny, when she heard voices from the saloon, and turned to find Ben coming up the companionway behind her.

For a moment they gazed at each other as if glimpsing a longed-for Christmas present at the top of the wardrobe and out of reach.

'Oh, I didn't know you were here!' they exclaimed simultaneously, and then laughed in embarrassment.

In the ensuing awkwardness Madge proceeded to make an elaborate fuss of Bodger, while Ben muttered that there hadn't been much chance to speak to Danny since he'd inadvertently won the art competition, and went for'ard to congratulate him.

'What will you do with the art prize money then?' he enquired. 'How about buying a bulk lot of lunch boxes? You could flog 'em to galleries for a thousand quid a time.'

'Going to spend it on getting my Yachtmasters', Danny informed him earnestly. 'With that sort of qualification I'll be able to deliver boats, or work on some of these big yachts in the Med. Then I can earn enough to make my old girl seaworthy.'

He wanted to hear about Ben's week in London, and was clearly hungry for news about Natasha.

'Is she not coming back?' he asked wistfully.

'No, I don't think so', Ben told him gently. 'She's a London girl, Danny. That's where she belongs, it's clear when you see her there. It's a different world.'

Ben's familiar world was all around. Astern, Rundleston's dwindling houses were dominated by the tall maltings buildings. His own family's maltings were a monument to their years in the town, a history to be proud of, he reflected. If he became famous enough as an artist, maybe his paintings would also be a legacy. Just a different sort. The splash of water from the bow, and that wonderful salty, muddy scent in the air connected to his innermost being, as did the fields and woods, the little bays and marshy reedbeds that he'd known all his life, sliding slowly past. It was nearing the top of the tide, giving plenty of water and, despite the breeze on the nose they could have tacked upriver with ease. No fault had been found with the engine, but at the wheel Flitch didn't seem inclined to turn it off and hoist sail. They had the dinghy in tow too, which Ben didn't see any need for.

'Where are we headed?' he asked him now.

Flitch just shrugged. 'See how we go', he said with uncharacteristic woolliness, just as Jamie made his way aft to them.

'I'd love to collect some shells from Woodshey Bay', he said shyly. 'To remember Rundleston. Do you think... I mean would it be possible to pick up a mooring buoy, so Mum and me can row ashore in the dinghy. Just for a few minutes.'

No chance, thought Ben, admiring the boy's chutzpah and hoping he wouldn't be given a flea in his ear. But Flitch must have had an unsuspected soft spot for small red-headed boys about to be flown across the world against their will.

'Yeah, we could do that', he conceded indulgently. 'You'll have to be quick about it though.'

Danny and Ben had successfully made the Hetty Jane fast to a buoy close in to the bay, hauled the dinghy alongside, and Jamie, hair matching his lifejacket, was about to join his mother when Tricia commented, 'Are you sure that's safe, just the two of them?

She and Flitch exchanged glances. 'No, you're right', he said at once. 'Ben, you go with them, just in case.'

Anticipating a rabbit hunt in the woods, Bodger had to be discouraged from leaping into the dinghy too. Tricia held on to him.

Jamie pulled manfully on the oars, and the boat was soon beached.

'I'll stay with the dinghy', Ben suggested as Madge stepped out of the bow, and he was surprised to see a look of alarm on the boy's face.

'Oh. No! There's something I saw last time I wanted to ask you the name of. It's up the end of the beach. Where the shells are. Can you come. Please!'

Madge took off her shoes to feel the scrunch of sand between her toes, while Ben hooked the painter round a seaweedy stump. This was all he would have left in two days' time, he reflected, an aching, imprinted memory of this special girl walking barefoot on Woodshey Bay.

'Hurry up Mum', her son urged impatiently. 'We're keeping the skipper waiting.'

They set off at a good pace, but only a third of the way along the bay Jamie suddenly exclaimed, 'I've left my camera behind! Catch you up,' and ran back towards the dinghy.

'Beautiful evening', Madge remarked, to fill the silence.

How has this happened? thought Ben sadly. All we can talk about is the weather. He looked round as Jamie reached the dinghy, only to see him shove off and begin rowing towards the barge as if pursued by a giant octopus.

'I didn't know he'd left his camera on the Hetty Jane!' Madge was startled. 'Nor did I. Will he be all right on his own?'

'Course he will. Had a good teacher didn't he', Ben assured her with a faint smile, just as his mobile rang.

'We're off now', Trish's voice was unmistakable, and loud enough for Madge to hear. 'Going to have some great burgers. We'll come back when you two numpties have sorted yourselves out.'

'The bastards!' Puzzling elements now made sense to Ben. 'We've been set up!'

'You mean Jamie was putting all that on!' Madge anxiously watched him reach the safety of the Hetty Jane. Admiration for her son's acting skills was vying with heartache that he was so desperate about her decision to leave. And to make him happy she only had to say yes to the man standing next to her, whose close proximity was now affecting her like an electrical force field, endangering rational thought. But the fatal flaw in their relationship would be her knowledge that Natasha was his real love. No, there was no going back now.

'Trish means well', she concluded. 'It's just that...well, there's nothing to sort out. We'll have to walk back to Rundleston.'

'No', Ben broke the ensuing awkwardness. 'Why don't we wander along to the end and get some shells for Jamie. You never know, he might really have wanted some!'

The dinghy was being tied astern, and Danny went for'ard to release the mooring rope as they walked slowly along the beach, the lowering sun now tingeing the horizon with soft orange between dark smudges of cloud, as if some painter had been cleaning his brushes against the sky.

'At least it gives me an opportunity to thank you for what you've done for the shop. All the changes you made were spot on.'

'Trade's looking good, isn't it.' Madge was glad to know her efforts had been appreciated. And this was an easy, safe subject as well. 'How about more cards and prints of your paintings now?'

'Rabson talked about the reproduction rights, but I haven't signed anything yet', Ben told her. 'At Rab's party I got the impression a lot of those who bought originals were principally interested in making a good investment, so public appreciation is a real boost.'

'Told you!' Madge couldn't resist. 'Ordinary people love your paintings. You could really clean up by selling the images commercially.' She'd almost said 'we'.

The Hetty Jane was now moving off, Jamie waving from the deck. His mother gave him an embarrassed wave back.

'Tell me more about London', she prompted, as they continued walking between lines of seaweed, as if a giant had amused himself by scribbling down the beach in psychedelic green and brown. The woods above were dark and silent. 'Nora and I listened to as many interviews as we could.'

'I let you down though, didn't I', Ben said apologetically. 'You told me to be myself, and instead I pulled my punches about all the contemporary rubbish that passes for art.'

'Yes, I noticed.'

'I did it because...well it doesn't matter now.' Making extra money for a marriage that wasn't going to happen was not something he wanted to dwell on.

Bending down he pulled experimentally at a length of coir rope, but the sand stubbornly refused to give it up. 'Pity that wasn't there before, it would have looked good on GARBAGE', he commented.

'Arabella's thrilled the festival now has an installation by a famous artist, by the way' Madge told him mischievously. 'Should be worth a fortune.'

'I wish. Although it's unbelievable how much money Rab and Natasha have managed to sell my paintings for. Not bad for a no-hope dork.'

'Tony had no right to say that!' Indignation trumped thought. 'I'd have punched him!'

Ben stood still, staring at her. 'How did you know...?'

'I... I was by the back door when you were arguing, and couldn't help overhearing. Well, I could have,' she admitted guiltily, 'but... That's why I'm going away.'

'What?

'You warned him off Natasha. So I know how you feel about her.' She shrugged helplessly, adding in a small voice, 'It's why we could never work.'

From among the trees came the piercing song of a wren, as Ben recalled Tricia's assumption that it was Natasha who'd turned him down, and Madge's words on Saturday, 'it's no good if only one person is in love.' He'd thought Madge didn't love him. Now the wonderful realisation sank in − she'd meant the opposite. Everything was going to be all right!

'Natasha...' he said, and a smile of pure delight suffused his face. 'Is that what you think - that I love Natasha!' He bent down to rescue a shell from the encroaching water. 'Well you're right.' Straightening up, he saw her stricken expression. 'You wouldn't like me much if I didn't. She's my daughter.'

Sitting on the sand with Madge, their backs to the same jutting tree root where he'd perched in June, he told her about Gaye's devastating rejection of him on his return to art school, swiftly followed by her marriage to Oliver Rabson. Then how a chance remark by Natasha this summer about her birthday had caused him to wonder about the girl's paternity. And Gaye's unwilling confirmation at The Dutch House. Finally this past week in London bringing home the realisation that things had to stay as they were.

'I've given her away', he said simply. 'To him, of all people. She must never know, because that's best for her.'

They sat in silence for a moment, the low rays of the evening sun lending a glow to that wonderful hair. She took his hand in sympathy, and then somehow forgot to let it go.

'Natasha's going to be selling my paintings, so I'll see her. That's something. But it'll be hard. And saddest of all for Nora. She really wants grandchildren.'

'It's not too late, you know', Madge said softly, giving his hand a meaningful squeeze.

A more sophisticated man would have taken this as the best of all cues.

'I've made a complete hash of things', Ben admitted. 'Got it wrong at the beginning, and that skewed everything else. A real dork, Tony's right.'

'We could make you a very successful dork', Madge assured him fondly.

'We?'

'Natasha and I between us – she with your originals, me with the prints.'

'And mouse mats', he teased, 'don't forget the mouse mats! I should have snapped you up as soon as you left school.

You'd have made us rich by now. Except you wouldn't have even looked at me. Probably won't now'

'Is that a proposal? Because I'm not cancelling expensive plane tickets without one you know.'

'Right.' He put on a serious voice, 'Madge, would you marry a complete dork who loves you very much and is now known as a giant rabbit. And don't say I've oversold things.'

'Mrs Reginald Rabbit', she tried it out.   'Irresistible. Especially as I'm the one with long ears.

Ben was lost in the bliss of kissing someone wonderful who was loving him right back, when Madge suddenly broke off in consternation.

'Oh crikey. Do you think they've got binoculars on the Hetty Jane?'

The inspiring outline of the sailing barge against a setting sun, the grey sea purslane and a faint haze on the water made a perfect picture. Ben barely glanced at it, and the slow smile that he gave Madge came from deep happiness.

'Stuff the Hetty Jane', he said.